# TRYST

## Based on Actual Events

Aaron Eldritch

The names of various people, places, and things have been changed to protect their identity.

# Contents

Prologue............................................................vii

Chapter One: Initiation......................................1

Chapter Two: The First Sign..............................19

Chapter Three: Descent.....................................23

Chapter Four: A Visitation.................................49

Chapter Five: A Victim Born of Fruitfulness............59

Chapter Six: The Year of Games.........................73

Chapter Seven: Revelation.................................95

Chapter Eight: Homecoming..............................137

Chapter Nine: Red Fear....................................157

Chapter Ten: Dark Fear....................................165

Chapter Eleven: The Face of Fear.......................183

Chapter Twelve: Twins of Fear...........................201

Chapter Thirteen: Voices of Fear........................213

Chapter Fourteen: Remnants of Fear...................245

Chapter Fifteen: Game of Fear...........................275

Chapter Sixteen: Rebirth..................................285

# Prologue

He had always harbored some unceasing fear of over-arching watchfulness, a sort of inescapable, and yet at the same time, condescending, consciousness of his every action. What made the feeling worse, what gave it its curious poignancy, was the image of the being – or beings – that he was accustomed to connecting to these watchers, combined with the fact that he could never explain to himself how that image originated. That image, which had lain at uneasy rest beyond the forefront of his thought for ten years, was suddenly exposed to him late one night, forcing upon him a dreadful recognition of that whose existence he was desperate to deny.

He and his friend, Matt, sat in the living room of the latter's parents' house. He and Matt were both thirteen years old and often found themselves telling or analyzing stories of what many would call 'aberrant phenomena', even when those discussions took them later into the night than their parents would prefer. Each exchanged what he thought was an interesting or eerie account, whether they arose from various folklore, or from recent, informal testimonies of eyewitnesses of varying credulity. Matt, however, was about to reveal something which was to top it all, and which was to finally bring to the fore a horror his unprepared friend had carried all along. "There is a book my mom has read, and after reading it, she told me not to read it for myself," Matt said. "In fact, it disturbed her so much she did not finish it." This was particularly discomfiting, because it was not in the nature of Matt's mom to get 'disturbed'. If it had been somebody else, it may have been less worrisome.

"So, what is that book about?" he asked, curious but becoming genuinely afraid at this point.

"All I know of it is what she told me about it, and it seemed hard for her to explain it," Matt answered. "It is a guy's story about how these strange beings start intruding upon his life. It's odd but to me it sounded as though the man liked it but didn't, you know? And I guess the book is roughly about his trying to come to terms with this – what's the word – ambivalence towards these beings. Even the title captures that I think."

"How can you both like and fear something?" he asked, as a person told the box given to him contains a harmful trap yet who wants to open it anyway.

"Well, my impression of them was that the creatures – if that's what you'd call them – were very smart, and that one reason he kept encountering them was that they were both learning from and teaching him. For some reason they just never stuck around for very long during these visits. But it's almost as if the guy was their student, informer, *and* victim! One of the creepiest parts to me is how numerously and randomly they would visit him, without any warning. He seemed to be at their mercy – and yet mercy just doesn't..."

"Do you... have the book here?" he half-reluctantly asked, interrupting his friend.

"If it is here, it will be upstairs in the room next to my parents' bedroom," Matt said. "Let's go see if we can find it, just be careful not to wake my parents, and don't step on the top step – it creaks."

The two of them crept up the stair, as though on a forbidden errand, Matt in front. Matt stepped over the top tread, and he followed, a peculiar sensation that an old acquaintance was about to rejoin him. For Matt's words had begun to evoke oppressive imaginings within him – or were they deep memories?

"Wait here," Matt said, standing at the threshold to the room in which the book was supposedly kept, while the other stood at the top of the stair. The hall and stair and room with the book were all dark, as the two had turned on no lights to be more secretive.

After several long moments, Matt returned from the dark room carrying a small flashlight in one hand and in the other, a book. Some creaking came from behind the bedroom door. "I've got it. Let's get back down now," Matt advised before the other had a chance to glimpse the book.

When the two were finally downstairs and back into the living room, that enigmatic book was brought into the dim lamp light. And then he saw, there on the cover, that image which somehow he knew all along would appear on that book, and all of his primordial horrors and wonder came rushing back to him, for that image was of a familiar and utterly unfamiliar bust, with shoulder, neck, and head – naked, beige, placid, imperturbable – staring with two knowing abysses, portals into another world. Into those portals he was suddenly pulled, or rather yanked from an abyss in which he had lived up till now and had believed himself secure and unknown, being placed on a high pedestal exposed to a terrible gaze. From that gaze, from the insecurity those eyes caused by unconcealing the world's levity, there would be no hiding.

Dying now a sacred Tryst
Abandoned realm foreshadows this:

Common theme of mimicry
Within and of a Story

Secret aide sought out from past
Not for long will either last

Darkness befriends the rhythmic sound
Power lost but doll is found

Invitation from the Unknown Force
From this world was space divorced

Song of Steel from concrete tomb
Baby new from mother's womb

Horse's imitator opens door
One's beliefs not yet matured

Now and then, words from afar
Sadly, alien to the Bizarre

Time sees itself in mirror
Certain twins soon appear

Dead Man summoned in the night
Asked to vanquish 'flame of life'

On the Strange Day one can no longer hide
That in which a hoax resides

Worlds collide, minds suffer
All an effort to learn; discover

Dark sky divided
By what was the Red Line guided?

Subtellurian voices rebound
Extratellurians walk the ground

Plastic ponies upon the ears
Not reserved for early years

The Monster comes to life on wall
Its face was gazed upon in awe

Old friend pays a visit
This revelation It brings with It

Decay and slow regression
Occasional self-annihilation

Mozart dances on a red ball
Shown freely, the ninth eye saw

Independence Day fast approaches
Haste must be made: the Nothing encroaches

Hands of Mockery lose their strength
though
Onward grows their lifetime's length

Final attempt toward some ill goal
Game is played to save a soul

\*\*\*

Alas, this world has met its end
Much this omen could portend

And such it does amidst all strife:
Past gives way to new-found life.

# CHAPTER ONE

## Initiation

### July 2000

"Well, Zeb, the loan was finally approved," Mr. Eldritch told his son. Zebulon looked up from his book and blinked thrice, allowing his engrossment in Schopenhauer's concept of Will to lighten momentarily. "Did you hear?"

"Approved, huh? I guess that means the land's yours now?" Zebulon asked, in a tone that belied his disgruntlement. Though clear with sight, a fog yet hung.

"Well, not quite, but it will be. Before you know it, we'll have a nice house there and we'll be fishing off the dock from sunrise to sunset," his father mused as he left the living room and entered the kitchen. Zeb was happy his parents would someday live where they had always really wanted to. But being a philosophy major in college, his thoughts were too immersed in the abstract to come to a full reconciliation with moving away. What few times he allowed himself to acknowledge the eventual change, he was ambushed by feelings which did not sit with him easily. He had lived here his entire life - over two decades - and to be quite honest, the thought of it was not only saddening but distressing.

The Eldritchs' modest rancher was the second house to go up on Attica Drive, more than thirty years earlier, in the rolling hills of the Piedmont region of Maryland. Buffered by a large forest to the south and pastures to the west, there was always adventure to seek out. Since the days of youth Zebulon and his younger brother Aaron had been playing in the woods;

building forts and taking journeys were the most memorable times. Even the oldest of the three brothers in this family, Daniel, would go there when he would visit.

Being a single father who taught classes during the day and attended them at night, one or two weekends a month was about as much time as Daniel could muster for these trips. But they were worth it – and preserving family ties was only half of the purpose. The forest was the other half. Entering 'the woods' as the brothers called them brought a sense of tranquility and offered some much-needed therapy.

And it evoked fond memories too, memories of less troubled times. Zeb and Aaron would often lead the way, being younger and more agile, and so it was on this occasion as well. He wondered how his younger brothers felt on these walks. Aaron, especially, would be ignorant of the sanctity of these moments in all their ephemerality, he thought. If only he could carry that blissful spirit again, even for a day! Zeb probably carried some of this ignorance but unlikely enjoyed these walks with the same degree of aloofness, Daniel imagined. He was seven years older than Aaron, and while Daniel knew that he had yet plenty to discover about adulthood, university studies and summer jobs had certainly broken him by now of that precious whimsy only childhood affords. He wasn't wrong.

It hadn't been long ago for Zeb. Only a handful of years ago, the biggest priority was figuring out how to raise the ridge beam on the fort he and Aaron had been building. It seemed so recent that to entertain the idea of finishing that child's project required only minimal denial... denial that things would never be like they had been growing up, denial that a grimace would form on his father's face when he saw his son return home with a shopping bag full of parts for another tabletop game instead of for an automobile. He asked himself with frustration why he continue dragging himself to town every day for such droll activities. With each dragging, the memories of youth became less clear, though he couldn't imagine they'd ever be lost. Those days were pure; innocent. When trouble did come in its rare moments, it would go no further than the woods' edge. Though he had not forgotten Daniel's stories of the Shadow Man of the forest – dark, sooty, never fully seen but always with wide-brimmed hat – nor his own encounters, the woods represented all that was sacred, right, and fearsome with the world, and instilled a desire for adventure.

Yes, these feelings were still in him and even these days, finding himself preoccupied with studies and planning for life after university, they could be recalled with relative ease. This was less true for Daniel who required a bit of coaxing, which a long walk through the forest or a few puffs on the tobacco pipe in the basement with good music usually accomplished.

And yet, the air tasted differently than it had. Perhaps it was just him, but he remembered it tasting sweeter years ago. The honeybees seemed to agree; he saw less of them too. It wasn't just the air either. It seemed to him the autumn colors of the forest had been brighter, the frosts bluer. The winter snows, deeper. But he stood here now, amidst the towering oaks and hickories, the quartz outcroppings, the bubbling creek. He knew them all like the freckles on his arms. His eyes followed the gnarled roots as they wove themselves deep into the earth. He liked that. Standing there silently he could have mistaken his feet for those roots as he let himself take in the forest's ambience, and for an instant he was overcome with a sense of communion with not only the trees and birds and insects but also his own Anglo-Teutonic roots. With raised goose pimples, he looked to his younger brother Aaron. The blood they shared was the most apparent quality but equally salient was their passion for the folklore and mythos of the Old World. It imbued most of their activities with a spirit of wonder, charm, and sometimes even fear. Even now, his mind swirling with the words of Kant, Sartre, and Derrida, inevitably forcing him to examine his own passions at a deeper level, he could not disregard his love for the forest nor his desire for adventure. Zeb knew the same was true for Aaron, even if he was still too immature to confirm it without the expected teenage hard-headedness. But now, Daniel was making reference to the lowered sun in the sky, and that it would be time to return to the house soon. And so this particular walk came to an end as did many others that summer, each ending back at the house on Attica Drive.

***

The house itself was home to many memories. Four children had been raised there: Theresa, who had since moved out and married, was first and her three brothers followed, one every seven years. The house saw their friends come and go. Some of the greatest moments were in the basement, particularly video games and role-playing games. Throughout each of the males' youthful years, they and their friends found themselves occupied with one of these, right up to this time which found Aaron and his friends playing Dungeons and Dragons at the poker table in the back corner.

Alex Wilkinson, a role-playing veteran, grew impatient as Aaron fumbled through the manuals. Greg Logan, being somewhat new on the scene, just waited and sang some anime tunes. His growing love for fantasy kept him patient. "Just another minute, guys," Aaron reassured them.

"Sure..." Alex responded with a hint of sarcasm. At that moment Zeb proceeded down the basement steps in his typical stride. As if having already sensed the growing sense of boredom in the room, he gave a suggestion.

"You want to go in the woods?" he said as he approached the table.

"Yeah!" Alex said, standing up. Now Aaron fumbled faster through the pages. He didn't want it to end so abruptly. But Zeb always seemed to work in a strange manner. He looked at Greg.

"Yeah, sure!" Greg exclaimed, jumping up and nearly knocking his soda can off the table. "I've only been in a couple times. Oh, but this game..." Aaron shut the book in defeat.

"That's alright, we'll come back to this later," Aaron said with resignation. "Let's go!"

Off to the woods they went, without hardly a bit of preparation, as excitement usually has it. Zeb and Greg grabbed a walking stick as they passed through the green wall of the forest and into its depths. Zeb led, as usual, with Aaron at the rear. "I'll take you somewhere new, Greg. I haven't been there myself for quite some time," Zeb explained. Onward they went, through the first corn field and down into the wooded valley where a deer path met with the main path.

They crossed the stream, continuing over into the part that had been subject to some logging not more than fifteen years earlier. Few ancient trees remained here; most were young to middle-aged. As the path meandered more or less parallel with the creek, they proceeded to pass a branch in the trail that led to an area where many forts had been built over many years.

"There's that weird stone," Alex said, giving a nod toward the bifurcation.

"Weird stone?" Greg asked, wondering if he was being played.

"You mean you haven't seen it?" Zeb asked with astonishment.

"Oh, you gotta show him!" Aaron said to Zeb as Greg shook his head. And so, he did. Greg followed right behind him, down the hill into a darker, older part of the woods. He stopped near the base, next to a gigantic stump. He pointed, and there, across from the stump, was a stone of blue slate protruding from the earth like a tombstone. It was natural in form, and aside from its beauty, Greg wondered what was so special about it.

"Look closely," Zeb began. "Not everything about it is natural." Greg moved closer and knelt before it. Then he saw, disguised with age and shadow, masterfully etched into the rock, two letters: I F.

"What?..." Greg started.

"If. Or I and F. Who can say?" Zeb pondered, asking himself again just as much as he was asking Greg. Aaron and Alex smiled for they enjoyed the moments when Greg would become so enthralled with wonder.

"What could it mean?" Greg wondered aloud.

"It's hard to say," Zeb continued. "Could be initials, maybe just a coincidence. Or maybe not. Or, perhaps, it is part of a larger message... and we see only the most curious part of it... 'if...'"

But the mystery would have to remain unsolved, as it had been for many years, leaving them with only the option of continuing the main trail. "So where are we going?" Greg asked, beginning to pant. They were now climbing a large hill, and more light was seen ahead.

"It's another stone," Zeb began. He paused and looked back to see Greg's reaction. It was one of confusion. He continued. "Well actually, there are two stones, very large, very close to each other. I've always called it Twin Mountain. There's also a strange gorge between them. I tumbled quite a distance once when scaling it."

"Okay..." Greg said as he attempted to make a mental image. They emerged into a large field. Far on the other end could be seen another path disappearing into the forest's depths.

"That path leads to the Mountain. My memory is less reliable beyond that point," Zeb told the others.

"I'll do my best to help," Aaron said. He had been there a couple times before. Soon the field was behind them, and they found themselves on a wider path, which seemed to follow a creek at some distance. They eventually came to a split. One of the two paths would lead to the geological feature, but whichever it was Zeb could not remember. Aaron believed it was the right-hand path, going mostly off intuition. So right they went. A couple more splits in the trail were encountered, both of which had no place in the memory of Aaron nor Zeb; both of whose path was decided on a whim.

Before long, the trail brought them to the creek at which point it was fordable. After crossing and going on just a bit further, a large grey shape disrupted the horizon of the opposite ridge. "There it is! One of the Mountains!" Zeb announced.

"That means the other must be nearby..." The trail continued onward, but a side path here also led to the stone outcropping visible through leaf and limb.

"Let's go look at it first, in case we get lost," Alex suggested. They agreed and headed for the rock. It appeared to grow not only larger and larger as they grew closer but more ominous as well. Aaron felt the shadow envelop him, and it made him uneasy. Greg, however, was in awe, and hurried forward behind Zeb. From the top, a distant horizon could be seen all around. But there was no other rock to be seen.

"It must be lower in the valley," Zeb explained. Aaron bent over.

"I've always wondered what these are," he said, as he pointed to some unnatural looking pockets in the rock's surface. Alex remained silent. They climbed off the rock and stepped heavily back down the path. But things seemed different coming back.

"Aaron, which way did we come from? This doesn't look familiar..." Zeb said. Aaron just stared with a perplexed look on his face.

"Uhhh...." he muttered. He was lost.

"I think we came from that way," Alex said flatly. He pointed across the stream.

"I guess so," Zeb said. "I could have sworn the path diverged to the other way, yet the ridge is over there... Anyway, let's go up this path. It probably leads to the other Mountain."

They did just that. But after several minutes of walking, no mountain was found. In fact, Zeb and Aaron had the sense that they were moving in the wrong direction, away from both rocks. "I don't think this is right, Alex," Zeb insisted. Alex remained silent, and just kept looking forward. He moved up to the front, looking ahead.

"Let's go a little further," he said.

"Alright, just a little, I don't want to get lost," Zeb replied. "With all the clouds covering the sun, I'm beginning to doubt my sense of direction. Of all times to leave my compass at home..." Aiming for higher elevation so that they might better orient themselves, they made for the nearest hill, while

Alex fell to the rear.

"Going to take a breather, guys," he said, though he didn't sound winded in the least. It grew lighter ahead as they approached the crest, and now at the top, the forest opened into a circular clearing of tall grass, whose homogeneity was disrupted here and there with burnt-looking patches. Greg was once again awe struck. Zeb was surprised as well.

"Well I've definitely never been here before, but I'm always glad to find something new here." Toward the center was a mound of what appeared to be earth and twigs, looking out of place but not necessarily artificial. Zeb moved ahead of the others. "It looks like some sort of shelter! Stay here, I'll take a peek." Aaron and Greg talked quietly wondering who would be living back here – if indeed it was a shelter at all, while Alex stood with his hands on his hips, nearly halfway down the hillside. Circling around behind the mound, Zeb was now out of sight.

Suddenly there was a cry and Zeb, with a fit of stumbling, came racing back. He was flailing his arms in a gesture as though telling the others, without giving away their presence, to run back up the trail. Aaron and Greg, having understood the gesture – and the fear in Zeb's eyes – wasted no time and stampeded down the hill, nearly plowing over the still motionless Alex in their haste. After nearly a minute in full retreat, Zeb caught up with them. The three were out of breath and surveilling their surroundings revealed that they were on a small trail that zig-zagged its way toward the valley's creek. In between heavy pants, Zeb said, "There was... someone in there! In bits of dirty, tattered cloth..." Then he chuckled, clearly amused with how easily he had let his imagination get away from him. "For a moment I thought it might be a witch!" Greg and Aaron were too tired to respond with anything more than a look of horror; ordinarily such vagaries would demand elaboration. But by the time they had recovered some energy, Greg felt there was another mystery needing answered first.

"Hey, where's Alex?"

"Oh, he stayed back there. We left him in the dust it

seems," Zeb said. Then Aaron pointed down the trail in the direction they were headed.

"There he is," Aaron directed. Sure enough, he was about five feet off the trail when Aaron noticed him stepping out from a dense thicket and onto the trail, walking stick in hand. Greg was in disbelief.

"How the...? What are you doing up there Alex? How did you get ahead of us?" Greg asked as he wiped the sweat off his glasses. Alex didn't respond. Greg simply looked toward Aaron for support, but Aaron was still confused. Greg whispered to Zeb and Aaron. "Aaron, he was well behind us, and not far in front of you, Zeb." Alex was still waiting ahead, staff in hand like a sentinel. Greg continued. "We beat feet back here, so how did he get so far ahead of us?... And what's with that stick he's got? He wasn't carrying that before..." He said this all very seriously. Aaron and Zeb, realizing the bizarre nature of the event, were about to laugh in disbelief as they were accustomed to doing, when Alex called out.

"You guys coming?" The three looked at each other.

"Yeah..." Greg shouted. They proceeded down the trail to meet with him. Greg whispered to Aaron. "I know it may sound weird, but I'm getting a bad feeling, like, like it's not really him... like one of the doppelgangers from Dungeons & Dragons, you know?"

"I know what you mean... It's pretty weird... Him getting behind us like that and all... Not to mention the weird thing Zeb saw..." Aaron whispered. "And Alex sure is quiet, and acting real plain too, like nothing is wrong." But nothing could be done about the fact, so they moved on.

Somehow that trail ended up taking them back to the main trail that they had been on earlier; perhaps they had come down one of those off-branches that they had not taken before. With navigation again possible, they returned home, having seen only one of the two Mountains, and with a person that they were beginning to suspect of sorcery.

Alex showed no more enthusiasm for fantasy nor for role-playing with his friends Aaron, Zeb, and Greg. In fact,

9

within a short span of time, he lost nearly all interest in those people, and soon, he stopped communicating with them altogether. Aaron would never have his company again.

*\*\*\**

It was roughly two years later now. Zeb had since graduated from college; his wisdom had grown but the world seemed indifferent. Aaron had just finished his freshman year, with hardly a care in the world. Greg had just graduated from high school and with renewed optimism, was excited to start his summer job at the gas station. This day found the three remembering that adventure with Alex two years earlier.

"We didn't quite see it at the time, but that day marked a significant change in his character," Aaron said of Alex.

"He had all those new friends from out of town all of a sudden and just stopped talking to us..." Greg remembered aloud. "Went full goth or something."

"Reminds me of Wendell," Zeb said, as if Greg already knew of this person. Aaron was the only other one who did.

"What's... Wendell?" Greg asked, having never heard such a name. Zeb laughed and answered,

"Wendell was once a good friend of mine. He, Gareth, Lars and I were all great companions. I've told you about the others, yes?"

"Gareth was your old neighbor you grow up with if I remember. And Lars is the one down the road on the farm? Has some trouble keeping his stories straight you said," Greg recalled. "Looks up to you and wants your validation even if he has to bullshit you on occasion."

"Ha! You remember well. You'll meet him one of these days, I'm sure," Zeb said, looking rather humored with the prospect. "And yes, Gareth was the one I knew since I was forming memories. Oh, there was Matt, too. But he never quite opened himself to the possibilities we four saw and never really became part of the fellowship." Now his face darkened. "Wendell was the most intense of the group, the most pensive. He proposed adventures even I thought might be too extreme.

Then one day, just like Alex, everything changed." Greg looked at Zeb with intrigue. Aaron leaned against the tree to whose shadows they had all retreated from the hot sun. "You see, he was a quiet boy who lived in a very noisy house," Zeb began. "And a very strange house. He was one of a dozen children and from what I gather from the one time I visited, there was utter chaos within those walls - the children, I mean - crazy. Which is weird, considering the parents valued order so much. It was their own strange idea of order, though. They could care less if their children threw knives at their walls, but if certain rules were broken, harsh disciplinary action would follow. Yeah, his parents gave me the creeps. There was every indication that they were involved in some sort of cult, referring to 'God' often enough and biblical stories, but always with their own weird twist on it. Like one of those movies, you know?"

A concerned look was on Greg's face. It amused Aaron a bit. It was fun to watch someone else hear this story, especially considering that it was true. "Why would, how did you ever become his friend?!" Greg clamored.

"I met him in middle school," Zeb explained. "I learned of him gradually, mainly through others who would laugh at him and tease him. I pitied him. You already know how, even at that age, I could see right through the superficial nature of middle-school culture; the social expectations, the small world view, you know. Well I wanted to show him that; I wanted him to see it for what it was, you understand? And at the same time show him that there was a world of wonder out there – one of ancient trees, heroes, and adventure. Who knows, maybe together we'd even meet the faerie-folk my grandparents talked about if we showed them our hearts. So I sat by him when I could; got to know him better. And I let him learn more and more about me. A lot of it was virgin territory for him – these were ideas he had never been exposed to and it seemed to make an unexpected impact. He became so intrigued by me and my ideas that he saw me almost as a mentor; perhaps even as a shaman of sorts."

"Well, you are intriguing sometimes," Greg said with a smile. "I'll be the first to admit that you've taught me plenty."

Zeb laughed again. His humility was of a special kind. Zeb continued.

"Wendell was always saying how strict his parents were, and how he hardly ever had the chance to come over here to play. So I went there instead."

"You didn't know what you were in for!" Aaron interjected, laughing.

"No, I didn't. I'll never forget it either: a dark mansion on top of a dreary hill – so foreboding!... And if you already didn't think the place was weird, how would you like to find an old lady watching a little T.V. screen in the attic all day long, then be taken outside by the father for some structured games of shotgun blasting?!" Greg didn't respond with more than a look of disbelief and disgust. "Yeah, that's what I mean - weird. So anyway, he I guess my influence was rubbing off on him. And because it didn't jive with all of their family values, he apparently became more rebellious at home and it was obviously not welcomed. One day in school, he was very sad. I asked him why, and he said that his parents had taken from him that which he cherished most, his puppy, and was then forced to read from law books, a common punishment there."

"They took his puppy..." Greg told himself sadly. Zeb went on.

"And possibly worse. I didn't press him on it. He finally confided in me that he was planning to run away and asked if he could come home with me. He said he could live in the woods for a while, until things got better. I agreed, and even offered to bring food to him. Wendell wasn't one to exaggerate or back out of things. He did just what he said and took off for the woods after the bus dropped him off on our road. It wasn't long though before his father called our house, with more anger than concern. He had called the police to find him and demanded that I tell them where he was. When the police arrived, I said I wasn't sure but believed he might be in the woods. They made me go in to find him. This is what's funny: after searching for him in good faith, I came out empty-handed, shrugging, but just then, somehow, Wendell emerged from the forest right behind me!"

"Kind of like how Alex got ahead of us somehow..." Greg said, again with a look of intrigue.

"Yeah..." Zeb sighed in agreement. "And that's not even what makes this story so much like Alex's." Aaron nodded as Greg's expression turned to shock. "It's what happened in the following month. See, Wendell was not in school for the next two weeks. When he returned, there was something disturbingly different about him. He was even quieter than before, and it was hard to find out where he had been. Finally, he found the strength to recall the last two weeks. Quite unexpectedly, he had been sent to a mental ward. And the things he said of it were very disturbing indeed - there's no need to go into detail."

"A literal nightmare," Greg noted.

"It gets stranger. In some ways he ended up sharing a similar fate to Alex, now that I think about it. You see, within a day of his return Wendell was acting much differently, even dressing differently. He was suddenly challenging all my ideas and beliefs and showing signs of opposition to me for no reason at all. He talked to me less and less, began dressing in dark clothing and randomly developed an intense interest in mimes. In fact, I heard he was even training to become one, or at least that's what someone thought he had said. One day, he was doing something right in front of me, something he knew I would push my buttons. This was spitefulness, and I knew his actions were only a pantomime, you might say, of high school culture. This actually made me angrier because he didn't simply forget the things I had taught him: like I said, it was in spite; it was hate." Zeb turned and breathed out heavily, looking to the sky. After a moment he continued. "I could have killed him then... put him through that third story window. I'd never felt so pure a rage as I had at that moment... but I resisted. I saw the last several years of my life wither away behind me; they meant nothing now. All I could do was forget about the poor guy and move on. That's just what I did. I never forgot what was important. I guess that partly explains my obsession with philosophy."

"That makes sense," Greg said, rubbing his chin and

nodding. Zeb clasped his hands together.

"See, now, how similar their stories are, he and Alex? We see people grow up and change all the time, all around us. It happened to most of my friends. But something is different with these two... The change is more out of spite... or something. So unnatural, so abrupt..."

"I never made that connection before!" Aaron exclaimed, and with a grin said, "I knew your philosophy would come in handy."

"I don't know what to think!" Greg said in bewilderment. The three stood silent for a moment. Aaron took a seat now against the tree. Greg continued. "Those woods... change people... Someone goes in... and someone different comes out..." Aaron jumped back up.

"...Greg!" Aaron stammered. He alone had yet to contribute to the mood of insight the others were enjoying.

"The woods... It sure seems to be the case," Zeb said, as he rubbed his face. "But what exactly could be happening, if that is the case? What's going on down there I wonder?" He paused for a moment in thought. "All the way back to when Dan was little... the Shadow Man... Could He be a factor?" He asked this last question more to himself than anyone. Sadly, no one could answer, but he did remember something else now. "Wendell did claim to have encountered him at least once..." Aaron and Greg's mouths hung open. Neither had heard this before. "When he first started visiting, I had told him to be wary of the Shadow Man if he ever entered our woods. Ironically, it was in his own woods where he had the encounter, and he fled home. Yet even as he sat in his kitchen, he saw a shadow for a moment out of the corner of his eye, and knew the Shadow Man was present... He became very ill the same day, and could barely explain over the phone to me what happened... This was all long before his change."

"So, was that the last of him, then?" Greg asked. Zeb struggled to come up with an answer.

"Uh, pretty much. Well, actually, not too long ago he did drop by... uh, you know, for old time's sake. Pretty weird, I guess. He definitely wasn't the same person I once knew...

Yeah, it was a pretty surreal visit..." Zeb's mind ventured into the past as he recalled that evening.

It was like he was there again. All the noises, faces, everything. His mother called for him as he lay on his bed, reading. "Zeb, there's a friend here to see you!"

"What...?" He rolled off his bed and turned off the lamp. But since it was darker now than it had been when he had begun reading, he had to move cautiously as he exited the room. His attempt at a confident stride fell short as he moved down the hallway, for wonder was the dominant feeling in him. He rounded the corner and saw his mother standing there, waiting for him. She turned and went into the kitchen after gesturing toward the front door, arousing his curiosity further. Zeb anxiously entered the living room with his head toward the front door. It took a moment, but as the clock chimed its hour, brought to Zeb's consciousness was the dark, slender figure of Wendell Hearn. His pallid countenance immediately brought a dead past into the living present, along with a whole slew of memories and feelings. He stood there like a shadow in the incandescent light, a dream in waking. Zeb's stride was abruptly halted, and he stood silent for a quick moment. Routine got the best of him and forced a look of pleasant surprise on his face, not representative of the feelings within him.

"Hi Zeb," Wendell said quietly. "Long time no see." Unwilling to let his deeply buried rage boil up, Zeb instead attempted to maintain a peaceful reunion. The years that had passed apparently had made this easier but also made for a greater disruption to whatever serenity he had achieved; the surprise visit had now even begun to nauseate him. Why was this old friend here?

The whole visit was a strange one, Zeb now remembered, but the memories became increasingly cloudier. They had gone into his room to reminisce... He saw fear in his mother's eyes... Wendell had apparently been involved in criminal activity since he dropped out of high school... He had taken one of the knives off Zeb's dresser and slid its blade across his hand... and he wouldn't sleep outside under the stars as he once loved... No, instead... The stairs... the basement stairs... What was he doing?!

"You okay, Zeb?" Greg asked, pulling Zeb's mind from the past and thrusting it right back into the present.

"Yeah, yeah, fine... Just remembering..." Zeb said, squinting at the sun, which had moved somewhat. "You know, you kind of remind me of him."

"What-? Not Wendell, I hope?!" Greg cried.

"Well... yeah. Don't get me wrong, I don't see you going in his direction, but just something about you. You share some physical characteristics as well. The dark curly hair, the lankiness, your pale skin."

"Thanks for that," Greg groaned. Zeb laughed.

"Nothing to worry about," Zeb assured him. "It doesn't mean anything."

The group migrated across the lawn, around the side of the house, from where the road out front could be seen. Aaron looked toward the end of the street, which ended at the forest's edge. The house at the end of the street, in particular, was the object of his attention. He moved in front of the others, and gesturing toward the house said, "I'm thinking about that weird house. I wonder, if there is something weird with the woods, I wonder if it's had any effect on that house?" The house was nestled in seclusion, at the far end of the neighborhood, buffered by the forest on almost all sides. Even the front lawn was filled with thick evergreen trees, further stealing the house from people's awareness. It was abandoned, and apparently forgotten by everyone.

"This isn't the Scary Book, Aaron," Zeb teased. The Scary Book was a collection of captivating stories of horror, decidedly unique in style and full of ideas one could ponder for days on end. They had discovered this wholly new universe only recently.

"Scary... Book?" Greg asked inquisitively.

"Oh, yeah, it's this book of spooky tales Zeb and I were gifted with a few weeks ago. We'll have to show you tonight. It's kind of always on my mind," Aaron laughed.

"If 'gifted' is what you call receiving something that was obviously not wanted any longer by the gifter," Zeb clarified with a clever smile. Greg's look of confusion and perhaps even fear demanded a quick elaboration from his amused agemate. With a chuckle Aaron said,

"So there was this kid around our age who lived over at that house..." He gestured to the secluded rancher at the end of the road. "...Never saw much of him, or the rest of his family for that matter. I was taking the trash out one evening when this fellow, who's never spoken a word to me at this point, walked right up to me and said 'I heard you enjoy adventures. You'll want this.' And then something along the lines of 'Yeah, I meant to give this away sooner, but things have been hectic and this might be my last chance...' Something like that. Anyway, before I can even ask about it, he shoves it in my hands and then abruptly walks away. So much for introductions, I'm thinking." A thoughtful look to the sky revealed less blues than there had been earlier in the day. With only a brief survey of the hills to the west, one might even observe a strand or two of mist in the vale, as Aaron now did.

"Um... okay," was all Greg could say initially. After a pause, "Well I'm glad you're enjoying the Book. Maybe we can watch that anime I brought over too. What do you think Zeb? Zeb...?"

Zeb had left the conversation. One might have mistaken him for a mannequin he stood so still, staring toward the house at the end of the road. Aaron approached his brother, and put a hand on his shoulder, startling him.

"What's up?"

"I, uh... it's nothing. Just some shadows over there," Zeb answered.

"What's up with that house?" Greg asked, now becoming a bit alarmed over all the intrigue with what was normally a quiet little street.

"That house has a bizarre history," Zeb began. "In particular, it has a reputation for housing strange people. My father told me about a policeman who once lived there. One day he went mad and blew the back door out with a shotgun. He ran off into the woods, and helicopters were flying all around looking for him. I don't think he ever turned up."

"Another victim of the woods..." Aaron said softly.

"Maybe. We can't jump to conclusions," Zeb explained. "Now, the next person was believed to be a sexual predator, one who preferred children specifically. My dad chased him off once. He didn't stay long. The next residents were just plain mean. A very mean old couple that was abnormally secretive and protective of their property. The last people were perhaps the most normal, though they apparently had some 'family issues' because during their stay we could here shouting coming from their direction most nights. It was this family that left the house in the state that it is now, and left us with the Book."

"And what state is that?" Greg asked. Aaron jumped in with the answer.

"See how high the grass is? The home's been abandoned. What's stranger is that no one around here seems to care. That grass just keeps getting taller and taller." He moved a few steps closer toward it, moving steadily down the hill. "Maybe we'll check it out later, what do you think?" Zeb didn't answer.

"Uhh, I'd rather not..." Greg said. But Aaron insisted.

"We may learn something. Mainly I'm just curious as to what it looks like. Zeb tried to investigate with our nephew, but he was too scared, so he didn't get very far. We'll be quick about it." Greg's silence was agreement enough for Aaron. They would descend upon that forsaken place at dusk, as would an aggressive mist. And just prior, they had set the mood for themselves – not with an anime, but rather with a solid two-hour introduction between Greg and the Scary Book.

# CHAPTER TWO

## The First Sign

Zebulon's nap was violently interrupted as Greg threw off his blanket and let the accusations fly. Aaron sat on the floor of the family room, having just entered the house with Greg. There was a problem. A big Problem.

"Why'd you go disappearing on us like that?! Oh, don't look so tired, you can't have been asleep long, Zeb!" Greg shouted, giving Zeb a shove then dropping to the floor by Aaron, in frustration. Aaron just stared at Greg in confusion. Zeb responded in a drowsy voice.

"Huh-what?... What's your problem?" He asked, a bit annoyed that his nap was stolen from him.

"Yeah, what's this about, Greg?" Aaron added. A sneer grew on Greg's face.

"Oh, yeah, just play dumb, guys. Won't fool me," he said. Aaron and Zeb just looked at each other. Zeb sat up now, rubbed his eyes, and put his glasses on. There was silence for a while.

"Can you explain what the matter is?" Zeb asked him in a collected voice. "You're beginning to concern me."

"Well it is concerning you!" Greg said firmly. Aaron slid away a bit.

"Greg," Aaron began, "there's already so much to tell him about what we saw down there, why don't you talk about that instead?"

"I am talking about that, Aaron," Greg explained while trying not to burst. "And I don't have to tell him anything because he was there!!"

"Woah, woah, whoa," Zeb interrupted. "What's this now? Where was I? And why is it an issue now?"

"Greg, are you crazy? He wasn't with us!" Aaron said. His look of confusion was more focused now, for he now knew what Greg's problem was. He could not understand, however, how the problem came to be. His comment, now, only angered Greg, which explained his responding only to Zeb.

"You were with us only five minutes ago! Now don't deny it!" Zeb fell back into the sofa with a sigh of agitation.

"Zeb, listen. Greg and I just got back from the investigation, like we planned. But he's insisting that you were with us," Aaron explained before looking over toward Greg. Aaron, sensing the sincerity in Greg's voice, was now beginning to feel something strange, something new, something... wondrous. He was feeling fear, real fear. His friend shared in this, though the mounting frustration overwhelmed his awareness. And if Greg sensed any sincerity in Aaron or Zeb's voices, it was only just beginning to surface.

"Wow, you guys are great actors," Greg said, humored by what he believed was a stunt.

"Look, Greg, it's hard for us to believe you," Aaron said softly. "I mean, for me, maybe he could have been around and I didn't notice him, but it's impossible for him to – "

"No, Aaron, he was right there with us. You were talking to him, even. Don't deny it," Greg demanded. Aaron shook his head.

"There's nothing we can do for you," he began, condescendingly. "I believe that you speak what you believe to be true, but all I can say is that we were the only ones down there."

"Sure, sure," Greg shot back in sarcasm. But in actuality he was beginning to sympathize with them. "My memory isn't hazy one bit. It is still all very clear, and you two are the only ones not making sense."

"Alright Greg, believe what you want," Zeb said, growing frustrated now himself.

"Anyway, tell me what you found, Aaron. Was there anything new?"

"I came out with more questions than answers," Aaron sighed. "The place is abandoned without a doubt. But it's more than that. You were right - the place is trashed, trashed beyond mere abandonment. It almost looks deliberate, and I found trash even in places that seemed strangely inconvenient, such as the roof top. It was too dark to see much inside the house, but I could make out some metal frames of a sort, and a mattress or two leaning against the wall. All the doors were locked. Another observation I made was that of 'decapitation'."

"The headless doll? You saw it then..." Zeb said.

"Yes, and a headless statue as well," Aaron added.

"Interesting... Well, all that matters is that we have all seen that place now, at one time or another, and in one way or another. We have all beheld its demise," Zeb concluded. But that was not good enough for Greg.

"But what you two don't realize," Greg began, "is the fact that that house definitely has an effect on behavior, and memory as well. And that's the biggest discovery of all. And I'm the only one who knows it." Aaron looked at Greg with a smile.

"Well, I'm beginning to see that that is the case with you, at least," he said to him. Once again, another long silence. The large windows in the walls were now very dark, and the drone of the ceiling fan became more apparent.

"Well, I'm sick of this. Let's play a game or something," Greg said.

"Sounds good," Zeb said.

And so the day ended without further discussion of the events. In fact they would not be spoken of for more than a year. But the memory never left, and each of them carried some worry that perhaps one of them – or all of them – had become 'victims', akin to Alex and Wendell.

# CHAPTER THREE

## Descent

The fall semester was more than half completed for Aaron and Greg. The cold of winter was fast approaching, and it would bring to Greg dreadfully dark times. Noteworthy are the pastimes he preoccupied himself with, when he could afford to. Namely was the reading of the Scary Book, which began to leave lasting effects on his world view. Greg was a receptive young man and was known to become unusually affected by things that most would simply pass by. The influence that Story was having on him is of special interest to this story, in that he soon found himself comparing his life experiences to those of the characters in the Book. It was never far from thought.

Zeb and Aaron had been reading it too, and the three of them usually spent hours talking about it when they would gather, which was becoming more frequent as the months passed. Sessions of Dungeons and Dragons and walks in the woods, on the other hand, had nearly ceased. The surreal, the macabre, the tragic – these were the new curiosities. It should come as no surprise then, that Greg reacted with intense emotion when he was faced with similarly strange phenomena in his own world.

One night that world was Aaron's house. He and Aaron had just gone to bed after a long night of videogames and discussions. The bed was just wide enough for two, but one could still find sleep to be elusive in these conditions. It was not the size of the bed, however, that kept sleep at bay for Greg on this night.

Sleep had almost come. Aaron was fast asleep, motionless and breathing quietly. Greg had entered a tranquil twilight. There he was greeted by a soft sound, nearly imperceptible.

Quick and rhythmic, it's repetitious droning would have been almost hypnotic had it not forced itself any further upon him. Yet it did. It came to a point at which he realized he was hearing this, and at that moment he was fully returned to waking. He remained silent, listening, waiting for delirium to fade. Yet as it seemed to do so, he became conscious that the soft metallic clanging had not left.

He held his breath, listening for Aaron's. He heard this still, and it seemed to suppress the softer noise almost completely, unless he focused his attention on it solely. He wondered if he was even still hearing it. As if out of graciousness or perhaps malevolence, it made itself known to him as it slowly grew louder. Now there was no denying it. His only concern now was of its origin.

Surely there would be some simple explanation, he thought. The noise was now perceptible enough to be an annoyance; it would likely give him trouble returning to sleep. So he decided to rouse Aaron from his sleep, in hopes to put to rest the mystery and the noise itself.

His sleep, he thought, would be disrupted soon anyway, at this rate. He whispered softly in Aaron's ear, causing him to stir.

"...My son?..." Aaron mumbled in his sleep, who had none. Then he woke from his slumber and managed to speak with a slurred tongue. "...Huh?... What's wrong?"

"Aaron... listen... Can you hear that?" Greg whispered.

"What?" Aaron whispered.

"Listen..." Greg insisted quietly. There was silence while Aaron listened. Silence except for a familiarly quick and rhythmic tapping.

"No... It's back..." Aaron whispered in a despairing tone.

"You've heard it before?" Greg said, a bit too loudly

considering the hour.

"Yeah... It just started recently... not more than a few days ago," Aaron explained. The tapping continued.

"Well... what is it?" Greg asked, quieting quickly as he listened intently for the answer.

"I... don't know..." Aaron admitted. I walked all around the house in search of an origin but found none. I couldn't seem to pinpoint the location." The two lay silent for a while. The noise seemed to fade for a while, and then grew again, this time louder than before.

"You know, I can hear it better when I press my ear up against the pillow," Greg said. "Try it." There was another moment of silence.

"You're right... It seems to be coming from below, more than anywhere..." Aaron said. "...From the basement."

"The basement..." Greg said with reluctance.

"That's the one place I didn't search out," Aaron said hesitantly. "Should we check it out?" The deliberation time was short, and Greg replied,

"No." So the two agreed to pass it off as something not worthy of further inquiry, eventually falling back asleep. The next morning the noise was gone, and the rest of the visit went untroubled.

It was perhaps two weeks later when the three again gathered. It was pleasurable, as always, as they shared varying experiences of interest and sipped on coffee. They wanted to play some videogames, particularly a scary one that Greg had not yet seen. Among a pool of below-average horror games, this one's horror was almost comparable with that of the Scary Book.

Now, they were accustomed to playing video games in the family room, for its entertainment center was of the highest quality that any of them had access to. Its large television, however, had recently stopped working. The only option, now, was to relocate to the basement, where the other television was kept.

"Uh... Well, your basement's kind of creepy but I can

25

handle it," Greg said as he chuckled. Zeb looked relieved.

"I'm glad, actually," Zeb said as he was following the others out of the room. "This room troubles me more, for some reason... Those large windows... Those portals..." He shut the door behind him, and looking forward, found himself looking down the basement steps, these being illuminated by the two lamps that hung on the side. The others had turned left into the kitchen, to get some drinks ready.

"Do you want anything, Zeb?" Greg asked. Staring down into the cellar, Zeb didn't seem to hear him. "Hey, you want anything?"

"Oh, no, no. I'm fine," Zeb answered, blinking. "Let's go." The three descended the wooden stairwell, which was housed on both sides with wood paneling. When they reached the concrete floor, the first thing to do was make some light. Aaron flipped the switch on the far wall, creating a sanctuary of incandescence that cast dark shadows against the back walls.

"We'll keep it on until we're all settled," he said. Greg let out a sigh of reluctant agreement. He popped in the game disk and took his seat. Aaron flipped the light and quickly took his seat next to Zeb on the couch.

The three watched the screen intently, wrapped in blankets. Greg's sweaty hands gripped the controller tensely. Zeb advised him when necessary. Occasionally, Aaron would remember where he was and check his back, particularly during the scarier moments of the game.

There was a sable emptiness behind them all. The light of the television screen only rarely illuminated the back wall, and one could never see around the corner to the section where they had once played Dungeons and Dragons so often. For the most part, he could only make out the glinting of metallic objects, such as a hat rack in the corner and the doorknob to the laundry section.

Aaron looked back toward the others, to find Greg staring at him with a troubled look on his face. Aaron didn't know how to react. He looked to the screen for a reason but found none. Assuming Greg was reacting to something he had missed, he gave him a look of acknowledgment anyway to maintain the mood. It seemed to work, and Greg slowly turned back to the onscreen action.

Perhaps twenty minutes passed. A segment of great interest was now playing, as the game was a mystery story as well. Suddenly, Greg whipped around, taking hold of Zeb's leg.

"Whoa!" Zeb yelled. A look of horror was on Greg's face. He then looked over to Aaron. Aaron looked back.

"Yeah, it's getting pretty good now, huh?" Aaron said, again unsure if he was responding appropriately. Either he was not, it seemed, or Greg had a strange manner of expressing his fear.

"Don't you guys...?" Greg began, looking at each of them in shear horror. Aaron and Zeb stared at him, waiting. "Ah, never mind." He returned to the game.

Now, after not more than ten minutes, he once again wheeled around. This time he had a look of horror as well as disbelief. There was no indication at all that the game had evoked such a response. For it hadn't. "You guys don't hear that?!" Greg nearly screamed. They stared at him, their blank faces becoming concerned. "How can you not hear that?!"

"Hear what, Greg?" Aaron asked.

"You hear something?" Zeb asked.

"I thought I had heard it earlier, but I wasn't sure. Neither of you reacted. I heard it a second time, and I was sure it wasn't my imagination. But you two still didn't acknowledge it, so I rubbed it off as nothing important. But now, now this last time it was almost absurd, and absurd that neither of you heard it!" Greg said, growing more frustrated as he went on.

"What, Greg?! What did you hear?" Zeb asked fearfully, almost laughing at the situation.

"It – it sounded like... the monsters in this game!" Greg cried. Zeb seemed to relax.

"It was probably just the sound in the game bouncing off the walls. You know, an echo, basically." But Greg was not content.

"No, that sound should not have played at that part... and it sounded too realistic. And why would this sound start traveling funny all the sudden?!" He was still panicking. Zeb could not answer him.

"The furnace makes some noises sometimes and the fridge as well. In fact, I may have even heard it. Yeah, I guess I'm just used to it," Aaron said, in a comforting voice. Still Greg was not convinced. He stared at Aaron in utter disbelief.

"Oh, I get it - Your furnace makes high-pitched squeals, like an animal?" Greg asked flatly.

"Well..." Aaron started.

"It probably *was* an animal," Zeb said. Greg had no pets at home, so this seemed more credible. It could even be their little terrier, Hazel.

"Yeah, I hope so," Greg said as he turned back around. "I hope *so* much." He was having a hard time now focusing on the game and began performing somewhat poorly. He soon began to dread the darkness behind him. What if it wasn't an animal, he thought? Ridiculous, of course, he then thought. But it was at that moment that another shrill cry called to him from the darkness. It seemed to come from somewhere behind him. He turned to Zeb and Aaron once more, and still neither of them seemed to notice. "You guys have bad ears or something. It just happened again!"

"I'm... sorry," Aaron said, with a look of genuine concern. Zeb stared with intrigue. Then Greg remembered the noise that seemed to have come from the basement two weeks earlier, and he grew fearful. He paused the game.

"Turn on the light, Aaron," Greg demanded.

"I'm not getting up now, after you've said all that!" Aaron said, laughing in ridicule.

"I can't play this anymore," Greg said, standing up. The two brothers just stared. "There's something wrong with your basement. I just can't do this..." Zeb remained silent.

"C'mon, Greg, we'll pull through this. I'm sure everything's fine. Nothing's... wrong with this basement. Let's keep going for a little longer. We'll be going to bed soon," Aaron said.

Greg sat back down, willing to give it another shot. He was gradually drawn back into the game, and the rest of his night in the basement was uneventful. He did, however, find his sleep troubled when they had gone to bed. This time, it was a random, metallic plucking sound from immediately under the bed. It was as if the wires of the mattress springs themselves were popping, though too subdued. He reached over Aaron to turn on the lamp, hoping to reveal some cause. This it did not do, but it did bring some comfort. The light roused Aaron from his sleep, and he angrily turned it off. This happened several times that night, but nothing more was learned.

Greg had not forgotten the events of the previous night when he awoke. He said nothing more of them, however. Perhaps the best thing to do was forget about them. But as he left the Eldritchs' house, he could not help but realize he was beginning to develop a different relationship with it. What was once simply a place of fun had now become, to a degree, a place of fear. This was, of course, due primarily to the recent activities with which they occupied their time. But there was still something more which could not be overlooked. Strange things were happening in Aaron's basement, things that only he was experiencing. For the first time since they had become friends, he felt a sense of relief as he left.

This was not enough reason, he believed, to visit less often, however. He had good friends in Aaron and Zeb, and truly loved engaging in discourse with them, especially that which was philosophical. It was ironic, he realized. Even though these conversations often left him feeling depressed or disturbed, he desired them. They were inquiries into truth, knowledge and being. Time could be spent in no better way. And it made sense now why it was so natural for good games and books to follow. They themselves were vessels of truth, and to enter those worlds was to see his own world from that same perspective. He couldn't deny that the Scary Book was among these.

Thus, he would again visit, for such richness in experience was rare elsewhere – at least, this is the justification he had been offering himself. During this next visit, perhaps another couple weeks later, things went about in much the same manner. Still, the television in the family room was unusable.

"I hate playing in your basement," Greg said bluntly, and the brothers laughed.

"I'm sure it'll be fine," Zeb told him. But it was growing darker, and the darkness brought fear to Greg, especially now at the Eldritchs'.

"We leave the light on," Greg demanded. Aaron let out a whine.

"Only for a while," he said. "That light makes it hard for my eyes to focus on the TV."

The three found themselves in a familiar situation: Greg in the seat, controller in hand, and the two brothers wrapped in blankets on the sofa. The light was now off as well, as Aaron was being quite stubborn. And once again, being absorbed into the world of that game, Greg was not expecting to have an encounter with the anomalous. So when he heard what sounded like a muffled scream come from somewhere behind him, he jumped and began to shake with fear.

"What is it now?" Zeb asked. Greg simply looked at him in horror. "Oh no... Not again..." he said, shaking his head. Aaron threw his head back in frustration.

"What is it this time?" Aaron reiterated. Still Greg was silent. There came another noise now that Aaron and Zeb seemed to hear. "Now that just then was the fridge back there. It was probably the fridge before." Greg responded in such a way that made Aaron's comment ridiculous.

"Does your fridge go: 'Eeearrrghhh!'?" He said, trying to imitate the muffled scream as quietly as possible so as not to wake the parents. Aaron and Zeb couldn't help but laugh since no refrigerator they'd ever encountered made this sound and they suspected the same was true for anyone. Then Aaron simply shook his head for an official answer. Greg managed to amuse himself with it, as much as he could, and continued playing. But it became too personal to be amusing. From somewhere in the darkness, there came an inhuman voice that uttered but a single word, in a questioning tone: his own name, Greg.

He wheeled around, grabbing Zeb by the arm this time. But Zeb remained ignorant, and only jumped when Greg made the sudden move. "...My name!" Greg cried. "It called me by name!"

The others demanded an explanation. He tried as best he could, his voice now quivering. "A voice out of nowhere called out with one word: my name! Asking it like a question, you know, asking for me!" Zeb's eyes widened.

"The exact same thing has happened to me before!" He said, his eyes filling with tears. It was time for a discussion. "It was at Dan's apartment. He, I, and his girlfriend were all sitting around the table, talking about a movie we had just seen, when all of a sudden, it happened just as you say: I heard a voice call out to me by name. There's more, though. First of all, all of us heard it. But we each heard it from different spots. To me it sounded distant, like you said – kind of muffled. Yet it was right in my ear. Very weird. Even stranger, is that the voice was familiar to me."

"What...?" Greg said, still shaking.

"It was my mother's voice. In fact, the very first reaction I had was that of annoyance, because, even though I was at Dan's, I thought she was calling on me for some chore," Zeb explained. "You know, these very first thoughts all happen in an instant, before you can put them in their context." He looked up in thought, smiling to have made this insight. Greg looked away and grew very quiet.

"Why... me?..." he said, with a tone of despair none of the others had heard from him before.

"Hey, it's okay. I've gone through the exact same thing. Well, close enough anyway," Zeb said. And it did serve to comfort him some. At least he wasn't alone. He managed to continue with the game, but not with his whole attention.

Apparently, however, he was not allowed to feel this

comfort. In less than an hour, he heard something that cast him into a deep state of despair. It was a sound that he immediately associated with the Scary Book, having been described therein, and attached to it all of the same meanings. It was a train whistle, a siren's call to the unknown whose allure was strong not in its attractiveness but rather in its authority – whether he comply or not, the beckoning suggested a beckoner and therein lie his dread.

Accompanying this irruption was an industrial cacophony, a mounting torrent of crashing machinery. This, together with the residual numbness left by the train whistle, was for him a signal of a crumbling in the fabric of reality, a shift in worlds, and of evil presence. It may not have had such an effect on him had he not correlated his experience with those of the character in the Book, but it is hard to say whether he would have even heard this noise, had he not already understood it in such a way.

Essentially, then, it was not simply the noise his own associations with it that made it nauseating and dreadful, but also the possibility that it was meant to be understood and presented in such a way that it would be.

He let out a wail of despair as yet another whistle sounded off from some incalculable distance. And as this phantasm faded from perception, it left Greg with a sense of confinement rather than freedom. He looked to Aaron and Zeb, if nothing more than a subject of curiosity, to see if they would even be with him still. He saw them there, staring at him, if that meant anything. The nauseating discussion from earlier flooded back into his mind. What was reality if there was only subjective consciousness? And what was truth if meaning was arbitrary? What was his purpose, and how did he ever end up in this basement?... The images of the two people before him became clearer, and he remembered they were 'friends'. They were Zeb and Aaron, and this was their basement. Greg fell into his seat.

"I need to go to bed," he said.

"What...?" Zeb began. Greg cut him off.

"I'll... talk about it tomorrow." And so the three retired

for the night, and whether Greg slept restfully or not he could not recall, for what would have been torments before would have at this time been as appropriate as anything else. Only sleep itself seemed to bring him from that state and restore him to the person that had been known by others.

Golden light brought him into a new day. He squinted up at the window behind and over him. Birds were chirping. Wasn't something supposed to be wrong? The moment felt so perfect... Then he remembered that the night before had been quite disturbing. He wrapped the sheet around him, at peace, and with a feeling of newness. Now was now.

Aaron stirred as the sheet had been pulled from him. He rose from bed and got ready for the morning. Greg was wide awake now, deciding what fun thing he would do first. Aaron would not let his mind go here. "You feeling better?" He asked hesitantly. A sense of having been breached came over Greg, as if a facade had been attacked.

"Yeah, yeah, great. Shew, last night was weird, huh?" Greg said with a lack of genuine intrigue. He wanted to forget about it all. He had managed to keep the details out of his mind, particularly the moments before bed, and wanted it to remain so. But Aaron persisted.

"That's great, considering how bad off you were doing. We'll talk about it with Zeb after we've all woken up a bit." Greg decided to do his best to recount the experiences but would do so in little detail lest he accidentally relive them.

They left the bedroom and went to the family room. Greg pulled out a Japanese comic, while Aaron waited for Zeb. He knew his behavior must have seemed strange to his friend, judging by Aaron's perplexed expression. Perhaps he was countering his emotions too aggressively – their concern might grow if he came off as *too* normal. The right balance was never quite hit, and the others were lost for words as they watched their friend blissfully flip through the manga's pages.

After Zeb had woken and entered the family room with

a glass of orange juice, he looked toward Greg when he had his attention. His look was of acknowledgment, and a similar look from Greg meant a confirmation of discussions to come. Greg seemed to acknowledge his own thoughts more easily in Zeb's presence, for whatever reason. First, they enjoyed a breakfast of waffles and eggs that Mrs. Eldritch had prepared. After some idle chit-chat they then returned to the privacy of the family room, at which point Greg decided he was ready to give a brief account of the night before.

"Yes, they were noises," he affirmed. "And neither of you heard them. They were definitely unnatural, too." He knew there was more - but feared remembering the details. The others seemed to know as well.

"Something bothered you very much just before we went to bed," Zeb said. "You wouldn't tell us what happened... maybe you couldn't tell us..." Zeb said, looking into the depths of Greg's eyes, which could not maintain contact with his. Greg raced for an escape but found none. His mind slipped into the past, and there the train called for him.

"It was a train," he admitted. Aaron wasn't sure he had heard correctly.

"A train?" As in the kind on rails?"

"Yeah..." Greg said for him. He looked up at the windows, sunlight shining in brightly. It kept despair at bay, and further reflection, too. Don't actually think about it; he thought to himself, at a level so deep that perhaps he didn't realize it.

"Why... a train?" Zeb wondered aloud, looking very inquisitive.

"I don't know..." Greg said, trying to appear intrigued, but in truth the ruminating was opening him to a slew of feelings he was hoping to resist. Much to his dismay, his friends would not relent.

"Isn't there a story in the Book about a train?" Aaron asked with a grave expression. "I seem to remember something like that."

"Maybe. I don't recall." He returned to the comic, and the subject soon changed. "This is a pretty great fantasy manga," he managed to say with some enthusiasm. "It's hardcore medieval stuff. You know, we need to have a D&D campaign soon. It's been too long."

"You're right," Aaron conceded. "It's just... I don't know, something's been off. But maybe if we get out the chips and salsa and play some soundtracks, we can get our mind off the Scary Book for a while." One may have guessed, albeit incorrectly, that Greg already had managed that much. The rest of the visit went on quite blissfully, and there was little if any discussion of Greg's troubling experience.

It was not until a phone call that the topic came up. He and Aaron kept in close contact not only when they talked at the college, but also over the phone, and had always had an understanding that they would be open with one another. This time, Greg was alone in his home and he admitted his fear.

"You were never like this before, Greg," Aaron told him, though a bit of static on Greg's end forced him to repeat it.

"I can't help it. I can't deny that I've experienced what some may call paranormal," Greg sighed. "I sometimes begin to fear my own home, even though these things have only occurred in your basement. I guess talking to you makes me feel just a little safer, as irrational as it may be."

"I fear it is irrational," Aaron sighed, sympathizing with him. There was silence for a moment. Aaron broke it. "I wonder what your problem has been, lately?"

"I don't know... I think that the question is more pertinent to your basement, than to me," Greg said in retaliation.

"What could that *be*?..." Aaron asked in the tones of both wonder and despair. "Let's say there's something going on – for example, say, I don't know, a poltergeist making these sounds. I doubt you'd come over here very often knowing that!" Greg laughed.

"Would that surprise you?" And now Aaron chuckled. There was another silence. But before he could open his mouth, Greg heard in the earpiece someone call him by name, and it was not Aaron. It sounded almost electronic.

"Uh, Aaron...?" Greg said, feeling his heart fall right into the knot of his stomach which had just formed. He listened for any sign of concealing in Aaron's voice.

"Yes?" Aaron responded. There seemed to be only ignorance.

"You didn't just..." Greg began, but he stopped when he again heard his voice spoken, this time in a different pitch, but still electronic in tone.

"What's wrong with you, now, Greg?" Aaron asked, beginning to laugh in disbelief. But another voice called out to Greg once again while he laughed.

"It isn't funny, Aaron!" Greg cried. Aaron stopped laughing. There was silence for another moment. Greg wondered if it had passed; already it was beginning to seem like a dream. That illusion was immediately destroyed when he heard it again, and now several more times, each at a different pitch, and with variation in timing. Then he remembered that this, too, was something he had heard from another story. It was the game, in fact – the game he had been playing in Aaron's basement recently.

"What's with this mockery, all of a sudden?!" Greg cried out. He explained to Aaron this strange fact, and his doubts that it was mere coincidence. "It seems so... intentional..."

"Maybe you've been playing it too much," Aaron suggested. Greg felt no guilt whatsoever and, not wanting to hear this, gave his fervent opposition.

"No!" And he heard the calls continue, after a temporary silence. "NO! I can't believe this is happening... Your house is..." A string of calls silenced him. This time it sounded almost as if they were right at Aaron's mouthpiece. Now they began to quiet down and become less frequent.

"What's going on? Are you there?" Aaron asked with concern.

"Yeah...I think," Greg said, feeling doubtful about this. Perhaps he was beginning to lose it. That's what Aaron really must have meant, he thought. "I can't believe this," he said again.

"Now even the phone is having problems. It just keeps getting worse."

"I wish I could help," Aaron said. But both knew nothing could be done. Anyhow, the calling had since stopped. And soon the phone conversation came to an end as well. As Greg closed his flip-phone, his stubbornness gave him a shred of hope. This hope was a double-edged sword, however, as it would still sicken him. He hoped that Aaron had somehow done it, even if it meant that Aaron was capable of such a cruelty. The actual experience, however, seemed incapable of being faked without access to expensive telephony equipment. The idea was still a small comfort, and it was something he would play around with in his mind from time to time.

Aaron was pleasantly surprised a bit to find Greg still expressing a desire to visit. They were still enjoyable, for the most part, he guessed. But it was something Aaron just couldn't understand. Would he accept the ofttimes-ridiculous explanations while he was away at home, allowing him to come back with renewed ignorance? Hopefully it was not that he believed it all to be foul trickery, Aaron thought. Hopefully, also, it was not a state of denial Greg was entering. Perhaps it could still be something more... Only time could tell, and even that was no certainty.

It was apparently not denial, for on this evening Greg had new demands. "I'm not going to play that game anymore. I don't care. I'm simply not playing it, and that's that."
"What do you mean?" Aaron asked. "What's wrong with the game? You don't like it?"
"No, it's not that," Greg began, scratching his head. "There might be a problem with the game, and maybe not. I don't know. All I know is that my worst experiences happened while I played it, and I want to rule it out." Aaron nodded with a frown.
"Makes sense I guess... Just a shame, because such a good game deserves to be played through completely, and you'll miss out. Guess I would do the same, though."
"We'll play that other game you were in the middle of, you know, with the zombies," Zeb said. They all agreed and left

the room. They stood at the top of the stairwell.

"I still dread going down there," Greg said. Zeb gave him a pat on the back, also hoping to make him laugh, which it did.

"I know what you mean." The three scampered down as quickly as possible, hoping their speed would protect them more than caution. It also helped ensure that the effort would be carried out in full. These types of things were rituals of a sort, and it helped band the group together. It wasn't always necessary to explicitly name their fears.

They began to play a different game this time, and Aaron allowed the light to stay on for a longer time. By the time it had been switched off, they had already become immersed in the fun.

Greg didn't seem to mind the light going off so much. Perhaps it was punishment for his poor judgment, then, when a familiar high-pitched squeal cried out from the darkness behind him.

"It happened again!" Greg cried. And again, the brothers did not seem to notice. "I just heard the same noise, even though I'm playing a different game!" And so, the possibility that the game was in some way a cause was now disregarded, whether it was ever reasonable or not. "It definitely wasn't the game... It's this basement!" The others watched as he stood up.

"What are you doing?!" Zeb cried.

"I'm going upstairs," Greg said firmly. He turned the game off, and Aaron turned the lamp on.

"You heard him, Zeb," Aaron said. "Upstairs we go." The three raced upstairs, Greg first. They entered the family room straight ahead of them. Zeb cried out when he entered.

"Shut those blinds!" He said, pointing to the large, dark windows all around him. The other two obeyed. When the windows were covered, they sat. "Still nothing we can do about the skylights..." He looked up at the two windows on either side of the ceiling fan and stared into their emptiness.

"What's your problem, exactly, with these windows?" Greg asked, still shaking.

"It's just a phobia I've had since I was little," Zeb responded. "I can't help but imagine there being watchers of some sort out there in the darkness. Over the years I've heard many stories of people actually encountering such beings." Greg looked at him in horror. "But don't worry, because there is no proof that they are indeed watching, or that they even exist." They huddled on the couch. "So it happened again, huh Greg?" And the three discussed it a bit. Greg even brought up the phone incident.

"I just can't get over the fact that my experiences are so similar to these other horror stories, be they games or books," Greg said. "Especially that one." He pointed to the Scary Book which sat by itself on the table. "Can't life start imitating, I don't know, Lord of the Rings or Star Wars maybe? I'd much prefer one of those. Even desire it!"

But with all eyes now on the beautiful and terrifying simplicity that was the Scary Book's cover, the young men couldn't resist their temptation to read from it a little more. An hour or more went by, as the three analyzed its artistic approach to horror. But as the night grew later and their minds grew weary, they began to act silly. Greg, most of all, made light of the Story by acting out some parts he thought would look funny. He did it very well, they all agreed, making a great effort to actualize that world. Everyone laughed.

Greg looked through the window over the big television, at the clock on the wall of the kitchen. "Wow, this night wasn't so bad, spending it up here like that," he said. Now it was time for bed.

Zeb retired to his room for the night, while Aaron offered half his bed to Greg. It was expected, by now, that they would double up in Aaron's room. And so again they would on this night. After the lamp was switched off and his eyes had adjusted to the darkness, Greg began to think again of the correlation between Story and reality. Could the Book or even the videogames be causes, in some way, of his bizarre experiences? He thought how the one noise even occurred when its correlating game was not being played. Maybe a creature from that world had somehow become manifest in this one... and it would remain now whether the game was played or not. But then why would only he experience it? And why did the encounters seem to be limited to hearing? Was some sort of other world encroaching on his? Finally, why had it been only dreaded things threatening to surface, and not the wondrous fantasy stories he had grown up on that had always brought such joy and serenity? It really did all seem like a bad dream.

He comforted himself again with the things that had made him laugh earlier. He smiled, now, as consciousness slipped from him. Then a metallic bang rang out. His eyes widened, but there was only darkness. He reached across Aaron and turned on the lamp. It seemed to have come from the closet. How was it that Aaron didn't hear it?

"Can you hear?... The train is coming," Aaron murmured in his sleep. Perhaps he had heard the boom in his sleep. Greg turned the light off and lay down. He was upset that his pleasant drifting off had been disturbed. He closed his eyes. Perhaps ten minutes passed. Now he heard, from somewhere distantly below, the familiar metallic clanging, soft and rhythmic.

"No... Please..." Greg said softly. But the noise grew louder. Now he heard also the sound of the popping springs, twanging randomly. The clanging seemed to become almost soft booming now, like a drum, but still fast. His heart raced. He began to hyperventilate. What was happening to his world!? There was another bang now, from within the closet. It was more violent than before.

"What... was that?!" Aaron said, as Greg felt him sit up in bed.

"Aaron... It's crazy in here..." Greg whispered.

"What now?" Aaron asked. They both listened. Now it seemed to Greg that the rhythmic noise had died down but was still present. There was no more metallic plucking. "That beating sound... It's back," Aaron discovered.

"It was worse before you woke up, Aaron," Greg explained. "The closet was banging, and the plucking was back."

"Are you serious!?" Aaron cried softly, trying not to wake his parents. Of his parents Greg also wondered.

"I'm surprised your parents don't wake up! Are we the only ones hearing it?" Greg asked, breathing erratically.

"They've got a box fan in there that drowns out noise. You can hear it's hum slightly. It must do the trick," Aaron explained.

"Why does this only happen when I'm here?" Greg asked in despair.

"On the contrary, last weekend when you weren't here, this rhythmic noise was the loudest yet. It was louder than now for sure. And remember: I was the first to notice it," Aaron said softly. "Last weekend I actually vowed to make another investigation if I heard it again."

"No... You can't..." Greg stammered. Aaron turned on the light and climbed out of bed.

"Yes. Come if you want," he said. Greg watched as Aaron put on his shoes and unlocked the bedroom door. He considered waiting, alone, for Aaron's return. In this house, which was growing stranger by the moment, it was the last thing he wanted. It was even worse, he believed, than... exploring the basement.

"Alright," he said hesitantly, as Aaron opened the door. They stepped into the hallway, as quietly as possible. The floor creaked under their feet as they passed the door to Zeb's room.

They rounded the corner, moving away from the parent's room as quick as they could without making too much noise. They did without a hall light, as the glow from the halogen lamp over the kitchen sink was enough to see by, even in the hallway. They peered first into the dark living room, then around the corner into the kitchen. The way was clear.

Around the corner they crept. They approached the counters on the opposite side. To the left, was the passage to both the family room in front of them, and the basement. They saw their reflections clearly in the window over the sink, for only darkness lay beyond. As they reached the counter, however, Aaron saw a third reflection in the window.

He wheeled around in horror, unable to keep himself from shrieking. There stood Zeb in his underclothes, scratching his head of messy hair. Greg nearly fell toward the staircase as the shriek startled him, and both he and Aaron were in need of breath as they stared at Zeb.

"What are you guys doing out here? I thought you went to bed," Zeb asked. Aaron shook his head.

"You scared us to death," he began, and then said accusingly, "What are you doing out here?"

"I heard creaks in front of my door... I needed to know," Zeb explained.

"I see..." Greg added. Surmising the rest seemed wiser than risk having his friend summon an aberration into the world by invoking its name, if such a thing could have one.

"Well, we're here for a similar reason. We heard that rhythmic sound again, and decided to check out the basement," Aaron told him. Zeb looked unsure of him. "I've looked everywhere else already. It's the only place left."

"There were other things happening too. That room was getting bad," Greg said.

"Well, can you come with us?" Aaron asked him. Zeb hesitated.

"Strength in numbers," Greg added.

"I'll go a little ways, but I should really get back to bed. Have a hard time getting back to sleep when I've woken up too much, you know?" The three loomed over the stairwell. They expected utter dark, but there seemed to be a soft glow on the concrete.

"What could that be?" Aaron asked. Greg leaned closer.

"Do you hear that? It's subtle, but listen... Something..." Greg said. The three listened in silence. They could hear faint static.

"Turn on the light," Greg told him. Aaron flipped the switch and... nothing. He tried again. And again. The light would not come on.

"Great," Zeb sighed. "Looks like we need a flashlight." Aaron and Greg looked at him in dismay.

"Well, there is one in the family room. Let's get it," Aaron said.

"Uh, that's okay, you go on ahead," Zeb told him. Aaron shook his head and opened the door, reached in, and flipped on the light. At least it worked. He entered, and returned a moment later, turning off the light. Then a dimmer light shone forth. It came from the flashlight he held in his hand. The two others parted for him.

"Gee, thanks," Aaron said as he pointed the light down the stairwell. The concrete looked yellow in its light. "Something's going on down here. You guys ready?"

"Just go," Greg said. Aaron stood there hesitantly for a moment, then descended very quickly, almost to the bottom. The others began to follow, Greg checking the switch for himself as he passed. But suddenly Aaron, turning his head to the left, where the noise seemed to be emanating from, jumped back against the wall. The stairs here on the lower half had no wall, and one could see into the television section before fully entering the basement. He had seen something. Greg, who had followed almost as quickly, was almost able to see at this point. He decided to take a look for himself before Aaron came running back, which he had already begun to do. He ducked, and though it was for only a short moment, beheld an unsettling – and unexplainable – scene. The television was on when there was no reason for it to be but displayed only snowy static.

This snow cast a soft white light on the surrounding area, and the dark silhouette of the chair was in front of it. But he didn't have time to think about it. He would not be the last out of the basement, so up he went, with Aaron right behind him.

"What is it?!" Zeb cried.

"The T.V....It's on," Aaron gasped. Zeb shuddered. [1]

This was an outright attempt to scare, Greg thought. He suspected Aaron. But how?

---

[1]     This incident in which the television was found to be displaying snowy static for no apparent reason may have been on a different night. No one quite remembers whether it actually occurred during this search; Aaron has a vague memory of this incident occurring on the same night and has written it in the story as such. This incident was not documented in the audio log, which seems to suggest that it in fact happened on a separate night.

"We must have left it on," Aaron said. Greg's suspicion faded. "We ran up in such a scare. Let's continue." And so they did. Aaron reached the bottom, where he reached around the right corner, fumbling for the next light switch.

"None of the lights down here seem to be working," Aaron said. "Come on down here, and we'll turn that T.V. off." They met him at the bottom.

"Creepy..." Zeb said as he saw the white television screen for himself. Aaron held the flashlight in front him, scanning the room as he entered. As he panned to the right, Zeb pointed to the two windows at the top of that far wall.

"What's all that?" he asked. Aaron didn't seem to hear him. Greg looked, unsure if anything at all was different. Perhaps... There appeared to be some kind of plastic sheeting covering the window, but it was hard to tell for sure.

Aaron moved to the television, leaving the others in what was mostly darkness. They hurried into the light. As Aaron approached the television, the field of light grew smaller. He turned the television off, and for an instant there seemed to be no light at all. He quickly spun the light around behind him, lighting up much of the room. After a scan, he checked behind the television for anything unusual. Finding nothing, he returned the light to where it could reveal most. They moved together, toward the back corner where the poker table was. A quick scan with the flashlight revealed nothing.

"Only the laundry and work sections are left," Aaron said, stepping closer to the door that led here. He reached for the doorknob and wrapped his fingers around it. As he slowly turned it, Zeb backed off.

"I can't go on," he said softly, and suddenly took off up the stairs.

"Zeb!" Greg called out. But he was gone. [2]

---

[2]   Here the memories of Zebulon, Aaron, and Greg differ. The way in which Zeb left the others is described the way he and Aaron remember it. In Greg's memory, however, the experience was much stranger. It seemed that Zeb was there one second, and then gone the next. Aaron, in Greg's experience, didn't seem to notice or care.

"What about strength in numbers?" Aaron said angrily. "Nothing we can do about it. We were going to go anyway, just the two of us." Greg sighed, and moved closer. He focused now on the door. What lay beyond it? Hopefully what he expected. But then, what did he expect?... He wasn't sure anymore. The door swung inward, as Aaron released the knob. In front of them hung the punching bag, which startled them a bit at first. Aaron peered in with his flashlight.

"Hey, don't leave me in the dark back here," Greg said.

"Everything seems normal enough," Aaron said, pulling back. He then stepped into the room fully, and Greg wasted no time in following. But there, Greg saw a room which he would not exactly call normal. The flashlight darted back and forth as Aaron surveyed the area. In the bouncing light he thought he saw a large canvas-covered heap against the shelf to his right. Many things were under it and they looked something like... human bodies. What was going on? Didn't Aaron see it, he thought? But Greg said nothing of it.

Aaron moved toward the narrow passage that led to the work section and the furnace, the furthest removed corner of the house. Greg felt a panic now and was ready for the jarring clamor of a train to burst forth. But what he desired was an end to the suspense, and none came. They went further into the back, and the light was now illuminating the room as much as it would. There, Greg glimpsed something unusually white lying still on the floor, as the pressure in his head was ready to burst.

Aaron would not settle his light upon it, either not noticing it or paying it no heed. But for one moment the light remained on it long enough for Greg to identify form in it. There he saw, lying in the middle of the floor like a corpse, a doll-like figure. It's stark-white limbs looked far too thin to bear its own weight, should it try to walk. Whether it did or not he had not the chance to see, for Aaron turned around and shone the light in his face, blinding him. Aaron saw a look of horror on his face, and having finished the search, raced back to the door into the previous section. Together, they scampered up the stairs, and back to the security of the bedroom. Zeb had apparently returned to bed as well.

"Well, I don't know what to make of that noise now," Aaron said in disappointment, still catching his breath. Greg was silent. What was going on with Aaron? he thought. Then he began to question his own sanity. He could do nothing but sleep it over. And they did just that, being left in peace for the rest of the night.

Greg woke up quite early, despite his adventurous night. As he got ready for the day, he wondered how he should go about explaining things to the others. He realized that he would probably need to always explain things to his friends, since they never seemed to share in his experience. He resigned himself to this fact, and decided that, since there seemed to be no way of knowing whether or not it was a question of his sanity, he would do his best to accept what happened and not dwell on it.
Aaron arose a while later. After Aaron had woken up a bit, Greg explained everything that happened. Aaron was much in disbelief.

"Are you sure it was a doll? Because I think there is a utility belt lying around on the floor around that area." Greg rejected this.

"No way. I saw the joints and everything," he said sternly. "It was a little wooden dummy." He decided to take Aaron downstairs and show him. It would still be there, naturally.

They ran down the steps. This was much easier to do during the day. At that moment, Greg remembered the electrical malfunction they had experienced. He flipped the light. It worked fine. He and Aaron looked at each other, shaking their heads in disbelief. Then he pointed toward the bright windows on the back wall. "Zeb saw something weird up there, and I may have too. It was too dark to tell."

"Well, it looks fine now, whatever it was," Aaron said. Greg opened the door to the laundry section, and they stepped in.

"There should be that heap here, still! Where is it?!" Greg said in frustration.

"I never knew a 'heap' to be here. It looks as it should," Aaron said. "Now show me, where was this doll?" Greg led him back to the work section. It was a little hard trying to see things from the same perspective as the night before. It was so dark then... So many shadows... Did it even happen, he wondered? For there, approximately where he swore to have seen a lying doll, was the utility belt of which Aaron spoke.

"But it didn't look anything like that, except for the size, roughly," Greg said angrily.

"I'm sorry, Greg. I just don't know," Aaron said. Greg sighed.

"Ah, maybe it could've been, I guess..." But he doubted this very much. They returned upstairs and found that Zeb had since woken up. After breakfast, they gathered in the family room and Greg recounted his experience of the night before for Zeb. This was becoming routine. Zeb's perspective, however, was a new one.

"A doll... What could it mean?" he asked. The thought was unsettling. Greg had only briefly entertained the possibility that it meant something. Only the dread of the Train had made him do this.

"How do we know it meant anything?" Greg asked, thinking from an existential standpoint. "Perhaps I experienced it, and nothing more can be said of it."

"That's no more comforting," Zeb replied. "For then all of experience, remember, must be understood likewise. No event could hold significance, no experience would be more meaningful than another." A cloud must have passed over the sun, as the room darkened. "A world of order as only an illusion of the mind, with only chaos reigning." Zeb would always explain these viewpoints as if they were in fact true. "Of course, it still could mean something. You'd only then need ask yourself if this meaning came from above – from God I mean." Greg now wondered which was better. The answer was not clear. They talked only a bit more of it, then busied themselves with other activities.

After the visit, Greg decided that there must be something wrong the Eldritchs' house... Something with it, or something with *him*. He preferred the first. Something was particularly unnatural about their basement, and now Aaron's room. He would not sleep in that bed again, he decided. Mostly, it was simply the difficultly with peaceful sleep that made up his mind. He could deal with nightly mysteries, he thought, if he could at least get some damn sleep.

# CHAPTER FOUR

## A Visitation

Aaron came into art class one morning, telling Greg that he had had a rather unnerving experience himself the night before. The torment from doubting the faculties of his mind were becoming apparent in Greg's demeanor and Aaron hoped his story could mitigate this. He recounted the experience when class was over.

He and Zeb had been in the family room, watching "Rear Window" with their father, for the television had since been fixed. Under normal conditions such a film would have earned the Eldritch brothers' attention. This time however, they were forced to break from the screen-induced hypnosis when a huge bang came from behind them, as if the deck adjoining the house had been struck. Their father didn't acknowledge it.

"You heard that, right?..." Aaron asked his father.

"I guess I did," his father told him. Aaron waited for more, but that was all. He and Zeb looked at each other.

"What do you think it was?" Zeb asked his father. He only seemed to be bothered by Zeb, not the noise, nor the accompanying tremor.

"It was the deck," he said getting out of the recliner. "Time for me to go to bed. Good night."

"Good night," his sons answered, then looked at each other once more, in confusion. "The deck?" Zeb said when his father was gone. "What's that supposed to mean?"

"Yeah, it was obviously the deck that was hit so hard," Aaron added. They tried to watch the movie a little more. Aaron moved from the couch to recliner. Zeb took the seat of the other, on the opposite side of the wood stove. Then there was another hard knock on the deck, right behind Aaron. It must have occurred just on the other side of the window. He and Zeb leaped from their chairs. Aaron began to shake with fear.

"I can't believe this either!" Zeb cried.

"I'm getting my sword," Aaron said. He did just that, returning with katana in hand. As he entered, he flipped the switch to the deck light. All the blinds were shut during this time. "I'm going to take a peek out there, Zeb." Zeb moved aside, as Aaron approached the blinds.

He slowly pushed several of the blinds to the side, making just enough space so that he could stick his head between them and get a good look at the deck. He stuck his head through, rolling his eyes from side to side as he did this. The deck not only looked completely undamaged but was empty as well. "Huh," he said as his fears left him. He withdrew his head out from between the blinds, and began to turn away when *bang!*, another hard knock on the deck shaking the floor and sending Aaron running across to the opposite corner of the room in fright. He was now on the verge of tears. "To think what Greg must be going through..."

"And yet he continues to visit. Strange isn't it?" Zeb said, almost as if he was going to reveal the answer. He didn't.

"What the hell is out there? I had *just* looked out that window before the crash!" Aaron cried.

"I have only one guess, and if I am wrong, then it is most likely nothing," Zeb answered. But he said no more.

And so Aaron finished his tale.

"You see, it's your house, not me," Greg said.

"Perhaps. Though I still say that there is at least very little objectivity to the experiences. Please don't let that be a reason to stop visiting," Aaron responded.

"I don't see that happening," Greg guessed. What had happened, however, was that he had developed an intrigue with not only the house, but the people who lived there. "I don't get your parents," Greg admitted, breaking the short silence.

"Huh?" Aaron clearly had not interacted with many other parents.

"They're so... oblivious or something!"

"Oh, right. Hmm. Yeah, I guess you could say that. But I have to wonder if they are even experiencing the same things. I mean, what more can I do than ask them? They seem not only ignorant but bored as well."

"I just... Maybe that's what happens when you're middle-aged," Greg hypothesized. "And we'll be like that too." Aaron nodded with a sigh.

"For better or worse."

The two began to speak of lighter things. Incredibly, fortune had blessed the young men with a rare smile – and this smile would make manifest what, after so many months of separation, was beginning to seem futile: an actual sit-down game of Dungeons and Dragons.

"Derik said he has another friend interested in playing D&D with us," Greg said. Derik Young was a fairly new friend of Aaron's, having met him at Greg's birthday party, and the three of them had talked about their love of fantasy and medieval Europe. Inevitably, the subject of Dungeons And Dragons had come up and soon actual plans were in the works. Before this, it had not been since the days of Alex that Aaron and Greg had played, a terribly long time it seemed.

"Another friend?" Aaron asked.

"Yeah, his name's Royce. He used to be a Game Master but wants to get back into character playing," Greg explained.

"Royce like the Rolls-Royce?" Aaron asked sheepishly.

"Yes, Aaron," Greg chuckled, "like the car." Aaron shrugged. "Anyway, we probably won't be able to add him to our group for several weeks."

"That's okay, we'll do fine, just the three of us. When's our next gaming session going to be?" Aaron asked, looking out a classroom window as students walked around the campus below.

"I can come over this weekend, but we can't have a D&D session for another two weeks," Greg said.

"Sounds good," Aaron said, looking back at Greg now. "I'll call you before we do anything."

But Greg called Aaron first. There was a problem. And it wasn't about the get-together.

"So I was sitting in the gas station watching all my customers come and go, when my phone buzzed. I looked at the menu, and your number was listed. Are you sure you didn't call?" Greg asked.

"Positive. I wasn't going to call until tomorrow," Aaron told him.

"Your house... I'm telling you," Greg said. Aaron chuckled. They went ahead and finalized plans for the weekend.

"I'll see you then," Aaron said.

"I'll see ya, and do something about all that static. It's very annoying." The weekend came in a flash.

It came with one as well. Aaron and Greg sat in the family room. Zeb was on the telephone in his room. Twilight had passed, and darkness reigned. The blinds were still open. They would be shut, for sure, were Zeb with them. A stare toward the windows offered now only a scene reflected back at them. Aaron turned the light off to improve the lighting as they prepared to play a video game, upstairs at last. But suddenly, the walls were struck with intense white light. Both Aaron and Greg looked out the window, as they saw a most interesting thing. To Aaron it appeared as an orb of light, and to Greg it seemed to be more of a projected light. In any case it glided from one side of the yard to the other, very smoothly, and perhaps no more than twelve feet off the ground. It then suddenly vanished, as quickly as it had appeared, leaving the room once again dark, and the young men blind.

Neither knew what to say to the other. Finally, "I'm about to cry..." were Aaron's words. Greg simply nodded in agreement with a gaping and frowning mouth. Then, Hazel, the family dog, began barking at the front door in the other room. Zeb's voice could be heard now.

"What is it, girl, what's out there?" They heard him say. A door opened, and the barking faded out. "Darn it!" Zeb began to call to the little terrier, which had apparently run off into the night. When he heard Zeb come into the kitchen, Aaron called for him. And when he entered the family room, he welcomed him with news.

"We've got trouble," he said. And the two gave their accounts of what had happened. Zeb looked to the deck more than once during this, and the skylights too. It was not what he wanted to hear before going to bed.

When this time came, Greg went with Zeb as he had planned. "I sleep by myself every night, and yet here now with all of you it seems hard," Aaron said, entering his room alone. Both doors were shut, and everyone climbed in bed. Zeb's bed was a bunk bed, for Aaron used to sleep in it as well. Now, Greg took the top bunk. The bed was set against the wall, and it gave Zeb a feeling of protection. From what, Greg did not want to know. But he would soon learn more.

The desk lamp went out first, and then the study lamp by Zeb's head. The two talked for a while, asking each other who their favorite Lord of the Rings characters were and who they thought they might have been based on in their author's life. Greg heard a strange snore below him.

"What was... that?" Greg asked. He was paranoid of noise, now, though sight had also become problematic recently.

"Don't worry, Greg," Zeb said laughing softly. "That's just Hazel breathing." She had returned home earlier and now lay at the foot of his bed, her belly gently rising and falling as she slumbered. Soon however, there was another noise. Very subtle, but both heard it. A soft creaking outside, in the hallway. "Oh, no..." Zeb said in dismay.

"Zeb... What.... What is that!?" Greg said quietly, but terrified.

"Greg, it's.... it's not Hazel..." Zeb choked.

"Does this happen, often?" Greg wondered aloud, in

terror. He and Zeb were both pressed up against the wall, staring at the door.

"Only in dreams, I think. Hope, Greg, that no more of the dream materializes," Zeb said strongly. They listened in total silence. Even the soft breathing of Hazel made details hard to hear.

"Where did you say your parents were, again?" Greg asked. He was pretty sure he knew the answer.

"They went to look at their new property. They stay at a little motel near there, pretty often. They do a lot of work there," Zeb explained. "I'm sorry. It is not their footsteps we hear." Suddenly, there was a great scamper heard in the living room, just on the other side of the wall to which they had their backs.

"Oh God..." Greg moaned softly.

"Greg... I fear that – that my nightly dream may be realized on this night..." Zeb said.

"Why, why can't they leave you alone?" Greg sighed, while trying to hold his breath. Zeb remained silent. "Yeah, let's just listen..." There was creaking again just beyond the door.

They thought they heard the knob rattle, as if something had just made contact with it. "Turn on the light!" Greg rasped out, which Zeb did immediately.

"Greg, I am blind, tell me: Is the door shut?" Zeb asked. His vision was very bad, especially in artificial light like that which dimly lit the room. Now it looked like it was shut, but before Greg could answer, this was revealed to be false as the door was pulled shut fully with an indulgent click in the jamb.

"It is now," Greg said, on the verge of tears. He mustered up enough courage to leap out of bed and lock the door. He returned to bed, just in time to hear a great scampering immediately outside the door, and they heard another door - perhaps Aaron's - get thrown open violently, followed by a loud moan of despair.

"Aaron!" Zeb said with concern. Now they heard normal footsteps, and a light went on somewhere outside the door.

"He's gotten up," Greg said. Just then, their door was

thrown wide open, despite being locked, and Zeb screamed as he saw a shadow enter the room.

"Aaron!" Greg said.

"Aaron?" Zeb gasped. "What's wrong?"

"I'm sorry guys, but I couldn't do it. I'm going to have to bunk with you guys - I just can't do it," Aaron told them, holding a pillow and blanket. He threw these on the floor and lay down. "I can't say I've ever had my door thrown open like that before. Hopefully we'll all fare better here."

"Yeah, sure..." Greg sighed. And the three eventually fell asleep. They would sleep in that room, huddled together, nearly every sleep-over thereafter.

Just a few days later, Greg was sitting in the gas station earning some extra cash after his classes. He looked at his cell phone. Four missed calls from Aaron's? he thought. "Strange."

But there was something more. Not only were they impossibly close to one another in terms of time, but there was also a text message attached to it. It was a long string of nothing but ones and zeros. He called Aaron.

"No, Greg, I never called. Besides, how could I even do it that fast?" Aaron said.

"I don't know... I just have a hard time believing it," Greg sighed.

"Those ones and zeroes are called binary code, yeah?" Aaron asked. "It is probably some computer error within your phone."

"Somehow I doubt it," Greg said.

"That's understandable," Aaron replied. A loud cluster of static exploded in Greg's ear.

"Ow!" He shouted.

"Huh?" Aaron asked.

"Nothing, just static again," Greg said.

"Anyway," Aaron began, "I'll bet there's websites out there that could help decode it. I can try to find one if you want."

"Go for it," Greg told him, curious to find out if the message translated into anything meaningful. After a few minutes,

Aaron had found a website and Greg slowly read the numbers one by one. He was nearly a quarter through. "Well, is there anything there, yet?"

"Well, the numbers are translating into letters, but so far it seems random," Aaron explained. "Miami."

"Miami?"

"That's all it says. It's just going to be an ad or something when we finish." Another string of numbers was translated.

"What about now?" Greg asked anxiously, hoping that it would still mean nothing.

"Uh, Greg... Just keep reading me the numbers, and then I'll tell you," Aaron said. Greg felt a knot form in his stomach as he complied. A couple minutes later, then he said, "Alright. It's done."

"Well?" Greg asked impatiently.

"Now Greg, don't get upset, but there is a message... a short one," Aaron began.

"Great... Go on," Greg said hesitantly now.

"It's not an ad. And it doesn't say Miami. It says: 'I am, I am, I am.'"

"You're kidding..." Greg said, almost laughing.

"No, I'm sorry..." Aaron said. This was too much for Greg. He began to accuse Aaron.

"You...You did this!"

"What? No, how can you say that, Greg?" Aaron seemed hurt. Greg calmed down.

"I'm sorry; it's just too hard to believe!" Greg said. "Don't you see what this means?"

"Yes," Aaron said. "A consciousness... A will..."

"There is a presence there, in your house, Aaron. And it called my phone," he said.

"I can't believe it either," Aaron said solemnly. "This is incredible..."

"Wait until you tell Zeb about this," Greg said.

"I know," Aaron agreed. "I may just go and do that now."

"Alright," Greg said.

"But listen," Aaron continued. "Try not to let this get to you... and don't tell Derik, okay?"

"Yeah..." Greg answered.

"We need to keep it together if we're going to play D&D this weekend," Aaron explained.

"Derik should be fine... I just hope I can still do it," Greg sighed.

"Me too," Aaron added. "I'm sure everything will be fine. I'll see you then, okay?"

"Yeah. Take care," Greg told him.

"I will," Aaron said. And the conversation was over. Could there really be some presence there within his house, one that recognized itself? And why was it revealing itself to him? Greg wondered. It seemed things were only getting more complicated, but one thing was becoming clear. The problem indeed lay in the house more than in his mind, and any shadow of doubt in this matter had been vanquished by the gracious light of obliging visitors from another world.

# CHAPTER FIVE

## A Victim Born of Fruitfulness

Greg arrived at Derik's house. He hesitated for a moment. What would his bringing Derik to Aaron's house entail? Hopefully nothing more than a good time. He'll like Zeb, probably, Greg thought. There was only one way to answer these things. He knocked on the front door. It soon opened, revealing a diminutive young man. He pushed his long frizzy hair from his sea-blue eyes, revealing a pointy, freckled face with the hint of a mustache.

"Oh, hey," Derik said, smiling. "I was wondering when you were coming."

"You ready?" Greg said.

"As ready as ever, I guess. I've never been to Aaron's, before. It should be interesting," Derik said, putting on his shoes. He grabbed his bag and, after giving his mother a good-bye hug, left his home.

He watched the side mirror of Greg's car as his house disappeared from sight. A strange feeling of alienation came over him, and for a moment, he thought he was in a strange land finding his way home. This passed just as quickly, and to Greg it appeared as nothing more than a cold chill. "You okay, Derik?" he asked, looking away from the road for a moment.

"Yeah, yeah. Just a little anxious, I guess. You know, meeting his family and all," Derik said.

"Ah, don't worry about it. They're all pretty normal. Well, good people, at least; nice people. We'll be playing D&D in no time," Greg assured him. They continued to talk about this and that, as they enjoyed the country ride. Before long, they pulled off onto Attica Drive, coming down off the high ridge from where the surrounding county could be seen. Greg pointed to Aaron's house on the right, up the hill, as they drew near. He parked the car on the street's edge, in front of the house like usual. Derik looked up at the house through the window, as the sun lowered behind it. He was captivated by the scene, though it brought him a sense of insecurity for a moment.

"Hey," Greg called to him, who had already gotten out of the car. Derik came out of his daze. "Get your stuff. Come on." Greg slammed the trunk of his car, as Derik got out. The two walked up the driveway, the house looming over them. Greg paused for a moment to gather his thoughts. He prepared himself for what may come.

"What's wrong, Greg?" Derik asked, looking back as he walked ahead.

"Nothing, wait up," Greg said. The two ran up to the front door, playfully shoving one another. Greg gave a few knocks on the door, then he and Derik hid to the side. They saw someone come to the door, then open it. It was Aaron. They jumped out in front of him, growling, but with big smiles on their faces. Aaron jumped back, then lunged forward at them, laughing as he mimed a zombie.

The three came inside, and Derik surveyed his surroundings. He saw Aaron's parents right ahead of him, in the kitchen. They had turned around to welcome the guests. A small, weathered man with a graying mustache and an awkward woman with a friendly demeanor were the percepts that stayed with him after he was greeted. He noticed also, a distinct difference in the personality that was revealed in their faces. The father seemed rather calm, perhaps even lacking in general enthusiasm, while the mother seemed to carry a constant look of worry. He found both, however, to be very kind and accommodating.

They first went into the family room, where Zeb sat playing a video game. Derik's eyes met those of Zeb, and for a moment it was like they had known each other already. They introduced one another, and three younger men stood and watched as Zeb played the game. Derik watched this, reflecting on what he saw in Zeb already, for Derik was very sensitive to social relationships. He seemed so mature, even as he sat there with the game; so charismatic. When Zeb and Greg spoke a few cryptic words to one another, he sensed a deep friendship between them.

Zeb soon ended the game, and the four went downstairs to set up for the role-playing session. Greg had not spoken to Derik of his experiences, but Aaron was willing to speak partially of his. He did not want Derik to be in total shock, should even the slightest deviation from normality take place. "Yeah, sometimes some pretty creepy things happen around here," Aaron said, as if it was expected that scary stories would be told in a basement. Greg gave Aaron a look of concern. "You know," Aaron continued, "footsteps, creaking, stuff like that every now and again. Don't go running off if some things happen that you're not used to." Derik laughed nervously in partial agreement. They sat around the poker table, where the greatest role-playing in history had taken place.

"So this is the proverbial table," Derik said. The others laughed.

"And there's Frankie," Zeb said, pointing to something on the wall by the table. Greg nodded, with a wary laugh, for he had heard the story before. Derik simply stared at Zeb blankly, then at the wall, then back at Zeb.

"Look closely," Zeb began, "and you will see a grotesque face painted in great detail."

Derik looked hard. Then he saw it. The wall was white, but there were spots of patching that were even whiter. These white patches suddenly became the highlights of a deeply shadowed face, grotesque as Zeb had said, but with the most subtle of smirks.

"Amazing..." Derik said, for he was an artist, and recognized the talent that must have been required.

"Now I imagine you must think this was done by someone with great skill," Zeb said to Derik, who then nodded.

"Here you have made a hasty assumption," Zeb continued, looking now to the face upon the wall. "For this image was painted only accidentally by my father, who lacks an artistic mind, as he was patching the wall. That's what he suggested in any case when I asked him about it." Derik stared in disbelief and couldn't help but laugh.

"That's probably why you didn't see it immediately," Aaron added. "You can see all the other patchwork that doesn't have any recognizable form." Aaron now directed his attention to the lower portion of the accidental masterpiece. "This part looks like a large, dimpled chin to me. Zeb however, sees something more."

"Well it looks like a half-shadowed space-alien face," Derik said. Zeb trembled.

"It, um... could be described that way..." he confessed, darkly. "This whole image has been here for some time. Can't remember exactly when I first noticed, but it was around ten years ago."

"Well..." Derik said, unsure of what to add. They settled in their seats and spoke of other strange things. Zeb recounted the story of Wendell for him. Then Derik described a few people in his own high school that were creepy themselves, many of whom focused on the arts or drama. Zeb nodded.

"There was quite an interesting fellow in one of my classes," he said, looking first at Aaron then Derik. "His name was Bennett, Mark Bennett." Aaron looked at Zeb with an expression of concern. Zeb smiled and continued. "He always dressed very formally, amidst all the trendy fashions around him. Aside from this formality, he was a very normal looking young man. You would never guess that he was in fact one of the most eccentric individuals alive." Aaron laughed.

The others waited for an explanation. "First of all, he could be found reading from thick philosophical tomes almost any time. When he wasn't, he was writing in his own tome. This he would let no one see, not even I, who became a close friend. He showed me only one page, and it had a strange diagram drawn on it. When I asked him what it was he called it the 'Wa-Wa'."

62

Everyone laughed, but Aaron rubbed his face nervously. "He also had strange tales to tell me almost every day," Zeb continued. "He called these 'mind adventures' and they were apparently journeys that took him to other worlds. He encountered various beings in these worlds, and even spoke to some. There were also certain beings he learned of, in these worlds, that he never personally encountered. He called them the 'Pirates'. It was hard to tell if he meant it in the literal term or not. Whatever he meant he was very ambivalent toward these beings. He said that though they were pirates and he did not admire what they did, they still demanded respect, perhaps for their mission. It was a bit hard to understand." Zeb let that sink in for a moment. "He had some odd expressions, too. Let's see... One he said often, to me anyway, was 'you'll never know.' And sometimes, this guy would come into class looking completely normal, except for one thing that would unravel the world's order. I remember one time he came in with his glasses upside down. He wasn't trying to be funny, either." The others were much entertained.

Derik began to think of good stories he could tell the others, particularly any scary or strange ones. One came to mind. "It was when I was on a Church retreat," Derik began. "In fact, it was there that Greg and I met. Anyhow, we were sleeping outside in our sleeping bags. I dreamt that I was running around in the woods, in madness. When I woke, my feet were covered in leaves and dirt." Zeb looked intrigued.

"Are you known to sleepwalk?" he asked him.

"No, that's the thing that worries me," Derik answered. It was evident he was still distressed over this old mystery.

"Even if you were known to," Zeb started, "it doesn't necessarily mean that's what happened. It could..." But he left the rest trail off, realizing that what he was going to say would probably find little relatability in Derik. He knew how to maintain his charisma, and thankfully Derik wasn't stubborn.

Unsurprisingly, the conversation at some point transitioned to one where they were asking each other what they believed scared different sorts of people. Zeb emphasized how thrill was separate from true horror. Derik was not as much a philosopher as the others, and he mainly focused on stories. The point Zeb made on shock-horror brought one of these to mind.

"One of my friends gave one of his friends quite a scare one time. It was late and we were outside," Derik explained. Now he tried to hold back from laughing. "We were about to get in that friend's car, but little did he know that one of his friends was hiding under the car. As soon as the one guy was close enough, my friend reached out from underneath and grabbed his ankle. He screamed so loud!" Everyone laughed. Aaron cupped his chin in thought, looking at Derik.

"Has Derik heard of the Scary Book?" Zeb asked.

"I've heard of it from the others when we were at Greg's house," Derik began. "Apparently it's the most disturbing tale ever."

"Yeah..." Zeb said.

"Honestly though Derik, like we've said, it would be best if you don't read it," Aaron told him. "Greg and I tell you this, having learned from experience. Learn from our mistake," he said, trying to humor him while remaining fully honest.

"You don't understand how much that story changed us, Derik," Greg said, not thinking himself how much it may have truly changed him. Still, it was true. "We didn't necessarily want it either. It's just that when you're exposed to such traumatic material, it has long-term effects." Zeb was now laughing to himself. "Don't you remember, Derik, don't you remember how different I used to be?!" Greg said, his face becoming tense. Derik looked concerned, noticing beads of sweat having formed on Greg's forehead.

"Yeah, I do actually... You do seem a little different. More downcast," Derik replied.

"You see? You don't want to read it!" Greg said in a more of a commanding manner this time.

"Alright, alright, geez," Derik said. "Anyway, it's getting later. We should get to playing soon."

"He's right, I guess," Zeb said. "My parents have already left for their trip." The parents had again taken a trip to their new property. "I actually have to get going, too. But I'll be back soon. Just need to make a quick trip into town." He left the three to their game.

"Now," Aaron began with a huff, "let's get started!"

The three were excited to be playing again, especially at the famous poker table. Still, Derik was left wanting. Having long considered himself sensitive to other's feelings, he sensed something was amiss with his friend Greg. That jovial and energetic person just wasn't there. Perhaps it was the role-playing. Could the personality of his character be bleeding over into his creator? He admitted to himself that he might be over-analyzing things. They had reached a rather serious moment in Aaron's campaign, after all. With that, he concluded it would be unwise to bring it up again – interrupting the game would most likely only see Greg's bowl of salsa dumped over his head.

As the minutes fled by, their enjoyment kept them from feeling any dread of the basement until Greg happened to look over toward the cellar door. He remembered the horror he once had in him when opening it. Then he saw that it was slightly ajar. "Hold on guys," Greg told them, seemingly out of the blue. He ran over quickly and pulled the door shut. "There," he said, returning to the table. The others waited for an explanation, though Aaron was less in need of one. "I can't stand that door. If I'm going to be sitting by it, it needs to be shut." Derik looked inquisitively at Greg, and let a small chuckle escape him. They returned to the game.

Several more minutes passed. Aaron rolled his dice, leaving his imagined world's circumstances to chance. Just then, there came a soft tap from the direction of the door Greg had just shut. Everyone looked at each other, for they had all heard it. They ignored it and continued on with the game. It involved a lot of voice acting, much of which was quite loud. It had now died down a bit, probably because they were actually still listening out for any further knocks. This was perhaps the only reason they now heard another knock, which seemed to be on the door itself. Everyone jumped. Greg jumped back against the wall, nearly knocking Derik out of his chair.

"Everyone heard that, right?!" Aaron clamored.

"Yeah!" The other two cried out. They all looked at each other in disbelief. Derik was amused, slightly, at the situation. The other two, having before discovered what such seemingly innocuous occurrences had become precursors to, were not feeling so jocose.

"Could it be Zeb, you think?" Derik asked, beginning to shake now.

"I hope so," Greg said. "But I doubt it. He's never done anything like this before."

"He's gone anyway," Aaron realized. "And he would never stand in that dark room by himself – never." The three stood for a while in silence. Now Greg realized the danger of role-playing at such a time.

"I want to play, but I want to be alert as well... I hate this!" he whined. They deliberated quietly for a few minutes. By that time, the fear had begun to fade, and they decided it was safe to resume, though only at a softer level. This, they now discovered, was a big mistake. As if out of anger for their inattention, the door now swung steadily open as they all stared in horror. As they jumped out of their seats to run for the stairs, the opening door revealed something terrifying to Derik and Greg. There in the middle of the doorway, its plastic surface glistening in the lamplight, stood a rocking-horse. It seemed to be impossibly in the way of the opening door, as this opened inward. Yet there it was, staring at them with wide-set eyes. There was no time to think about this, however, as the three were already running for the steps, leaving the horse behind them.

At the top of the stairs, they each grabbed a knife from the knife set on the counter. They looked at each other in horror, breathing wildly.

"That door opened... all by itself!" Aaron cried, unaware of the horse the others had seen.

"No – the horse... There was a horse!" Greg screamed at him, in frustration and horror.

"There was a horse in the doorway!" Derik affirmed in a

quivering voice, though a hint of frolic remained in his eyes.

"What...?!" Aaron asked, in confusion and terror. "Let's get out of here!" He ran to the front door, knife in hand. Throwing open the door, he ran out into the darkness. The others followed right behind, running across the dew-soaked grass in only their socks. Aaron raced around the house. "There's a back door into the laundry room," Aaron puffed as he ran. They came around the bend, where a large bush grew. Around the corner, they saw concrete steps, surrounded by a metal railing, leading down to the back part of the cellar. "Let's go!" he shouted. The others followed, feeling they had no other choice. They would certainly not stand alone in the dark after having seen what they did.

Aaron reached the bottom and opened the door. His trembling hand reached around the corner and flipped a switch. A halogen light flickered on. They entered the room, shutting the door behind them. Everything was normal. The door was shut, just as Greg had made it. To Greg and Derik's horror, however, they did see the horse. It sat, however, where it belonged, whether they knew it or not, and this place was not in front of the door but on the side, rather, against the wall. "That's the horse!" Derik shrieked, pointing at it.

"But that's not where it was! And the door is shut!" Greg added.

"You're right! This door was open when we left it," Aaron observed, as he looked around. "It's as though it never even happened..." Now he examined the horse. "You say it was this horse? Are you sure you didn't see it here against the wall as you ran by?"

"No, it was definitely in the doorway... and facing us," Greg explained, still shaking.

"Strange, since I am sure I saw nothing but the dark room beyond the door," Aaron said. "And it would even seem impossible for the horse to be here," he said, standing in the spot where they claimed it had stood. "The opening door would not have been able to fully open, which it did, had it been obstructed by the horse here."

"Yet we saw it there all the same," Derik insisted.

"I just don't know…" Aaron sighed. He opened the door in front of him.

Everything on the other side was normal as well, just as they had left it. "We would never have guessed, ten minutes ago, that we would be the ones emerging from this door." They regrouped in the club part of the basement, closing the laundry room door tightly behind them. They looked at each other, as they held their knives, still in disbelief.

"My… gosh!" Derik said, with a laugh of disbelief. That was all he could do to sum up his feelings.

"My feet are soaking," Greg said. Aaron chuckled. He and Greg sat down on the bar stools next to the bar.

"Sorry, Derik, but I did warn you," Aaron said.

"Yeah, I know. You couldn't do anything more," Derik responded. "I've got to go to the bathroom, I'll be back."

"Heh, I bet you do. Be careful now," Aaron told him. Aaron and Greg could only wait.

Derik crept up the stairs, knife in hand. He could see only the folding-door to the family room ahead. He reached the top and peered around the corner. The kitchen was still and silent. Only the light of the halogen lamp over the sink allowed him to see. He passed the knife set, still holding the knife. He would take it to the bathroom with him. He stepped across the floor, looking through the doorway ahead and into the living room. He saw his reflection staring back at him in the window of the front-entry door. It drew nearer as he came to the doorway. Suddenly, a figure stepped from around the corner. Derik jumped back, his throat chocking out any attempt to scream. Then he recognized the figure. It was Zeb.

Aaron hopped off the bar stool, with an inquiring look. "Listen," he said, signaling Greg for silence. They stood at the bottom of the steps. "Did you hear that?"

"No, what?" Greg asked, his forehead wrinkling with worry. He moved closer.

"It sounded like… Derik… talking!" Aaron stammered. "Listen!" Greg obeyed him.

"You're right!" He turned to Aaron in shock. "There are

definitely voices up there!"

"Not only that, but they sound very calm... Who could Derik be talking with?" Aaron wondered aloud.

"Maybe we should hope it's Derik," Greg said. "Because if it's not him, well, then..."

After a minute, the faint conversation ended. Then, a minute later, footsteps were heard approaching the top of the stairs. Looking up, they saw Derik proceed down the steps. Derik seemed confused as they backed away from him cautiously.

"What's wrong with you two?" He asked them. Looks of uncertainty were on their faces.

"Who were you talking to?" Greg demanded in a stern, slow tone. Derik seemed confused by this.

"Who was I talking to?" he asked.

"Yes, Derik, who were you talking to up there?" Aaron asked him in a demanding manner. Derik looked at Aaron like he was crazy.

"No one, why?" Derik said.

"Oh, great..." Greg muttered. The three returned to the poker table, Aaron sighing heavily.

"Derik," Aaron began, "we heard... voices, upstairs. We were almost certain it was you, talking with somebody. Are you sure it wasn't you?"

"Positive," Derik said. "That's pretty weird... What's going on around here?" he asked.

"Your guess is as good as mine, actually," Aaron said. Now they heard footsteps upstairs. "See?! There's someone up there!" Derik, with a gaping mouth, nodded in agreement as he listened. The footsteps came closer now, even to the top of the steps. They all stared in this direction, holding their knives in front of them. Down the steps came Zeb, swinging his keys.

"Hey, I'm back," he said. Then he saw them huddled together, all with knives brandished. "Woah, what's with you guys?" He began to laugh. "What, uh, happened... to your game?"

The three explained the whole story, in detail. Though disturbed by the story, Zeb was not surprised. "I guess all this is pretty new to you, Derik?" Zeb asked.

"Well, uh... Yeah!" he answered, as if the answer was obvious. In any other house it would have been.

"You get used to it after a while," Zeb assured him. "Don't let it get to you."

"I'll do my best," Derik said, chuckling nervously.

"Well, should we try to resume the game?" Aaron asked.

"I don't think I can..." Greg sighed. "Not after all that."

"Well that wasn't one of our better sessions, to be sure," Aaron said. "Let's go upstairs then."

The four entered the family room, after turning off all the lights and returning the knives to their proper places. They began to talk, and soon it was a full-blown philosophical discussion. Derik was not used to this, and the emphasis on reason and logic annoyed him a bit – he had always worked better on intuition. But as he listened to Zeb more and more, he began to look up to him. He really was wise, he thought, just as Greg had told him. He would have preferred, of course, that Zeb have a less dismal view on things... Was this necessary, he thought? More than once he heard Zeb refer to the 'Nothing'. It was a concept he had a very hard time understanding. He looked out the skylights, which were now only voids of ebony, in an effort to understand. A feeling of anxiety began to fill him slowly, until it made him weary. The others noticed after another hour or more of talking that Derik was very tired, and now made plans for bed.

Zeb retired to his bedroom, while Aaron and his two guests prepared the family room for sleeping. "This is not my favorite room to sleep in," Aaron said. He told Derik the story about the knocks on the deck. It wasn't as if Derik would think the place normal if he left his friend ignorant. The lamp was turned off, and the three were soon asleep. Their night went undisturbed.

The next day, after the guests had left, Zeb approached Aaron. "Aaron... about what happened last night..." he began.

"Yes, something unexpected happened..." Aaron replied

in anticipation.

"It's Derik... he believes the horse incident to be farce, and my doing," Zeb explained.

Aaron nodded. "I see..."

That night, Aaron called Derik on the phone. "Oh, hey Aaron," Derik greeted him.

"Listen," Aaron began. "I was thinking about your story of your friend scaring the guy by the car..."

"Okay, go on," Derik said.

"Well, I was wondering if you could do something for me," Aaron said.

"Maybe. What is it?" Derik asked with curiosity.

"Well, regarding the unusual things that happen here..."

# CHAPTER SIX

## The Year of Games

Greg was talking to Derik over the phone. "Aaron wanted to know if you could make it this weekend," he said to Derik.

"Yeah, I think I can," he replied.

"I know I probably shouldn't let you do it," Greg told him, "but at least you'll finally begin to understand what we're talking about all the time." He was talking about the Scary Book.

Over the last few weeks the three had been holding their role-playing sessions in Aaron's basement, and without any 'trouble'. During this time, Derik's curiosity of the Book had grown so much as he heard the other three make constant references to it, that he had suddenly jumped up from the table, insisting that the Book be read aloud. The others reluctantly agreed.

"You think they'll let me just buy a copy of the Book and read it for myself?" Derik asked Greg.

"Well, we've been reading from it as a group for over a year now," Greg explained. "I've since finished, but there is another Book of bonus chapters coming soon. We like to discuss it as we read, and they'll probably want to see your reaction. It amuses them."

"I can imagine..." Derik said, more to himself than Greg.

"Alright, then, I'll pick you up Friday evening. Does that work?" Greg asked.

"Sounds good... Oh, and Greg. Have you ever noticed all that static on the phone when talking to Aaron?" Derik asked somewhat hesitantly.

"Yeah, I have. I'm sure they'll call in a service ticket for it," Greg told him.

"Right," Derik said. "Well, then, I guess I'll see you Friday?"

"Yeah. See you then," Greg said. The phones went back on their receivers and the call ended.

Daniel and his son Carson were there for the weekend when Derik and Greg arrived. Derik had not yet met them. He wondered why Daniel was dressed like popular character from a movie about archaeological adventures. Aaron laughed when the question came up.

"Well, it's because he *is* an archaeologist, or was for a time at least. But it may be that he chose that path only because of the movie. It influenced him a lot, you see?" Aaron explained. Derik was humored. "He actually has quite a few interesting tales of his adventures. Some are even a bit frightening."

Everyone sat together in the family room as Aaron reluctantly brought the Book to the center, though still with a smile. Though worried about what effect it may have on Derik over time, he was still excited to show it to someone new. Finally, when everyone was settled, Zeb began to read from it. Carson listened, and grew scared. At this point, Daniel took him and the two left the room. Now it was only the four of them.

As the hours passed, Greg noticed a change in Aaron. His face looked weary of worry, almost as if over something other than the story being read. After the three drank some coffee – Zeb never drank it for it had only ever interfered with his mind – the reason seemed clear.

"I'm getting bad stomach cramps," Aaron said.

"Just don't gas us out of here," Zeb teased. The others laughed. Before long, they were the only ones awake now. The house was so full that every bed was taken, and they would have to sleep in the family room whether they wanted to or not. There was no point in stopping yet, for the coffee was now taking effect, except for Zeb who had handed over the reading to Aaron.

He lay down in the sofa and shut his eyes. Before long, Aaron could no longer read.

"I'll be back," he said, rubbing his belly. "These stories are tearing me up." He handed the Book to Derik to read for himself, then left for the bathroom.

"Hardly anyone's listening, now," Derik pointed out.

"When you get to a good part, we'll stop and wait," Greg suggested. Derik continued reading. Aaron returned in a few minutes.

"It's not over yet," he said, grinning. "Honestly, I almost feel like vomiting." Zeb laughed, surprising everyone since they thought he was asleep. Aaron let Derik continue reading, as he no longer seemed able to do so himself. Derik slowly began to get a feel for the style of the Book. Aaron had to jump up again. "Time to try again," he said. The others pretended not to hear him. They were now a group of just three. After a few minutes, Derik paused.

"I'm kind of thirsty," he said. "Let's get a drink and wait for Aaron." Zeb got off the sofa and the three left the family room, entering the dark kitchen. Zeb turned on the light. They heard the vent in the bathroom and came halfway down the hallway. The odor coming from behind the bathroom door was impossible to ignore.

"Ah, let's get out of here!" Zeb gagged, the others laughing and running ahead of him. They began to pour their drinks when the lights flickered for a moment. "Everyone saw that, right?" They nodded. Remembering the electrical malfunction several weeks before, during the doll incident, Greg walked over to the stairwell to check the same switch. As he came around the corner under the kitchen light to reach for the switch, he could not help but glance down the stairwell.

In the dim light that was cast by this overhead light, he

saw there on the floor at the bottom of the staircase something most unexpected. He quickly withdrew his arm from the stairwell and stood there speechless as he beheld the peculiarity. There, squarely on the concrete, was a portal of sorts. It had a wide frame that seemed to be made of plywood or some solid material, weighing heavily upon the concrete. On the left and right sides of this frame was something that looked like a coiled wire. Within the frame, he perceived what seemed to be depth, in that he could see that what lay beyond was well below the concrete slab. Because of the frame, however, he had no sense of the thickness of the slab. He saw only what was beyond the portal which looked something like large white tiles. Due to the poor reach of the incandescent light above, he couldn't be certain. Now, on the close side of the square border, coming out from under the framing, there were two appendages that looked almost like bicycle handles, as if the whole thing was to be lifted off the ground and carried away by someone. The monstrosity in its entirety was very symmetrical.

He observed all this in nothing more than a short moment, and only Derik noticed that he had seen something. Greg turned away, facing the others, with a stern face that seemed flushed of true strength.

"Zeb... Come here. You have to see this," he said. Derik stood there with a blank face, as Zeb approached the top of the stairwell. Greg backed away for him, as he leaned in. He gave a quick scan of what lay before his eyes, then withdrew.

"What? What's the matter?" he said.

"What?!" Greg exclaimed. He pushed Zeb out of the way and looked down into the cellar. Everything was back to normal: the anomaly was no more.

"It's gone!" he cried out, putting his hand to his forehead in dizzying disbelief. "Oh my God..." He tried the light switch. It didn't work.

"The light isn't working!" Zeb said in despair.

"Something's still wrong here... but this is not what I wanted you to see," Greg explained.

Zeb grabbed his drink and retreated into the family

room. The others followed him, Derik glancing down the cellar as he passed and shutting the door behind him. "It must be Aaron," Greg said in disgust. "He's up to no good." Zeb could see that Greg was truly bothered. Derik just stood and watched; his mouth parted as if confused.

"Greg - What did you see?" Zeb inquired. Greg continued to shake his head in disgust.

"...Up to no good..." he said again. "There was something very weird at the bottom of the steps." He began to describe it, when they heard a toilet flush. Soon they heard someone coming through the kitchen, toward the door. The door opened and Aaron walked in, with a look of relief.

"All better," he said. "...I think." His smile faded when he saw the angry, flushed face of Greg.

"There's trouble, Aaron," Zeb said.

"So, you're playing your games again?" Greg added angrily, remembering a similar situation in the very same room some time ago.

"Games?" Aaron asked.

"You know what I'm talking about, Aaron," Greg growled.

"Aaron," Zeb began, "Something really weird just happened."

"Let me at least defend myself!" Aaron said, growing angry himself. He sat down in the recliner, with a sigh of either frustration or relief. "I've been in the bathroom for nearly fifteen minutes, now. How can you accuse me!?" he asked Greg in defense. Greg was silent for a moment.

"Now from the way you're behaving, I'm actually starting to believe you. I'm growing very sick as well," Greg began. Aaron let him continue. "Look," he said. "I'm just feeling flustered, is all. Give me a moment to think." Derik and Aaron exchanged glances.

"Tell me what happened, whenever you can," Aaron said gently. There was silence for a moment. Derik sat quietly on the floor by Greg, and Zeb sat in the sofa staring up at the skylight.

"Well first the lights started to act up." At this moment

he quickly stood up. "Look." He beckoned for Aaron, who followed him to the opening at the top of the stairwell. Greg reached out and flipped the switch. The light worked fine. "Well now it's back to normal. Anyway, it wasn't working." He turned it off and they quickly returned to the family room. "I guess you saw, guys," he said to the others as he entered. "The light's working again." Zeb shook his head.

"The world has settled back into normalcy," he stated solemnly.

"Is that what has you so worked up?" Aaron asked.

"No," Greg began. "You haven't heard the worst. I saw something very strange at the bottom of the steps." Aaron looked at Zeb, who now listened intently. "It's hard to describe, but it was almost like a hole in the floor. It was hard to tell. I could see something down there that looked like your basement ceiling tiles, as if it were a mirror reflecting up."

"A mirror..." Aaron echoed.

"But it could just as easily have been the wall of a tiled shaft, if you know what I mean, especially the way the light hit it," Greg explained. He then described the details as best as he could remember, including the frame, wires and handles.

"You were right about it being weird..." Aaron said. Zeb looked up at the skylight again.

"So it was almost like one of these portals up here?" he asked.

"Yeah..." Greg said in disgust. "A portal." Aaron got out his sketchbook so Greg could replicate what he saw as best he could. Before long, an image was drawn that would never be forgotten.

Even several days later, Greg was still feeling confused and distraught over his personal encounter. He decided to give Derik a call, since their drive home had been a relatively quiet one.

"I just can't help it," he said. "It's so hard to believe that I actually saw it. No one else goes through this. And when they do, they're labeled as crazy."

"You're not crazy, Greg," Derik insisted. "It's his house,

remember? Not you."

"I guess you're right... What's going on over there?..." There was silence for a moment. "And still, it was only me. Why was I the only one?"

"Don't worry about it. Maybe you'll find out one day," Derik said, in as comforting a tone as he could manage.

"And I wonder about Aaron, too," Greg said. "Could it have been one of his games?" He hoped this was true. He just didn't see, however, how this could be. Derik further confirmed this doubt.

"It didn't seem like it to me," Derik began. "We've talked about it. He's worried about you." Greg sighed heavily into the phone.

"I just miss the days when we could just play games and have a good time," he said. "It all started with the Book. Maybe I should never have read it."

"That's silly, Greg. It's scary, but it's still only a book. The problem is either with our infatuation with it, or Aaron's house itself," Derik stated. Greg offered a third possibility.

"Or both..." The phone call ended. Derik hung up the phone and with a sigh, allowed the spirit of melancholy to claim the remainder of his day.

It was winter break now for Aaron and Greg. Derik was still finishing up his second last high school semester. Greg gave Aaron a call on the phone. He was greeted with a scramble of static, and all he could manage in response was a "Wow."

"Hello? Hello?" A voice said. It was Aaron's.

"Hey..." Greg said. The two talked about various things for a while. Inevitably, it seemed, the subject of the portal came up. "I still can't believe I saw that..." It had been several weeks, now, since his visit, as exam time had made them very busy.

"Nor can I," Aaron replied. "I'm still trying to figure out what it means, if it means anything at all." He waited for a response. Soon he heard laughing.

"...I just... can't believe it!..." Greg managed to say, still laughing. He was now nearly hysterical.

"Greg..." Aaron said empathetically.

"Oh, Aaron..." he continued, as if in delirium. "I wish something would just come and blow out my flame of life!" He laughed madly now.

"Greg! Greg!!" Aaron shouted into the mouthpiece. The laughing eased a bit. "What do you mean by that!?" Greg simply continued to chuckle, until he finally calmed. Aaron had never heard him behave so maniacally before. "Greg, are you ready to talk?"

"Yeah... I think so..." he said softly, chuckling now and again.

"Did you want to drop by, sometime?" Aaron asked hesitantly.

"Sure... How about next weekend? I'm busy this weekend," Greg answered. He seemed to have returned to equilibrium as quickly as he had left it.

"Alright. I think Dan will be here again, so I have to double-check," Aaron said. "My parents need space sometimes, you know."

"Yeah. Well you do that, and get back with me, okay?" Greg said.

"Sure," Aaron responded. They hung up their phones. Aaron managed to persuade his parents to let Greg visit even when Daniel and Carson would be needing a bed. The only condition was that only he could come, and Derik would not be allowed. It turned out that Derik was too busy that weekend, now in the middle of exams himself, so it worked out anyway.

When Greg came over, he felt a sense of relief almost, as there would be no reading from the Scary Book this time. Daniel and Carson were there as well, and Aaron's mother was playing Christmas music over the speakers. There was a sense of celebration, one he had not felt in some time. It was nice. Even the basement had become a place of comfort and socializing as the three brothers and Greg all sat around the bar smoking their pipes, sipped on blueberry wine, and listened to renditions of colonial-era music. Carson watched whimsically from a distance, enjoying the aroma against his father's wishes.

"It's too bad we don't do this more often," Daniel said. "One day we won't be able to anymore."

"You mean because of your parents, right?" Greg asked him. "Since they've got that new property I suppose." Daniel nodded then blew a smoke ring.

"You may not be able to feel it now," Zeb began, "but the Nothing is on the boundaries of this world that is our home. The moments are fleeting by infinitely fast, and nothing can be done to stop it." Greg made a noise of disgust, and for a brief moment it seemed that the basement, in its nothingness, twitched, and he was surrounded by only barren concrete block walls – or had he merely felt gloomy? A little more time could have allowed an assessment, but the haze dispersed almost instantly.

"But we're here now," Greg said, "and we see the good and beautiful things around us. That must matter." Zeb didn't answer, but just breathed out a cloud of smoke. Greg stuck his pipe back in his mouth.

The three laughed and spoke of myth well into the night. Sleepiness fell upon them, and they decided it was time to end the night. They went to bed. Greg and Aaron piled into Zeb's room, and the three slept a restful night's sleep.

Greg would stay another full day and leave the next. The sky was cloudy, but the day was once again rich and satisfying. As evening drew near, Zeb made a decision on a whim. "Let's go in the woods," he said. "I like it this time of year. It's not too hot. Great for journeys." Greg had not gone into their woods for some time now. He had heard from Aaron that the latest fort was further along in construction. This fort could hardly be called a fort, unless one meant it in the true sense. It was constructed of logs, some halved and some whole, and stood nearly eighteen feet tall. Alex had helped them build it initially, but when his interest wore off and Zeb began working, little progress was made. Aaron recently experienced a renewed interest in seeing it to completion, mainly for the sake of practice for future endeavors. And so the three embarked.

They followed a new path through the woods that led more directly to the newest fort. It took them along the old path first, through the first section of woods. But here they followed along the edge of the cornfield, to the opposite side, rather than cutting across the corner down into the wooded valley. It took them generally along the hill's ridge. The stream was somewhere downhill and far to the left, they knew, and they were roughly following it. The walk did not seem so far when the trees were leafless, as they were. As the trail took them closer to the ridge's edge, they saw ahead through the trees a bone-like form. They had arrived at the fort, its large, wooden poles standing with silent integrity like ancient monoliths.

"It's been a while," Greg said. "You guys sure have come along."

"We really did pick a nice spot for it. It's a shame we haven't been able to devote as much time to it lately," Zeb said. It was built near the edge of a rough cliff, at the bottom of which was a steady slope that lead to the stream. This stream could be seen from where they stood. Zeb stood at its edge, looking out to the far ridge. He pulled his pipe from his deep coat pocket. Grinning at each other, Aaron and Greg did the same. They puffed away as they enjoyed themselves in the darkening wood.

Suddenly Greg heard faintly an agonizing scream, far off in the direction from which they had come. He looked at Aaron to see if he would acknowledge it. He didn't. Perhaps it was too far off, Greg thought. He looked to Zeb now. Zeb had pulled the pipe from his mouth, staring intently from under his hood in the direction of the scream. "You heard it, didn't you?" Greg asked him. Zeb turned to him, and nodded, with dark eyes.

"What did you guys hear?" Aaron asked. Greg told him about the scream. "Interesting..."

They continued to smoke their pipes. It was now nearly twilight. They could still see, however, into the valley. Then, another blood-curdling scream echoed throughout the valley, this time much closer. "Woah, I heard that," Aaron said.

"Um, guys, I'm kind of horrified," Zeb said, which meant he was, in truth, absolutely terrified.

"This is weird," Greg said. "For once we are all experiencing this together."

"Unfortunately, I noticed that," Zeb responded. They looked at Aaron. He was staring down into the valley, with a most fearful look on his face. They turned to see what he was looking at and found their answer. There was a humanoid figure stumbling through the creek. It clumsily moved downstream, closer to them, though it was still down in the valley. Aaron screamed in horror.

"What- What is that!?" he cried, stepping back. The others grabbed hold of him. Now they heard a strained moan come from the being. It snapped its head in their direction, and swung around, climbing out of the cold water.

"Is it a crack-head!?" Zeb said, almost laughing.

"You know what I think it is! You know... what I fear!" Aaron said. This was the undead he spoke of.

"Guys, he's uh... coming up toward us!" Greg said, beginning to hyperventilate. The three scrambled away, further up the hill, and hid behind trees. Peering around, they saw the figure relentlessly in pursuit, though it was unclear whether it had a specific destination. It stumbled up a gentler part of the hill, though if it had more intelligence, it could have found an easier way still. As it drew nearer, they could make out more details in the dying light. It was extremely pale and wore a long-sleeve red shirt covered by a tattered and soiled T-shirt, and blue jeans. It also appeared to have dark, short-cropped hair. Greg watched as it tripped, and its head smashed right into a rock.

There, on the ground, it began to eat leaves and dirt, like a man dying of starvation who is driven to do such desperate things. It slowly and unsteadily rose, then continued uphill, moaning now more excitedly.

"How is this happening?!" Aaron cried out, and ran further along the ridge now, deeper into the woods. The others ran right behind. The ridge fell away now, and with an adrenaline-fueled dash, they raced for the lowest-lying and most camouflaged area within sight. This they found, and here they hid in a shallow hole. Aaron grabbed a rock while Greg grabbed a long stick. "Greg, don't get close to it..."

"I won't be threatened by such a thing!" Greg said bravely, if not stupidly.

"Greg, I'm serious... If it is... one of them, you can't get near it," Aaron reasoned with him.

"You could get sick..."

Greg ran out from cover and some distance up the hill despite his friend's warning. The hominid was nowhere in sight. "Away with you!" he cried. "If anyone's trying to scare us, he's going to be seriously injured! I'll not hesitate to use this weapon!" he cried, his stance bellicose and firm. He saw for a moment, a pale head pop up from behind a rock, as if the creature had some intelligence after all. It seemed to be stalking now.

"Get back here, Greg!" Zeb called out. Finally, Greg obeyed and returned to the hole.

There they lay in hiding for perhaps fifteen minutes. It seemed like forever. "It's getting very dark," Greg said. "If we wait any longer, we will be in much more danger."

"But to get back home, we have to pass through that area again!" Aaron groaned.

"Pull yourself together, man!" Greg said to him. "We have to act like men at a time like this." It was a strange change in character for him. His courage had come at a much-needed time.

"I guess he's right, Aaron. We need to leave now," Zeb said.

"Alright... Let's be quick," Aaron said. The three rose quietly. They heard nothing but the chirping of myriad nocturnal insects around them. Twilight would soon turn to night. They cautiously made their way back up the hill, moving from tree to tree. The figure was nowhere in sight. Greg was now at a spot where he would have been able to clearly see the figure before, when it appeared to be hiding. It was no longer there.

"We'll move away perpendicularly from the ridge, toward the farm," Zeb detailed. "That way we'll be out of the woods and have a little more light."

He began to lead them in this direction, when they entered a strangely spacious area within the forest. Here there was a wide circle filled entirely of dead saplings, and the grass within the circle was scorched and unhealthy. In fact, it did not seem to be grass at all, but rather stringy, tangled weeds. Greg felt a flash of déjà-vu. Could this have been the clearing they had found some years ago? Hadn't there been some kind of structure here before? But there was scarce time to dwell on it, for here Zeb suddenly became lightheaded and began to fall. Aaron caught him before he hurt himself. He struggled to keep him off the ground, but Zeb was too cumbersome in his long coat and Aaron was forced to drop him.

"Great," Greg said.

"No, not now..." Aaron said. He shook Zeb violently, but he was stricken with delirium. He muttered only gibberish. Now, he slowly rose, with intent.

"We need to go," he said.

"You're right," Aaron agreed. "Let's do it then! Up on your feet! That man could be anywhere around!" Zeb did not seem to remember where he was. He simply began walking, with a lightness that almost made him seem to hover right over the brush. He had turned sharply left. "Hey- wait! Where-? You're going the wrong way!" Aaron called. He and Greg ran up and grabbed him by the coat.

"Get back here, Zeb!" Greg growled. But Zeb resisted strongly, even as he held his head in apparent pain. Greg had not seen Zeb like this since the incident at the abandoned house. The two managed to pull him back, all the way across the small clearing, and further up into the woods. All the while Zeb resisted, though he spoke very little. And then he fell once more, nearly breaking his cherished pipe that stuck from his pocket. Aaron slapped him across the face.

"Ow!" Zeb cried out, blinking in the darkness. "Woah, why am I on the ground? And it's become dark so quickly!" Zeb now remembered only up to the point where he entered the circle. The others explained what happened as they helped him along. They eventually found their way out of the forest, without any further sightings of the shambling creature.

They walked up the hill of the neighbor's yard that buffered the house from the forest. At last they came to the house, where they walked up the steps of the deck and into the family room through one of the two side doors. After settling down and drinking some water, they reflected on what had just happened.

"Could it have been one of the local farmers?" Zeb asked. "Drunk out of their mind?". For only a moment it seemed plausible.

"Drunken men don't eat dirt, nor do they survive strikes to the head like that," Greg observed. He explained how the being fell as it climbed the hillside. Zeb had seen it eating dirt but had been looking away during the creature's collapse.

"If one were on drugs he may," Aaron suggested. This seemed reasonable.

"Or if he were just plain nuts," Greg added. "But how would these individuals find themselves in the middle of the forest?" The three sat in silence, pondering this. Suddenly Aaron shot up, with a look of horrifying realization.

"Aaron, what is it?" Greg asked.

"Are we in danger?" Zeb asked.

"We may be," he said. "You, most of all." He pointed to Greg, who grew fearful now, if not indignant.

"Have you forgotten your words on the telephone? 'I wish for someone to come and blow out my flame of life'." Greg dropped his head in shame. Zeb looked at him in disbelief. What he had previously seen as a display of courage in Greg had now become sick hypocrisy.

"...I don't know what came over me when I said that... I didn't mean it," Greg pleaded dismally. Then denial overcame him. "No, that's silly," he began. "My words could not have had such an effect." The others simply sat silent. Zeb began to draw the shades.

"I hope so, for your sake alone," Aaron said. "Personally, I would feel safer that way, since its mission would involve you and you alone. If it is simply... one of the undead... then it is a threat to everyone. But don't be surprised if this is not the end of it. For its mission would not yet be complete." Now Aaron smiled, but still said in seriousness, "We may find it plastered against one of these windows within the hour." Greg laughed in horror as these very windows were removed from sight one by one.

The holidays had come and gone, as well as several sessions of role-playing with their newest member, Royce. Derik and Royce were well into their final high school semester, while Aaron and Greg were getting busier and busier with college.

"We should get together with just Derik," Greg suggested over the phone. "He needs to get further in the Book."

"Yeah, it's been a while," Aaron said. "He's probably forgotten a lot already." But they found out that Derik had other business that weekend, so both the Book reading and any role-playing were out of the question. They made plans for the weekend anyway. Zeb and Aaron also had a new videogame to show Greg. That was always fun to do. "We could go in the woods, too," Aaron suggested, with a wink.

"Oh yeah, right, great idea!" Greg answered, playing along.

"I hope we can feel better about going in the woods soon," Aaron sighed. "I'd like to take Derik there some time." Greg agreed.

Greg arrived that Friday evening, filled with excitement. He marched with Aaron into the family room where he dropped his luggage. Aaron's mother greeted him and told him where to put his stuff. He did this after talking to Zeb for a few minutes, who read in the chair. Mrs. Eldritch graciously left the room for the boys, retreating to the study by herself.

"I hear you guys have been playing a lot of Dungeons and Dragons lately," Zeb said. "I wish I still had the time. One day it'll happen, I'll see to that." This was because he and his two brothers had recently begun looking for real estate themselves, somewhere in the wild where they would not be disturbed by the spread of the same urban sprawl they were seeing beginning to encroach on their beloved countryside, and all the trouble that came along with that. They had their eyes set mostly on the state of Kentucky, for land was beautiful as well as conveniently cheap.

"Good luck," Greg said sincerely. "We've had some of the best sessions ever, at least as far as I know. The only problem is that it won't last much longer. After this summer, who knows what will happen to Derik and Royce?" Zeb nodded sadly.

"That's how it always is... With everything..."

They lightened their darkening moods with some video games, then watched a movie Greg had brought with him. When it grew darker, Greg was even willing to resume with the horror game that he had stopped in the middle of, the one he had begun in the basement but refused to finish. But soon, they found themselves in a familiar situation when Aaron began to complain of cramps. They pardoned him as he left the room, and they resumed.

"Wow, he was serious," Zeb said. "He's been in the bathroom for more than ten minutes."

Something seemed oddly familiar about this, Greg thought. After another couple of minutes, he said, "Well, let's take a short break." He waited for Zeb to follow. They opened the family room door and peered down the stairwell before entering the kitchen. It seemed normal enough, thankfully. They continued on and got their drinking cups from the cabinet. Zeb walked to the fridge near the doorway to the living room to get ice cubes. Greg, out of curiosity and perhaps to make himself feel more secure, went to check the light of the stair well. Before he accomplished this, however, he beheld something both perverse and appropriate.

He saw there on the basement floor a new portal. It was different than the last he had seen. It was roughly in the same spot, as far as he could remember. And it was no longer so alien a form, for now it was simply a square cutaway in the concrete, revealing absolute darkness below. The concrete looked to be only an inch thick, and there was no shaft whatsoever, only a void below. Instead of coils, now, there were strips of chain-link fencing along both sides, holding on to what little bit of concrete they could. The gap between these strips, he observed, seemed just big enough for him to slip through if he had wanted. This offer he refused.

He stumbled back, a dizziness taking him. He put his hand to his forehead as he slid away, calling to Zeb.

"What's wrong?" Zeb asked, apparently not understanding the seriousness of the matter.

"...Look!..." Greg cried out weakly, but when he looked back to the stairwell, the portal was no more. He stumbled away, still holding his head. "No... Don't worry about it... It's gone..." He nearly fell into Zeb, who now withdrew into the living room.

"What is wrong with you?!" Zeb asked concernedly. Greg stood swaying for a moment.

"I saw another portal," Greg said, nearly crying, and failing to make eye contact with Zeb. "What is happening to me?..."

Zeb walked over to the top of the stairs, Greg following. "It was right there, you say?" Greg nodded with a shaky head. Zeb dashed into the family room with Greg, shutting the door. "Let's turn the sound of this game off for a while so you can rest for a moment," he said, muting the sound system. "Let's just wait for Aaron." Greg simply fell into the couch, feverishly. After a minute or two, just like the time before, they heard a flush, then heard someone come through the kitchen, and now saw Aaron enter the family room with them. But instead of being accused, Aaron saw his friend looking very ill, and noticed the sound was muted.

"Uh... What happened here?" he asked. Zeb gave a look of acknowledgment, and Aaron knew something had gone amiss.

"Just sit down, Aaron," Greg began softly. "I'm about to explain what just happened, to both you and Zeb." And so he did. The others comforted him as best they could, and it seemed to help. Zeb started to say something but stopped.

"It'll be okay," Zeb said. "Trust me." After a drink, Greg

looked a little better.

"I just can't believe it..." Greg began. "I really saw that, right there in front of me. I could have jumped in if I wanted..."

"Well we're glad you didn't," Aaron said, smiling sympathetically. "And don't do it, still, if it happens again."

"It will, I'm sure," Greg sighed. "I do wonder, though... What would have happened?... Where would it have taken me?..." The others could not answer, though they pondered over this for many months.

Greg would still visit. Perhaps it was stubbornness, perhaps stupidity, or maybe it was that something had exercised some control over him and drew him there. Whatever it was, two other friends coming with him made it easier. This weekend Aaron's parents were gone, and only the three brothers and Carson would be there. Seeing an opportunity, Aaron invited the whole crew over, which consisted of Greg, Derik and Royce. It would prove to be most interesting.

Royce listened as Derik read aloud from the infamous Scary Book. They sat huddled on the family room's carpeted floor, surrounded by windows that grew darker by the moment. It came to a point where a light of some sort was needed. But as Zeb got up to turn on a light, a great boom came upon the side door. Royce had heard that Aaron's house was known for 'bizarre happenings' but he still did not expect this. "Okay, that was weird," he admitted with some surprise, since he considered himself skeptical and level-headed.

"Hey, where's Dan and Carson?" Greg asked.

"They're camping outback," Aaron answered. A suspicious look grew on Greg's face.

"Dan wouldn't do something like that, would he?" he asked.

"It's not like him, but anything's possible," Aaron said. "Although his son is with him, and he gets frightened very easily, so I doubt he would." They continued with the reading for some time, well past dark.

"I need a break, I think," Derik said. "Just need to walk around, or something." This sounded like a good idea to the others.

"Let's go see what Dan is up to," Zeb suggested. So they put their shoes on and stepped out of the family room through the side door. They could see a bright orange fire at the back of yard, near the wooden fence. A couple of dark figures could be seen sitting by it. As they approached, they heard that there were also audio tapes playing a theatrical performance of some kind. The two figures were revealed by flickers of flame-light to be Daniel and Carson, and after a moment it was clear the audiotape was a rendition of Daniel's favorite book in the Lord of the Rings trilogy.

"It's been a while since a campfire has been made here," Zeb said.

"I don't know why we talk about doing things like this but never actually do it," Daniel said. "I just did it."

"We're having a good time out here," Carson said.

"I bet you're a little scared, too," Aaron said with a guessing smile. Carson's silence was as good an answer as a 'yes'. They all talked for a while, but then Greg noticed that Derik was not with them.

"Hey, Aaron, did you see where Derik got to?" he asked him. A look of confusion crossed Aaron's face.

"No, actually. That's weird... When did he slip away?" Aaron wondered aloud. Royce was not paying attention to their conversation. Aaron nudged him.

"Do you know where Derik went?" he asked Royce. Royce hardly seemed to care.

"Probably went to the bathroom," he said, and turned back to the conversation with the others. Aaron nudged Zeb now.

"We're going to go back inside. Derik must be waiting for us," he said. Zeb nodded as he spoke to Daniel and Royce. This must have been an acknowledgement, Aaron guessed. Aaron and Greg left the others, returning to the family room. There they found an empty room. "Guess he's in the bathroom," he said. They left the room, passed through the kitchen, and peered into the dark living room.

He was not here. Aaron flipped the hall light on before entering, then proceeded down the hallway, Greg following. The light in the bathroom was not on.

"Where could he be?" Greg asked, growing disgusted with what he suspected might be tomfoolery. Aaron shook his head. They continued down the hallway and turned the corner. They peered in each room as they went by, including first the parent's room at the corner, then Zeb then Aaron's room on either side around the corner. Only the room at the end was left. As they approached, they could hear strange, soft laughter coming from behind the door. Aaron slowly opened the door, making the laughing more audible. As the room opened to the right, all of it could not be seen from the door. He could make out, however, movement just at the edge of sight. He stepped in, turning on the light. There was Derik, sitting in the rocking chair and facing the wall, his back toward them. He did not acknowledge their presence, and simply sat there laughing and rocking his head from side to side. Greg had not yet seen this, and only saw Aaron from the back. He knew he had found Derik however, when he called out.

"Derik!" Aaron called. Greg ran in and beheld the scene. Derik still did not respond. Now Greg called to him, but still there was no response. Aaron could do only one thing. He ran up, and hoisting him up onto his shoulder, carried him back to the family room. Derik laughed deliriously the whole way.

Aaron dropped him on the floor, before a bewildered Zeb and Royce who had just entered the house. Derik rolled on the floor, still laughing. Everyone watched in silence. Slowly he calmed, until it became more of a stupor, and the others believed he was nearing the end of his fit. But suddenly he raced for the stairs, and after standing there at the top for a short moment, descended. Aaron alone watched in amazement, for only from his angle could this be seen.

"Uh, guys, he just went into the basement," Aaron said. Greg ran up to see, but Derik had already gone below sight.

"He went in the dark!" Greg cried in disgust. Suddenly they heard a shrill scream from the basement. Aaron wasted no time in chasing after Derik. He turned on the basement light and found him standing there in the middle of the floor. He looked to be in a panic.

"I woke up to find myself in your basement!" he cried out. Aaron helped him back upstairs. He told the same story to the others. He said he could not remember anything from before. When he saw the bookmark in the Book, he did not remember having read so much.

"Nothing has ever happened to me like this before," Derik said. "Except for that dream I had which seemed to affect reality."

After a breather, the others convinced him to continue, except for Royce who seemed to be in a daze now. He left the room as they read, failing to turn on any lights where he went. "Doesn't he need light? His vision is bad enough," Zeb said, for Royce had a dead eye.

Ten minutes passed, and still he did not return. Zeb decided to find him. He began to leave the room, but then slowly stepped away from the door. Royce entered, holding a knife. He turned off the light as he did this, shrouding the room in darkness. "Woah," Zeb said. "Easy..." Royce approached the group slowly, with his head down, his long straight hair concealing any expression, if he even had one. He seemed as though he was unsure of what to do with what he held, as he would look at the knife, then at the group, then the knife again. Zeb rested his hand upon Royce's shoulder. "Easy, now," he told him. He slowly went for the knife, but Royce withdrew suddenly.

"What, this?..." Royce asked, perhaps mockingly though he seemed genuinely confused. Suddenly he dropped the knife and grabbed his face. He cried out and Zeb, thinking quickly, snatched up the blade from the floor while Royce slowly melted into his seat.

"What happened?" Derik asked Royce. Royce looked up as Zeb returned the knife to the kitchen, then turned the light back on.

"I don't know... A weird feeling... Then my bad eye flashed, and everything came back to me," he explained. The others had never seen him like this before. Usually he was so cynical and care-free. Greg was in near-hysterics, but not wanting to appear fearful in front of his friend, sat on the couch and allowed the reading to go on.

He heard something else, too, however. It was a soft whisper from behind him, through the open window. He spun around, but the window was veiled by the blinds. He jumped away, grabbing the fire stoker propped beside the woodstove. "This is ridiculous!" he shouted out angrily. The others looked at him in silence. Aaron jumped up to calm him. He had just seen Royce holding a knife, and now Greg was wielding a heavier weapon. He would not allow this to continue. As Greg raised the stoker at the window, Aaron grabbed him and pulled him back. But Greg managed to get a swing in, knocking the blinds aside for a moment. And during that short moment he saw there a figure hunched low, just outside the window.

"There's a man!" Greg shouted. "A man is out there!" The encounter in the woods immediately came back to him.

"A man!?" Aaron cried, still wrestling with Greg. Everyone else stepped back. "Relax, Greg, and we'll check." He did this, and Aaron immediately opened the door, and turned on the porch light. He and Greg ran out, checking the area in which Greg had seen the figure. The only thing Aaron saw was the charcoal grill.

"Could you have seen this grill, Greg?" Aaron asked. "Perhaps you thought this was a man." Greg's response was plain.

"No." They returned into the family room. "Nothing," he told the others. Despite everything, the reading resumed. They heard Daniel and Carson return to the house through the front door a while later. They must have gone to bed for they did not see them again until the next morning. What a strange night, Greg thought. Absurd, even. The Eldritchs' house was changing Derik, and even Royce. He could expect nothing now, and shuddered. It was even unclear what choice he would make should another portal offer itself to him. What *was* clear, and needed no witness, was the smile he now bore.

# CHAPTER SEVEN

## Revelation

Summer had finally arrived. Another semester was over, and it was of special significance for Aaron in that it was his last at the local college. For Zeb, too, this summer bore significance, for he had recently begun employment at an office outside of Baltimore. While commuting was nothing new – he had commuted to university and back daily – this marked the beginning of a new life and for him, a new low. This would test him in ways he had never guessed were possible, but through it all he always kept close his lessons from his past, and even more importantly, his memories. They would become one of three sources of whatever will he had left in him. Another was the new debt he had taken on that, along with his student debt and other expenses he had before not known existed, necessitated the office job. This debt was the result of a recent purchase of acreage in the Appalachian foothills of Kentucky – one shared between him and his two brothers, Aaron and Daniel. It was a risky decision the brothers made, especially for the younger of these, and only time would tell if there would be wisdom in it. For now, it was something to be excited for; something, perhaps, they could even learn to *live* for. And for Zeb, it was the second source of will. The third, well, one need only read on a bit longer to understand.

Greg, despite having been dwelling all semester on the paranormal experiences he had been personally involved in, was feeling generally well. There was something about being unable to form expectations that made each day feel somehow fresher, even if it did give him reason to feel more anxious and paranoid. Derik, however, was distraught over something, something that had been a burden on him for several months. He had noticed that Greg was beginning to question his Catholic faith. He didn't joke as often. He didn't return calls as faithfully nor show up movie night as frequently. He would attempt to return Greg to a mindset he had presumably long since abandoned and relieve himself of this burden once and for all. On a warm and clear day, he did this.

He had made plans with Greg to talk with him at the local café. To his surprise, he showed, arriving about ten minutes later.

Greg entered the establishment and was greeted by the wholesome aroma of fresh coffee. After ordering a cappuccino he surveyed the sparsely populated room and found his friend sitting toward the back. Derik gestured him to sit with him at a small table by a window. They simply sat for a while, sipping on their drinks as they watched the outside world. People of all kinds were doing their daily things, passing briskly by this way and that, oblivious to the angst on the other side of the glass. What was it like to walk in that world? Greg had nearly forgotten. The sun shone brightly through the pane and upon the table. Derik pulled the blinds and allowed their eyes to adjust. They occupied themselves with some small talk, but Greg knew he had been brought here for other reasons. Derik seemed nervous.

"Alright, Derik. What's going on? What did you need to tell me?" he asked. Derik feigned a laugh. Then he grew very serious.

"Greg, there are all different kinds of people," he began. Greg looked at him, giving him a confused look. "And many people we know have many different sides." Greg waited for more. "And sometimes what we believe to be a true side is really one among many."

"I'm not following," Greg said. He gulped the rest of his

cappuccino. Derik rolled his coffee around in its mug.

"Okay. Listen to me, from start to finish, and don't go stomping out of here," Derik demanded. Greg agreed. "After the horse incident of several months ago, I got a call from Aaron..."

"Oh, hey Aaron," Derik greeted him.

"Listen," Aaron began. "I was thinking about your story of your friend scaring the guy by the car..."

"Okay, go on," Derik said.

"Well, I was wondering if you could do something for me," Aaron said.

"Maybe. What is it?" Derik asked with curiosity.

"Well, regarding the unusual things that happen here..." Aaron began.

"Go on..." Derik insisted.

"They have all been farce."

"I kind of knew, actually. I knew that the horse incident was his doing, anyway. But everything else, too?" Derik asked.

"Well, let me rephrase that," Aaron said. "Almost everything. I want you to understand that you still may experience some things unnatural, minor things. These will be very obvious. Everything that Greg has told you, however, was my doing."

"Wow... You must be pretty good with that," Derik complimented.

"I guess so..."

"Well what was it that you want me to do for you?" Derik asked.

"First, tell me you will keep this a secret," Aaron requested.

"Sure, I can do that."

"Good. Now, I was wondering if you would be able to help me, even, with this hoax of mine..." Aaron said cunningly.

"Uh, well, I don't want to ruin it by accident," Derik said.

"You believed the horse incident to be farce right from the beginning, correct?" Aaron asked.

"Yeah."

"From what I saw in your performance during that incident, I believe you would do quite well," Aaron told him. Derik laughed modestly. "And I can tell from your stories that you enjoy tricking others and giving them scares."

"Yeah, I guess," Derik agreed.

"Alright then. Greg is beginning to think that all this is happening in his mind. I want him to continue thinking like this, you understand?"

"Yeah," Derik said.

"So if you see or hear things, try not to react. The best thing to do in most cases is to simply not say anything, and he will think you are easily confused." Derik understood.

"I think I can manage that," he said.

"Now, I'll probably be pulling another stunt before long. I'll prepare you for it when I've got all the details ready," Aaron explained.

"Sounds good," Derik said, and he began to chuckle impishly.

"Heh, heh, alright. That's all for now," Aaron said chuckling himself. "Oh, and Derik... Thanks..."

"No problem..." Derik said. "See ya."

Greg sat silently at the table, looking down. Derik patted him. A few stray rays of sunlight poked through the blinds, revealing what looked like a tear in Greg's eyes. "That fool..." was all he could say. His whole idea of who Aaron was had suddenly been turned upside down. Could he even be considered a friend? Even if he could resist hating him, did he even know him still?

"Remember," Derik said, "everybody has many faces. This was only one. I'm sure you still know the real him. I'm sure the true sides of him have surfaced many times." Greg nodded but doubtfully.

"I just can't believe it... and yet I can. It's what I initially thought. I should have trusted my gut," Greg told himself as much as Derik. "So it was all fake..."

"Pretty much," Derik affirmed. "Even Royce was in on it

last time." Greg looked up, now with an expression of acceptance.

"Entertain me, Derik. Tell me how these things were done," Greg said, for he realized now, that it must have been very hard indeed.

"Most of it was done with great preparation and what may be considered obsessive practice," Derik explained.

"I never knew Aaron had the time, what with college and all... And Zeb! What about him?!" Greg asked in disbelief.

"I'm not sure so much about him," Derik explained. "I think he knew what Aaron was up to, but he at least was behind the horse incident. Neither of them told me exactly how they went about accomplishing these feats, as one may call them, but they required precise timing and manipulation even." Greg looked sick. "This latter part was what sickened me. That's why I had to tell you. I couldn't bear to see you be manipulated like that."

"Well thanks," Greg said sincerely. "Although I feel more ill now than I did an hour ago."

"I'm sorry about that," Derik said, "but I thought it was in your best interest. I've been worried about you, if I'm being honest. You're not the same person you used to be... I miss the happy-go-lucky, passionate, smiling Greg armed with a thousand Star Wars quotes!" He managed only a feigned laugh from Greg, but perhaps it was progress.

"Well you have to know how grave these occurrences were to me – the implications I mean," Greg began, feeling a bit defensive. "I figured I was just starting to lose it... and I guess I was somehow trying to warp that into a good thing." Now the defensiveness was transforming into anger toward his deceivers. "I've been wronged."

"You have," Derik agreed without hesitation. "There's no denying that. I noticed that you haven't been praying as much lately, Greg. Before meals and such. Or wearing your Rosary. I don't want to tell you what to do or believe but I have been making these observations and, well, knowing that they were coming from a place of falsehood I just couldn't allow it to continue."

"Finding truth is the most important duty. I'm glad you have done this..." Greg said sighing. "I would have thought Aaron would have known this... He is a philosopher like Zeb... He understands the importance of truth... Or maybe he doesn't. Perhaps he is nothing more than a sophist; a manipulator."

"You have every right to be angry. But I'm trying to understand Aaron, too. Perhaps he's needing guidance right now. Heck, there's even a chance it was all in good faith. Maybe he just wanted to have some fun and have something to laugh about with you in the future," Derik supposed.

"He intended, then, to reveal this himself at some point?" Greg asked. Derik didn't answer, but just fiddled with his spoon nervously. Greg looked down. "He didn't then... I just don't understand him... Why would he do this?" Derik remained silent. "I don't mean to make this hard for you, Derik. I know it was hard enough for you just telling me. I could have freaked out on you, for all you knew. I really appreciate it. Thanks."

"Yeah. You're welcome. I hope we can all still be friends," Derik said.

"I would hope to. I'm just having a hard time knowing who my friends are..." Greg said, letting out a melancholic breath.

"It doesn't bother me with Zeb so much... He was behind the horse thing, okay. But Aaron went too far... Those portals... I should have known he was up to something... Tell me, how did he do it?" Greg looked at Derik intently.

"He showed me many things, Greg. It was a mirror, he said. He actually showed me the frame for it he made. I'm surprised it fooled you. It was only cardboard," Derik said.

"A mirror?... Cardboard..." Greg said to himself. He seemed a bit confused. "And the second one? The hole... How...?"

"It was a painting, nothing more. He showed me this as well," Derik told him.

"A painting looked that convincing?... Amazing..." Greg said, almost becoming impressed with Aaron now.

"It surprised me as well that a simple painting like that would look so realistic, yet it did," Derik added.

"It was so dark..." Greg again said to himself. "And all the noises – the doll, the monster in the woods..."

"He showed me a tape he recorded and played it for me. It had all those noises on it. And he made that doll. He showed that to me too," Derik revealed. "And the zombie was a friend of Zeb's... Aaron had planned all this beforehand."

"Such simple devices... They worked so well... I am a fool..." Greg said as he lowered his head and sunk into his seat.

"No. You're wrong. When someone goes as far as he did, it would happen to anyone," Derik said comfortingly. "You don't realize how far he went. In fact, we even started working on this video tape together. We were going to play it on the VCR while you thought I was playing a game. The game was recorded on it. But Aaron filmed a mock portal and I took segments of this and put them into the game footage. It would have looked like the game was cutting in and out, and we weren't going to acknowledge it. He ended up deciding against it, for whatever reason."

"Wow... You were really in on all this... You bastard, you!" Greg said jokingly. Derik laughed.

"Hey, maybe we can get him back, too," Derik suggested with a grin.

"We'll do something... Just don't let him know that you told me," Greg said. Derik nodded.

"Right."

Greg was feeling too nauseous, still, to eat anything. He talked with Derik for a while of lighter matters, then they left. Greg breathed a deep breath of fresh, summer air as he walked out of the café. Derik felt relieved as well. Hopefully Greg's mood would soon lighten, he thought, and his faith strengthen, now that those distressing events were revealed to be nothing more than games. They got in their cars and returned home. They both knew that they would go to Aaron's again, eventually. Greg, especially, knew it would not be easy, but it would be worth it in the end.

Not more than a week later, Greg had gathered enough courage to confront them. He would not let Aaron know what he knew, however. He was still unsure of how he should react to the next prank, for one would surely come. Perhaps he would continue to play-act, and gradually let it sink in that he knew, or, better yet, turn it around on Aaron in some clever and surprising act that would have them all laughing together.

He arrived at Aaron's, under an overcast sky. He felt knots form in his stomach. Aaron still would behave as he always had, and Greg would have to go along with this, for a while at least. He would begin by seeing what Aaron's reaction would be if Greg suggested that all the 'problems' were because of something going on within the house itself - not necessarily plotting and orchestration which would be too forward, but something more subtle... something even darker... Hopefully this would even leave Aaron feeling guilty if he read into it enough, and he would stop his games.

Aaron and Zebulon welcomed him into the living room, and there they sat and talked for a while. Inevitably the subject of the house's 'problems' came up, with an interpretive and analytical standpoint. This amused Greg, to see them put so much effort into making it seem as if they would truly spend much of their time thinking about their 'problems'. In fact, as he listened to Zeb's impressive synthesis of philosophy with the experiencing of aberrations, it seemed for a moment that they could not be separated. He was impressed with both him and Aaron, if he was being honest. Now he would present his own supposed beliefs.

"I think I know what's going on here," he said. Aaron's eyes widened. He leaned forward, waiting.

"I am reluctant to tell you..." Greg continued. Aaron insisted that he speak his mind. At this moment, with a grim face, Greg made a gesture with his arm, as if drawing upon their floor. Aaron did not understand the meaning. "Something evil... in this house..." Greg said. Still Aaron waited, looking very intrigued. "Certain things being done in secret... Behind closed doors..."

"What...?" Zeb said. Aaron looked to share in this confusion. Hopefully now he thinks I know, Greg thought. Hopefully he'll become guilty now...

"What was that gesture you made?" Aaron asked finally. Greg now would 'reveal' to the others that he 'in fact' did not know of Aaron's hoax.

"A pentagram..." he said grimly. Aaron's mouth dropped. Zeb tilted his head, apparently still confused. Greg continued. "Devil worshiping..." Zeb stood up now, barely able to hold back his rage.

"This is ridiculous! You-!" he sat back down, calming. "I'm sorry, but you can't really think that? What would make you think something like that?"

"It's obvious that there are secrets here," Greg said, now thinking that perhaps that was a little too obvious.

"We keep a lot of our experiences to ourselves, Greg, that's about it," Aaron said, seeming hurt himself. "And we've respected your privacy by telling others nothing of your own strange experiences. These would be the only secrets."

"Well, it's just a theory. But such dark practices would surely bring evil into this house, as well as malevolent spirits," Greg said. Zeb looked up in thought. Then he began to nod as he spoke.

"I suppose that would be possible - if such practices were held," Zeb said. The three sat for a while in silence. Aaron looked out the large bow window toward the grey skies, deep in thought.

They moved into the family room, but Aaron's parents were watching a movie. "We'll play a game downstairs," Zeb said to Greg. "It's better down there anyway, during the day at least. It's too bright to see the T.V. with all those windows." Greg pretended to agree with reluctance, but did not hesitate to follow him down, for he was now without fear.

He dropped his bags by the couch and they sat for a while, in the dim light. Trying to relieve himself of some stress, Greg paced around in the basement. His nervous behavior was noticed by both brothers. The tension had built up to the point where he wanted to do something very dramatic but could not think of anything more clever than scaring Zeb into admitting what he knew of Aaron's hoax. What a joy it would be to scare these guys, he thought. *Really* scare. Looking at their faces began reminding him of the hurt, and he grew indignant. The indignance became rage. He pulled his pocket knife out from hiding and unfolded its blade. He turned quickly, and approaching Zeb, raised the knife. Zeb watched as he came closer, with knowing eyes. Greg brought the knife down with great speed toward Zeb's neck.

"Greg, *nooooo!*" Aaron cried out, leaping forward to try and restrain the weapon. When he realized his knife would pierce flesh, Greg stopped the blade's advance just before it did. Aaron, who must have known he would have been too late, was looking quite frazzled. Zeb, however, had not flinched. With only a look of awe, the satisfaction Greg hoped for never fully came and he now felt panic set in. What had he just done!? Awkwardly, he attempted to regain control by returning Zeb's look with a more deviant one. Only silence and wonder reigned at that moment, and so Greg backed off, slowly, and ambled over into the laundry section. Aaron and Zeb stared at each other, dumbfounded.

Now Greg would try to find empirical evidence of the hoax, pretending to have come upon it accidentally. Maybe it was in the back where he had seen the doll... But Aaron and Zeb now followed him into the room. They're following me, he thought. 'They don't want me to find everything.'

"You're acting very strange, Greg," Aaron said. "Are you feeling okay?" Greg just feigned a look of delirium. Then it seemed to pass. Greg thought that maybe bringing Daniel into the picture would help ease the topic along.

"Maybe it's Dan," he said. "Maybe he's the cause of all of this..." Zeb looked at Greg inquisitively. Then he seemed to approve of the possibility.

"Right... You mean because of his archeology, right? Perhaps he has disturbed spirits throughout his various digs," Zeb said. Greg shook his head.

"No," he bluntly replied, with a very serious look now.

"I mean like maybe he has pulled pranks on us. Like that time when Royce was here... and I saw that guy out the window..." Zeb seemed to struggle with accepting this. Greg continued. "Maybe he's a real sicko."

"Uh, I don't know..." Zeb began. "That's not what I know him to be. Perhaps he could have played a part in the events on that particular night... but this would not explain all the other things." Greg pretended to play around with this thought.

He began to pace again, and he now walked back into the utility section where he had seen the doll. Strangely, as he walked further into the darkness, he felt an uneasiness growing in him. Perhaps it was lingering feelings from before, which still could not be shaken. Anyhow, he scanned the room for any evidence, finding none. He withdrew, returning to the others. They were looking at him very strangely. I must seem so weird right now, Greg thought. 'That's okay for Aaron. He's done enough to me himself. But Zeb doesn't really deserve this...' Aaron shook his head and left the room. The others heard as he walked upstairs, on some errand probably. Greg walked up to Zeb and looked at him face-to-face. He would now explain his behavior.

"Derik told me everything, Zeb. About Aaron's ingeniously orchestrated hoax. You knew of this, right?" Greg did not expect his answer.

"No comment," Zeb said, neither showing surprise, guilt, nor any sign of amusement regarding the hoax. Why wouldn't he simply say whether he knew of it or not? Greg wondered. He probably didn't want to spoil it without Aaron's consent. Greg continued.

"Derik's not going to help him anymore, but we don't want him to know that Derik told me, not yet anyway," Greg explained. Zeb nodded, looking at Greg intently.

"I see..." he said.

"So don't tell him I know, okay?" Greg requested.

"Sure..." Zeb said, crossing his arms. He looked very serious. Perhaps he didn't know of the hoax, Greg thought, and was angry for having been played by his own brother.

They left the laundry room and returned to the television section. Greg turned the game on, and began playing, not waiting for Aaron. In several minutes, the phone rang. It rang a couple times, then someone apparently picked up. A couple minutes later, they heard someone come down the steps. Turning around, they saw Aaron. He stopped about halfway down, and they could see him standing there where there was no wall enclosing that part of the stairwell. He leaned over, holding a phone to his ear.

"Zeb!" he called out to him, beckoning him. "I need to talk to you for a minute." He walked back upstairs, talking to someone on the phone. Zeb got up from the couch.

"I'll be right back, Greg." Greg nodded, and returned to the game. Several minutes later, the two brothers came down together. They seemed to be having a personal argument of some type. "Truth above all else, Aaron. Remember that." Aaron was breathing heavily. He was very quiet as Greg played his game. Greg wondered what had gotten in to him, all of a sudden. He gave Aaron a look of confusion, then continued the game. "So much for the progress," Zeb muttered to Aaron.

"All for the best, probably," Aaron responded. What were they talking about? Greg wondered. He wouldn't worry about it. He had enough on his mind. He just wanted to play a game, at last in peace.

When a pound was heard against the wall to their left, Aaron was quick to react. "Don't worry about that noise, Greg," he said. "That was the furnace, I am sure. You have nothing to fear here." He said this a bit nervously. What was all this about?

"Oh, I'm not worried Aaron. I'm just fine," Greg said.

"That's good... That's very good," Aaron said assuredly. Greg returned to the game. Aaron never left that strange state of behavior that day and Greg found himself talking more to Zeb. Greg slept over once again, and sleep went uninterrupted. Not even a creak was heard. He slept restlessly, however.

So many doubts and obsessive thoughts now beleaguered his weary mind. Though he had believed himself to be quite accepting of the recent discovery, he was obviously disturbed by it. He was still dealing with his relationship with Aaron and the house. And why did Aaron begin behaving so strangely, so suddenly? Did he figure it all out somehow? He certainly was admitting that there was nothing to fear... as if nothing strange had ever happened... Eventually his thoughts led him to remember what Derik had told him, and here they floated for a time in a whirlpool of anguish. Could he have been wrong maybe, or even have lied? No way, he thought. He knew Derik too well, and he could tell that Derik was indeed vexed himself and was being completely honest about everything he had said. But what was Zeb still hiding? Something... These incessant secrets became so taxing on Greg that finally he could bear no more, and sleep claimed him.

A new morning brought new strength, and Greg would try to learn more from Zeb. Aaron's behavior was still obviously inauthentic, though it remained unclear what that meant. Again, this day Greg would converse with Zeb more than Aaron, before departing. They found themselves talking on the deck, leaning over the railing while they watched the rippling water in the pool.

"I'm having trouble understanding what is real, I guess," Greg admitted. "I believe Derik, but I sense something is still being kept secret."

"Reality..." Zeb muttered. "It always seems to come down to perspective, does it not? When one attempts to corner it, he finds himself either overwhelmed or denying its ambiguity. Truth is often implied when reality is spoken of, as it, too, is hard to isolate." A breeze blew through now.

"Are they not the same?" Greg asked.

"What is true is really true, and what is real is truly real," Zeb said. "Reality may be elusive in this world, but truth is always there."

"I suppose I seek both..." Greg said. A leaf fell into the water.

"A great task is before you, then," Zeb told him. "I can be your crutch for only so long. The rest is your duty alone."

Greg nodded. "Let me tell you, that I am sure Derik has done what he believes was best for you. I am also sure that he has spoken truthfully. As to this reality he has spoken of, I can say no more." Greg looked at him desperately.

"Why...?" Greg said, drawing closer as he looked deeply into Zeb's narrowed eyes.

"Time will tell," Zeb answered. "For time destroys everything, and walls of disguise are no exception." Greg nodded, and stepped away. He paced the deck.

"Well," he began, "these new discoveries will probably not leave my mind in peace. Until I know, until I understand, I will have no rest."

"Such it is," Zeb said. "Forget not, still, your friends. For they were brought into your world without your asking, and so should they remain. In time you will find yourselves united in strength, and I will be there with you." Greg smiled, and returned into the house, to spend time with Aaron, who was still a friend to him. As Zeb stared into the water, he shuddered, for he was lost as well.

The next day, Derik opened his front door to greet whoever had knocked. It was Aaron. This is weird, Derik thought, coming here out of the blue like this.

"Oh, hey Aaron!" Derik said. "Here, come in." They walked into Derik's living room and sat. "I've got a new video to show you," he said. Derik's hobby was digital video, and he hoped to someday become a film director. He and Aaron watched the video, which was a documentary on a combat sport his friend had invented. Both he and Aaron had participated in the fights that were shown, so it was very amusing. But after the video was over, there was an awkward silence. Finally, Aaron broke it.

"Hey, the main reason I came is that my brother wants to see the video we made, you know, the one with the portal, the one that we're going to play to scare Greg. Do you have it still?" Derik looked at him cautiously.

"Yeah... hold on," he said, turning and walking to the cassette shelf to look for it. "Ah, here it is." He handed it to Aaron.

"Great, thanks," Aaron kindly said. "I should probably get going. Have some things to do at home." Derik walked him to the door. "Thanks again," Aaron said, walking through the door. He held up the tape, with a sly grin upon his face. "Because this was the only thing you would have been able to show Greg to prove to him what you told him." Derik looked at Aaron in disgust.

"I thought it was weird, you coming over here like that... You've played me now, just like Greg," Derik said. "I won't deny that I told him everything... I just wonder how you learned..." Aaron surveyed his friend for a moment. Finally, he said,

"I didn't have to do anything." He walked out onto the porch. "Let's just say I have my ways." Aaron beckoned him to follow, and Derik stepped out onto the porch with him. "It's your word against mine, now, Derik," Aaron said. "Now that I have this, you can do nothing but persuade him with words. And as you know, I excel here." Derik stepped closer, eying the tape. Aaron stepped back. "Oh no, don't think about that!" Aaron said. "After going as far as I have, don't you wonder how much further I would go to keep this from you?" He laughed now.

"Is that a threat?" Derik asked challengingly.

"It is whatever you want it to be," Aaron said.

"I just don't understand you anymore. I thought I knew you. I thought I was your friend. I thought Greg was your friend!" Derik looked down, feeling sick. "How can you do this to your friends?!"

"Don't try the guilt trip on me, Derik," Aaron retaliated. "For it was you that betrayed me, remember. I had faith in you, and you failed me. You are to blame for this, you are to blame for Greg's dilemma!" Aaron drew closer. "For Greg is now more distraught than he has ever been, and only the world he knew before can restore his sanity." Derik shook his head and was not intimidated.

"So you'll continue this, then? You'll continue using him like this? Have you no conscience?" Derik asked, becoming quite emotional though he concealed this fairly well. Aaron laughed.

"Feelings... Are they not more than inconveniences; interferences? They have no place in objective studies!" Aaron said passionately.

"Then he's nothing more than your lab rat... Sick..." Derik said.

"If you understood the nature of the Study, you would not disagree," Aaron told him. "And you are wrong to think that I do not value his mind. For I will restore him. Only you threaten this. Only you are destroying his mind."

"That's not true..." Derik said timidly. Then he looked up with sudden strength. "You didn't create his world! You merely changed the way he saw it! It's not your place to tell him what is real and what isn't!" Aaron shrugged innocently.

"I haven't done anything for him. He has reached his conclusions all on his own. His reality is just as sound as any other, including yours. It is only because he is alone there, that you worry for him...Derik, is it that you are envious of him? Do you desire what he has found?"

"What-?!" Derik started. "That's... ridiculous!" Derik was quite taken aback by this. "You throw around these words, trying to confuse me, but you know just as well as me that we all live in the same world!" Aaron's eyes grew stern.

"No!" he shouted passionately. "You know nothing of reality! You are alone in your world and can say nothing of others'. Your personal world is the only thing you will ever be able to fathom, and as for an 'objective world', this does not exist!"

"I just can't agree with you..." Derik said. Aaron closed his eyes, letting out a long breath.

"Then there is nothing more I can do for you. You have been faced with 'truth'. If you cannot accept it, then I can do nothing more but wish you happiness in your bliss." Aaron began to walk down the steps. Turning back, he had one more thing to say. "And if you care for Greg, then you will obey me and not speak of this visit of mine, nor anything we discussed. Leave everything to me, and I will heal what wounds you have made."

"Farewell to you as well," Derik said as Aaron stepped off the porch. Aaron gave a gesture of farewell.

"I'll be seeing you around, again. I have nothing against you, Derik, and you are still a friend to me. But I will do what I must." And with that he left.

"What was that all about, Derik?" his mother asked him, stepping out onto the porch with him. "He sounded like a completely different person." As he watched Aaron drive off, Derik wondered for a moment if there was still something noble in what Aaron was doing.

"Playing mind games, that's all," he said to his mother. "I'm sure we'll talk it over later."

He returned to his room, where he could think in peace, wondering if he indeed was living in a bliss. He would talk with his parents about all the things that had brought him so much distress in the last year or more, leaving out no details. "Some people are like that," his father said of Aaron. "Follow what your heart tells you, and you can't go wrong." Derik nodded, but he would still obey Aaron's orders.

The four did not again gather for a few weeks. Greg had visited once, and it was almost like the old days. But without Derik, there was no reason to read from the Scary Book. In these recent times, the Book had been deemed by Derik to be damaging to Greg's mind, though he had no problem with the Book itself and could even say he respected its handling of the horror genre. When he heard that Greg was rereading it, there was no point in keeping his own reading on hold. After all, he was nearing its completion. It would help, he hoped, to lessen any feelings of awkwardness, as these feelings would inevitably be felt while in the presence of both Greg and Aaron. That was going to be fun, he thought.

Surprisingly, the three seemed to get along quite well, even managing to summon a laugh here and there. Still, there was a lingering tension between Derik and Aaron. Derik felt as though Aaron was always there, holding him by the leash, ready to pull him back should he venture into territory unwelcome. He remembered the words he had told Greg: people have many sides. He tried not to think about the ugly side of Aaron, that side which had seemed so foreign, but rather enjoy the sides with which he was presently shown. This left him feeling dissatisfied, for he realized this was only denial: that ugly side must still be there, whether hidden or forgotten, and it was a problem. Two things he knew: he would be manipulated no longer, and he would not hesitate to discover the truth if such an opportunity manifested.

It was only natural, then, when he and Greg found a curious cassette player sitting on the living room speaker box that, with no one else around to guide his actions, he hit the play button. There was a recording, a journal entry of some sort. The speed was set too fast and the volume was too low, so he adjusted these to listen in. The voice spoke very clearly, the entry being either pre-scripted or professionally recorded. The content itself, he would discover, was disquieting.

"...Young, seems captivated and fearful as well."

This was Zeb's voice he realized now, though the first half of what he was saying was not heard. Derik looked at Greg, feeling immediately breached as he heard his last name spoken. They listened in.

"These outsiders are becoming a bit troublesome, but I suppose the world must know sooner or later. My brother and his friends were having a social night in the basement. Upon just returning home from an errand, I was told of a bizarre event which they had all experienced. Apparently, they had experienced noises from behind the cellar door which would be shut tight one minute and then slightly ajar the next, even after being shut again. Then, I am told, the door swung wide open revealing a toy horse, which was impossibly in the path of the opening door. Later, I was lost for words as Mr. Young approached me and asked how I accomplished this feat. Realizing that he thought it was a hoax and believing that it was probably best this way, I acted quickly in my given part: I 'admitted' that it was I, and to make myself even more believable I made it seem as though I wanted to keep it a secret from the others. My only hope now is that Mr. Young does not realize the silliness in believing orchestrating such an elaborate hoax is possible given that no one here is a trained illusionist."

The recording ended, Derik and Greg looking at each other, each speechless. Derik was almost laughing, while Greg simply stared in disbelief. The recording immediately picked up again with a more recent recording Aaron had made.

"Though I find the recent phenomenon intriguing, I do not have the same conviction as Zebulon in revealing this to others," Aaron said. "I personally believe that the well-being of the human mind is also a factor and should be preserved by any means necessary. With that said, I have noticed my old friend, Mr. Logan, beginning to suffer in mental functioning, and my new friend, Mr. Young, expressing an obvious dissatisfaction with the recent occurrences. The Study is important and shall continue, but first I must preserve my friendships and the minds of those who are my friends. After all, Mr. Young should have no reason to fear this house. The hard part, without a doubt, will be fabricating a coherent story that will make Mr. Young feel more comfortable. Mr. Logan seems more willing to accept it, but I should at least present it in a manner more appealing to him."

This session of recording ended, and the tape continued on with the next. It was Zeb speaking this time.

"The Doctor called. He suggested we gather for a discussion this time. I still have several more notes to gather together, but it should make for some interesting insights, as he is a very insightful person. Lucinda will not be able to make it, but we should be able to get in touch with her later."

This session ended, and the next one began. Greg and Derik continued to listen, both speechless. Zeb was again speaking.

"Mr. Logan is not inaccurate when he says the experiences are similar to the 'Scary Book'. In fact, I have often wondered if it is not our close familiarity with it that has caused many of these phenomena. It could be that I find the Book interesting only because it accurately depicts the ambiguous nature of reality, but I think it is more likely that the Book itself is having an effect on reality. After all, my brother and I had what we call 'the Scary Book day' which was when, after reading it nearly all day long, the environment itself took a likeness to that of the Book. But then, other people must read it without experiencing such things, so I am presently unclear as to what is happening."

At this point Aaron came out from wherever he had been, completely unaware of what was happening. When he saw them there holding the tape player and heard what was playing, he stopped short. He tried to say something, but nothing came out. As his stomach twisted, he glared at them with eyes both furious and terrified. He quickly moved past them, retreating to Zeb's room where he found Zeb. As the tape continued to play, they heard Aaron counseling with Zeb in desperation. They had missed some of the recording, but now listened in. There were three voices: Aaron, Zebulon, and a now also a very strange one that sounded like it was either electronically doctored or generated.

"...pretty much just looked like a shadow with some rags around it. I'm not even sure it was a person." This was Zeb.

"Interesting," Said the strange voice.

"Yes," Zeb said. "Now what's very interesting is how my brother here has a different account, as well as his friend." Now Aaron was heard.

"Actually, if it weren't for my friend, there would be no problem with the accounts. We probably would assume we went at separate times. Okay. Basically, I went with my friend–"

"Mr. Logan, I presume," the strange voice said. Aaron continued.

"Yes. We went to that house. I went with him, and him alone. We saw all the same things Zebulon described and went about the investigation in pretty much the same manner. Mr. Logan started acting a little funny, and I decided it was best if we return. Upon returning, he seemed dumbfounded to find Zebulon taking a nap as he usually does at that time of day. He woke him up, asking him why he was acting weird, and was soon insisting that he had gone with us. When I reminded him that it was simply he and I, he grew angry with me. It is obvious that he believes now that both me and Zebulon had accompanied him. So, that's the strangest part about all this. How we all have different accounts. Mainly Mr. Logan's account and how it disrupts ours. It has actually got us questioning whether it even really happened."

"I'm not sure what you mean by 'real'," the strange voice began. "In any case, you have experienced something. All of you. These experiences were real."

"But people can usually relate with things in the same way," Zeb explained.

"They can talk with each other and both give and receive affirmation of the experience. In this case, the stories aren't correlating..."

"Indeed," the strange voice said. "The cohesive threads of your worlds seem to have been torn. But obviously no longer. Not at the moment, anyway."

"This isn't the only case of our stories not quite

matching," Zeb said. "Well, let me tell you about a more recent incident. This one is quite strange also. Then Aaron can tell you how there is definitely a subjectivity to the experience, since it is mainly his story. I was out running an errand. It was evening, when..." At this point the recording stopped and immediately resumed at a later point. The strange voice was in the middle of talking.

"...caught you by surprise, but there was no reason to lie to Mr. Young. It would have been better to have simply told him the truth as you knew it. But that is intriguing how quick he was to presume you to be the cause, despite empirical contradictions."

"Yes, it really goes to show that seeing is not believing," Zeb said.

"Yes. Remember, believing is seeing," the strange voice said.

"Well, brother, why don't you describe the subjectivity in this occurrence," Zeb suggested.

"This time I was the one who had an account different than the others, though I think I'm better off with my experience than theirs," Aaron began. "Zebulon was talking about Mr. Young telling him how the door swung open revealing a toy horse. This is the part that is not coherent with the others' stories. I had heard some noises coming from beyond the cellar door. Mr. Logan also insisted that the door had been shut and it was now open slightly. Maybe I hadn't paid enough attention to that. Now, the door did swing wide open, but I didn't see a horse standing in the doorway. I didn't get a good look either, but I think I would have seen it. Both Mr. Young and Mr. Logan insist on it. I know of the horse they spoke of, it is an antique toy of ours, but I did not see it in the doorway. It would be impossible for it to be there anyway, since it would be in the path of the opening door."

"Impossible to arrange," the strange voice said. "But not impossible to experience."

"Well..." Aaron started. Zeb cut him off.

"This isn't the best example anyway. Tell him about the 'doll' incident. Remember?" Zeb asked.

"Oh. Uh, yeah, this one involves Mr. Logan as well," Aaron said. "Once again, it was he that experienced the bizarre, not I. For the most part anyway..." Here the recording was apparently paused and resumed at a later point. "...So, basically, except for the electrical malfunction, and the noise, things seemed normal enough for me, but obviously not Mr. Logan."

"I see, I see. This is very interesting indeed. I'm glad I know you two," the electronic voice said as the others laughed. The strange voice continued. "Yes, this experience of his you describe to me... it consists of things that normally cause fear in the perceiver. It is obvious, then, that there is something different between these and other experiences. Now, since sensation is already in constant flux, then it is in perception where the change takes place. Usually, perception remains relatively constant despite this flux. But it is in experiences such as yours where perception is in flux as well. It is a rupturing of context, that which forces human minds to operate coherently."

"I have often thought of context as well," Zeb began. "It does indeed seem to be a key factor in horror, and even humor, I would add."

"Yes, as well as issuing in a whole set of conflicts, dramas and revelations," the strange voice said. "Context serves to bring us toward Being by organizing our sensations into meaningful things, beings. Yet, by adopting this meta-perspective, it also alienates us from Being."

"I wanted to add that visuals are not the only mode in which our perceptions are ruptured, so to speak. Audition has been a major factor as well. You remember all the noises we told you about..." Aaron said.

"Hmm... Yes," the electronic voice began. "Audition, as it is often considered less trust-worthy than sight, serves as an introductory stage in Tryst. It... eases one in... more comfortably."

"This 'introductory phase' to me suggests some kind of purpose or perhaps even a will behind the phenomena," Zeb said.

"No, there isn't necessarily a single, outside will causing these phenomena," the strange and knowing voice said. "Remember, all sensations are, in a sense, random. This is true even down to the most miniscule level. Most modern physicists will confirm this for you. It is only our relationship with these sensations that changes. This results in a change in perception; our world view, you might say."

"Is there a cause, then, for this change in perception, or our relationship with sensations?" Zeb asked the mysterious person. "I cannot fathom a result without some kind of – "

"There is indeed a cause for this," the mysterious voice interrupted. "It is the way in which we participate in the Wa-Wa. You know of the Wa-Wa and how it is an endless, ineffable cycle. It is when one becomes aware of the utter futile nature of it that he begins seeking out alternate realities. This is when the Tryst forms. It is a mutual relationship in which each side seeks the other."

"I see," Zeb said. "Apparently it is rather effective."

"Oh yes," the voice said. "It is the result of a person's most desperate efforts to change his place in being."

"Then we ourselves would be desperate. But one cannot not be aware of the choices he makes. We have never made such choices," Aaron said.

"Oh, but you have," the strange voice insisted. "One can be a completely willing member in a relationship without even realizing it. It is like a baby in the womb. It does not realize that it is the child of its mother. It is also similar to those who do not realize that they are conscious. It may only be a matter of time, however, before the obligations of the relationship are fully welcomed, on all levels."

"But Mr. Logan strongly states that he wants nothing to do with any of the recent occurrences," Aaron said.

"That doesn't matter," the voice said persistently. "There is a deeper will inside us all that deals with those matters of which most people's states of mind are not aware. Or, stated another way, the Wa-Wa has the property of inciting, given sufficient time and a compatible disposition, a certain set-back willingness in the subject."

"Perhaps Freud was right after all," Aaron said.

"Wait, this is not similar to Freudian psychology," the mystery voice said. "The only thing he said that relates to us is that there are forces beyond the conscious self that influence the direction of our will. You will see... as I have. This is not some buried motive nor desire. It is blossoming as we speak."

"Okay..." Zeb said. There was a brief pause.

"Now," the strange voice began, "I have several things left for today but do get in touch with – "

"Oh yeah, we'll definitely keep you updated..." Zeb said interrupting.

"We done?" Aaron asked.

"Yes," Zeb replied.

"I look forward to – " the voice began to say, cut short as the recording was ended here.

Derik finally managed to speak. "That voice...What is up with that voice?! It's obviously not a natural voice..." Greg was nearly laughing himself now. He could hardly handle any more.

"I just don't know what to think! Just don't know what to think!" he repeated, flabbergasted. The recordings continued. Following was yet another more recent session, one of Aaron's.

"As Mr. Logan has grown fearful of the cellar stairs, I have begun to understand more fully the relationship that grows in Tryst. He has had an obvious sentiment for it. And now I see that the Tryst is very personal indeed.

"I almost knew that he would finally have intimate engagement in it. Because of this, I prepared Mr. Young for the experience as best I could. Going along with the 'hoax' bit that he had established with Zebulon, I went to great lengths to ensure that Mr. Young would feel comfortable. As part of the hoax idea, I constructed a frame of sorts, mimicking that of the window Zebulon described having seen. I made it rather ambiguous, so that in the case of any new manifestation being slightly different, it could still be a credible gimmick. My plan could not have worked more perfectly.

"Just as I had predicted, Mr. Logan had a very intimate experience. I hid in the bathroom, waiting. I could feel the time was ripe, but I was a bit nervous since I may have to tell my friend that I could not do it. But there was no need. Mr. Young thought I was preparing the hoax. Zebulon brought he and Mr. Logan out into the kitchen. And then Mr. Logan saw it. I don't believe Mr. Young could see it, which confused him a bit. I returned from the bathroom a few minutes after hearing their commotion in the kitchen.

"Mr. Logan's first words with me were somewhat angry. He must have been so upset by the experience that he believed it was a hoax! At this point I became sure that he had had an experience. It was not my intention to hide it from him, as it is with Mr. Young, so I tried to get him to explain his experience in full detail. This seemed to reveal to him that it was in fact not a hoax, and he had a very hard time telling us his story. I eased him as best I could, for I needed to know all the details so that I could make it work for Mr. Young. I believe the first word to describe what he saw was 'mirror'. Yes, he said it looked like a large mirror, with a very large frame surrounding it. He then said that there were coils of wire on either side of this, which itself was sitting symmetrically at the bottom of the steps. He added that there were also handles of sorts, similar to a bicycle's. These were two, on the close side, and he said they were there as if the whole thing would be lifted off the ground and carried off by someone. I had expected something a little more similar to Zebulon's experience, but all in all it was fairly similar.

"All three have been squarish, sitting at the bottom of the stairs, and glass-like, with framing. Then, however, Mr. Logan began to describe the thing as more of a portal. I think he was not sure if it was mirror-like or simply a hole. In any case, these 'portals' seem to be evolving in some way. The first was barely identifiable, if at all. The second, from what Zebulon tells me, seemed to 'open up' a bit, becoming something more familiar, a window. Now, the wires, according to Mr. Logan, have apparently coiled into a more distinct form, and it is a bit more understandable, in that at least it had unmistakable handles, though their purpose is unknown. I carry the burden now of making all of this coherent for Mr. Young, who is amazed at 'my' ability to produce such phenomena. I am amazed, however, at how convenient this was for me. I almost feel as if something was working with me to make it happen the right way. I mean, it was almost too perfect."

Greg had been looking at Derik throughout this whole recording, shaking his head from side to side in disbelief. Both of their worlds were suddenly turned not only upside down, but leftward, rightward, right side up then upside down again. This was simply so preposterous and disturbing that it was hard to take seriously. They continued listening. Again, one of Aaron's sessions played.

"Per the advice of the Doctor, I have gone to even greater lengths now to ensure Mr. Young's comfort at my home. In addition to the frame I have made, I constructed a 'doll' as best I could. I am no doll-maker, but I think my work may be of good enough quality to satisfy Mr. Young.

"As for the many strange noises that Mr. Logan has been hearing - and hearing alone - I told Mr. Young that I had been playing a radio in the back. Or maybe a cassette tape. I can't remember at the moment. But as long as he does not inquire into the subjectivity of the experience, it should remain plausible. At the moment he seems totally accepting of my explanations. He has, however, begun to show dissatisfaction in that he thinks it is a 'mean joke'. He is awaiting my supposed revealing to Mr. Logan that it is a hoax.

"Unfortunately, this cannot be done since me doing this will not put an end to the anomalies. I do agree, though, that Mr. Logan is beginning to suffer in mental ability, and I am considering having Mr. Young tell him what I've told Mr. Young. Zebulon is strongly against this, thinking that knowing the truth is the main concern. I think he is mostly interested in Mr. Logan's budding relationship with this alternate reality, and would like to study it, protecting it from any conditions that would otherwise not have arisen."

Derik laughed hysterically. He could manage nothing more. "Wow," was Greg's vocal impulse. "He's done something quite brilliant, that Aaron. It seems so realistic, too." In reality, he was only *hoping* that what he was hearing was a masterfully thought-out and crafted addition to Aaron's supposed long list of hoaxes. The recordings continued. Next was a story he had heard before. Zeb began speaking.

"I have often thought back to an old friend of mine," he said. "His name was Wendell Hearn."

Greg looked at Derik. "Now this is true," he told Derik. "Weird..." The whole story that Greg had been told was again spoken to him.

Near the end of the story, Derik and Greg heard Zeb's door open. Aaron came marching out of the hallway, looking very nervous and very distressed. Greg noticed that the Wendell story was not yet over. What more was there to say? he wondered, though his thoughts were not nearly this clear at the time. Aaron came right up to Greg and snatched the tape player from his hands. He turned it off, and with a wild snort, retreated again to Zeb's room. A faint and urgent discussion could be heard behind the wall, now.

Greg's face was beyond grim. But Derik's radical rejection of this entire study rubbed off on Greg, and he was soon laughing again, disgusted with Aaron and at the same time greatly impressed with what he believed Aaron had accomplished.

"Well the voice was obviously an actor or faked somehow..." Greg said. "And it was spoken so well, it must have been scripted."

"But Greg, how do you know that that isn't what he wants you to think!? I'm telling you, he's a manipulator! You can't trust anything!" Derik cried desperately.

"I don't know..." he said. They walked together, down the hallway and into Zeb's room.

Aaron backed away from them, to the corner of the room, very quiet. Zeb sat on his bed, looking at the two with inscrutable eyes. Greg had no care and even allowed himself to enjoy the momentary spotlight, in whose center he knew he and Derik stood.

"I am very impressed, men, very impressed," Greg said sincerely, though also flustered and still struggling inside. Somberly, Aaron looked at him but avoided eye contact.

"Yeah... well, I'm glad...." That was all he could say for a while.

"Aaron, you may as well give that act up," Zeb told him. "Cat's out of the bag."

"Look, I just don't want to lose my friends!" Aaron cried. "That's all I've really cared about all along! You care more about the Study! You could care less what these guys are going through... But I have done nothing but try to make their stays here as welcoming as possible! I've done so much, and still, I see my friendships crumbling... It's not my fault!" Zeb looked at him condescendingly.

"Aaron... That's why I've been telling you all this time that truth is the highest of aspirations. If you had simply told them the truth, you would have been friends always," Zeb said.

"...Until they stop talking to me because I live in a freak-ish house! Until they fear for their lives, whether they should or not!" Aaron vented. Derik walked up to Aaron.

"Aaron... Answer me plainly: Was everything real, or was it all fake?..." he asked, looking right into Aaron's nervous eyes. Aaron was silent. Derik waited.

"I... I can't say..." Aaron said. Derik turned around.

"Then I will no longer be any part in this," Derik said simply. "When you two can be honest with me, then I will talk. Until then, good-bye." He left the room, distraught, and walked out the front door. He got in his car and drove home. He watched in the mirror as the sun set behind the Eldritchs' house. He had seen this before, but it was a new house the sun now fell behind, one he would try and forget about lest he un-ravel entirely.

Greg still stood in the room, staring at Zeb and Aaron. His look of disgust had been replaced with that of concern. "You didn't go after him," Greg said to Aaron. Aaron plopped down on the bed by Zeb.

"I know..." Aaron sighed. "As hard as it was, there was nothing I could do. He must come to terms with truth all on his own." Greg now remembered Zeb's words on the deck from more than a month ago. He looked at Zeb.

"So is this truth, then?" he asked Zeb. Zebulon looked up, with much wisdom upon his brow.

"Truth is still unknown, and it shall remain so," he said. "As for reality, you have only to accept it, and it will be yours."

"Is it yours?" Greg asked. Zeb nodded.

"It is."

"It's just... so hard to believe... All this time, I had no idea... There's been so much going on outside of our little cir-cle... and I was a topic of discussion..." Greg fell to the floor, and sat there, stooped. "I feel sick...." he said. "...It's Friday the thirteenth, you know..." He looked up at Zeb with a weak smile. "My universe *would* come crashing down today."

Aaron jumped up, looking down at Zeb in fury.

"You!... You did this!" he said, speaking through teeth both clenched and bared. "Somehow you knew they would play the tape! You simply went ahead and did what you thought was best, without first consulting me, and totally contrary to everything I was trying to do! The audacity..." Zeb grew angry himself now, and stood up, looming over even Aaron now.

"Relax your tongue and be angry with only your own foolishness!" he said, powerfully. "For only a fool could believe that I have such control over others' behavior, and it is this fool's deceit alone that has brought an otherwise avoidable disaster down upon him." But Aaron stood with resilience.

"You have forgotten something, brother," he said to a now smug Zeb, who waited and listened. "It was your deceit that started all of this... when you told Derik that the horse incident was your doing." But Aaron's sense of victory was short-lived.

"That may be true," Zeb said, "but he approached me already having these beliefs. I did not lead him from truth. I merely let him remain blind." They both sat down. To Greg, he said, "Fate has seen that you discover the truth and allowed me to become careless for a moment..." Now he turned to his brother who was still red with anger. "...for I was merely making a copy of that tape and had forgotten to put it away." Aaron looked down now, while his brother returned to Greg. "What you've heard is the true history Aaron and I both share. It is now for us all, together, to discover which *reality* is most coherent... You have already told me your desire to find it."

"I have," Greg said.

"What about Derik?" Aaron asked. "I do hope we see him again. I can't bear to lose his friendship. But what should we tell him?"

"You already know what I think," Zeb said.

"I agree," Greg said. Aaron nodded with reluctance.

"I suppose so, but it will be hard. We will have to reveal it to him gradually," Aaron said.

"But we can do nothing to keep the Tryst from surfacing... He'll be welcomed by a most surprising aberration from normality, one we will be slow to explain," Zeb said.

"And any attempt to explain it as a hoax, Aaron, would only work if I pretend to be a victim still, as I believed I was before," Greg said. "And I will not do this. I am not saying that I will approach him and tell him that I believe everything I heard on that tape of yours, but I will make it clear that he is in need of enlightenment."

"Then I guess that's that, then," Aaron said, almost as if in defeat, for great efforts he had made were now all for naught. "There will be no more conspiracies, and Derik will have to learn this on his own." Greg stood up again, feeling a little better, although still nauseated by the sudden change in gestalt that had occurred.

"I still find it so hard to believe... and yet Derik had never fully convinced me. He told me many things, but there were still many questions... still many things that he failed to explain, either because he was never given a story by you, or because his explanations left me unsatisfied. I have believed for more than a month now, that all of those experiences were nothing more than games... and now I see that you knew much more about them than you said even then..." Aaron gave a weak smile.

"Sorry," he said, possibly seeing the chastising expression on his friend fade a bit. "I just wanted to keep my friends, even if it meant endangering the Study..." Aaron sat in thought for a while. "I guess you heard all about it, then. I grabbed it from you when I had enough guts to face you, but you must have heard lots..."

"Well I was so shocked and, honestly, amused, that I had a hard time paying attention to some of it. I mean, what the hell, Aaron? This isn't you! And you too, Zeb! 'The Study'? Since when did you guys become scientists? I see you two in front of me but right now you're strangers to me."

"Please don't say that, Greg," Aaron pleaded. "It's much

more complicated than you think. I've done things and seen things others haven't and I hid things from you. But I promise I haven't been faking who I am or anything like that." Zeb was being unusually conservative with his commentary. At last he spoke.

"Greg's not wrong. We clearly sound different in those moments, like in that recording. Our temperament, our sense of purpose, even."

"I regret the whole thing," Aaron declared.

"Don't be so brash, Aaron," Zeb responded.

"I do. I wasn't made for something like this. I'm supposed to be drawing, sculpting, building. I'm supposed to be peering into deep pools in the creek somewhere in the woods, not peering into the depths of - "

"Mind your words, brother!" Zeb interrupted. "You've had plenty of opportunities for protest. What makes you think you can simply walk out of this, anyway? I'm personally not ready to accept that as a... reasonable option." Greg was flabbergasted.

"Listen to you two! It's a total joke," he laughed in disgust. "You guys have a long way to go if you think you're going to be researchers. But I don't think you even know what you want, do you?"

"Maybe I don't, Greg," Zeb admitted. "My life isn't what it used to be. The world I remember from my childhood is no more. Everyone around me tells me that I'm doing everything correctly, but every day brings more misery..." His entire frame quivered for an instant, his eyes lowering. The others had never seen him like this. "Every commute to the office, every bit of small talk in the elevator, every lunch I pack before going to bed... each is a small chink in my heart. And now, imagine, if you will, that you find yourself at a low moment, when suddenly a whole new world opens up to you... What do you do? Well I can tell you – I jumped all over that. Was I scared? Of course. Was I wondering if perhaps my behavior was inauthentic? I was. But this was my chance, okay? *Our* chance. Maybe I will regret it, but when I think of the alternative..." And now Greg could see that Zeb's eyes were glistening, so he put a hand on his shoulder.

"I can respect that, Zeb." Looking to Aaron, now, he said, "As for you, I'm not so sure."

"You can look past his involvement when he isn't even remorseful but for some reason for me it's a cardinal sin?" Aaron responded, his voice breaking with emotion. "I thought you'd at least try to understand."

"Well, I'm still here, aren't I?" Greg said in return.

"Look, the Study... I've had misgivings about it since the beginning," Aaron began. "It never felt right treating you like a test subject and it was only at the behest of others that I continued. Obviously, I ignored my conscience and kept on. I'm sorry for that. If I ever thought you were in danger I wouldn't have." Greg was shaking his head and frowning.

"I don't know. This could have gone on forever if we hadn't found the tape."

"If I'm being honest, it's possible," Aaron admitted. "I failed you as a friend. It's true. But my concerns were there and there was a lot of pressure to continue. I can't overstate that."

"We don't need any wishy-washiness in the Study, Aaron," Zeb interjected. "You can count yourself out now."

"Are you really so surprised?" Aaron said. "You saw how cautiously I came on board. You knew I wanted to preserve my friendships. You also had to have seen that I really do hold a great intrigue for these... occurrences... But I can't go on like this." He lowered his head now, in reminiscence. "It's always been hard for me... This sort of, I don't know, sequestering part of myself and then letting it right back out at the appropriate time. Even walking into church for Mass and leaving an hour or two later requires that I act as if nothing of significance has really happened – while anyone around you would tell you that the most significant thing in all of the world had just transpired during that hour. I wasn't planning on things unfolding this way but here we are." Now he turned to Zeb. "Maybe I should be thanking you, Zeb, since now I won't be forced to live this dual life any longer – but the life I live from here on will be one not with secrets but one shared with friends." And he looked to Greg, who in every respect was his best friend. "So yes, my friend, I can say that I regret my part in the research because I love my friends and I know I'm not the person I pretend to be during these study sessions. That's why I'm going to make a promise now: I will never use you or any other person like that again. I hope you can take this as my apology."

Greg gave a compassionate look. "I forgive you. Tensions are running high right now. We're all pretty upset. I guess I'm just still hurt and I still don't understand how you got involved in all of this."

"I'll tell you as often as I need to that I'm truly sorry for how I handled things and that I allowed you to endure so much on your own," Aaron began, thinking hard on how to word his next thoughts. Greg waited, watching his friend fiddle with a Rubik's-cube. "It isn't so easy to explain how I got drawn into this. Sometimes you just want so much to be something special... To stand before the unknown, one amongst the lucky few. To stand there, as a man, looking into that abyss and be able to comment on it with that scientific coolness, that lack of personal investment. Maybe it was my admiration for Zeb," and he looked to his brother, then back to his friend, "and I wished to emulate that. Seeing the way Zeb was handling everything was maybe the only thing that kept me from completely losing it after it became clear there were some unnatural things happening around us. There was no one else I'd be able to talk to without raising some big concerns, you know? I don't want to end up in psych ward like Wendell." He gave a melancholic stare out the bedroom window now. "I miss the old days too. I guess I'm not ready to say goodbye to those times, and I haven't been forced to, either, like Zeb here. If I had my way we'd be playing D&D and going in the woods every day. Somehow, all of this started, and it's crept its way in rather sneakily. And that's where all of this gets so complicated for me. I'd be lying if I said watching these, er... troubles... develop hasn't become an adventure too, in its own way. Dangerous perhaps, but still an adventure. But I'm not going to log any more sessions for the Study. I'm done. It's fascinating, for sure, and maybe I'm a fool. But I'd rather stand with my friends. I know that might not count for much, but all of this has nearly put me in stupor and I'm afraid that's all I know to do."

"Put *you* in a stupor? Ha!" Greg scoffed. But he wasn't truly angry like he had been only moments ago. "Look, I think I might understand. I'm not going to make you guys say any more. I just hope you understand that I still have a ton of questions."

"We do," Zeb assured him. "And Aaron, I won't hold that against you. I have to admit that the whole thing doesn't feel right for me either, but I've made my choice and will follow where it leads me. My lifestyle will probably not allow many more sessions, regardless."

"You may be thankful for that later," Greg said cautiously. "But seriously, someone needs to tell me: what the hell is going on with that weird voice on the recording?" Greg asked, feeling is curiosity begin to pique as well as his nausea. A smile grew on Zeb's face. He never disappointed.

"This person wishes to remain anonymous, and thus had his voice doctored," Zeb said.

"Oh, I see..." Greg sighed.

"But I will tell you if you can keep it secret. Consider it my thanks for being so understanding."

"I can keep it a secret, but if you don't trust me enough, I respect this person's wish to remain anonymous," Greg said. Zeb smiled.

"I trust you," Zeb said. "You have heard me tell of this person before, though I described him in such a way that you would never guess that he has been a close acquaintance for several years now. His name is Bennett. Mark Bennett." Greg's jaw dropped.

"Wow... *the* Bennett? The odd guy?" Greg said in astonishment. Zeb nodded.

"The same one who told me all those stories. He was a few years my senior. We both had an obvious passion for philosophical and esoteric conversation and while small talk was never possible with Mark, some of the most mind-blowing

130

talks I've ever had were with him. After high school he went right into university. He double-majored in anthropology and journalism, while I continued my pursuit of wisdom in a more scholarly fashion. But somehow by the time I finished my fourth year he had already been awarded his Doctorate! He's a bit odd if your standard is, I don't know, somebody you'd pluck out of the mall or off the beach but trust me – he has a genius." Zeb laughed now. "And he hasn't gotten much easier to understand over the years! This should be evident in his words recorded on our tape." Greg nodded.

"I'll probably want to listen to that tape again. It sounded pretty dense," he agreed. "How often do you see him?"

"This may sound strange but I haven't *seen* him since high school," Zeb answered. Now Greg was entirely flummoxed. "In the literal sense, at least. I've visited him a dozen times or so and Aaron probably half that. Would you agree?" He looked at his brother.

"I'd say so." Greg was still waiting for an explanation.

"Oh, so what, you went blindfolded or something? Now he's part the Cartel, is that it?" Greg asked, growing frustrated with the digressions.

"No, nothing that dramatic," Aaron began. "Like Zeb said, he's very private. Perhaps even paranoid. It's hard to gauge things like that when you can't see their face. But he accomplished this by sitting behind a curtain while he spoke to us during these meetings, and kept the room very dark. It probably should have seemed weirder to me, huh? I guess it just sort of reminded me of a confessional, and eventually I got used to it as another one of his peculiarities."

"You meet some... interesting... people," Greg noted. His friends laughed now. "You know, it should have dawned on me when I was listening to that," and he pointed at the cassette player. "I thought I heard someone mention the Wa-Wa... I knew that sounded familiar. You know what this is, then?" Zeb's expression was doubtful.

"I hardly understand it..." Zeb said. "It seems to be at the center of his metaphysics as well as ontology, and everything stems off from there, like the spokes on a wheel. I am on-

131

ly beginning to grasp the concept."

"And did I hear something about a Tryst? What's that about?" Greg asked. Aaron fell back onto the bed, sighing. After a moment of silent calculation, he sat up and looked squarely at his friend.

"We don't necessarily believe in this Tryst, Greg. It is, after all, just another human's theory..." he said.

"Just?" Zeb returned, with a squint.

"This 'Doctor' of yours doesn't exactly seem like a 'mere human' to *me*," Greg retorted, eliciting a laugh from Zeb. Aaron continued.

"Well, regardless of how you feel about him, I have only considered it like I would any other theory. In the Study it seems that I am quite accepting of it. This is more because when you do a study, you must take a position and make analyses from that standpoint. You can't go changing your hypothesis while in the midst of research. It is the foundation for everything else," Aaron explained defensively.

"If you insist. I still want to know what it is. I get the feeling it's not about romance..." Greg said.

"From the way Mark described it, it seems to be a relationship of sorts, but not *necessarily* romantic," Zeb began. "You know how I am always talking about context: well, this seems to bring it all together. Now, where is my dictionary?" He sifted through various books on his desk, and then found it. Greg braced himself, and Zeb continued. "He chose this word very carefully I would imagine. Here we go... Tryst... First it could mean an appointment to meet at a certain time and place, especially one arranged in secret by lovers." Greg looked at him in disgust.

"Love is the last thing happening here," he declared. "Continue."

"Also, it can mean an appointed meeting of any kind, or the place itself in which the meeting takes place..." Zeb read. Everyone sat in silence and dwelt on that for a moment.

"Finally, it can also be an appointed station in a hunt or ambush, it says."

"That's the one I find unsettling," Aaron said.

"What does any of that have to do with us?" Greg asked in disgust.

"I am not sure exactly," Zeb said. "I remember he said something very full and concise which was recorded during one of our conversations. It was very hard to understand. But I sense that there is also much more. Basically, it seems that there are two seekers: we, and it. Or they. This other side is what requires the most questioning. Somehow, he says, we willingly submit to this relationship, though we may not know it, and a very intimate process then ensues. Here each side seeks out the other, in a desire to discover alternate reality. This may or may not be realized, and I am not sure if the Tryst depends on it."

"Interesting..." Greg said, cupping his chin in his hands and rubbing the small patch of hair that the others were sure had not been there a month ago. He took a seat in Zeb's desk chair. "Where would this place of meeting be? And what be the object of the hunt?"

"I am not sure that the hunt is even a part of his understanding of it," Zeb began. "But I do sense that there is an emphasis on the meeting place. This must be the moment when the two worlds interact... or perhaps when two minds interact." He sat in thought for a moment. "The portals... They must have something to do with it..." Aaron pulled out the cassette player.

"Greg, you need to understand something about these portals," Aaron said with hesitation. "You aren't – "

"You aren't going to be hopping through any, okay?" Zeb interjected, and grabbed the tape player out of his brother's hands. "We won't let you."

"That's good to know I suppose," Greg said amusedly. "Does something about me scream 'I jump through otherworldly portals?' I need to work on that," he joked – though in truth it wasn't very funny to him. That even such statements were being said aloud suggested that this was clearly going to be a long and toilsome road and would require the greatest strength of will. "I can hardly believe we're saying these things right now," he continued. "It's going to be a while before its really sunk in that those... things... were real."

"It's... pretty incredible," Aaron said. "And if you were wondering, they were the hardest things to make Derik believe to be fake... I would not have been able to do it without certain unexplainable aid..."

"What do you mean?" Greg asked.

"I really can't say... It's unexplainable. Somehow, it was far easier than it should have been," Aaron said.

"I find them to be most interesting, actually," Zeb said. "The portals I mean. Perhaps they are portals to the Tryst itself... or maybe they simply are an outward sign of a Tryst in which one is already part of. The latter seemed to be closer to what Bennett was saying, though even he could be mistaken." Aaron asked his brother for the tape player back, and after an odd exchange of looks, he handed it over.

"There is someone else, as well, that we have consulted and of whose existence you were unaware," Aaron said.

"Go on," Greg said. He was no longer surprised at this point.

"Her name is Lucinda. She is a para-psychologist," Aaron said. "You know, those weird people that are obsessed with the paranormal and – "

"You mean people like us!" Greg broke in, laughing. Everyone laughed.

"Yeah," Aaron said. "Like us. But these people go about their studies in a mostly scientific manner. I have to say, though: little seems to be empirically verifiable."

"I personally don't believe science is the best approach in these matters," Zeb said. Aaron continued.

"Dr. Owens, I mean Lucinda, has views that are quite different from her friend Mark's. She was particularly intrigued by Zeb's deepest fears... I think you know of what I speak," Aaron said. Greg nodded hesitantly.

"She seems to believe that we are ultimately the source of these manifestations," Zeb said. "Like a dream kicked up a notch or two."

"So, there are lots of theories going around," Aaron said. "When it comes down to it, you're alone, Greg. It's up to you to find your truth."

"But you are not alone in your troubles," Zeb added. "Though many of the experiences you had were no one's but your own, we too are immersed in a world that seems to follow no rules."

"I was wondering why Derik never explained why he couldn't hear some of those noises I was hearing. I guess he just couldn't," Greg said. 3

"There are many inconsistencies between your experiences and the props I created to fool Derik," Aaron explained. "I have learned of these one by one, and each time he noticed, I explained it away to him by simply telling him that you were 'just crazy', and that your memory was very faulty. This made even large inconsistencies a problem of yours, not mine. This obviously back-fired on me, though, since he thinks you are more in need of psychiatric help than you really are."

"Gee thanks for telling him all that," Greg muttered. The brothers laughed, and Greg smiled.

"Anyway," Aaron continued, "I just wanted to tell you one last time: I'm sorry for not being honest from the start and treating you like a specimen." Zeb made a small sound of annoyance and rested against the headboard of his bed.

"It's okay," Greg said. "These things come about invisibly, almost. Maybe I would have done the same. Maybe I *will* do the same."

"What? I don't understand," Aaron said, giving his friend a scrutinizing look.

"The Study... Look, I'll make a deal. You can continue

---

3    This was an experience of Greg's that was not described in the story at the time it was had, this being done for the sake of drama. It was an early occurrence, before Derik was told about the hoax but after Greg had already had numerous aberrant experiences of an auditory nature (nearly all the others were described). Greg was apparently hearing bizarre sounds from the darkness while in the presence of both Derik and Aaron. Neither of these two heard the noises and must not have been informed of his experience until later, since Aaron never had to deal with this difficulty when convincing Derik of the hoax. The telling of this experience was skipped so that the reality of the phenomenon would not be so evident. Greg had in fact realized this, and it was one of the few things that lingered in the back of his mind during the time of the hoax, never allowing it to be fully at ease.

with it... only if you allow me to join in."

"Oh boy," Zeb muttered, with eyes closed.

"Greg, I really don't know if that's a good idea. Like I said, I don't think I even *desire* to go on with it. I'll remain open philosophically speaking, but I don't think I'm going to sit around with that tape player and wait for something to happen."

"Well, if you ever feel the need, make sure I'm there," Greg said.

"I will. No promises on meeting the Doctor, though." This got a laugh out of Greg.

"Remember that strength you told me about, Zeb? The one you said we would all unite in?"

"I do," Zeb said.

"Well, I think I can feel it already..." Greg said. "We only need Derik here with us now."

# CHAPTER EIGHT

## Homecoming

It was October, and the annual Renaissance Festival was being held. It was something Aaron and his brothers had been attending for years now, and it would be Greg's second time. Derik had never gone. It would be a good way to heal wounds, Aaron thought, if Greg would bring Derik with him this time. They would go as friends, and he would see Greg as still a good friend of Aaron and Zebulon. This would help ease Derik's troubled mind, he guessed. What needed less guessing was the extent to which the trouble afflicted him.

Derik had thought of his last visit at Aaron's less and less as the weeks went by, but it still plagued him like an infection lying dormant. While the nauseous feeling that he had left the house with was now gone, he longed for the days when he could look into the eyes of his friends, without awkwardness. For they were still his friends, he knew. He wanted only to understand and be able to trust them.

Greg had talked to Derik only several days after the vexing incident. It was not hard for Derik to see that Greg had returned with a change in heart and belief.

"Are you okay, then?" he asked Greg.

"I'm fine... Let me just say that there was a great misunderstanding."

"Do you believe what was on the tape, then?" Derik asked.

"It shouldn't matter what my beliefs are, Derik, as long

as we can trust each other and share good times again," Greg said.

"How can we trust them?" Derik asked.

"I cannot make you trust them," Greg said. "Let me just say that you were a victim more than I, but this is over. There are no more victims."

"I hope so," Derik sighed.

When Greg asked him if he wanted to come to the Renaissance Festival with Zeb and Aaron, he agreed to it without hesitation. He even was willing to return to that house, which was an object of so much angst, though he was doubtful whether he could do this without Greg's accompaniment.

"We'll go together," Greg assured him. "It'll be fine. We'll be able to enjoy each other's company, I know it."

"You're probably right," Derik said, and now an impish smile appeared. "Maybe we can even find a cute Ren-Fest chick for Aaron!"

"Ha! I can hardly imagine!" And the two friends had a laugh together. Greg later told Aaron the good news.

His assessment had also proved correct. Aaron and Zeb were glad to see Derik again, as he walked through the door in pseudo-medieval clothing.

"You need to update your wardrobe, friend," Aaron said smiling. Derik laughed.

"I can do that at the Festival," Derik said, and everyone laughed. Aaron walked up to Derik and rested his arms on his shoulders.

"Derik, I know I've put you through a lot," he said. "Let's not think of those times. Everything will be explained before long. Now is a time for celebration." Derik nodded, and they all trampled out onto the deck for some good pipe-smoking.

Dan came over with Carson that evening, and everyone had a great time in the company of the others. Dan had his brothers drooling as he excitedly spoke in anticipation of the meat pies, cinnamon rolls, wines, cheeses, ales and mead. He took special care to emphasize the food, as he was wont to do. Everyone was excited.

Aaron went off-topic for a moment when he made a suggestion to Derik. "You know," he began, "you're almost done reading the Scary Book. You could probably finish it tomorrow night when we get back." Derik felt an icy sting in his chest at the very mention of the Book, and expressed his hesitation.

"I don't know…" he said. "I'll think about it later. I'm feeling too cheerful right now to talk about the Book."

"That's okay; it's not that big a deal. We have a fun day ahead of us in any case," Aaron said. Aaron, Greg, and Derik slept in the family room; their sleep being disturbed by nothing other than their own excitement.

***

The Festival was more than Derik had expected, perhaps a result of the Eldritchs' tendency to understate. Not simply a thematized section of a modern town nor a quick mashup of cardboard façades, this was nearly a legitimate town built from the ground up, all in the fashion of the high middle ages and full of the songs and smells he imagined such times had seen. And the people – how alive they seemed! Persistently in-character, charitable with jokes, eager for spirits: this was the change in society he needed for at least this day. And while he struggled to get his friend Aaron to cavort with the female attendees, he did manage to collect a few phone numbers for himself!

Amid the revelry, it was hard to feel resentment toward Aaron. God willing, the dark times might even be put behind him – lies and all – and the friendship would see a reset.

Greg, too, welcomed the change of scenery. For one, it offered several opportunities to bond with his friends – including the Eldritchs – over subject matter that had become all too rare these days. Old European traditions, especially those imagined through a fantastical lens, had been what originally brought these three together. It was good to know that these aesthetic preferences had not been killed off entirely by the events of the last couple of years. To think of those months now was to dredge up images of a nightmare he was happy to keep submerged. The contrast with the pensive gloom of the Eldritchs' home had not been lost on him – how could two so very different worlds exist concurrently?

He most enjoyed the traveling congregation of medieval-looking monks with whom he would cross paths from time to time during the festival. Remembering now that the Church's beauty was of near-equal import to the dogma itself, Greg resolved that he would do everything in his power to ensure that he would never be far from such sights – nay, he would one day become the very thing.

Such clear callings had passed Zeb by. Fighting a headache, perhaps from too much pipe-smoking, he found himself desiring a dark room more strongly than the incense-filled alleys of the Renaissance Festival. Don't let the pain muddle your reasoning, he thought to himself. He knew he had a love for the medieval aesthetic – perhaps it wasn't the headache, but rather the self-adopted delusion he felt was necessary for truly enjoying the festivities. Try though he may, every effort only served to bring greater distress. These short-lived acts of theater were not of the same passion that had seen him and his three friends – Wendell among them – gathering in the woods as teenagers with torches, feasts, libations, and *plans*... No, those gatherings had formed out of a greater desperation, and in a space far more sacred. These games in which he now partook caused him only frustration – for looming constantly was the knowledge that this wasn't the real world, and tomorrow morning nearly everyone here around him would be fighting traffic on the interstate... and nobody would do a thing to change it.

Aaron was less despondent, though there was no doubting that he was having difficulty fully embracing the merriment his friends had found. The conflict with his friends was too recent, and left knots in his stomach that simply would not come undone. And of course, it was hard to forget that, just a few dozen miles away, was a place where true wonders were flourishing. He had not decided that these were indicative of either malevolent or benevolent forces at work – Mark had shown him caution in such judgements – but was not so naïve that he would ignore the threat it posed to his friendships. On the contrary, he now considered that perhaps it would be best not only to discontinue the Study, but to ignore the phenomena altogether. What good could come of immersing himself any further? He had no answer. Meanwhile, he was actually laughing and smiling with his friends despite the commonly understood fact that everyone here was role-playing. And why should that be so strange? They had enjoyed role-playing in a basement nook hundreds of times, with only their imaginations providing the scenery. Now was no different, other than the presence of strangers and physical visual cues to the fantastical. And so, if only for a day, he would allow himself to embrace the atmosphere. If absurdity must find him, it would be in the form of jugglers and jousts.

He had maintained this for the better part of the day, even flirting with a girl or two. At one point, while they sat listening to a pub song, he commented to his friends that this was perhaps the best Faire to date. "Just seeing that things like this are possible... It makes me think. I mean, I have that land in Kentucky – Who says we can't do something like this? Imagine, an entire medieval town to ourselves! We'd hardly have the need for role-playing!"

"I'll pester you until you make it happen!" Derik said in a cheerful slur, handing a drink to the young lady with whom he had just made acquaintance. "And don't think you can hide from me, either!" That evoked laughter from everyone at the table, including Derik's new friend who had found humor in the exchange despite her ignorance to the men's history and nuance of relationship.

Soon the joust began. It was always the climax, of sorts, during these Festivals. And as if fate had not already deemed this day to be one that would be remembered fondly, the men had secured seats on the front bench for the best view of the action.

From opposite ends, heavily armored men burst forth on muscled steeds, charging toward the center with lances raised. A glint of sun on steel, and *CRASH!* The lance splintered in myriad shards, sending the warrior to the ground, his armor now made imperfect by a large dent at the pauldron. But the fight had not left him. Drawing his sword and yelling, he charged his now dismounting enemy, whose back was turned. But just before the blade came crashing down on flesh, the opponent ducked and kicked his leg out, sending the former flying over him.

Now the two engaged on foot, swords swinging. Blade struck shield, shield battered helm. *Crash! CRASH!* Aaron felt a jolt for a moment. Shaking his head, he refocused. On the battlefield blade met blade. *CRASH!* Another jolt. A heart palpitation. Something was not right. Metal clanged before him yet again. *CRASH!* He was beginning to panic. And again, again, again. *CRASH, CRASH, CRASH!* There were only hulking monstrosities in front of him now, abominations of iron mindlessly colliding with one another. Sweat rolled off his brow and into his eyes, burning them, but he could not shut them for the terror that had beset him.

"Damn, THAT was a show!" Greg exclaimed, slapping Aaron on the back. Suddenly they were two armored knights again, the victor having been named and arms raised in glory.

"Yeah, that was something," Aaron managed. The merriment was over. He said nothing of it to his friends nor to his brother, but he was scared. Two years of ever-deepening excursions into the Bizarre had clearly left their mark. And now, fear turned to despair as Aaron wondered if he would ever again be able to enjoy the things that had once brought only unambiguous happiness. An entire day of good news, he thought, had been too much to hope for.

*** 

Derik had to return home that night, so he would not be

able to finish the Book. He assured Aaron that next they meet, this long-awaited moment would come.

"Yeah, you really should. After all," Aaron started with a chuckle, "the bonus chapters will soon be on shelves." Derik laughed, again assuring him, then gave his good-bye. Greg would again stay the night. He would now bunk with Zeb, and Aaron would sleep on the floor by the bedroom door.

They lay in darkness, speaking of myth and fantastical things. Despite Aaron's distress, it had truly been a good day for mending wounds and revisiting familiar passions. Greg and Derik had indeed 'updated' their wardrobe, as well, and Greg spoke of his excitement for his new garments. "I'll don this cloak when I visit you in Kentucky," Greg said.

"Yes," Zeb said. "Be our ambassador, for our realm will be much secluded." Greg laughed joyfully, for he knew Zeb was one to stick to his word. Gradually, they spoke less and less, as sleepiness came over them. A new era of phenomena was about to begin.

A plucking from the mattress was now in Greg's awareness. He sighed in frustration. Could this really be happening again? Hopefully it was simply the bed settling. But the plucking continued. Then, there was a scuffling noise on the headboard, just by his ear. He sat up in frustration. The noises faded.

"Zeb..." Greg said quite loudly, enough to wake him. He managed to mumble out a 'huh' noise. "The plucking... the one I used to hear in Aaron's room... I hear it again..." Zeb seemed too tired to care. "And there is a scuffling on the headboard right by my head... Zeb!" Now Zeb was awake.

"Noises?" he asked.

"Yeah... Really annoying..." Greg said.

"It may be an animal in the wall," Zeb suggested.

"Maybe... I hope it's not, well, you know..." Greg said.

"Me too," Zeb said. "Now go back to sleep." And Zeb rolled over, wrapping himself in his sheets. Several minutes later, when Greg himself was returning to sleep, even louder scuffling now woke him. He was fighting fear with all his strength. For he again had reason to fear Aaron's house: he was not alone in his experiences and no one could explain it. There were only distressing theories to mull over. This did not help.

He heard the scuffling, now and again. The plucking was less rare. He did his best to ignore it. But soon, he felt threatened as the bed itself began to tremor. "Woah!!" Greg cried out, leaping from the top bunk. Aaron cried out as he felt a weight suddenly fall upon him; this was Greg. Zeb let out an awful moan as Greg's cry scared him out of his sleep. He turned on the light. "There you go!" Greg applauded him, though full of terror now.

"What's going on here?" Zeb asked in weariness.

"I don't know... It's crazy in here! The bed started shaking..." he said, grabbing the bed himself and shaking it violently. "You see? Like this!"

"Woah, easy Greg!" Zeb gasped as he attempted to secure himself. Greg calmed a little.

"It sure hasn't taken long for things to start up again!" Greg said in disgust. The other's looked at him, growing fearful.

"Let's all try to get back to sleep," Zeb said. "Perhaps it was nothing more than a small seismic tremor." Greg gurgled as he climbed back in the top bunk.

"If you jump down again, try not to land on me this time," Aaron said. Greg laughed a little but was still not in the mood for jokes.

Several more minutes passed. No one was yet asleep. A high, soft noise of short duration was heard by everyone for a moment. No one spoke. Then another was heard. This one was a little clearer, and it sounded perhaps like a whimper.

"Did you hear that, Greg?" Zeb asked.

"Yeah... Unfortunately I did..." he said. "Aaron?... Aaron?!"

"I'm here... I'm awake... I heard it too... I'm just trying to listen..." Aaron said, and while he spoke, Greg thought he heard yet another whimper.

"I just heard it again!" he cried. The others listened.

Now they heard from the direction of the window, where their feet were all pointing, yet another whimper. This one sounded more... human. A collective gasp meant everyone knew and let everyone know that everyone knew. Now there was a whine from behind Zeb's door, and now in the closet. The noises had evolved into something less like whimpers and more like the cries of babies.

"It's all around us!" Aaron groaned. "From the window... the door... and within this very room!" They listened further. Now, a long, drawn-out baby cry was heard, and it was hard to tell how close it was.

"Turn on the light, Zeb!" Greg demanded. "Quick!" The light went on after only a couple seconds, and nothing out of the ordinary was seen.

"We're not going to see anything..." Aaron said softly.

"We're not allowed to..." Greg added.

"Does everyone agree that those were babies?" Zeb asked. Aaron and Greg did, much to their disappointment. "This is almost as bad as that short time ago, Aaron. Remember?"

"How could I forget?" Aaron said.

"What's this, now?" Greg asked.

"Zeb and I were in the family room, and the windows were open. It was dark, and we had a light on inside the room, about to play a game. Then we heard, out of nowhere, many babies crying, right outside of the window," Aaron recounted, nearly in tears of horror.

"Oh, wow..." Greg said.

"They weren't wails of protest, but more like sobs and whines... squeals..." Zeb described. "It was much too close to be from the neighbor's, and we didn't bother looking, since we doubted there would be a visible source anyway."

"That's why you didn't turn on the light yourself..." Greg realized aloud.

"And because it is sometimes easier to deal with the experience if you can avoid a visual encounter, even when one is possible," Zeb added. Greg shuddered.

"The light seems to have helped, in any case," he pointed out. The others surveyed their surroundings and agreed.

"But we can't be forced to leave the light on all night. We must try to sleep," Zeb said. And with that, he turned off his light, even as Greg cried out against this. "Sleep," Zeb repeated. But the baby coos were back within ten minutes. Aaron let out a moan of despair.

"What does it mean...?" he asked himself aloud.

"I cannot help but think of rebirth..." Zeb began. "Something is beginning anew. I only wonder what this could be..."

The coos seemed to fade away after a while. But just as Greg was about to find sleep, as Zeb had commanded, he was violated in a manner most unnerving. He felt a single prod upon his belly, for just a moment. He lashed out, hitting nothing, and with a great wail at the same time. "Nooo!" This cry yanked Aaron from his twilight in a most horrifying way.

"Wha, what is it?!" Aaron cried out.

"I- I was touched!" Greg gasped. Now Zeb was wide awake.

"Touched? That's different..." he said.

"Turn on the light, you fool!" Greg again demanded. Zeb began to speak.

"Greg, we can't keep turn – "

"Turn it on now!" Greg cried. The light went on. Again, Greg saw nothing that would explain this new form of violation. After a few moments of silence, Zeb spoke.

"Is it alright? Can I turn it off?"

"Yeah..." Greg sighed acquiescently.

"Hang in there, Greg," Aaron said. Greg was silent for a while.

"Nothing like that has ever happened to me before..." he said. "I hate it..." Just then Aaron remembered something from his early childhood, and he decided to share it in the hopes it would show Greg that he was not alone.

"This reminds me of something from long ago," he began. "When I was little, something similar happened... I was lying in bed, having a bad dream. In the dream I was watching somebody. This person was in utter despair about something and fell to his knees in a dark gloomy world, as if unable to continue. I woke up from this dream, much relieved, but then something far worse happened. I felt a gripping force around my ankles very suddenly – not like hands, but just a force of pressure. Then I was slowly pulled against my will down toward the foot of my bed... I remember resisting with all my strength, and the force releasing me just as my legs went over the end." Zeb remembered his story from long ago and nodded.

"And the porcelain mask– " he began to say.

"That's not important," Aaron interrupted.[4] "The point is that I had forgotten it until now," Aaron told him. "So don't feel alone, Greg. It has happened to me as well, this unwelcome touching."

"I just wish I at least knew why... Why is this happening?... And why to me?" Greg asked.

"Many people deal with the paranormal, Greg. I'm sure there are some people out there who struggle with even greater disruption," Aaron said. "And it may even be that *everyone* deals with it, whether they realize it or not." Greg merely sighed. He was so troubled by this new manifestation, that he began hoping it just may be Zeb.

He hated returning to these thoughts, but he couldn't help himself. Even if it would put a strain on their friendship tomorrow, right now this mindset was looking attractive. But when he felt another prod, now upon his arm, no self-imposed belief was going to check his instincts – he leaped out of bed

---

[4]    In actuality, there was a third facet to the experience, in addition to the dream and the pulling 'force'. When Aaron awoke from the dream, he believed he could see something right in front of his face, something so faint that the he wonders if it may have been nothing more than dim flashes in the eye, like those after staring at a light. He described it to Zebulon as a 'tin-face' or 'porcelain mask', whose recesses were utter black and soft protrusions were catching only the smallest bit of light. He said it looked like a stage mask, those used to represent comedy and tragedy (happy-sad masks, he called them), except that it had no expression whatsoever. Only after it faded into darkness did he experience being pulled down the bed. Aaron did not know what to make of it, and at the time, Zeb said nothing of his personal fears. Aaron later told Greg about this third 'facet' to the experience, when the time was more appropriate.

and sat by Zeb.

"It happened again!?" Zeb asked, still disoriented, and turning on the light. Greg nodded, trembling.

"Can't I have a full day of peace and joy?!" Greg cried out, now wondering if he was being punished for something. He sat there for a while, in the light.

"I can't leave this on, Greg. I'm going to turn it off... Look on the shelf up there. Should be a small flashlight you can use if you need it," Zeb said. Greg stood on Zeb's bed, leaning over the top railing, in search. He returned below holding the flashlight. "Good," Zeb said. "Now you can look whenever you want to but try not to disturb us too much." The remark left Greg feeling a bit incensed, for it seemed as though his concerns were not being acknowledged. Perhaps his friends here had truly become numb to the anomalies. Zeb turned off his light. At this precise moment, Greg felt something grab him on the shoulder. He immediately whipped on the flashlight, and lashed his arms out at the same time, hoping he would catch one of the brother's in the attempt. Neither his arms nor the light struck any such thing.

"Wow!" he said disgustedly. "I turned on the light immediately, and nothing was there! I had *just* been grabbed!" He began to breathe unsteadily.

"I don't know what you were expecting to find," Aaron said. Greg climbed back up in the bunk and turned his flashlight off. When the bed began to shake again, that was all he could take. He again jumped out of the bunk.

"I'm getting out of here!" Greg said, as he grabbed a blanket and pillow and stepped over Aaron, reaching for the door.

"Where are you going?!" Aaron stammered.

"Out of this room!" Greg said angrily. "I'll risk the living room couch." He opened the door, as Zeb wailed, then left the room, closing it behind him. As they heard Greg walk down the hallway, they spoke of his behavior.

"It must have been really bad for him, if he's willing to do that," Aaron said to Zeb.

"Indeed, I feel sorry for him. I hope he is safe out there.

Though there is really no reason to think he is safer in here," Zeb replied. They returned to sleep.

Greg walked down the hallway, in frustration. He guessed that he would not have been able to muster up this sudden courage had he not had such a wholesome day. He fought off dread as hard as he could, as he came into the dimly lit living room. He lay in the couch, putting his pillow under his head and covering himself with his sheet. Alone, in the Eldritchs' living room, he guessed that there were few places that would be more frightening to sleep in. As he shut his eyes and asked for peace, he noticed that it was still and quiet. This did not rest his fears, however. Instead it became dreadful suspense, and though the remaining night went uneventfully, it was this absolute absence of the aberrant, this *nothing*, that made it perhaps the most horrifying night he would ever endure.

The following weekend, Aaron gave Derik a call. He would do his best to explain to Derik what he could and hope that this would not keep him from ever coming back.

"Are you sure you are ready to talk about it?" Aaron asked.

"I am... Are you sure you can be honest with me?" Derik responded similarly.

"I am," Aaron parroted. "You must be understanding, and I ask forgiveness for the foolish things I have done to you, and for the foolish efforts I made in my attempt to preserve our friendship."

"I forgive you," Derik said. Aaron breathed a sigh of relief.

"Thanks... I should have listened to Zeb and just let things happen on their own... Instead I lied to you. I became obsessed with making you feel safe, for you seemed timid to me. But now I see your strength. It was wrong to deceive you... You neither needed nor deserved my comforting lies."

"So it was all real then...?" Derik asked clearly but reluctantly.

"...Yes."

"Then it still is..." Derik said. Aaron was silent for a moment, then spoke.

"I will not lie to you. You must know this before you come back: There is nothing I can do to keep the paranormal at bay. We are powerless before it."

"I see..." Derik said.

"Then... you will not come back?" Aaron asked.

"Do you have such little faith in my strength? No, many visits to your house will come," Derik said.

"I knew you wouldn't go down that easily," Aaron said, and they laughed.

"That tape was so hard to believe, though... not just what you guys were saying, but, well, that voice for example..." Derik began.

"Who's? Bennett's? Oh, shit!..." Aaron said, just as he remembered that Bennett had asked to be anonymous.

"That was Bennett?!" Derik said with a laugh of disbelief.

"I wasn't supposed to say that... He wanted to remain anonymous. We told Greg, and I guess I forgot that you weren't there... I've never actually heard his true voice. He had it electronically altered right there on the spot, so he could remain anonymous even if the tape was played for others."

"It seemed like it was there for us to find," Derik said.

"I believe it was," Aaron explained to him. "If you had stayed with us that evening you would have learned all of this with Greg. Zeb may have put it out for you to find, without my knowing, though he denies this."

"I don't see how he could have predicted everything that followed," Derik returned. "I very nearly left that cassette player alone!"

"Maybe I'm just frustrated still with how everything transpired," Aaron reflected aloud. "Either way, he seems to have gotten his way." The two sat now, with the purest representation of the enigmatic – silence – hanging all around them.

"There is something else, too," Aaron continued. "I want you to understand that you did nothing wrong in betraying me before. You saw me hurting another person, and you stepped in for the greater good, rather than mine. I admire that."

"Thanks... I don't feel bad about it," Derik said. "I knew I was doing the right thing."

"You simply didn't understand that I was in fact not doing anything to Greg, other than studying his involvement in the bizarre, mostly because of my great acting on your doorstep," Aaron explained.

"Yeah, what was with that? You seemed so serious..." Derik remembered aloud.

"I was," Aaron said. "I knew you wanted to do good, but I also knew something you didn't: that unexplainable things were in fact going on, and Greg's involvement was of great interest, to me and to Zeb especially. It was the only thing I could do, besides telling the truth, that would keep you believing and leave Greg experiencing."

"Wouldn't he experience those things in any case?" Derik asked.

"Not necessarily," Aaron replied. "One's beliefs may be a necessary factor in experiencing these... unnatural things. I noticed that Greg was having fewer complaints of such things shortly after you told him everything... this may imply that it was his *belief* that it was all fake which prevented it from manifesting as an actual experience."

"Or there could be a presence behind it that knows when the time is right..." Derik suggested. He had borrowed this theory from Greg, of course. It fit more neatly into the Christian world view they both held.

"I have considered this, actually," Aaron said. "In fact, this seemed very likely, at times when it would seem impossible to hoax you. Were it not for convenient circumstances, I would have failed many times. These conveniences have made me think along those lines, more than once."

"There must be something that helped you... Your story you gave me was flawless... It fooled me in every way possible," Derik said.

"If I have misled you into believing that my story was

flawless, this was not my intention," Aaron said. "For there were many discrepancies and inconsistencies between my story and Greg's actual experiences that I could only hope you would overlook."

"Inconsistencies?" Derik asked.

"Yeah. Many times I would tell you 'how I did it' or I would show you some material thing, before learning the details of Greg's experiences, or even having misunderstood his accounts. Whenever you did notice the inconsistency, I could only say 'Greg's just crazy', if you remember..." Aaron revealed.

"I do now... I believed you, too. You would even point out the inconsistency and then tell me how it was evident of him losing his sanity," Derik remembered.

"And was it not that which worried you? Him losing his sanity?" Aaron asked.

"It was... and I thought you were making it worse," Derik said.

"And the whole time he was quite sane. This was what I didn't want you to know," Aaron explained.

"I remember one, now, a small one. It was a tape with noises on it you showed me. You recorded noises on it from a game, and had yourself call out his name," Derik said.

"...From the wrong game, and in a very plain voice, both deviating from what he would later tell me," Aaron said. " I was assuming the voice experience was like that of my brother's, so I made the voice speak normally. In reality, however, the voice was inhuman, he tells me. I did the recording before learning this and failed to update in time before I showed it to you."

"There are many others, I suppose," Derik said.

"Plenty," Aaron said. "And even without the inconsistencies, I would still have been surprised that you fell for it, since some things seemed like they would be too hard to believe, and since some of my stories failed to explain certain things."

"Like what?" Derik asked curiously.

"Well, like believing that I would be able to run all around the house without anyone hearing or seeing," Aaron said. "Like the night Greg saw the first portal. My dad was sleeping in my room, yet you still believed I went in there to get a mirror and was running all around the house with it without making a noise... but I guess this was more believable than a portal in the floor."

"Then the portal was real too..." Derik said.

"Everything was real, Derik. Everything..." Aaron said. "I can't tell you how I managed to predict what Greg saw as accurately as I did, but you may have noticed that his description was a bit different. I even made the frame I showed you ambiguous so that it would fool you even if Greg's experience would differ slightly, which it did."

"Why can't you tell me how you predicted it so well? Why are you still hiding things?" Derik asked, growing frustrated now.

"I'm sorry, Derik, but there are some things which I still cannot tell you," Aaron said.

"That's what bothers me... I feel like I still don't know you..." Derik said, saddened.

"You don't need to hold these doubts, Derik," Aaron said. "Maybe you should talk to Greg. He's sensitive to the fact that this is difficult for me, too." Aaron had become upset himself.

"I'm sorry... I guess I don't feel quite like that... I'm just getting upset again, that's all... I wish I could understand..." Derik sighed.

"I would tell you if it concerned you, but it is a personal matter, and has no relevance to you. Think of it this way: you would not inquire into the personal life between husband and wife, would you?" Aaron asked Derik.

"No, I wouldn't..." he answered.

"Then you should understand now as much as you need to, for it is deserving of comparable privacy," Aaron said. Derik seemed to accept this.

"I'll try not to be upset," Derik said. "I know you're doing all you can to make things better." They were silent for a while. "I'm still curious about some of these other stories you told me... How were they not good enough?"

"Well, take the creature in the woods for example..." Aaron began to say.

"You told me it was that friend of Zeb's," Derik said.

"Lars, right. And this would have been a good explanation except for several things," Aaron said.

"Go on," Derik insisted.

"Well, first of all, Lars was on a road trip with some friends that week. I had tried to find an alibi that could at the very least confirm that he had been in the area. I discovered this instead and could only hope you wouldn't investigate for yourself." He let that sink in for a moment. "He sent Zeb some photos of their trip, if you decide my word isn't enough."

"Oh boy... I – I'm good," Derik mumbled. Aaron continued. "And then there's the more visceral details."

"Like?"

"Well, only the most fool-hardy would wade through such cold waters as were those on that late autumn day. And only that same person would risk being attacked. This person would not, however, survive the fall this creature suffered. His head bounced off a rock. There was no way for me to explain this to you. Luckily you overlooked it. Even the way the creature ate dirt and leaves would seem hard to believe, but I guess it sounded good to you." Derik allowed a laugh, though it was one tinged with dread as he realized the horror of the event.

"W-what – was your woods that day?!" he cried, laughing hysterically.

"I... don't know..." Aaron said. "And don't forget the words Greg had spoken that seemed to summon it... It – it could still be down there, for all I know." Aaron thought now for a moment.

"What's the matter?" Derik asked him.

"Nothing..." Aaron said. "I was just thinking about the first unexplainable experience you were exposed to."

"The horse?..." Derik asked hesitantly.

"Yeah... The horse... I never did see that horse," Aaron said. "But do you remember the way you approached Zeb upstairs, after the event? You asked him how he did it... You presumed it to be a trick... Zeb was not expecting this, but he was quick in keeping you unaware. He had nothing to do with any of it. He had just gotten home before you saw him."

"My...gosh!... So that's when it started..." Derik said in amazement.

"That's right," Aaron said. "Then I took the ball and ran with it, if you will."

Derik laughed in astonishment, and he was also beginning to feel ill from these revelations. "Your house, Aaron... Your house...!"

"It is an interesting place, without a doubt," Aaron admitted. "But don't fear it. There is no reason to think that there is something wrong with the house itself. It could be the people who gather there, including you and Greg. Perhaps something... happens... when we gather and collectively think or dwell on things."

"Or when we read certain Books..." Derik added.

"Yeah, I was thinking the same thing," Aaron revealed. "But I just can't see how that would matter, reading the Book I mean. Others read it, right? And yet no one else goes through this, as far as I know... Maybe it's that we connect with it at a much deeper level than anyone else..."

"I wonder if I should still read it..." Derik said.

"This is just conjecture, Derik. We can't take it to heart. Besides, you're almost finished. It would be a dishonor to the work, in my opinion. And all peculiarities aside, it really is just a good story that I think you'd be satisfied seeing through to the end."

"I guess I'll finish it," Derik submitted. "It really is well-written, but I just worry sometimes. I think it had made me a bit demoralized." Aaron laughed.

"You and me both," he said. There was a brief moment where Derik and Aaron just listened to each other laughing. "Well, I guess I better go. I hope I haven't troubled your mind too much, but I can't imagine you leaving this conversation the same way."

"Well, at least that much is true," Derik began, "but I prefer this over those awkward moments and deceitful times." Derik cleared his throat. "Actually, I had one more question, a big one really."

"Go on," Aaron said.

"The video we were working on..." Derik said. "...The one with the mock portal... What was your reason for doing it?"

"That video no longer exists," Aaron said. "And I can say nothing more of this."

"I see..." Derik said.

"Just trust me... That is all I ask," Aaron said. "Take care, now. And don't dwell on anything too much – it's not healthy."

"Alright..." Derik said. "See ya..." Derik hung up the phone. As he was very close to his parents, he would later tell his father all of this.

"I think he's still pulling your leg, Derik," his father said. He was a small man with a huge heart.

"I know you are concerned for me... but I can sense that he speaks the truth. I know him better than you, Dad," Derik said.

"I hope so," his father said. And they sat together and watched from their back porch as the waxing moon came up over the hills.

# CHAPTER NINE

## Red Fear

There had been so much doubt; so much hurt. Though these things would still surface occasionally, the general phenomenon of doubt and suspicion as a whole was over, and it would be a journey of shared experience; a union of strength and friendship in the face of Fear.

After having just seen a deeply moving religious movie with Greg, Derik did not want to read from the Book. He had suggested to Aaron that he may be able to drop by for a while after the movie, but that would probably be all the time he could manage. The evening after the movie, he and Greg arrived at Aaron's. They were deeply disturbed from the movie and its story. Zeb had seen it as well. They talked about it for some time as they sat around in the family room.

Aaron sensed it was growing late and began to grow anxious. With Derik and Greg both in college now, there would be fewer chances to finish reading the Book. It had already been some time since Derik last read; he was probably forgetting some of its content already. If he didn't finish the Book now, it could be over a month before he would get another chance. So Aaron spoke his mind, for he was not one to keep secret his judgments. "Derik," he said, "I know you didn't feel that it was a good time to finish the Book, but you're in college now, and will not find the time to finish it any time soon. Perhaps it is best that you finish it while the rest is relatively fresh in your mind." Derik groaned.

"Aaron... I don't know..." he said. It was obvious he didn't want to. Greg however, was in agreement with Aaron.

"He's probably right, Derik," Greg said. "I know it's not the best time, but it's not like we're not feeling sick already."

"I guess so..." Derik said. "I don't know. I'll give you my answer later." When Aaron, Zeb and Greg returned to the family room after a trip to the kitchen, they got their answer. Derik was sitting on the floor, holding the open Book in his hands. He looked up at them with a look of resignation.

"I guess you'll be leaving tomorrow," Aaron noted rhetorically.

Derik said only one thing. "Let's finish this." And he began to read. Perhaps after twenty minutes, he had noticed something interesting.

"Have you noticed the use of color throughout this Book, particularly the last few chapters?" Derik asked.

"I have," Zeb said. "The color seems to change throughout the story. First grey, then greens, now oranges and reds..."

"Yeah... Reds now, especially," Derik affirmed.

"The colors set a certain mood, but they seem to be inextricably tied to the characters as well," Aaron said.

"And the world as the characters see it also changes over time," Greg pointed out. "Very organic terms are used near the end, as so many things are described as vein-like, or intestinal even."

"It's weird, too, the way the Book puts emphasis on different facets of the core conflicts and problems the characters face," Derik said. "At first it seemed so psychologically focused, yet by this point, religion has been heavily addressed as the central theme."

"I'm sure that's impacting you deeply, especially now, after having seen that movie," Zeb said.

"Yeah..." Derik admitted. He continued reading, with only several pages left. And then, in the presence of Aaron, Greg and Zebulon, he finished reading the Scary Book. It masterfully answered some questions that were raised in the first few chapters, but there were still many questions, and it was crying for a Book of bonus chapters. "Wow," Derik said. The others gave him a pat on the back.

"Well, what now?" Greg said. The others laughed. Surely, they could think of something else to do, other than read from the Book. Yet, after more than a year for Derik and three years for Greg and the Eldritch brothers of reading this Book, there was a definite sense of finality and transition. They would later correlate this transition to that of their experiences. This would not be the only correlation that would be made, however.

Greg and Derik slept side by side in the top bunk, with Zeb below and Aaron again on the floor. They would now always huddle together in Zeb's room. They lay silent for a while. Greg had not forgotten the flashlight he had used so vainly before. He had shown it to Derik, then kept it close, for it comforted him still, whether this was rational or not. Before Aaron and Zeb had closed their eyes for the night, Greg turned the flashlight on, creating an orb of light upon the wall. This more than startled the two brothers.

"Quit fooling around with that light! You could cause things to go wrong with those foolish actions..." Aaron reprimanded. "...It's just asking for trouble."

"Sorry," Greg said playfully, turning off the light. Derik chuckled softly. Everyone again lay in darkness. Perhaps fifteen minutes passed. Aaron and Zeb had drifted off to sleep. The night was unusually normal so far, Greg thought. Derik thought nothing, since untroubled sleep was normal for him. He guessed that it probably wasn't as often as Greg had made it sound.

Sleepiness came over Derik, though Greg was having trouble getting to sleep. Each lay still. There was absolute darkness. The moon must have even been covered with thick clouds, for no light whatsoever came through the window. Whether one's eyes were open or closed made no difference. Yet both Derik's and Greg's eyes were open at this moment, and both had their eyes set in the same direction, apparently. For they saw, appearing out of nowhere on the ceiling, not more than four feet over their heads, a sudden point of intense red light, which made the difference between shut and open eyes very clear. Neither knew that the other was seeing this, as each remained silent, having been caught totally off guard. Now, utter dread came over them as they watched this point grow in one direction, becoming an intensely red line. What seemed fuzzy initially became a thing composed of tiny wriggling capillaries as their eyes adjusted to the invading radiance.

The line continued to grow longer, as if the ceiling was splitting and revealing only a sliver of another world beyond, a brilliantly red one. 'Is this... the end of the world...?!' both of them thought to themselves, literally paralyzed with fear. They simply held their breath and waited. When Greg saw a crossbar of sorts appear when the line seemed to have finished its trek, he now saw before him what he perceived as a religious symbol, the Cross. This was indeed the end, he thought. Derik did not see this crossbar. The line slowly began to widen until there was now a gap in the ceiling more than an inch across, creating such radiance one might mistake the room for one illuminated by the setting sun. Then, as suddenly as it had appeared, it vanished.

The room was again in total darkness, and the only thing that made them believe it even happened was the state of shock in which the event had left their minds and bodies. They lay for several seconds in silence, then Derik managed to get some words out through constricted breaths.

"Uh...Greg...?!" he said.

"...Yeah...! I saw it..." Greg said despondently. It was also a recently formed habit to immediately accuse Aaron of anything similarly unexpected or unnatural, whether it was warranted or no. "That Aaron's up to his tricks again!"

"What?... You think it was him?" Derik could barely ask, still horribly shaken. Greg didn't respond, for already he was remembering the truth. Still, he pulled out the flashlight and shined it down in Aaron's face. Aaron cried out as the light woke him, and, realizing it was only Greg, groaned in anger and wrapped himself in his blankets. Greg was not done with him. He thought of the best way such a thing could be replicat-

160

ed, though there would only be a slight likeness, and accused Aaron of this.

"Quit fooling around with that laser pen, Aaron! I mean it!!" His fear-driven rage was bound only by his embarrassment in suggesting such nonsense. Aaron, however, was now angry for receiving such a rude awakening.

"Greg, you better quiet down, get that light out of my eyes and quit your accusations right now... How dare you wake me like that!?" he snarled in response. Still, Greg persisted.

"I would if you would quit it with your games! I thought all of this was over?!" Greg said angrily.

"Greg, I have no idea what got into you all of a sudden, but I'm offended you'd wake me with such presumptuous and foolish thoughts! It *is* over, and that should mean you blaming me no more. You're going to have to get used to it. Now, LET ME SLEEP!" Aaron cried out, perhaps the angriest Greg had ever seen him. Greg did this and turned to Derik.

"We'll tell him about it in the morning," Greg told him. Then he turned off the light.

"What in the world is going on?" Zeb asked sleepily, but now awake.

"Don't worry about it Zeb," Greg said. But Zeb could hear Derik's troubled gasps and knew something had gone amiss.

"Tell me in the morning, then," he said, and fell back asleep.

"You think it was a laser pen, Greg? You must think he used the mirror or something? I mean... it was a line... and it was like the ceiling was splitting open and - and..." Derik was not content.

"I just don't know if I'm going to bother denying it any more..." he finished.

"I know how you feel... It's still so hard to believe though... I mean, I really thought the world was ending, there..." Greg said.

"Yeah... so did I..." Derik said. They spoke little more of it before finally falling asleep.

The next day, with light – natural, beautiful, sunlight – shining through the windows, they found it easier to recount. In fact, it seemed almost like they were describing a dream, rather than a thing of reality.

"Veiny, you say?" Zeb asked Derik with eyes much intrigued. "Just like the descriptions from the Book..."

"Yeah, you're right... I didn't even realize that, at least not consciously, anyway," Derik said. "Right after I finished reading it!... I can't believe it... That's so weird..."

"And I saw a crossbar... We again experienced different things..." Greg said. Zeb seemed to have made another discovery.

"And you - you had just watched the religious movie..." Zeb said in disbelief.

"So it had religious significance for me... What does this mean?" Greg asked.

"It caters to the individual, somehow... for some reason..." Aaron said. "I am almost more disturbed by its apparent sudden disappearance – It felt like the end of the world had come, and then, just like that, nothing at all!"

"I know, it was weird," Derik said. "But it left me in the greatest suspense I've ever felt... Truly, when I saw that, it was the most horrified I have ever been."

"I can believe it, easily. But you need to accept it if you plan on visiting again," Aaron said. "I doubt this will be the last time you have a brush with the unexplained."

"I'll do my best," Derik sighed. They mulled over the event in silence for a moment.

"Greg... you had just played around with the flashlight before you saw this right?..." Aaron asked.

"Well, I turned it on, a little while before we saw it," Greg said with steadfast innocence.

"Perhaps I was right in suggesting you not do it, lest it cause trouble," Aaron said. Greg stubbornly denied this possibility.

"Why would it cause trouble? If Tryst is only a mutual relationship, and there is no will of any kind involved, what would be provoked by such silliness?" Greg asked.

162

"There is a will, at least one. This is your will. And my will. And Derik's and Zeb's. Perhaps our own ignorance punishes us," Aaron said. "It would be like some internal reminder, keeping us on the right track. We would do well to be respectful of such things, I would imagine, rather than make light of them." Greg mumbled something and said nothing more.

"What is this Tryst I keep hearing about?" Derik asked. "I remember it being mentioned on that tape..."

"It is nothing to be concerned with," Aaron said. "It is only a theory."

"I don't know, Aaron," Zeb said. "It may be of great concern."

"Well, we don't have to confuse him right now. Derik, we'll try to explain it to you gradually, a piece at a time if that's okay," Aaron said.

"Sure," Derik said, with a nervous chuckle. That, of course, did not happen. By sunrise, Derik had become the recipient of knowledge more esoteric than he ever imagined possible. He lay there during all of this completely limp, as though having been struck by a tsunami. And all the while the men still wondered if there was indeed another realm, a red realm, beyond the walls of Zeb's room that night, for their dread had made them its prisoners and they dared not leave it.

# CHAPTER TEN

## Dark Fear

The more recent era of great role-playing had seen its rich albeit plagued life run its course. Royce was away at college, as well as Derik, although the latter was close enough that he would be able to participate in occasional sessions if they were to be held. He was still dealing with living independently and felt an anxiety about his new life; thankfully this was tempered somewhat by the budding romance he was enjoying with none other than the young lady he had met at the Renaissance Festival, who went by the name of Tiffany, and referred to Derik now as her 'sig'.

Greg was busy between community college and his part-time job at the gas station. Lately he had grown anxious himself since his plans for life after community college were murky at best, and the reality that the life he shared with Aaron and the others would one day end was becoming hard to ignore.

Zeb had, after twenty-six years of living at Attica Drive, moved out. His commute to work was so long that after much anguish he conceded that living with his aunt, about two hours away, would be more prudent.

Aaron now had a new full-time job at an industrial park, still not used to his new work environment and trying his hardest to keep it from depressing him. Because of the job, he no longer had the free time to create the worlds of fantasy that had brought him so much joy, not only in their being acted-out by him and his friends but in their very creation. As if that wasn't enough to sour his spirits, he recently was also experiencing fits of panic.

This was because he had seen his parents looking at floor plans and house designs for over a year now and apparently, they had finally taken a contract out on a house. This house was for their waterfront property, and the only thing left now was to sell the house on Attica Drive.

And so the Eldritch brothers were now planning their own home designs, the homes they would build on their Kentucky property. They were feeling sadder and more depressed every day about leaving what had been home to them their whole lives. Zeb was trying to make meaning of all of this but found himself again faced with the Nothing. He was thrust into this world, he understood, and some time before long he would be pulled from it.

Encounters with the paranormal would grow grimmer too, in the coming times. Despite attempts to see the events as neutral and the personal involvement as valuable, as Dr. Bennett would have it, the friends in Tryst would instead find themselves becoming more and more fearful as their world grew darker.

Surprisingly, Greg managed to fit frequent visits to Aaron's into his busy schedule. There were fewer occasions when both Greg and Derik found time to visit, as Aaron had predicted. When a particularly distressing event occurred one night, only Greg was visiting. It was well into the evening, which had so far been quite pleasant. The bonus chapters of the Scary Book were now available, and Greg had already begun reading them. Zeb had just started. He would only read the Chapters when he visited, so that Aaron might share in the experience. They spoke of what they had both read so far. Greg had never done the reading away from Aaron's house, and it was surreal listening to Zeb read but not know for himself what was to come, as had always before been the case.

When it was time for bed, Greg was again taking lodge

in Zeb's room with Zeb in his bed and Aaron, who, in keeping with tradition, taking the floor.

"I look forward to this part of my visit less and less each time," Greg said. The others giggled.

"Oh, by the way Greg," Zeb began in a serious tone, "it followed me."

"What...?" Greg asked. He had no idea what Zeb was talking about.

"The Aberrant. Strange things have been happening to me at my aunt's, and it seems that no one else experiences it," Zeb explained.

"Oh no..." Greg said. "Go on."

"Well, I have heard a loud clanging just about every night – this being the only time I have to myself, which I try and use to fend off the despair that has crept in during all other hours. Frustratingly, the clanging wins every time. What you'll find more interesting, I'm sure, is that I had no way of explaining it, and my aunt had no idea what I was talking about," Zeb said. "Then the other night, I was fast asleep, when around three in the morning my bedroom door was thrown open."

"Just like me that one night..." Aaron said.

"They're still visiting you, Zeb," Greg said solemnly. Zeb sighed and continued.

"It gets stranger. Just a few nights ago, I had to go in their basement for something. First, their basement light had become very weak. Then, when I got to about the middle of the floor, I heard what sounded like a broken music box playing quietly and intermittently. I couldn't identify a location, and it only lasted for a minute or so. That may have been creepier than the door opening."

"So does this mean the house has nothing to do with it after all?..." Aaron asked. "Why else would it be that things get so crazy around here?"

"We already know that people all over the world have encounters with the paranormal," Greg said. "It doesn't mean that a particular location can't be more prone than others. I think there is definitely something here that brings out the, what should I call it – other-worldly forces? – more so than other places."

"Maybe nothing more than the people within it," Aaron said. "There have been many occurrences already that seemed to play on our individual fears. For example, all the things from the Scary Book that have manifested in this world..." Greg sighed in agreement.

"But again, it is only when I come here that I experience such things," Greg said.

"Yeah, I always forget about that. I guess the worst things happen when you are here," Aaron said.

"I suppose that much could be true," Zeb said. "The music box thing was relatively 'subtle'. But don't forget about Mom's account, Aaron."

"I *did* forget about it!!" Aaron cried out. "My gosh... It happens to everybody..."

"What's this about your mother?" Greg asked nervously.

"Our mother, as you know, is an assistant teacher at the school," Zeb began. Greg nodded.

"Well," he continued, "she was teaching the children in one of those portables, as they call them, which are detached from the main school building. It was cloudy outside and there was a distant storm. Now something happened which is very hard to explain, mainly because my mother had such a hard time explaining it herself. It took all of our efforts to get a detailed account from her but proved to be impossible to corroborate as you will soon understand. Anyhow, a bar of light, soft and yet intense as she described it, slowly entered the room through the window. She watched this bar enter the room, while none of the children seemed to notice it. This horizontal bar fully entered the room, slowly and steadily, and glided right over the children's heads. It continued to move across the room until it exited the opposite side. She asked the teacher if she saw it, and she did. But – and this may sound familiar, Greg – the teacher described the experience differently. She described having seen the bar high over her head, despite the ceiling being much lower than this. Mom made it clear that it was definitely not lightning, which was what we initially thought it must have been as she gave her story. She said it was one of the weirdest things that has ever happened to her, but it doesn't bother her really... Anyway, it's just another example of unexplainably surreal things happening at places nowhere near this house."

"Your mother's weird like that..." Greg said. "She probably wouldn't believe you if you told her about all the things that happen here, yet she experiences some of the most outlandish things herself..." The brothers were humored by this truth. Still, no one could explain the cause for such phenomena. All they knew was that strange things were now beginning to happen within their room.

A pattern seemed to be emerging. First the scuffling at the headboard was heard. Plucking, scraping and pitter-patter within the walls and mattress would be heard intermittently. One would comment on these, when no one else seemed to hear it. Then, much to their despair, the touching began. First Zeb thought that Hazel, who regularly slept at the foot of his bed, had jumped up on his bed. When he remembered that she was already there, he moaned in horror and turned on the light. Nothing was seen. When they again lay in darkness, Aaron felt a gentle pinch on his big toe, followed by a less gentle tug. Soon Greg was a victim as well, when he felt tugs on his sheets and something come to rest on the pillow, just to the side of his head. He dreaded feeling physical contact with his very flesh, but so far he had been spared.

There were new noises, too. While they heard no baby coos this night, there were other sounds. Now and again the closet would gently ring like a small gong. There also seemed to be some kind of subtle but ever-present droning, industrial in nature, as it sounded almost like generators coming from somewhere deep below. Aaron could even feel this as he lay on the wood floor. It was too loud to be the furnace, and neither the heat nor the air conditioning was running anyway. Then, there was suddenly a loud crashing sound, perhaps from somewhere off in the far end of the neighborhood, as Aaron would describe it. To Greg, however, it sounded very close. Zeb was not awake to hear it.

Aaron and Greg fell asleep some while later. They would awaken now and again to some bewildering noise, one even coming from right on the other side of the wall which would have been from the living room. When Aaron heard this, he sat up quickly, and began to sweat in a panic. Then, something happened which suggested dark motives. As Aaron knelt there, rolling his head in an effort to listen from all directions, he was spontaneously struck on the top of his head. He cried out and collapsed, holding his head. Zeb, waking with a wail of terror, turned on the light. Greg was now awake as well, and both he and Zeb found Aaron lying in pain as he held his throbbing head.

"Aaron!" Zeb cried out. "What happened!?" Aaron did not respond for almost a minute.

"I was... attacked..." he groaned.

"Attacked?!" Greg asked in fear. "What do you mean?"

"I had heard something that startled me out of my sleep..." Aaron said, gesturing toward the wall that the bunk was against. "No one else seemed to have heard it, even though it came from the living room... I was sitting up, listening around, then something hit me on my head, really hard!"

"My gosh... Aaron..." Zeb said. Greg now felt a sense of violation come over him. Seeing and hearing things was one thing, and touching was itself an unwanted violation, but inflicting pain... This was a threatening cruelty. "Let's see your head." Zeb examined his brother's scalp while Greg assisted with his trusty flashlight. "You've got a knot forming there, without a doubt. No broken skin, though."

"Oh, great, I'm not spurting blood! Yet!" Aaron scoffed. "It felt so solid. In fact..." Aaron continued, "my head was by the railing of the bunk... It was as if – as if *you* hit me, Greg!" He looked at Greg with growing rage, and Greg looked back, offended.

"Don't place blame on me!" he said. "I was sound asleep! Look, I don't know what's going on here, but it's getting really nasty... It's starting to hurt people now... And it's always making us blame each other!"

170

"I'm sorry…" Aaron began. "It's just that… my head hurts so much… and I don't want to think that it's something going on in my own house… or worse, my own mind…"

"We obviously need to stay on guard, guys," Greg cautioned.

"And yet we can't function properly without adequate sleep," Zeb noted.

"And there's nothing we can do about it, probably. If we are to be attacked, then we will suffer pains," Aaron submitted.

"How can you just let it go like that?…" Greg asked, feeling subject now to a dark and threatening force.

"What am I supposed to do, Greg?" Aaron barked, now irritated. Greg stammered, but had no answer. "It's not like I can just run next door. Or ask 'it' to stop."

"You haven't tried," Greg murmured.

"I guess that's true…" Aaron conceded. "I've just never had to think about it like this before… Being in real danger, I mean."

"We've all been kind of assuming that anything and everything can happen under this roof but for some reason we draw a line when it comes to physical harm," Zeb noted in a philosophical tone. "We clearly had a mental block against that possibility. But why? And I'm not suggesting that there's any malevolent forces at work here – but we were fools to think that there wasn't at least the possibility of someone getting hurt."

"So… does anyone want to leave?" Greg begged. "Next door, or…?" No one answered. "Right then." Before long, everyone was again asleep.

Now, Greg was awoken when he felt a great weight suddenly bearing down upon him. He flailed his limbs out in horror, knocking away some large object. Not a half a moment later, there was a loud crash on the floor of the room, immediately followed by two wails of terror. Greg sat frozen, panting wildly, when Zeb turned the light on. The scene was one of mayhem. Aaron was now sitting upright again, and there, next to his pillow, lay on its side a large ceramic jug. This was the wine jug which usually sat as a decoration on the floor at the side of the door.

The most reasonable explanation seemed to suggest that this jug was the weight Greg had felt bearing down upon him, and was the object tossed over the edge of the bed. Luckily, it seemed, the jug had missed Aaron's head by only several inches. A direct hit would have resulted in at least a crushed nose and broken teeth. Strangely, the jug remained wholly intact.

"That was the last straw," Greg growled with failing strength. Aaron simply sat with a greying face and wide, terrified eyes.

"What in the hell just happened?!" he asked, taking hold of the jug. "Did this just fall?! I heard a great crash beside my head... It was probably the most jolting thing in all my life!" Greg described what happened to him, for Aaron as well as a bewildered Zebulon.

"Somehow that jug was suddenly over me and began to bear down on me. I don't know how it happened!" he said in disgust.

"I was thinking that you somehow got hold of it and hurled it down upon me," Aaron said, looking up at Greg cautiously. "Are you sure you..."

"Don't be ridiculous with that stuff! I'm getting really sick of it! I simply reacted out of fear and threw it off of me! Don't you get it yet?! I'm as scared as you, Aaron! And I'm scared *for* you! You could have gotten seriously injured!" Greg was saying hysterically.

"I know... I'm sorry..." Aaron said. "But all of a sudden, you know? I'm being physically threatened..."

"It may have been only your guardian angel that saved you, Aaron. That jug, it seems, was intended to land on your head. It was not I, however, that willed this," Greg said. "I'm sorry, but there's a dark force at work, and there's no denying it. Loving relationship my ass, something wishes us harm!" Aaron slumped quietly. Zeb sighed in disbelief. "We need to keep vigil, friends," Greg said. "There will be no more sleep had this night. That has already been determined. We may as well stay alert... And yes, Zeb, with the light on!"

"Alright, then, for a while... Only situations like this demand it," Zeb said reluctantly. All he wanted to do was sleep. He would be able to, he believed. After all, he had never been harmed. Aaron was just doubting, probably. It was his doubt that manifested in such violent forms, he thought. But he left the light on anyway, for a whole other hour. The rest of the night went smoothly.

For the next several visits, their nights would play out in similar ways, except for the obvious physical endangerment. Some nights there was no scratching at the headboard, and some nights babies were heard. Other nights were dominated by industrial clangs and tremors from somewhere deep below. On one particular night several new phenomena began.

There were the usual creaks, scuttles, and rumbles. There was even a hard knock on the window, an anomaly which had never surfaced before. This was particularly troubling for Zeb. Then, it seemed that objects within the room were again being moved and thrown around. While they were apparently not as heavy or large as the ceramic jug – which, to their dread, had in fact relocated several inches over – they still made for some loud crashes and startling scares. But it was not until these things began to dwindle away for the night that a new phenomenon surfaced. It had been dead quiet for more than ten minutes; a rarity in itself. But sleep would not yet come for Aaron nor Greg.

First was a noise immediately on the other side of the bed-wall. It was the sound of a bouncy rubber ball being dropped from only several inches above the wood floor. It was heard bounce many times. Sometimes it was very hard to hear. After a time this stopped and sleep seemed like a possibility at last.

Deep voices suddenly began bellowing out, heard at differing distances to Aaron and Greg. To them, it seemed that there were two voices, both obnoxiously loud. One seemed to be distressed, while the other, still deeper voice, seemed more angry or frustrated. Neither Greg nor Aaron could make out the words of the conversation, but for seemingly different reasons. To Aaron it seemed that the voices, though loud, were distant, and it was this distance that muffled the voices. But to Greg, the conversation sounded very close, as if two people were standing in the hallway with no regard for waking others. These two voices he heard were speaking total gibberish. It was as if the voices were stupid and only pretending to make conversation, or perhaps it was some super-intelligent language. Then again, it sounded like it could have even been the voices of two whose mouths were bound shut yet still desperately trying to speak.

No one said a word until the conversation seemed to be over. Then, the two revealed to each other that they had been awake and heard it. They woke Zeb to tell him what had happened, but he didn't seem to care.

"You just slept through one of the most horrifying things yet!" Greg cried in disgust. But Zeb just wrapped himself in his sheets and returned to sleep. It would not be until the next morning that he would hear the story. Aaron and Greg told the details of what they heard to each other, learning the distinct differences in their experiences.

"Why do we always experience different things?!" Aaron said in fearful frustration. Greg had no answer for him. "Objective *and* subjective... It just doesn't make sense..."

"This may have been the worst thing yet for me, Aaron," Greg said. "Those were unmistakable voices... Does this mean there are spirits among us?..."

"It may..." Aaron sighed. "But not necessarily. They could be phantoms of some sort... Their words being so unclear... What could it mean? It made me feel like they weren't wholly there..."

"I still can't believe that your parents never hear any of this...They didn't even hear the jar crash that one time! And those voices just now were right in the hallway by their bedroom!"

"I know... The box fan they've got in there can't work *that* well..." Aaron said. "It really is like were in a world of our own when these things happen."

"I think we are," Greg sighed. "I think we are." They found themselves having a hard time of getting back to sleep after this.

Another new aberration made it still harder to find sleep, this one involving the closet folding-door. Not only would it make pounds from the inside now and again, but now it suddenly began shaking. Greg used his flashlight to investigate, but the shaking stopped. The closet door was still open, however. He reached over as far as he could and managed to push it closed.

Later, though, without commotion, the closet door again slid open, for it was like this in the morning. They found that the ceramic jar had also moved over several inches. What did this mean? Was it suggesting that it could have just as easily been thrown across the room or hurled again at one of those who slept? They feared it to be such a reminder.

Derik would know such fears the next time he visited, which was sooner than anyone had expected. In art school, his studies were focused on video and sound, for he wished to direct films one day. For one of his projects he wanted some scenes from the Eldritchs' house so he brought some of his recording equipment with him. He walked through the front door, dressed in his medieval garb and dumping his equipment on the living room floor, which had Mrs. Eldritch pacing around nervously. After some hesitation, she told him to put his things in the basement, which he did. He had also brought a couple tin whistles he had bought at the Festival from a couple months ago.

Greg arrived shortly after, finding a familiar setting: Aaron's house during Holiday season. The Christmas music was playing, incense was lit and the Christmas tree was wonderfully decorated. He found the others in the family room, with Derik looking at him through his camcorder as he entered.

"Ah, put that thing down," Greg told him when he saw the blinking red light, then advanced toward the camera lens like a wraith. The others were much amused.

"And how are things with the Lady Tiffany, good sir?" Aaron asked Derik, who smiled with satisfaction in return.

"Still going strong! She's great – I mean, really great. We have more in common than I thought possible."

"That's great. Send some of your luck my way," Aaron joked.

"Will do!" Derik said through chuckles. The men settled to the floor. "So I'll need you guys to do some simple acting for me," Derik began. "I want to describe this dream I had on video, but I want the conversation to come up kind of casually, if you know what I mean." The others nodded.

"I have this really funny movie I want to show you guys," Aaron said. They welcomed this idea gladly. It had been so long since they had done something purely for fun, they had almost forgotten the feeling. So they took the family room, sat down and did it – They watched the movie, laughing at all the best moments, especially those whose comedic element came from the fact that the director had attempted – and failed – to make a no-nonsense action-drama.

The movie left the men in a very funny mood. Derik stuck both tin whistles in his mouth and hooted away on them, creating a very discordant and almost carnival-like tune. It was rather jarring, especially considering he had started his little jingle with a horrible screech that sounded like a female scream.

"What the-?! Would you quit that?" Aaron said, hearing this. Derik kept playing. Greg now looked serious.

"Cut that out, Derik!" Greg said sternly. "You're going to *cause* things!" He seemed to understand now what Aaron had told him before. Still Derik would not listen. So Greg walked up to him and snatched the whistles from his hands. Derik seemed upset for a while. Aaron lightened his mood.

"Now we'll probably hear a whole symphony of tin whistles while we try to sleep," Aaron said jokingly. Greg cried in laughter at the thought, but Derik was still irritated.

"We better do that video thing," Zeb said.

"I'd rather just talk like we usually do," Greg said.

"We will. We'll try to fit in the dream discussion near the end," Zeb suggested. And so they did. Derik preferred the video be shot in their living room. Zeb, Aaron and Greg had already begun talking when they were pulled into the living room by Derik. They took their seats and talked for an hour or more about the nothing, and things.

"Someday soon this house will be, well, nothing," Zeb said. "As far as we are concerned at least. The phenomenon of this house as we know it will no longer exist. It's very *being* will have been annihilated." The others sighed despondently. Zeb then told a story someone had told him at work.

Apparently, an investigator had been conducting a background investigation on someone. He was talking to him on a subway trolley. The man had seemed to become more and more nervous, as if the investigator would soon discover something dangerous about him. And he would, only not dangerous to the investigator. The subject, who had seen that another train was approaching from the opposite direction, suddenly jumped up and opened the side door. 'Oh shit, I'm doing it!' he said. And with that, he leapt off, just as the oncoming train came rushing by. The investigator had no time whatsoever to stop him, and the man died instantly. Allegedly he had seen pieces of flesh scattered across the rails.

Derik filmed while they talked about this dead man's fate. Was it damnation? Or did he simply become nothing? Then they asked if he was already nothing, as some philosophies suggest. A very dismal discussion on Christianity ensued. No perspective seemed hopeful at all regarding the fate of a soul. Finally, Zeb remembered that he was supposed to talk about Derik's dream, so he brought up the story, but not as seamlessly as he would have liked.

Derik's dream was strange, to be sure. In it, he found himself in a dark graveyard. There before him was a burlap sack. But somehow, Derik knew this sack to be a portal, rather than a container. Out from the sack came a hideous monster, a giant arachnid with the torso, head and upper arms of a female. From out of nowhere Derik drew a sword. He tried to kill the monster but was cast aside like a rag doll. He tried once more, and this time he managed to cleave the head off the monster. He watched as the head rolled to his feet. There it stopped, but there was something that left Derik not with a sense of victory but rather despair: a mocking sneer was on the head, which he observed to be staring at him. He knew that, despite having beheaded the monster, he was still subject to its evil will.

After he filmed a few additional locations within the house they prepared for bed. This time, Greg and Derik took the floor and let Aaron have the upper bunk.

"I hate getting those sleeping bags from the basement," Aaron said.

"I hate walking into your kitchen," Derik added. "The reflections are so clear in that window over the sink... My reflection in general has actually begun to disturb me, and I feel as though it could be a separate entity merely imitating me." Aaron looked at Derik with intrigue, while Greg recalled in silence the bizarre incident with Alex several years ago. Then Aaron revealed something.

"I have been thinking about doubles lately as well," he began. "It was weird. I was at work and we were on break. The break room was downstairs. I went down just to get a cup of water and returned to sit in thought by myself. This took no more than two minutes. When all the others came up after break, they were shocked to see me. They swore they had seen me in the break room, just sitting there, and wondered why I didn't follow them. It was as if... I had a double myself..." Derik and Greg looked at him in wonder and fear. Zeb looked to be deep in thought. Then he spoke.

"A similar thing happened to me at work. A coworker and I were approaching the elevator, as its door closed. The coworker beside me looked at me in astonishment and saying something to the effect of having just seen me come from the same elevator. He was very confused as to how I came to be next to him, so it was almost more like I suddenly appeared to him. Come to think of it, he didn't pay much attention to me while I walked with him..."

"The same thing happened to me, actually!" Aaron said, shocked at this new phenomenon. "I was walking through the college hallway not long ago to use their gym, when something very strange happened. I was walking by a large doorway that led to a flight of stairs. I saw out of the corner of my eyes someone walking down from these steps and coming straight for the doorway. I continued walking, thinking nothing of this, as students walk these paths many times a day. But as the student came through the door, he nearly screamed and fell over me, and, after giving me a sideward look, apologized for not seeing me, and said how much I scared him! Just like you said, I must have suddenly appeared before him for him to react to my presence like that." Greg shook his head.

"What's up with you guys...?" he asked. Zeb laughed and shook his head, having no answer.

"I just thought it was an interesting story," Aaron said. But to Greg it seemed there might be untold context.

They spoke less and less now, as they grew more tired. But the familiar pattern of paranormal activity was soon recognized. Aaron was the first to notice when he heard the scratching on the headboard right behind his head. Then Derik, who had never been witness to the many sounds during these times, heard a bang from within the closet. It upset him greatly. An occasional crash or pound from the basement could be heard by all and felt by the two who lay on the floor.

"What's going on... in your basement?!" Derik cried softly.

"Try to ignore it, Derik," Greg suggested. But it was impossible for either of them to do this. An industrial hum was heard now and again. Derik lay frozen in fear. Aaron did the same, so as to be aware of anything that might be dangerous.

"Remember, Greg," Aaron said. "I was attacked before. I can't just ignore these things anymore."

"You don't have to remind *me*," Greg sighed. There was silence for some time. So far, the only things missing were attacks and voices. They were glad these had not surfaced. But the little joy Derik got from this fact was soon destroyed. For the first time in his life, he experienced feeling the touch of the incorporeal. At first, he did not realize it.

"Greg... did you just touch me on the belly?" Derik asked. Derik's question woke him.

"Uhh... no... You were touched...?" Greg asked. Derik began to panic.

"Are you serious?!... That wasn't you?... Oh no..." he said. Derik cautiously stood up in the dark and flipped the room light. Everyone was tucked away in bed. He could hardly believe what happened. He remembered the red line and began to despair. The light disturbed Zeb, and he grumbled for it to be turned off. So Derik turned off the light and quickly went back under his cover. Not five minutes later, he felt a hard poke on his shoulder and cried out.

"What's wrong, Derik!?" Greg asked.

"It happened again... on my shoulder..." he answered.

"That's so weird... I haven't been touched at all," Greg realized. "You're being singled out, I'm afraid."

"Why...?" Derik asked, not expecting an answer, though he did want one. Only a few minutes later and he now felt a sort of punch on his chest. Now Derik began to weep in horror. Greg turned on the light, waking the others. He put an arm around Derik and patted him. "I just don't understand..." Derik said. "It never used to be like this..." Aaron leaned over the railing.

"Derik...? What happened to you?" Aaron asked.

"I was punched," he responded. He pounded the floor in frustration. The others were silent.

"Truly there is evil here," Greg said. "I wish there was something we could do."

"Try not to be afraid, Derik," Aaron told him. "That might be making it worse."

"Easy for you to say!" Derik shot back. "I'm in pain right now, Aaron! Real, actual pain! I can still feel it!"

"I only say this because I've gone through it too," Aaron said reassuringly. "Staying calm seems to help. I'll help any way I can." Through sniffles, Derik said,

"Thanks, Aaron. I know you're trying. I just... I wonder sometimes why I even come here... I like you guys. You're my best friends. Family, even... But each day it gets harder to re-member what we all stood for... what we yearned for. We hard-ly ever had a chance to have a decent game of D&D, you know? Where we weren't interrupted by possessed toys or polter-geists with a penchant for hurling objects across the room... Even our trips into the forest have been tainted."

"The most important thing is that we stand with each other through all of this," Greg told his friend. "No one is ex-pecting anyone to put themselves at risk. Am I right, Aaron?"

"Of course," he answered.

"I'd offer you guys a room, but I probably shouldn't give away rooms that belong to my aunt," Zeb joked. "I'm sure you're dying to hear that music box." With some nervous laughter, Greg turned off the light and everyone returned to bed. Derik felt something grab him gently, now and again, but it would be for an instant only.

There was silence and darkness for some time. Then Greg felt a strange sensation come over him. He somehow sensed that there was a presence over him, and just as he felt this, there was a heavy prod upon him. He had begun to react even before this, yet he still hit nothing but air as he flailed his hands out with a holler. Again, the others were awake now, and he explained this horror. They returned to sleep once more, but the next aberration to rudely and horrifically wake them would be a shared experience.

As if in a dream, they all heard suddenly a playful tune. Its sound quality and tune were in the likeness of a carousel song one would here at an amusement park. There was some-thing foreboding about the tune, somehow, as they listened in horror. Derik jumped on and flipped on the light as the music played. They realized now that everyone was hearing it, as they looked at each other in sheer terror. They had seemed to enter a whole other world. The whimsical tune continued plucking along.

"It doesn't stop!" Zeb cried, but as he spoke, they seemed to lose the music, for it was no longer there when he stopped. No one could believe it had just happened.

"I'm just waiting for a clown to burst through the doorway!" Aaron said in horror, as the others jumped away from this door. Only a sliver of darkness was seen under it.

"Or something more like your plastic horse in the basement!" Greg said. "That was a merry-go-round tune!" It was understandably well into a new day when they finally found sleep.

Long after the sun rose on this day, they woke. They could hardly believe that it happened. But they all shared the memory, and that made it just as real as anything else. "Once again, another manifestation of the Scary Book," Greg said. No one disagreed with this. Then Aaron remembered something, as he looked up with wide eyes.

"And once again," he began, "it may have been caused by some action of ours: this time it would be Derik's little tune last night!"

"Derik!" Greg shouted, as Zeb looked at Derik in shock. Derik dropped his head.

"Come on...you can't be serious..." he said.

"I'm quite serious," Aaron replied. "This would be just another example. It has happened like that before. Something seems to be mocking us."

"Yeah, the red line... Right after completing the Book..." Derik sighed.

"It doesn't necessarily have to be mockery," Zeb said. "But it does seem to be a response of sorts to particular things." The others nodded unsurely. The phenomena seemed to be guided by a will of some sort, but doubt remained for its face had not yet been seen.

# CHAPTER ELEVEN

## The Face of Fear

A favor was asked of Greg. He was to retrieve the original footage of the mock portal from Derik, who had taken this when working on the video prank. Aaron felt he would not be trusted enough if he were to ask himself, after what he had done to get the finished video project from him before.

"Yeah, I was wondering if you had the original footage of Aaron's, you know, of the mock portal? The footage you put in the video?" Greg asked him over the phone, very carefully. But even this aroused Derik's suspicion.

"Aaron put you up to this, didn't he?..." he asked. Greg sighed, for he could not lie when asked such a direct question.

"Yeah, he did... He just wants the original footage back..." Greg said.

"What's with that video now? That was the one thing he said was proof of the whole hoax he had got me involved in... Why would he talk about it so openly?" Derik wondered aloud. Greg's answer surprised him.

"I can't tell you any more," he said.

"What...?" Derik asked. "Why?... You mean... you know the answer to this?..."

"I took a vow, Derik. I was simply given a task. Do you have it?" Greg asked.

"I'll look," Derik said reluctantly. "I haven't seen it around lately. In fact, I had forgotten about that... I wonder why Aaron never took that, too..."

"That's all I can do for him then," Greg said. "Thanks

for your help."

"Yeah..." Derik said. And the phone call ended. Derik later called Aaron regarding this matter. He was not only curious but suspicious too, and it was beginning to eat at him.

"Why do you want the footage back?" he asked.

"Oh, I don't know..." Aaron said. "I'd just like to see it again."

"Why would you want to see it?" Derik asked, growing frustrated. "What's so important about it? I thought it was just a mock portal." Aaron didn't answer. "That was a real portal, wasn't it?..." Still Aaron said nothing. "And to think I handled it... You know, it wouldn't be the only portal I've seen..." Aaron was shocked.

"You've... seen one?..." Aaron asked. "When...?"

"It was the first one Greg saw... I glimpsed it for only a brief moment, but at the time I thought it was your doing," Derik told him.

"My gosh..." Aaron said. He had never known that the portals could be seen by more than one person at a time. "Was it the same that Greg described?"

"I'm pretty sure," Derik responded. "I was expecting something more glass-like; I was thinking it must have been a great illusion... and by the time I glimpsed it, I think Greg and Zeb had confirmed that everything was back to normal, so I was a bit confused."

Aaron sighed. "Derik, remember I said there was something I could not tell you about?"

"Yeah, I remember..." Derik said.

"I think you better get over here, while my mind is changed," Aaron said.

"Woah... okay. This is kind of a late notice, but I guess given the circumstances I can make an exception," Derik said, laughing nervously.

"Alright..." Aaron said. "I'll see you soon."

It was already very dark when Derik arrived. He had never stood before that house alone in such darkness and took this as a sign of grim things to come. After Aaron greeted him and he entered, it seemed dark even inside the house. Why don't his parents turn some more lights on? he thought. And where was Zeb? Then he remembered that Zeb lived with his aunt and was here only on weekends.

"It seems so weird, him not being here," Derik said. "Every time I come, he's part of the group, but I keep forgetting that he doesn't really live here."

"Yeah," Aaron said. "For him, this house has already begun to slide into nothingness, phenomenologically speaking. It is not the same home it used to be. In fact, he's been wondering lately what home really means. He spends most of his time at work, sleeps most of the time at his aunt's, yet I feel he would still call this place his home."

"Sad..." Derik said.

"I know. But it's because he's not here that I needed to talk to you now," Aaron said.

"What...? What does that have to do with what you want to tell me?" Derik asked.

"The things you are about to learn are not only my secrets, but Zeb's as well. I considered them to be too personal to be a concern of yours or Greg's, and Zeb still thinks so. So, I must ask that you do not tell him what I am about to reveal to you," Aaron said.

"Yeah, I can do that," Derik assured him.

"Like I said, I thought it was none of your business, but then I learned something," Aaron said.

"Go on," Derik insisted.

"I've told Greg about these things already. I believed it was his business, though we still have kept it a secret from Zeb," Aaron explained. "But then I learned just shortly ago, during our phone conversation, that you had seen the portal...this was the only reason I told Greg what I'm about to tell you, the fact he had seen portals. Now that I know you have seen one, I can tell you, for now I know that we share the same fears and experiences."

"What do you mean...?" Derik asked.

"What we were thinking was very personal is no longer such a private matter," Aaron said. "Greg has seen two portals, you have seen one, and Zeb and I have seen them as well."

Derik was dumbfounded. "You... you've seen them...?!" he stuttered. Aaron nodded.

"Let me get the Study for you. It will make everything clear," Aaron said, getting out of his seat. He left Derik in the living room and returned to his seat after a minute or two, holding the portable tape recorder in his hand. Derik sat on the floor in front of him. "Brace yourself," Aaron told him. "It may disturb you." He rewound the tape to the beginning, then fast-forwarded it for only a few seconds. He hit play, stopped it, went a little further then hit play again. Zebulon's voice was speaking.

> "He is not the only one who has continued to ex-perience the aberrant. For now, perhaps one of the strangest of all phenomena has occurred, and within the walls of my own home. I have witnessed what appeared to be a window of sorts, anchored firmly into the cement floor. It was counter-intuitive however, having no visible purpose, which is to say, it had no reason to exist. There were also bars, steel bars perhaps, barely visible beyond the dirty glass. Should the opportunity arise again, I will make an effort to study it more carefully."

Aaron hit the stop button. "This was over two years ago," he said. Derik shook his head in disbelief. "Soon after, his opportunity came, though I am not exactly sure when or how. Listen." He hit play once more. Strange static was heard. "I don't believe he heard this while he recorded. The same goes for many of the things you are about to hear. Let's just listen."

> Zeb was speaking amidst a whining static. "I'm very fortunate to be able to make this recording... simi-lar to the last object, but not exactly... There seems to be less bars...... definitely larger... yes, definitely an...... I can also hear..." and at this point the quality of the static seemed to change to more of a rough sound, "...hear

strange noises from behind the glass as well," he said, and a tapping could be heard, likely upon the glass. "...Let's see... there are also several wires protruding from the frame-like border..... seems to serve as an anchor of some..." and while he said this, there was heard amid the static the wail of a baby. Now there seemed to be more than one baby, and they were crying loudly. It was hard to tell if Zeb was hearing it. He continued speaking during this. "I seem to have a clear mind, I seem to have, be in total control of my wits, so I don't think I'm delusional. No, this is certainly before me..." Now the sound began to cut in and out. The static was heard in bursts, yet the baby cries went uninterrupted. Zeb's voice was hard to hear at times now. "....now look......... Yeah, definitely a.............. much larger.............. The noises continue.... and............. more wires that.........................."

Aaron stopped the recording. His hands were quivering, as well as Derik's lips, as he tried to speak. "That's not it," Aaron said, as he fast-forwarded once more, through much material this time. He found the place he wanted and hit play. Aaron's voice was speaking now.

"I had my most intimate experience yet in Tryst. I saw my first portal. It did not quite match the description of either my brother or Mr. Logan, but it is evidence that an evolution is taking place. This portal, it had neither glass nor a mirror. It was a gaping hole in the same spot as all the others. It was small and square, and it was a shaft. I could not enter the hole, however, since the entrance was completely covered with thick, steel fencing. There was a tiny gap in this fencing which did offer me an opportunity to tear it open, but I refused the offer. At this decision, I could faintly hear what sounded like a train whistle, but I could not identify the direction. This noise actually served, in some way, to take from me my consciousness. I woke up in bed the next morning and, like before, it was gone."

Aaron stopped the tape player and sighed. "Now you understand what we have endured as well." Derik nodded shakily. "Neither you nor Greg have been alone in these experiences. Zeb and I have long since known about them."

"I... can't believe it!" Derik said, with a washed-out look on his face. "You were just waiting for us to finally see a portal of some kind..."

"And judging by the way each portal seemed to change, I could guess fairly accurately what the next would look like," Aaron said. "They seem to be opening up gradually. I suspect that soon, there will be nothing but a simple hole in the floor, very large probably, and no obstructions whatsoever."

"You wanted me to pretend I didn't see it..." Derik said.

"I was hoping you wouldn't even look," Aaron began. "But I was still glad you didn't get any closer. Surely you would have seen it for what it was. It was a good way of keeping you believing me."

"Not to mention what may have happened to either of us if we approached it..." Derik said weakly.

"Zeb and I did approach what we saw before us," Aaron explained. "They always appeared at night, just before going to bed. For Zeb, I guess he went to bed knowing that thing was still there. For me, as I describe in the Study, it seemed to have an effect on my consciousness. It made me fall asleep. Sometimes I wonder if the whole thing was in a dream..."

"Zeb came out with documentation, though..." Derik said.

"I know... I guess it wasn't a dream..." Aaron said. "They seemed to just vanish for Greg... Very interesting, in my opinion... Why won't they stay around as long for him, I wonder...? It definitely made it seem as if it was a delusion, which is what I wanted you to think that I wanted him to think, if you follow."

"Yeah... It's like something was helping you..." Derik realized.

"I know... I've felt that for some time," Aaron said. "But

now we all know the truth. If it happens again, be prepared for a closer examination." Derik shuddered and didn't respond.

"Zeb's documentation is not the only one we have." Derik looked at him, with an expression of understanding. "The footage of the portal..."

"I knew it," Derik said, nodding hesitantly. "I knew it wasn't a mock..."

"Do you remember how the camera couldn't focus on the portal?" he asked. Derik nodded. Aaron continued. "You thought it was a very creepy effect and wondered how I did it. I explained that it happened without trying. This was the truth, but it is not so hard for me to understand. You see, I didn't see the portal in front of me. I couldn't see it through the camera lens, either. All the camera saw was a flat concrete surface, so it had a hard time focusing... In the playback, however, it was there..."

"I remember hearing your mother playing the piano in the background, and your dad walk by, talking to you... They definitely weren't acknowledging what you were filming," Derik said.

"Yeah, you couldn't hear it on the playback on my camera, so I thought you couldn't on yours either. When it did, I was hoping that their ignorance would not occur to you while you were editing it," Aaron said.

"It didn't... I feel stupid..." Derik sighed.

"Don't feel that way. Anyone would have believed the same," Aaron said.

"Why were you filming in the first place?" Derik wondered. Aaron shook his head.

"Sometimes, Zeb and I have these premonitions... Usually they're in the form of dreams... then they become reality. That's how I knew Greg would be seeing his first portal. That's why I couldn't give the details of the supposed hoax until I saw them in my dreams... Then I would prepare you as fast as I could," Aaron explained. "I hate to say it, but I have had another dream, recently." Derik groaned. "So I guess that's another reason it was good for us to talk about this. I don't want you to lose it if you're there to see the next portal. I want you to be ready."

"I can't believe... you have to tell me that..." Derik said. Aaron gave him a pat.

"It's all very strange indeed. Something very special is going on here, and we should consider ourselves lucky for being part of it," Aaron said. Derik was not convinced of this.

"I would rather not be part of it," he said. "It may be 'special', but I don't think it's a good thing happening... I don't think it's even neutral..."

"It's hard to say," Aaron sighed. "It may have nothing to do with the more violent incidents. Then again, it may all be subsumed within a single phenomenon, a single cause. It's hard to say which anomaly would be a part of Tryst, and which wouldn't be - if not all unexplainable things are." There was silence for a while, as they sat in the dimly lit living room. "I wonder where that footage could be... It would be a shame if it was lost."

"I can't find it anywhere..." Derik said.

"And I looked through all of our old video tapes, just to make sure," Aaron said. "I don't think it ever came back to my house, though. I was positive I left it with you. When I took the final video project that day, I knew I had left the original footage. I hoped you would forget about it, or think I forgot about it... Now it's just gone..."

"Why did you take that video anyway?" Derik asked.

"It was a good way of convincing you, as harsh as it was," Aaron said. "I figured it wouldn't be long before we put it behind us and were having fun again. I didn't think you would ever learn the truth. But there was another reason, too. I felt very uneasy giving you that footage for the trick you thought we were planning. You didn't realize it of course, but I had decided from the beginning that we would never actually go through with it. Even the mere existence of that video made me sick. Now I stand here and wonder if it was even dangerous, since mocking these things has proved to cause abnormal events... Anyhow, I destroyed the tape, as soon as I got home. I didn't want it to exist anywhere." They sat in silence for a bit longer.

"Remember when Royce and I were both trying to scare Greg?" Derik asked. Aaron nodded.

"Yeah..." he answered. "I wasn't positive that you were acting, actually. Especially when you descended the stairs... Only Royce's strange behavior made me think you two were joking. I didn't think it was possible for the house to have such an effect on him so soon, and it would seem I was right."

Derik sighed, lowering his head. "I thought I was acting, too, until I descended your basement stairs..." he said. Aaron's eyes widened. "I don't know what came over me... It was like I was drawn down there... I was utterly horrified as I took each step, and yet I couldn't stop. I would never do something like that in my right mind..." Aaron looked at him with intrigue and fear now.

"The same thing happened to Wendell..." Aaron said. "It's something Zeb doesn't like to talk about. Wendell descended those stairs in much the same manner, though he did not seem to be fearful. It was the last time Zeb ever saw him. He had said something very strange, too... I can't remember..." Aaron lifted the tape player. "I believe Zeb describes it in here. Let me try to find it." He searched through the Study, until he found the Wendell story. "Here we go... Just a little further towards the end is where it should be..." He went a little further, then let the audio play.

"This time he arrived at my doorstep on an otherwise average day," Zeb's voice said. "He said he was here just to see me again, but I sensed other motives. He had become a criminal during those years, and had a perverted, cynical outlook on all the good things I had once shown him. He showed an obvious intrigue regarding me, particularly me in the context of my home. He exuded fear in everyone at my home but me, who was filled more with disappointment and frustration. We went to my bedroom to talk. I remember him eying my sword then picking it up. I looked at him with disgust as he slid its blade across his hand, drawing blood. He said he would stay the night, which my mother agreed to, though fearful of him. I asked if he wanted to sleep outside, under the stars, but he refused. Instead, he slowly descended the staircase that led to the cellar. Looking back toward me as he receded into the dark, he said, 'I don't know how you can give this up... But if I don't see you again, remember that you made it all possible.'

I slept out there, under the winter stars, dwelling on that. Only now am I beginning to understand his words. The next day Wendell Hearn was gone. I have not seen him to this day, though I believe I heard from someone that he had died. What am I supposed to make of this? All I can say is that he seemed to have a certain relationship with me, this house, and the Wa-Wa itself, a relationship that I was unaware of. I will take his advice, however, and open myself to Tryst as much as I can. He probably knew something."

Aaron gave Derik a grim look. "You are lucky the same thing did not happen to you, friend," he said. "Whatever that fate may be."

"That was the last you saw him?" Derik asked.

"Yes. I am not sure if anybody has seen him since. In fact, like Zeb said on the tape, we heard that he had died, although it is unclear if this happened before or after his visit." Derik shuddered.

"Why...? Why did I go down there like that?..." he said. Aaron could not answer. They sat for only a short while longer. Derik had indeed been enlightened, though it felt more like an endarkenment, if such a thing was possible.

He left Aaron's house the same night. It was an unusually short visit, he thought, and something had felt surreal for its entire duration. Although it made him sick, he was comforted by the fact that neither he nor Greg were being singled out. This did not lift the darkness they were in, however. Rather, it made them fear that house in a new way. And the new information regarding Wendell, of which Derik soon informed Greg, was unsettling to say the least.

Greg was well into the new Chapters. Interestingly, the story was taking a new direction, sharing some characteristics of traditional ghost stories. While psychological instability still seemed to be a factor, the emphasis on faith and religiosity was becoming more and more apparent. This was largely seen with the introduction of phantasmal beings similar to demons that were harassing the protagonist. While spooky, it was more of a mystery story and mostly self-contained. The more Greg read, the more enthralled he became. If he hadn't understood that the Book was authored by someone far away who presumably knew nothing of the Eldritchs, he would be inclined to think he had written it himself, inspired by the happenings within their house.

He sat in his friends' family room now. The parents were again on a weekend trip, and the men sat in the room feeling quite isolated. Zeb had just finished reading, closing the Book for the night.

"I can't get over how the phenomena become so universal... It's not just the main character's immediate surroundings anymore... It seems like the whole world is unstable..." Zeb thought aloud.

"That's what I'm beginning to think about the things going on around here," Greg said.

"People everywhere experience the unexplained... They are either too ignorant to realize it, or they deny it. And when they realize it, everybody has his own way of understanding it. The world's crazy!"

"I only wonder why it is so commonplace here," Aaron said. "There still must be something special in our situation, something in us, or this location; this house." They sat in thought for a while.

"You wait, Zeb," Greg began. "The story gets weirder." Greg laughed to himself. He wanted to say so much, so badly, but he didn't want to spoil anything for Zeb.

"It's amazing how the same things are expressed in such

different ways, from chapter to chapter," Zeb said. "My mood is constantly changing and my theories as well. It certainly helps me expand my views on reality." They spoke for a while longer, but sleeping time inevitably came.

"I don't particularly feel like going downstairs to get the sleeping bag," Aaron told Greg.

"Could you come with me?" Greg reluctantly agreed.

"Alright, then, let's just do it as fast as we can..." Zeb and Greg followed Aaron as he scampered down, nearly tripping over each other. They ran into the back section, grabbed the gear and raced back out. As they ran through the doorway and headed for the stairs, Aaron, who was in the rear, caught sight of something he knew to be different. It was some kind of dark shadow; more than dark, it was pure blackness, on the far wall near the poker table. Although that section was poorly illuminated, he could tell that something even darker was now there. He continued right behind the others, up the stairs, but grabbed Greg as he got to the top.

"Greg, Zeb, somebody... I saw something down there... I'm serious!... I don't know what it was, but I want someone to follow me back down there... I need to know..." They looked at him in horror, neither expressing desire to go back down. Zeb shook his head.

"I'll go only if you two are in front of me," Zeb said. Greg sighed.

"Just for a second," he said. "We come back as soon as anything funny starts to happen."

Aaron, his face white, held onto Greg tightly as they returned to the basement. They reached the floor, and Aaron slowly pulled the others toward the cellar door that divided the two sections, from where the shadowy entity could be seen.

"It was on the far wall... near the poker table... It should be coming into view..." he said. Greg wondered if what Aaron saw would even still be there. For him, it seemed that such things would be visible only for similarly short durations. He and Aaron were both surprised when the aberration was still present. And when they realized what it was, utter terror gripped their hearts.

In the darkness they beheld an even deeper shadow. It was the grotesque face they had known about for years, but now much more apparent. The highlights of the face remained white, but the negative space, which was usually hard to visualize since it was only a whitish cream color, was now black. This blackness brought to life the face in its entirety, including the chin which itself now seemed to be a separate face; half shadowed, with one, large, sable eye that pulled them closer.

As Greg began to withdraw in horror, Aaron stepped closer for a moment, enraptured. He stood before the face, now aware that the shadows were in fact tiny writhing tendrils which almost seemed to crawl on the wall. They were clustered densely where the shadows were darkest and thinned out as they distanced themselves from the face. The whole image rippled before him, like black ink on wet paper. He stared into the deeply shadowed eyes, while the face simply looked back, with an imperturbable grin that left Aaron drained of any courage or resilience he may have had. He was face to face with Fear itself and stood powerless before its knowing gaze.

A sense of submission immediately came over him and he nearly collapsed, when he heard Greg shouting for him.

"Come on, Aaron, what are you waiting for?!" he cried. Aaron's body jolted, as if coming out of a trance, and turned from the face. He sensed he had committed some offense as he ran up the stairs behind Greg. The three of them raced to Zeb's bedroom and locked the door behind them.

"What happened!?" Zeb cried. Aaron was stricken speechless. His eyes were filling with tears. Only Greg had an explanation.

"It's the face... Frankie..." he said. Zeb's eyes widened in horror as he waited for more. "It's become a real face... that's the only way I know how to describe it... It's much easier to see than it usually is. All the shadows of the face are pitch dark... It was like... like it was meant to be seen..." Zeb didn't know what to say.

"Let's just try to get to sleep. We're all very tired... Perhaps you two were having nightmares before actually lying in bed," Zeb suggested.

"*That's* definitely not what was happening, but you're probably right in saying we should get to sleep," Greg answered. He climbed up in the top bunk. Aaron slowly prepared his sleeping bag, saying nothing. When Zeb was ready to turn off the light, Aaron spoke.

"I have to go back," he said. "I have to know it's really there... Every other time we wait till morning, but I am going to stay until something happens..." The others shouted out to him as he unlocked the door and left the room. No one went after him.

Aaron drew a long knife from the knife set when he came to the top of the stairwell. He listened first, as he stared down into the dark emptiness. He heard nothing. It was such a traumatic experience, that he was beginning to forget the details of it already. A dread filled him as he again remembered. Was that face really down there, he wondered? Was the face of evil really on his basement wall? It was probably waiting for him, much displeased with the way he had left, though this would be concealed behind its devilish grin. He turned on the light and descended. He carefully rounded the corner, and was faced with a dilemma, but not a face. The image was still there, but it was now as it had always been. He pulled a chair up in front of it, and slumped into its seat, staring up at the blank wall.

He did not know how to feel. He was glad in a sense that it was gone, but he was also distraught. If it had stayed, perhaps he could have gathered the courage to rise against it, however this may be done. It would have become a presence known to all, over time, and it would no longer be such a personal dilemma, but rather a challenge for the whole family, if not all of mankind. But it was gone. The faint image stared at him mockingly, and Aaron sensed that there was still evil within it. Even though Greg had seen it, Aaron felt horribly alone and confined within the face's gaze. He knew there was a mind behind that face, and it was aware of him. Wherever he went, whether he was thinking about it or not, he would be remembered by it.

He dropped his head and wept.

Greg poked his head over the edge of the bed. "Zeb... do you hear that?" There was a bellowing noise now and again coming from the basement, but it was too muffled to identify.

"Yeah... Like guffaws..." Zeb began. "Or horrible weeping... It is too muffled to hear clearly..." They listened in silence for several more minutes as the noise persisted.

"What is happening to Aaron...?" Greg asked nervously. Then he became angry. "Why did he go back!? That fool... He should know better..."

"I guess he wanted to examine it closer... but what could have happened?" Zeb wondered.

"Zeb, what do you think he meant when he said 'we always leave things behind until morning'?" Greg asked. He knew the answer, and he knew Zeb knew. He wanted Zeb to know that everyone knew about the portals he and Aaron had seen.

"I don't know... The doll you saw, maybe?" Zeb replied. He now realized Aaron's comment was indeed revealing. "What do you think?"

"He told me about the portals, Zeb. And Derik too. We all know about the portals you and Aaron have seen," Greg revealed. Zeb sighed. He was not upset, but he was a bit embarrassed. "It's okay. We share a common bond."

"Derik, too?..." Zeb asked.

"Yeah... Only Derik knew at first. Then he told me, and then Aaron," Greg said. "He saw the first one I had seen... and the video footage that Aaron took..."

"I knew he was handling the footage, but I never knew he saw an actual portal before his eyes... I guess we're all in the same boat now." At this moment, their door opened, and they wailed in horror. The room light went on, and Aaron stood in the doorway, swaying a bit. He entered and shut the door.

"Is everything... alright?..." Greg asked. Aaron had only one thing to say.

"Gone... all gone..." and he turned off the light and

climbed under the sleeping bag. They heard him weep and mumble in the darkness until they were asleep.

The next morning, Aaron woke up with unexpected vigor and enthusiasm. Greg was still disturbed by what he had seen the night before, and Zeb was soon asking more questions.

"What happened to you down there?" Zeb asked his brother. Aaron looked at him confused.

"When?" he asked. The memory of the entire event from the night before was buried away in the depths of his mind, presently inaccessible. It had been replaced with one fabricated. This was now immediately apparent to Zeb and Greg.

"Oh, great... He forgot," Greg sighed. He and Zeb exchanged glances.

"What did I forget? I haven't forgotten anything," Aaron said assuredly. "Did something happen during the night?"

"Wow... It must've really disturbed you," Greg said.

"Don't you remember, Aaron? Before we went to bed? What you saw on the wall?" Zeb asked, trying to draw out any memory.

"What did I ever see on the wall?" Aaron asked. "Wait... I remember Greg thought he may have seen something last night... What was that again?"

"Never mind..." Greg said. He turned to Zeb. "He's completely repressed it." Zeb shook his head in disbelief.

"I did see something strange," Aaron said. The others turned to him in anticipation. "When Greg and I were coming back up with the sleeping bag, I saw someone sitting in a chair staring at the wall, you know, the wall with Frankie on it... I thought it was you, Zeb, and it was quite disturbing. I couldn't understand why someone would ever just sit in front of the wall like that..."

Zeb looked at him unsurely. "I went with you two when you got the sleeping bag," he said. "I was never sitting in a chair, and I didn't see anyone else doing this either."

"Well, maybe it was a dream..." Aaron sighed. "I

wouldn't have even mentioned it if you guys didn't bring up last night's events." Greg shook his head and got ready for the day.

He later took Zeb into the basement and explained exactly what he saw. "It was Frankie... His face was so easy to see... The blackness was like a grainy substance, that faded out as it got further from the face. It was horrifying." Aaron's eyes were wide.

"You saw all of that?!" he laughed, almost in disbelief.

"You saw it too," Greg said. "It bothered you so much that you can't even remember."

"That's crazy..." Aaron said. But it was true.

"I wonder why I never saw it?" Zeb said. "Maybe my eyes just aren't good enough. You said it was dark over there, right?"

"Yeah," Greg answered. "But the face was so dark, it was still easy to see."

"This has never happened before... not that I know of, anyway... What could be happening?"

"I don't know, but it sure is like the new Chapters," Greg said. Zeb laughed in fear as he realized the truth of this statement. "...There are always correlations..."

Aaron would not remember the true events on that day, but he believed that Greg had seen something. The more he heard, the more he wondered if he had indeed repressed the experience. The memories he had were already quite fuzzy and before long he knew even those would be reliable no longer.

# CHAPTER TWELVE

## Twins of Fear

The minutes ticked by as Greg stood at the cash register one evening. He was working in the store this time instead of the usual gas station just outside the building, because Holiday season had arrived and extra help was needed inside. Finally, his shift was over, and he went to say good-night to his supervisor. She stared at him in disbelief as he stepped into the doorway of her office.

"Why Greg," she began, "I thought you had already left for the night." She smiled and shook her head.

"Oh, no, I'm just now leaving," Greg said. "I just wanted to say good-night."

"Weird... I saw you walking out of here on the security camera," she said. "I guess you walked out for something else?"

"Yeah, I guess..." Greg said, immediately remembering Aaron and Zeb's similar stories. For he knew that he had in fact no yet left the building.

"Well good-night Greg," she said. He nodded and walked out. 'Guess she'll have to watch me walk out again,' Greg thought to himself amusingly. He got in his car and drove home, anxious to tell Aaron about his doppelgänger.

Aaron's job at the warehouse was a full-time day job, so Greg would only be able to call from work in the evening. Luckily, this opportunity came toward the end of the next day when he was put in the gas station, and he made the call. Mrs.

Eldritch picked up the phone when it rang and handed it to her son when she learned it was Greg.

"Hey, Greg, you calling from work?" Aaron asked.

"Yeah... you'll never believe what happened to me yesterday at work..." Greg said.

"Oh boy," Aaron sighed. He knew it would be disturbing rather than funny.

"Let's hear it." Greg recounted the event, conveying both its simplicity and its relevance.

"Wow... So now you have a double..."

"It looks like it," Greg said. He was thinking how only Derik was now without one. He was soon corrected.

"Derik?!" Aaron suddenly shrieked. Greg was startled.

"Aaron, what's wrong? What about Derik?" he asked. Aaron listened as he could faintly hear Derik's voice in the background. It seemed as if he was talking to Greg.

"Is Derik with you in the gas station?" Aaron asked hesitantly. Greg shivered as he looked around, apparently alone in the little station.

"No... I'm alone..." Greg told him. Then Derik's voice was right in the mouthpiece.

"Hey, Aaron, sounds like you need a chill-pill!" the voice said mockingly.

"Oh my God!!" Aaron cried, turning off the phone. He had not considered Derik having a double for some time. Something had happened several months ago that revealed this, but he initially did not accept it. Rather, he believed it was simply Derik exhibiting uncharacteristic behavior.

Some time after Derik had revealed what he thought was a hoax to Greg, in the café, Aaron got a call. It was while Greg was visiting, and in fact, just after he had explained to Zeb what Derik had told him. Aaron picked up the phone and heard Derik's voice greet him.

"Oh, hey Derik," Aaron said.

"Spelled with a 'Q'," Deriq said.

"Okay..." Aaron said, not thinking much of this. "Where are you?"

"Derik's far away, but *I'm* very close..." Deriq said.

"What do you mean? Why do you keep talking like you're not Derik?" Aaron asked.

"Derik can't tell you what I'm about to tell," Deriq said. "Whatever. Just tell me what you need to say," Aaron said, growing frustrated with this person.

"Derik has told Greg everything about the hoax..." Deriq began. "If you don't believe me, just ask Zeb - Greg just got done telling him about this. Go ahead, get him. I'll wait." Aaron did not know what to say. He was very angry with Derik for having betrayed his trust, especially since it seemed that he was finally coming to agree with him that not everything in one's world need have a naturalistic explanation. He walked halfway down the basement steps, still holding the phone to his ear. He bent over, and saw Greg playing a video game as Zeb watched.

"Zeb!" he called out. "I need to talk to you for a minute." He returned to his bedroom, and waited for Zeb, who soon came into his room with him. Aaron shut the door behind him. "I have Derik on the phone," Aaron told Zeb.

"That's Deriq with a 'Q'," Deriq said.
Aaron spoke to Deriq now. "Yeah, you already told me that." He looked to Zeb again.

"He told me that he told Greg everything about my 'hoax', and to ask you, because you would know." Zeb's eyes widened.

"He's right..." Zeb sighed. "How did he know? Greg told me this himself not five minutes ago... but he said Derik wanted to keep it secret... They must've planned this..."

"Why did you tell him, Derik?!" Aaron shouted in the mouthpiece.

"You're welcome," Deriq said. There was a click followed by a dial tone, and this person who was apparently not Derik - though Aaron had not yet realized this – was not heard from again until now, when he heard him in the gas station with Greg. Now he knew that 'Deriq, spelled with a 'Q',' was a different person, and had always been.

Aaron sat trembling in the family room, still holding the phone. After a minute, it rang. He was about to let it go, but then decided at the last moment to pick up.

"...Hello...?" Aaron said. Derik's voice answered.

"Hey, Aaron?" Derik asked. "Are you... okay?" Aaron gulped, and responded carefully.

"Is that the real you, Derik? Or is this... Derik with a 'Q'...?"

"What?" Derik asked. "What just happened? Greg called me and said you heard me in the gas station? Is that right?"

"Yeah... at least, I heard your voice... Then the voice spoke to me," Aaron said. Derik waited. "It was very short, and I can't even remember exactly what he said... but it was right up close, like you were talking right into Greg's cell-phone..." Now there was a patch of static.

"Ow!..."

"Are you okay?" Derik's voice asked.

"Yeah... Just static..." Aaron answered. "Derik, you have a double... that's all I can say. Just like me, Zeb, and even Greg... I've known this for a while, but I've denied it..."

"I don't know..." Derik's voice said.

"You may have wondered how I came to learn that you told Greg about the hoax," Aaron said.

"Not really," Derik's voice replied.

"If it was not you, then it was your double that told me," Aaron said. Derik's voice remained silent. "I assumed it was you at the time. I was very careful when I came to your house the next day to get the video. Greg had told Zeb that you wanted to keep it secret from me, yet you were the one who told me, so I wondered if you were perhaps having an internal conflict of some kind, and thought it best not to bring up the subject. When it seemed that you had no memory of calling me, I played it safe and treated you as if you never did. I still believed it was probably you...but you never came out with it. As all of us began to have 'twin' experiences, I wondered if perhaps it was your twin... Now I have no doubts."

"It wasn't *my* twin..." Derik's voice said.

"I know you don't want to believe it... It's hard to believe that *I* have one... but it's the only way to explain how the voice knew that Greg had just told Zeb what you told him," Aaron said. "In any case, he's back... and he was with Greg at the gas station." There was another interruption of static. "Alright, the static's getting worse... I'm going to have to go." He listened, but he heard nothing now but soft static. He sighed and hung up the phone. Aaron would later explain the same thing to the one he believed was Greg. Years later, he would discover that both Greg and Derik had never been told of this 'Deriq': he had been speaking to the twins themselves both of these times. An interesting fact was learned, however, at the same time. Derik used to spell his name with a 'Q' when he was going through a troubled time during his high school years. It was a complicated phase in his life, and looking back, he saw that he was essentially a different person then. He had kept this fact to himself until the time of this writing.

Whether or not this was mere coincidence could never be ascertained. The impression, given what was already known, was that there had been a split in personalities at some point, and this 'Deriq' continued to exist in some alternate reality, influencing the world of his twin from time to time; this all made possible by the enigma known as Tryst.

Greg was working out his own theory as well. He did not have all the experiences of Aaron to support a twin theory, though he could not deny his own experience at work. He focused on spiritual phenomena and was now considering the possibility that 'possession' had been occurring for some time. He thought about the incident at the abandoned house. Perhaps – and it pained him to even consider it – Aaron and Zebulon were possessed by demons. Zeb had been acting so strange... and then the way Aaron fell as he walked back up the steps to the family room... He had even mentioned hearing a train whistle before he collapsed... Maybe he, Greg, was the only one with a clear mind... Then he remembered his words that seemed to have summoned a creature in the woods that day a year ago. Perhaps something possessed him, for him to say something like that. And the same day when Zeb was acting so strange in the darkness... walking deeper into the woods like that... He certainly seemed possessed... And Derik descending into Aaron's basement that day when Royce was over... A twin did not seem to explain this, but demonic possession certainly did.

In any case, Greg's home phone rang one Saturday afternoon a month or more earlier. He had only recently begun to theorize about 'possession'. Greg and his mother stood before the phone, waiting for one or the other to pick up. His mother reached for the phone, then Greg saw that Aaron's number was listed on the caller-ID. "I got it, Mom," he said, reaching in front and grabbing the phone for himself. It was Aaron, but he did not expect to hear what he did. The moment he put the phone to his ear, he heard Aaron's voice which wasted no time in speaking.

"Greg, Greg!..." Aaron's voice said nervously. Greg had never heard Aaron like this before, for this was even before the face-on-the-wall incident.

"What is it, Aaron!? What's wrong?" Greg asked.

"You need to listen to me carefully..." Aaron's voice said urgently. "Leave all your doors and windows unlocked, and stay up late enough for – " and at this moment the voice was cut short by static. Greg hung up the phone, bewildered. He looked at the time. Quarter after three. He called Aaron's house an hour later. Aaron's mother answered and gave the phone to Aaron.

"Are you okay?" Greg asked. Aaron was confused already. He knew this was a weird way to start a conversation.

"I'm fine, why?" he asked.

"You didn't sound fine an hour ago, when you called me," Greg said sternly. Aaron wondered if Greg was playing with him.

"I never called you, Greg... Are you joking around?" Aaron asked. Greg laughed, then became very serious.

"No. I wonder if you are, though," Greg responded. Aaron was not convinced but did not know how to prove to Greg that he didn't call. Until Greg explained the story in detail, that is.

"At quarter after three, you say?" Aaron asked. "I know this is hard to believe, but that was the only time all day that I was not at home... I slipped out to get the newspaper and fuel up my car, and was only gone for fifteen minutes... It must've been as soon as I left..."

"As far as I'm concerned, it was you... Your voice, your number," Greg said stubbornly.

"Greg," Aaron began, "you can look at the station's security camera if you want. It will show me there at exactly that time. I don't know what else to say..."

Greg sighed. "Maybe you weren't possessed, then..."

"Possessed?!" Aaron cried.

"Yeah... I've been wondering lately if much of the strange behavior of us all, over the last few years, has been a result of possession by demons..." Greg explained.

"It's possible, I guess... but it would not explain this situation," Aaron said.

"I know... I was really hearing your twin, then..." Greg said despondently.

"If it was my voice, from my house, and the voice was in no way trying to hide these facts, then that would be the most likely possibility," Aaron said. "If you're telling me the truth, I think it is quite unnerving, really. I mean, not only for me in that something is either imitating me or is somehow me, but for you, too... The command itself... What does it mean?"

"I don't know... I should have known it wasn't you though," Greg said. "You always leave your doors unlocked... You wouldn't have known we secure our house so well..."

"So this twin knows things... knows more about you than even I do..." Aaron sighed, thinking about the many things 'Deriq' knew. He wondered if the voice calling himself this may have in fact not been Derik. Again, this was before the call from the gas station.

"Aaron, I just want to know what you think..." Greg began.

"Go on," Aaron said.

"Should I follow you twin's advice?" Greg asked hesitantly.

"I... I don't know..." Aaron replied. "You said the end of the phrase was cut short... We don't even have a complete message..."

"Stay up for..." Greg repeated in meditation. "Stay up for what?! How late should I stay up? And do you know how scared I'm going to be, staying up all alone with all my doors and windows unlocked, waiting for some unknown thing to happen?!"

"I don't know what to say... I don't know if it would be wise to follow or disobey the order," Aaron said.

"Well, I guess there's nothing you can do for me... I was just hoping it was you who called..." Greg said. Aaron laughed.

"Sorry," he said. "I wish it was... Well, actually I'm glad I wasn't possessed, but I wish you never got that call..."

"Yeah, me too," Greg said. "I'll have to make the decision some time tonight. I'll tell you what I did... if I come out okay." And Greg hung up his phone. Aaron did the same, wondering what he would do in the same conditions. He could not answer.

Greg decided to obey the command. He went behind his mother and unlocked each door after she locked them. He stayed up into the early morning, wondering what might happen. Perhaps the most dreadful thing of all happened – nothing. When he could resist sleep no more, he went to bed, leaving all the doors and windows unlocked. He gave Aaron the details the next day, and both simply shrugged without any understanding of what any of it meant.

What was perhaps the most outright presentation of, and obvious encounter with, Aaron's double was also over the phone and happened much later, well into the new year. Greg decided to give Aaron a call. He was greeted by the noise of many gleeful and rowdy children, shouting to one another and squealing with excitement, whilst carnival tunes could be heard. Amid the noise, Greg heard what he guessed must have been Aaron's voice, loud and joyful. "Who is this?" the voice said, apparently not recognizing Greg's voice. "Settle, children," he laughed, as the children continued to squeal.

"Greg! It's Greg!" he shouted into the mouthpiece, so Aaron could hear him over the racket.

"*Ooooh, Greeeeeeeeg!*" the voice said, now apparently remembering. And it was at this moment that the phone cut out, and left Greg with nothing more than a dial tone. He called again immediately, and Aaron picked up after a few rings, totally unaware of what Greg had just experienced. Greg didn't bother accusing Aaron, and simply explained what happened. Both of them could hardly believe it.

There was another phone occurrence whose strangeness seemed to be caused rather by some possession. It was a time when Aaron was talking with Greg on the phone in his bedroom. They had a nice, long conversation, in which Aaron learned several mundane things about this or that. Greg had been hearing strange things over the phone, including static, whimpers and even a female scream. He suddenly became silly and was saying funny things. Then there was a explosion of static in Aaron's ear, and when it was gone, Greg was normal. In fact, he had no memory of the entire conversation. Were it not for the several bits of mundane knowledge Aaron had gained from it, he would have thought he had imagined the whole thing. But he had had premonitions before, so nothing was being ruled out.

Sometimes, it was hard to tell what exactly was happening. All that was known was that Zeb and Aaron would both 'act weird' at times, as Greg and Derik would say. They would have no memory of their behavior. Perhaps they were not truly Zeb nor Aaron, but rather twins. Or, perhaps, they were possessed. The latter seemed more likely when their actual bodies would disobey the laws of nature. Such were the times Derik brought his camera to Aaron's.

One of these times, they sat in the basement helping Derik with a storyline for a movie he was making. Much had since happened to the friends that has yet to be told. The parents had gone to bed, and the group decided to take a break for some drinks. Zeb went ahead of the others, and when they reached the kitchen, Zeb was nowhere to be seen. Derik filmed as he joined in the search. They searched the family room. Nothing. They went through the side doorway of the kitchen, into the dining room. He was not here. They walked through this room and into the living room. He was not here either. They began to walk down the hallway, past the other kitchen doorway, when Derik felt a hand grab him from behind. He wheeled around with a cry, nearly dropping the camera, and there in front of him stood Zeb. Zeb did not seem to understand why they were startled to see him there, not realizing that, in their perception, he had just appeared out of nowhere.

Another time, Aaron, who had recently seen the face come to life on the wall and was presently unable to remember this, was the one acting oddly. He begged to use Derik's camera, but his reasons were unclear. The others were very cautious of him as they watched him reached for the device like someone in a drunken stupor. He chuckled, and tried again, but Derik would not let him have it. After a while, his behavior became annoying, so he allowed him to use it for a moment only. He immediately ran with it into the basement and began to record. He walked over to the wall on which the pale face of Frankie was painted, and pointed the camera right at it, documenting it and creating a piece of footage that would never be forgotten.

Aaron had no memory of doing this, afterward, and the others were sure that something had possessed him. They did not mention this to him, and it was much later, after Derik had put the footage on a disk, when Aaron saw the footage for himself. He could hardly believe what he was seeing on the screen. It was his voice without a doubt, though it seemed to quiver with fear. And he said something during the documentation that simply wasn't true. "It's been here my whole life," he said as he aimed the camera. Perhaps in his delirium he simply got his facts mixed up. The truth would never be known.

Ironically enough, one of the most visual of these occurrences was only on video and was never experienced first-hand. The four stood in the basement, in different spots, as they listened to something strange and faint. Derik document-ed the entire event, panning this way and that, moving from person to person as each reacted in his own way. He now fo-cused the camera on Aaron, though Aaron was not aware of this. Derik watched as he seemed to just stand there. But in the playback, it was quite obvious that his body had lifted off the floor at least several inches, then slowly returned to the ground. Aaron had a hard time admitting it. He did not like the thought that his very body was performing anomalous feats... but he also realized that it only occurred in the play-back, so perhaps it was some unnatural thing outside of him which had altered the footage. Hopefully, he thought, it was not revealing some truth to which ordinary sight was blind.

Yet another time, Derik's camera was recording as Aa-ron was again acting strange. Aaron suddenly became very impatient when waiting for the others to come with him into the basement for they had planned to play a videogame there. He stood up, and briskly walked to the top of the steps alone. Greg, taking notice of his strange behavior, went after him, and grabbed him by the shirt as he began to descend. But Aa-ron's legs kept moving, like a robot, and walked right off the steps while Greg continued to hold on tight. Aaron fell back-ward, spilling a drink he held in his hand all over himself and all over the steps, and tumbled nearly all the way down the steps.

Derik's camera managed to capture only the aftermath and recorded while Aaron suddenly rose from his crippled state. He rose steadily, then moved with intent into the dark-ness of the basement, mumbling something no one could hear. Derik followed with the camera, and found Aaron facing the wall in the back corner. Suddenly Aaron cried out, grasping his back, and fell to the floor. The others raced over to check on him, and he said his back was in horrible pain but did not know why. He had no memory of his attempt, nor of his fall. All he knew was the great pain in his back which, unbeknownst to him, would carry on for many years. These occasions of falling into a fugue state proved nothing and favored no particular theory.

# CHAPTER THIRTEEN

## Voices of Fear

The landline phone had recently become the favored place for the burgeoning Tryst to reveal itself. At Aaron's it had long since been a 'troubled' device, groaning with static now and again, and even making calls when it shouldn't. In addition to the static, strange and disturbing noises would be heard occasionally. These seemed to become more numerous, starting with the time Greg heard his name being called. Since that time there had been an plethora of noises – some recurring, some unique, and most being heard only on the other end.

A faint scream or whine was one that had become nearly expected and lasted for the better part of year. Now and again there was a noise that seemed to play on the fears of those who heard it. Some of these sounded like animal noises, like apes or wildcats, but one could only wonder what the true source was. Some were the noises of a party, such as party whistles or a celebration like that which had involved Aaron's double. Still others were subtle and industrial, almost like what would also be heard during the night. A particularly unnerving noise was one Derik first heard and was later confirmed by Greg. It was the sound of a broken music box, randomly plucking its discordant notes. This was the same noise that Greg had heard in Aaron's room, only much louder now and they couldn't help but wonder if it was the very box Zeb had heard at his aunt's. But none of these, aside from the times when a double would be heard, suggested the presence of a will or mind. This did not happen until now, when Derik talked to Aaron over the phone one night.

Greg had recently told Derik about his and Aaron's experience with the face on the wall. Derik wanted to learn for himself how much Aaron had forgotten.

"So you didn't see what Greg saw?" he asked him.

"That's right. I didn't see a thing," Aaron said. But Greg had told Derik that he *had* seen something...

"I thought you saw someone sitting in a chair?" Derik asked.

"No, I may have dreamt something like that..." Aaron said. But Aaron now remembered something more. "That's funny you ask, though, because I do remember now that there was someone sitting in a chair, staring at the wall... It was me!" But Aaron still had no memory of ever seeing a shadowed face. "After listening to Greg's account, I had to go and see for myself... I had to see if it would show itself to me. I went into the basement, pulled a chair up to the wall, and sat there waiting. Nothing ever showed up." Derik just listened, amazed at the story Aaron's mind had fabricated. Aaron sounded like he truly believed what he was saying. He guessed it was repression rather than simple denial. Aaron changed the subject. "While you're on winter break, maybe you should start reading the bonus Chapters of the Book. Zeb's nearly done. It's incredible, to say the least. There are ties to events from early chapters that you would never guess."

"Yeah, maybe I should... I can probably make it this weekend," Derik said. He heard a loud metallic bang over the phone as he spoke. "What was that?" he asked.

A strange voice, deep and obscured by static, answered. "*IT IS WHAT IT IS*," the voice declared. Derik's heart nearly leapt from his chest, then dropped into his stomach, only to be caught be a tight knot forming there.

"...Aaron?" Derik hesitantly asked.

"*WHAT?*" the strange voice said, as if it were itself Aaron. The whole time Aaron was hearing only static.

"Oh my God..." Derik said. His heart raced with adrenaline now; his eyes moistened with dread. The static now stopped and Aaron heard a much-distressed Derik.

"Derik! What's wrong? What just happened?!" he cried. Derik could barely speak, but after a minute or two of rest, managed to explain.

"It was speaking to me, Aaron..." Derik choked. "It was even trying to take your place..."

"I can't believe this... You say it sounded nothing like me... This is the only case of a voice speaking to us that is not some twin of ours," Aaron said. "It is an outside entity..."

"There's another thing too," Derik began softly. "What it said... It's exactly what my art teacher has been saying to the whole class all semester... It's what he says when trying to explain the essence of an object of art..."

"Weird..." Aaron said. "So it was definitely meant for you: Only you would be able to find meaning in this." The two were not in the mood to speak of lighter matters. They simply confirmed the plans for the weekend and left it at that.

The last holiday season Aaron and Zeb would spend at the house was now over, and the only cause for celebration was Derik and Greg being on winter break. Derik came over early, for he was already planning a video project for his next semester and wanted to get some video footage of the woods near Attica Drive.

It was a sad time for this, and this was reflected in Derik's finished project. A large section of the woods had been deforested, and Derik documented this as Aaron lamented the loss.

"The hardest part is admitting that I'm powerless against this," he began. "This is where the Kentucky property comes in: It will be the one place where we can make sure this never happens. We can make it our world – a reflection of our ideals." Then Aaron took Derik to the stone which bore the word 'IF'. Aaron explained his belief before the camera that the stone was somehow tied to the life of the forest, and then showed to Derik and the future audience that a spike had been driven into the top of the stone, splitting it right between its two inscriptions. "'IF' has been attacked, and so have the woods. Soon they will all be gone, nothing more than a memory." Numerous videos would be created by Derik in this theme.

When they returned after twilight, they beheld the full moon rising from the east. They climbed the hill up toward Aaron's house, and then sat as they watched the moon glowing through the branches of the willow that grew in the front yard. Derik filmed this last scene, then followed Aaron into the house. There he met someone who had until now only been a picture in his head: Lars.

Zeb and Lars came running out of the house, passing Aaron and Derik. They were laughing together, Lars nearly in tears. "We just scared Greg so bad!" he laughed, with a flash of his blue eyes, revealing a wildness that had served him well over the years. Zeb nodded with amusement, though there was an air of distress in his face.

"What??" Aaron asked, walking back out onto the porch. He wondered why Zeb was acting again. And had he just seen a wink?

"Greg just called," Zeb said. "Lars picked up and Greg didn't recognize the voice...Then Lars started saying all kind of wacky things and Greg didn't know what was going on! Isn't that what you said, Lars?" Zeb asked, laughing.

"Yeah! I just kept saying 'hello? Hello? Hello?' over and over! He thought it was so weird!" Lars was cracking himself up. "Then the phone rang again. Zeb picked up this time and it was Greg again, like I thought it would be. I kept pretending to be some kind of crazy person. God, it was hilarious! Greg was scared out of his mind!" Aaron laughed along, but wondered why Zeb was laughing, as did Derik. They looked at each other questioningly.

"Greg's coming over here now," Zeb said. "We can't let him know..." Derik was perplexed. It was as if Zeb was essentially the person he had once thought Aaron to be - a jokester and nothing more. It didn't make sense, and he nor Aaron had any idea what to think.

"I don't know," Aaron said. "That's pretty mean..."

"No, we've got to keep it between us, until tomorrow at least," Lars said. "Now, I gotta split!" He ran down to his car and went home. The others went inside.

"What was that all about?" Aaron asked his brother.

"Let's go in the basement..." Zeb said, now very serious. "Something strange has happened." To the basement they went. Derik now noticed that the concrete floor had been carpeted.

"My parents are making little changes to increase the value of the house," Aaron explained. "This house has only monetary value to them now." Derik allowed an ironic grin.

"How are we supposed to know if there's portals under there now?!" They laughed, now taking their seats at the bar. Now Derik found a message on his cellphone. It was from Greg. The message was very urgent.

'...you have to get out of that house, Derik! It's dangerous... Something strange is happening...' then there was silence. But the message was not over. '*Hello? Hello? Hello?*' Greg's voice said in a strange and nasal tone. Derik put the phone down.

"I'm going to call Greg and tell him it was just a joke," Derik said. "It sounds like he's losing it." Aaron nodded.

"Wait!" Zeb said. "You have not let me explain... It was no joke and I believe an anomaly has occured... Greg may be justified in fearing this house..." Derik's face contorted.

"But you and Lars... you were both laughing... You two played a trick on him!" Derik said, growing frustrated, for it seemed so obvious.

"No, Derik. What you saw was me acting in front of Lars. You see, there's something you need to know about him," Zeb began. "I'll tell you the same thing I've told Greg in the past. Now, Lars is my friend and I don't wish to cast him in too poorly a light, but I'll tell you this much: he has always tried gaining my favor and he's known to, well, bend the truth at times in pursuit of this. Over the years I've learned that he could probably be considered a pathological liar, though it's always been more or less harmless... Still, it bothered me a lot and it is for this reason that I stopped talking to him for the longest time..." Aaron nodded, for he already knew this, but he still did not understand where Zeb was going with this. "Greg called two times. The first time, I didn't pick up, and I'm not exactly sure what happened. I'll explain more about this in a moment. When Greg called again, I answered the phone. Greg was telling me that he had just called, but someone strange had answered, and just kept saying 'hello? hello? hello?', like that, in a nasal voice. Then, even while I was speaking with him, he said he was hearing strange voices, overlapping even, in the background. I told him Lars was with me, and that he may have heard Lars speaking in the background, but he would not accept this as an explanation... He said he was coming anyway and would be here before long."

"What about this message, then?" Derik asked. "And still, you were acting as if you knew it was Lars..."

"I don't know what Greg's message is about, but I haven't finished explaining yet..." Zeb said, standing from the stool. "After Greg hung up, I asked Lars about the first call." He paced now, clearly agitated. "I approached him as if he had played some trick. I could tell that he didn't know what I was talking about, but he took the blame anyway, for glory's sake, if you understand." Derik still seemed confused, for he did not know Lars so well.

"Yeah..." Aaron said. "Lars was probably just using the situation to gain your favor. He probably didn't do *anything*. It's just hard to believe someone could use a situation like that without reflecting on the situation itself. I mean, wouldn't he wonder what Greg was talking about?"

"You would think so, but this is Lars we're talking about," Zeb said, as he analyzed his idea of Lars's personality. "He already believes in ghosts, for one thing, and secondly, if he believes it will make for a good laugh or impress me somehow, then this would be his first priority. The implications may not even occur to him."

"I can see what you mean now..." Aaron sighed. "So Greg was hearing things even as you spoke to him?"

"Yeah... When I told Lars that he really was hearing

things, he figured Greg was simply paranoid, and insisted on taking credit for it. That's why he took off so fast. He probably either forgot that Greg knew he was with me and thought that if Greg saw him there, it would spoil the 'joke', or just did it to make you guys think Greg didn't know he was with me."

"I don't know... This is all so crazy," Derik sighed. "He really goes out of his way like that?... Doesn't even bother him that something weird was actually going on...?"

"I just wonder now if Greg is coming," Aaron said. But just then Hazel began to bark upstairs, and someone came through the door. After a few seconds, Greg came trampling down the steps.

"Hey, nice carpet," he said. He did not seem troubled in the least bit. Now no one knew what to think.

"Greg... Is everything okay?" Derik asked.

"Sure. Why?" Greg asked. Zeb slumped in the bar stool. "Oh boy," he said.

"What's going on, guys?" Greg asked. After a moment in meditation, they did their best to explain the whole story.

"I even have a message from you on my phone," Derik said. He flipped open his phone. "Oh no... It's gone..."

"I never left you a message, Derik," Greg said. The others stared at him, speechless. Then he smiled. "Just kidding!" he said, and they all breathed a sigh of relief. "It was just a joke, Derik. I don't know how the message vanished..."

"Maybe you should be more careful," Aaron said.

"Yeah," Greg sighed. "I don't know what happened, but I know it wasn't Lars." But the problems were not yet over.

Again, the phone rang. There was a phone right by the bar. Zeb picked up. To his surprise it was functioning like a normal phone now, for on the other end was a friend he shared with Lars who was looking to make plans for the evening. Zeb covered the mouthpiece and whispered to the others.

"It's a friend of Lars's," he told them. "The reason Lars came over in the first place is that he and this friend of ours want me to come over to watch some Pay-Per-View fight..." He closed his eyes, concealing what was probably an eye-roll. "That's all they ever talk about..." He uncovered the mouthpiece and conversed with his friend. But as they spoke of mundane things, his friend's voice cut out, and suddenly there was a voice saying something familiar. Zeb nearly dropped the phone, then called the others over to listen.

"*Hello? Hello? Hello? Hello? Hello?*" a nasal voice kept repeating. Suddenly Zeb's friend's voice came back.

"Oh there you are...What happened?" Zeb asked him. He was told that his own voice had cut out. They resumed their conversation, but then, several minutes later, the voice of his friend again cut out, and now something even stranger was heard. Again, Zeb called the others over to verify what he was hearing. Everyone was in agreement: it was Beethoven's Ninth. It was a poor recording, however, like those which are heard when being put on hold by a customer-care department. The music played on and on, and eventually Zeb, figuring it was now an endless loop, hung up the phone. Moments later it rang again, and Zeb once more went off-hook. There was a strange static, whining and whirring, with muffled words heard at times. Zeb hung the phone back up. Soon it rang again. Now Mr. and Mrs. Eldritch had grown angry, and Aaron's father came down the steps.

"Who keeps calling!?" he shouted. He walked over to the bar-phone and picked up. There was nothing but silence. "Pranksters..." he said, returning upstairs. The phone rang no more. Everybody looked at each other in wonder and fear.

"Rare are the times when our own house receives such disturbing calls," Zeb observed. "Usually it happens on the other end... Why the sudden change?" They pondered this in silence.

When it was still early enough, they had Derik begin his reading of the new Chapters. He immediately picked up on the mystery-like approach of the new story and was impressed with how it succeeded in maintaining the macabre atmosphere from the original Book. Horror would evidently continue to be found within its newest pages.

It was again time to bunk in Zeb's room. This time, Greg considered sleeping in the family room. "What do you

think, Derik? It might prove to be more restful," Greg suggested. Derik shuddered.

"No, I don't think I can... I'm beginning to understand
why Zeb fears this room so much..." Derik said. Greg sighed.

"Well, I'm certainly not sleeping out here alone," he
said, and followed the others into Zeb's room. They had
thought ahead this time and brought up the sleeping gear earlier. But Derik had forgotten a pillow. They had already shut
the door.

"There's one in my room, Derik," Aaron said. But Greg
had something more to say.

"Wait," he said. "We need a pass code. Two fast knocks
followed by a third one a few seconds later. Remember that
before you enter, or you'll be locked out."

"I guess it has come to that," Derik sighed. He left the
room, and Aaron locked the door behind him. After a few moments, the doorknob rattled.

"The pass code," Greg said. "We're waiting." But there
were no knocks. Greg leaned over the railing, looking at Aaron
who sat on his sleeping bag. "He's not giving the pass code,
that fool... He should know better than to goof off." Then, the
door suddenly opened, and in walked a figure with a large,
cumbersome object for a head. It was Derik, tilting his pillow-
covered head from side to side. The others shrieked in fear, as
Derik pulled the pillow off, laughing. The others saw nothing
funny. Aaron knew that Derik was imitating a character from
the Scary Book, and it made him nervous. He failed to realize,
however, what Greg found so upsetting.

"How did you get in here?!" Greg gasped. "That door
was locked!"

"No, it wasn't," Derik argued. "At least, not before I
opened it. I watched it unlock. One of you guys must have let
me in." They shook their heads.

"No, I was closest and did nothing of the kind. I simply
waited to hear the pass-code," Aaron said. Greg confirmed
this.

"Just like the time you came barging in here, Aaron,"
Greg said in disgust. "That lock lets anyone in who wishes to

enter!" This seemed irrefutable. And it was deeply disturbing. They had locked the door so many times... and now they knew that it could have opened at any time. Aaron locked the door again anyway. Derik lay next to Aaron, and Greg settled himself in the top bunk. Zeb turned off the light.

It did not take long for the room to become 'active'. The scratching at the headboard was soon present, and then something was tossed across the room. Even with the light on, the object could not be found. They were again in darkness. It remained peaceful for perhaps fifteen minutes. "I guess the worst is over," Aaron said, but even as he said this everyone heard a loud trampling of quick footfall from what sounded like the cellar stairs. Such a stampede it was, that it could be felt through the floorboards, as though an army of children had beset the home.

"You spoke too soon," Zeb said. The irony of the timing could not be denied, and it made them sick. It had to be done intentionally, they thought. But what did it mean to say this? If there were indeed beings using the staircase, did it mean that they all had super-sensitive hearing, and were waiting for such a comment to be made? This seemed silly. Perhaps some greater will could decide when such beings would manifest... or perhaps the beings did not exist in any objective sense at all - perhaps they were placed there to be heard for no other reason than to be ironic. This thought was indeed nauseating. In any case, it was only the beginning of a night-long session of scampering and tramples. Some were shorter, some quieter. Some consisted of many more legs than others, and some were even heard on the rooftop, but all were equally bothersome.

Derik kept the camera close by him all night, and even had it recording at times. But the camera saw nothing in the darkness, and the noises must have been too faint for the microphone to pick up, for nothing of interest was in the playback the next day.

The next day would involve further video recording. Derik arranged a set, of sorts, in the back room; the 'den', everybody called it. He found the colors and lighting in the room to be particularly interesting. The walls were covered in soft, pink wallpaper with subtle designs. Two windows were on the wall opposite the door. Facing southeast, these windows let in intense sunlight when the sky was clear and the sun had not yet passed over the house. Such it was on this day.

There were two small, wooden artist's mannequins standing on Aaron's desk, normally used to aid an artist in rendering images of the human body. One stood roughly eight inches high, while the other stood only three or four. Derik grabbed the larger of these and took it into the den. He set it on a dinner-TV stand and pulled a rocking chair up in front of it, facing the windows. The intense light fell upon the figure and the desk. He then proceeded to contort the figure into various positions. Aaron was with him, helping him set things up. Greg was in the family room talking to Zeb. After Derik had done some recording of the room and the wooden figurine, Aaron saw something peculiar under the room's door. It was the small mannequin, somehow wedged between the door and the wood floor. He grabbed Derik. "Did you do that?!" he asked. Derik saw it and laughed.

"No!" He was hardly afraid, probably because of the time of day. Aaron picked up the figure and placed it back on his desk where it belonged. He gave it a wary look, then returned to the den with Derik. He would keep his eye out on it from now on. Derik finished his filming, and the rest of the day went without incident.

It was not until Derik and Greg were back in school that Aaron's house again found itself in the world of the Bizarre, if it had ever left. This time, it tried to take Greg with it, and it was a sure sign of a malevolent will.

Greg's home phone rang one Saturday afternoon. It rang perhaps three times, before he could get to it. When he picked up, he heard only a dial tone, as if a call was never made. Yet the caller-ID showed that a call had indeed been made, from Aaron's house no less. Greg shrugged, and began to walk away. The phone rang once more now. Greg was still close to the phone and walked over to see who was calling. It was from Aaron's house again. He picked up, guessing that Aaron had tried calling the first time but somehow got disconnected. Yet once again, he heard nothing more than a dial tone. Whoever was calling had to be watching him, to know when to hang up just as Greg would pick up the phone. Yet the calls were coming all the way from Aaron's... Now Greg became uneasy. He considered calling back but hesitated. He stared at the handset for time, deliberating. Then he picked it up and dialed.

The phone rang a few times only to end with the familiar 'call error' tone. Strange, he thought. He was positive he had dialed the right number. He listened in as the typical pre-recorded female voice explained the nature of the error. "*The number you have dialed...*" the voice began, and then repeated the number he had dialed. Oddly, it was the correct number, as he had guessed. The voice continued. "*...is no longer of this world.*" Greg could hardly believe what he heard, and wondered if he had heard something wrong. But the message repeated. He had heard correctly. The voice said many other things that these kinds of recordings would never say, but Greg was so horrified that he forgot most of it immediately. Thus, little can be documented here, but one more thing the voice said remained with him. After giving some warning whose specific details Greg has forgotten, the voice suddenly ridiculed him. "*But I'm sure you'll be coming here anyway,*" the voice said sinisterly, apparently humored with itself, for Greg thought he had heard a little chuckle. It then said several things, attempting to entice Greg into coming to the house. Greg simply held the phone and listened, hanging up when the initial message began repeating over and over.

Greg was so disturbed by the call that he refused to believe it was a message from the 'other side'. As much as he hated to, he blamed Aaron, for he hated this other thought even more. The next day he called Aaron and cut right to the chase with his accusations.

"I don't know how you did it, Aaron, but I know it was

you," he said. Aaron could only imagine what had just happened to Greg that had him accusing him once again.

"What do you mean, Greg? What happened now?" he asked. But Greg was angry and wanted to hear nothing of this.

"Don't play dumb, Aaron..." Greg began. "You know what I'm talking about... The call-error message yesterday... the mocking voice, which, by the way, was obviously fake... telling me your house was dangerous, and in another world... and then trying to get me over there... Why don't you just tell me why you want me over there so badly?" Aaron didn't know what to say. He was exhausted of defending himself.

"Greg, please... It wasn't me... I really want to know what happened..." Aaron said. Greg's anger began to fade, but the memory of the experience was still too disturbing to accept.

"I can only wonder how you did it," Greg said. "...I keep forgetting that you don't have caller ID..."

"You don't have to wonder, because it wasn't me," Aaron insisted. "If you remember, I was working overtime yesterday... I wasn't even home..." Greg was not listening.

"You must have some high-tech computer software or something..." Greg rationalized.

Aaron gave up.

"Yeah... I guess..." he said. He was greatly disappointed in Greg. But he wasn't going to try to cover anything up. He would let Greg think whatever he wanted and leave it up to him to figure things out on his own. The accusations frustrated him, but they also made him sad, sadder than he had been in previous times. It seemed that no matter what he did, he could not keep his friends from losing trust in him. The preternatural influence that first seemed like loving aid now seemed to have revealed its ugly nature - that of mockery and violence.

"It's good to hear you admit it for once," Greg continued. He felt himself powerful and was taking advantage of this state of mind.

"Sure..." Aaron sighed.

"Well, take care then, Aaron," Greg said, spitefully. "I hope we can trust each other next time." He hung up the phone. He felt good to get it off his chest, but his anger toward Aaron immediately began to fade as he recalled the horror of the experience. He began to wonder if he should not have acted so fast in accusing Aaron... There would have been cause for this only if there was evidence that he was to blame, but there wasn't... He had told Aaron it sounded fake, yet he now remembered that it was this very characteristic – the mocking voice that other phone recordings lack – which made it so troubling in the first place. Within his heart of hearts he knew that it was not Aaron, but a malevolent entity from another world. He now regretted having reproached Aaron as he did, having done so only out of fear, and only hoping that perhaps it may have been his doing. Regardless, he did not yet have the courage to apologize.

Aaron slumped in the recliner, still holding the phone. 'Fake?... What could have happened to him?...' Aaron wondered to himself. 'It's like something wants him to think I'm actually to blame... Why is this happening...?' He now remembered that Greg had said something about the home being dangerous and being trapped in another world... A dread filled his heart, and he began to panic. Was he in grave danger? Why did Greg have to be so presumptuous?! Aaron thought, angry himself now. Then he had an idea. He called Derik.

"What's up?" Derik asked. He detected fear in Aaron's voice.

"Listen... Something horrible happened to Greg..." Aaron began. "He's okay, just flustered. It was apparently an encounter in Tryst, and he's blaming me..."

"Well, was it you?" Derik asked.

"No!" Aaron cried in frustration. "But it's like something wants him to think it's me... This would be a bad enough problem, even without the apparent danger I'm in..."

"What do you mean?" Derik asked. Aaron recounted what he could remember of what Greg told him. Derik groaned in despair.

"Yeah, I know..." Aaron said. "The experience itself sounds disturbing enough... but do you understand the implications? The voice told him my house is dangerous! It said something about it being in another world... I can barely maintain my composure, Derik!" This was quite evident.

"I don't know how to help..." Derik said.

"I need to find out more," Aaron said with a quivering voice. "I need to know how great of a danger I'm in... I'm sure Greg knows more but he won't tell me because he thinks it was my doing... Derik..."

"Go on, Aaron. I'm listening... Just hang in there..." Derik said.

"I want you to try and learn more from him... Don't tell him I sent you, or he may not answer," Aaron explained. "Try to elicit it out of him, and come back to me with the details... I need to know as soon as possible... It may be that I should have already fled this house..."

"Alright... I can do that," Derik said. Aaron gave a sigh of relief.

"Thanks... I'll be waiting," he said. But Derik would not play this game. He risked the chance of Greg remaining silent, and simply confronted Greg, over the phone, with the truth.

"Greg," Derik began, "Aaron is deeply frightened... He is ready to flee his house..."

"I think maybe he should," Greg responded. It was obvious now that Greg had accepted the experience for what it was, and this relieved Derik. But it was not good news for Aaron.

"He told me what happened to you, and feels like he is facing a great danger, and facing it alone, since you accuse him," Derik explained. Greg sighed.

"I'm sorry..." Greg said. "I never wanted that to happen..."

"He wanted me to learn from you whether or not he was in grave danger, and do this without letting you know that he spoke to me..." Derik said.

"You never listen to him," Greg laughed.

"I just have better judgment sometimes," Derik said. "He needs to learn still that telling the truth is the best way of doing things."

"I just can't believe what I was hearing... There is no

doubt in my mind now that at least one evil spirit is present within that house," Greg said. "And that, coupled with your recent experience on the phone..."

"I know," Derik said. "It'll be even harder going back to his house now... But tell me, so that might at least provide Aaron some direction: Is he in great danger? Should he flee?"

"I don't know," Greg replied softly. "It might not be a bad idea... If I were him, I probably would, but he'll be moving before too long anyway, when the house is sold."

"I guess that's true," Derik sighed.

"The message told me that at the moment of my call, the house was no longer of this world..." Greg remembered aloud. "This doesn't necessarily mean it's permanently left, though... Perhaps it is safe again, if you were able to talk to him over the phone."

"I heard a few noises, but nothing major," Derik said.

"Then tell him there's definitely something wrong, but that there's no more urgency to flee now than there already was," Greg said. "On second thought, I'll talk to him myself... I need to apologize."

Aaron had begun his work week at the industrial park when Greg called him. It was Monday evening. Aaron was tired, too tired to argue. He was worried for Greg, and himself, and held no grudge. "You okay?..." he asked Greg.

"Yeah..." Greg answered. "Let me apologize for the things I said yesterday... I knew it wasn't you... I was trying to convince myself of this, because it was so absurd... It won't happen again."

"All is forgiven," Aaron said. "It's hard to believe myself, what few things you said..."

"There really isn't much more to say...I forgot so much because I was so scared that I could barely pay attention...I remember the things pertaining to me most clearly..." Greg explained. He recounted the experience as best as he could remember. Some things that he had told Aaron only yesterday he had already forgotten, and Aaron reminded him of these things. Unfortunately, many details were still lost in the past.

"You should consider getting out of there as soon as you can," Greg suggested.

"I probably should," Aaron sighed. "But this house will be sold before long, and I'll be leaving whether I want to or not... My parents found a possible buyer already."

"Really?" Greg said, quite surprised. It was finally hitting home that his friend would not be around much longer. "It's all happening so fast..."

"I know... It's hard to imagine calling any other place my home. It will be tough," Aaron sighed. They were silent for some time. Then Greg made a suggestion.

"You should also consider having the house blessed, before you move out," he said.

"I don't know," Aaron began. "First, I'm not sure we're even dealing with spirits, let alone evil spirits. But the main reason is timing."

"Huh?" Greg asked. It was timing, he thought, that made it a good suggestion.

"My parents need to sell this house... They can't take any chances of people finding out about what has happened here... It could prove detrimental to their efforts."

"I see..." Greg sighed. They were silent again for some time.

"Things have changed so much these past couple of years," Greg commented. "For such a long time it just seemed like a fun thing to do, going over there... Always playing D & D, talking about Tolkien... I mean, it was you guys that got me into all that... And then it became so horrible... Ever since you got me reading the Scary Book... It changed everything... I sometimes wish we had never picked it up."

Aaron sighed. "Maybe we wouldn't have if it hadn't been given to us with such desperation. We didn't exactly want to take it that day, but by the time I knew what was happening it was in my hands and I couldn't bring myself to throw it away without at least skimming through it."

"I don't know... I guess it's true you couldn't have predicted the impact it would have on us all."

"Maybe if we all put in enough effort we can try and

have more positive moments," Aaron suggested. "Start making more trips into the woods again. Or hell, plan a trip out of state somewhere!"

"I don't see why it can't happen," Greg agreed. "We could start trying right now, even."

"You want to do something this weekend, then?" Aaron asked.

"Sure," Greg answered. "I'll see if Derik can hitch a ride with me."

"I thought he was spending the weekend with Tiffany?"

"Oh, she dumped him," Greg said. "Apparently overheard him talking to his friends about the 'crazy tryst' he was involved in and went bonkers. Nothing he said made a difference, he tells me."

"A shame," Aaron lamented. "She seemed nice. Well I'll be glad to see both of you, then. Call me when you're headed this way."

"Sure thing."

While Greg and Derik still had a bit of free time to spare – as single life now allowed – they would visit Aaron whenever they could. It would be hard, with their fear now greater than ever. They knew, however, that time was running out, and that they should cherish each visit as much as possible. No matter what they did, however, and no matter what attitude they attempted to adopt, the Scary Book would work itself into either their activities or conversations. Free will was a complicated thing it seemed.

Free will seemed mostly irrelevant to the quality of the visits for other reasons too. It usually happened that only one of them at a time would be able to work it into their schedule and coordinating these get-togethers was becoming increasingly difficult. One day in late winter, Aaron learned this would again be the case.

"So you won't be able to make it then..." Aaron sighed. "It's going to take you a while to finish the Chapters."

"Yeah..." Derik sighed, though he was in fact glad to take a break. He was to be participating in some medieval-themed live-action role-playing with some college friends that weekend and was very excited to get his mind of his recent breakup. Aaron figured as much but didn't want to mention Tiffany more than he had to.

While considering this and still listening to Derik with the phone against his ear, he noticed something peculiar in his bedroom. Sometimes he would put his wooden figures in different positions. This time he did not remember having positioned them in the way they now were. The larger of the two was lying flat on the desk, with an arm outstretched toward his coin-container. The smaller one, which was usually close by, was now on his dresser, positioned as if it was in the middle of a stride. He wondered if either of the guys had done it last time they were here and neglected to tell him. He considered asking Derik.

"Hey, Derik..." Aaron started, as he stared at the figurines.

"Yeah?" he responded. "What's up?"

"Never mind..." Aaron said. "It's nothing." Derik shrugged, and looked out his apartment window. He thought about the strange coincidence that he was now living in multistory apartment, just like the characters in the new Chapters... and then he heard a noise over the phone. It sounded like the squeaking of a window being wiped.

"Aaron?..." Derik started.

"Yeah?" he asked, still looking at the wooden imitators.

"I just heard something... and it's really weird..."

"Oh great... What is it?" Aaron asked. Derik explained the noise.

"And the weird thing is... I was just looking out my apartment window when it happened..." he said, his eyes beginning to water.

"My gosh..." Aaron said. "What could it mean?..." Like always, neither could answer.

They ended their conversation, and Aaron made plans with only Greg for that weekend. It would result in a confrontation with a will whose presence was more forthright than any other would ever be.

Zeb's room was crammed once again, with Greg in the top bunk and Aaron on the floor. The family had begun to pack some things up in early preparation for the move, and Zeb's room was now more cluttered than ever. They could hardly imagine what it would be like if they tried to cram Derik into the room. There was something else, too, that may have been a factor.

"Zeb..." Greg began. "Look at this picture frame hanging up... It's going behind your mirror... It's as if the room..."

"Shrank..." Zeb said, completing the thought. "I know... It seems to get a little smaller every time I come over..." He sighed. "You know, something else has been happening too," he began. Greg listened closely. "Things have begun to disappear... Some things quite important too, like the deed on some real estate I own where my parents are moving... But mostly minor things... pencils, old speakers, drawings, you get the idea..."

"He's not exaggerating," Aaron affirmed. "I was there when the deed vanished."

"Wait, you own more than your Kentucky property?" Greg asked.

"Yeah," Zeb answered. "I also own property near my mom and dad's new property. It's mainly just an investment."

"I see..." Greg said. "Strange..." They settled themselves into their beds and the light went off.

Surprisingly, this was not immediately followed by 'activity'. Instead, they rested peacefully for nearly a half hour - nearly a record-breaker. In fact, Aaron and Greg were fast asleep when they were woken by an auditory phenomenon that pierced their ears like a needle. Zeb, somehow, remained unconscious during this; an incredible feat considering the intensity of the noise.

The noise itself would be laughable were it removed from its context, and nearly so even at this very moment. It was right at the point where one could not decide whether it was comical or horrific. But these listeners were themselves not yet understanding it within the larger context, for there was still more to come.

In any case, what woke Aaron and Greg up could only be described as an electronic tune, like those made by synthesizers, and wildly off-key. It burst into their awareness with awesome might, like angels breaking through the heavens. The discord became apparent almost immediately, crushing their hearts and stealing their strength. Still, the music was so proclamatory and magnificent, that it seemed its purpose could be nothing less than serving as a glorious harbinger of the coming of some being deserving of such perverse heraldry. And as suddenly as it began, the song ended.

Aaron flipped on the light during this, making comment of his dismay even as the song-like noise continued. To their amazement and disgust, Zeb continued sleeping. Aaron shoved him.

"Zeb!... You just slept through one of the worst things ever!" Aaron cried. Zeb mumbled and rolled over, paying Aaron no heed. Aaron gave up. Sometimes Zeb would get like this, and there was nothing that could be done to change it, even if the others refused to believe that this aloofness was inconsequential.

"I wonder if it's all because of him..." Greg muttered, watching him. "Always sleeping through things... We might just be living his nightmare, like the characters in the Book..." Aaron just sighed, flicking the light switch off. But now there would be no peace, for a ruckus was suddenly heard in the basement. "Greg, I'm going to use your idea," Aaron said. He flipped on the light again and opened the door.

"What do you think you're doing?!" Greg cried, as Zeb moaned in fear.

"I'm getting the tape recorder," Aaron said. The last time Greg visited he had suggested that Aaron try using the small tape recorder to capture any occurrences or pick up anything they may have missed. Now seemed like as good at time as any, if not better. Aaron cautiously entered the hallway then slipped into his bedroom. He grabbed the tape recorder as quickly as possible, then returned. "That wasn't easy to do, by the way," Aaron said. Greg just shook his head. "Anyway, now were ready. I'll have it right by me and if anything else happens, I'll whip it out as fast as I can."

This didn't take long. The light had been off for maybe fifteen minutes, and Aaron was wondering if nothing more would happen. He hoped so, even if it meant bringing in the tape recorder for nothing. But before he or Greg fell asleep, there could now be heard a faint humming. It was coming from the basement, and almost sounded like a conversation. It was different than the muffled voices they had heard before, however. Aaron whipped out the tape player and hit the record button anyway, hoping the noise was loud enough to be picked up. It may even become louder, or other noises might follow, he thought. But neither of these happened. The faint mumbling went on for maybe a minute and could no longer be heard.

Aaron hit the stop button. He flipped on the light. "I doubt it picked anything up," he told Greg.

"Probably not. Let's hear it anyway," Greg said, leaning over the rail. Aaron rewound the tape and hit play. He had gone too far, ending up in the last entry of the Study.
"That's the Study," Aaron said. He let it play softly, since it was near the end, and the next recording would follow immediately. "The recording should be coming up now..."

And then it came.

First there was a crackling static. "I wonder if I had the mic's sensitivity too high?" Aaron said. "It sounds like sheets rustling..." But Greg knew that there had been absolute silence aside from what Aaron was attempting to record. A knot formed in his stomach as he felt a feeling of dread come over him. Then, after several seconds of crackling, a deep and staticky voice was heard speak amidst it.

"*I...*" the voice began. Aaron shrieked, and out of some reflex stopped the tape. His hands began shaking. Greg's face had lost all color.

"We need to get Zeb up for this!" he said, leaping out of the bunk and giving Zeb several shoves. He saw to it that Zeb would wake this time, and he did.

"What is it?" Zeb asked tiredly.

"Put your glasses on, Zeb," Greg told him. "We have a big problem."

"What?" Zeb asked, putting on his glasses as Greg commanded. "What's the problem?"

"I brought this tape recorder in here, while you were asleep, because we were hearing things, and we were going to try and record some of it," Aaron said, beginning to hyperventilate. "I tried recording something, b-but..."

"But something else ended up on the tape," Greg said grimly. "We just started listening to it, but Aaron stopped it short. Go ahead, Aaron, play the rest." Aaron hesitated for a moment, then hit play. The crackling static was immediately heard, and Zeb looked at the others in horror. The voice was heard again, still speaking amidst the static.

"..... *am* ................. *I*................... *am* ..................... *I AM!* ..................... *I* ................ *am* .............. *I am!* ............ ..................... *You* .................... *you* ..................... *you*........ ............ *you* ....." Now a horrible and loud static, like that of poor transmission, was heard over the crackling, and amidst all of this the voice said one final word. "...........*Wendell*.........." and it was at this point that Aaron had stopped recording, having no longer heard the faint conversation from the basement. It was also at this point where everyone gasped with terror. Now there was total silence, as everyone stood speechless. Aaron was rubbing his face.

"Yeah, I just pulled a jaw muscle on that one." But no one cared about that right at the moment.

"...Does everybody agree that the voice said 'Wendell'?!" Greg stammered. Aaron shakily nodded. Zeb shook his head in disbelief.

"It indeed spoke that name," he said.

"Play it again, Aaron," Greg said. Aaron's shaky hands held the tape player away from him.

"No!.... I... can't!" Aaron cried. "I can't hear that again!"

"We need to hear it again..." Greg said. "We need to hear it from start to finish." Aaron finally complied, and he replayed it. Nothing had changed – the paranormal record was there to stay. No one could believe what they now had on tape. Now they would try to understand what this was.

"Zeb... you have never mentioned Wendell's fate... Aaron told Derik and I, but you never would... What do you know?" Greg asked.

"Only what is recorded on that tape," Zeb said, pointing to the recorder. "And the one thing I failed to mention in the Study... Wendell's encounter with the Shadow Man..."

"You say he went into your basement and never came back?" Greg asked, still shaking horribly.

"Yeah..." Zeb sighed.

"And he's dead? Is that true...?" Greg asked.

"That's what I heard, but I've not confirmed it with his family," Zeb said. "Death by suicide is what Lars heard through the grapevine. A note was even found, mentioning 'leaving this world' and that sort of thing. I've tried to be respectful to his memory and not speak much of this.

"If that is true, it looks like Wendell is still among us," Greg said. "As a spirit. And you know what the Church says about the fate of a soul that chooses this path..."

"Stop it, Greg..." Aaron muttered.

"I don't see that as directly evident from what this voice has told us," Zeb said.

"How can it not follow?" Greg asked, now stubborn to deny this horrible possibility.

"First, the voice sounds nothing like Wendell... In fact, it almost sounds like you, Greg," Zeb began. Greg shook his head defiantly. "But mainly I say this because the voice never actually declares itself to be Wendell himself... It simply states his name..."

"Yeah, it is hard to understand the meaning of the words," Aaron said. "They're spaced so far apart... To me it almost sounds more like the voice is calling out to Wendell, rather than being the person himself."

"Whatever it is, it has a will... And it wanted to be heard," Greg said. "I wonder if we would have heard more if you had let the tape record for a longer time..."

236

"I don't know," Aaron sighed. "I get this weird feeling like it was all preordained, from my decision to get the tape player, to the moments I decided to start and stop recording... I think we heard all that we were meant to hear..."

"Yeah, I kind of feel that way, too," Greg said. "But I still think we have the voice of Wendell on that tape now."

"What about all the other words, though?" Zeb asked. "They must be equally important..."

"What was it again?" Greg asked. Aaron reminded him, as painful as it was to both of them.

"So should it be understood as 'I am', then, followed by some unfinished thought regarding us, when it kept saying 'you, you, you,'?" Aaron wondered aloud. "Or should it be understood as 'I am you'? The latter of these was actually my first impression."

"I don't know what to think," Greg said. "How could *it* be *us*? It just doesn't make sense..." Greg could not shake his belief that Wendell's spirit was among them. Even if the voice itself was not Wendell, it was still calling to him, and it would still seem that he would have to be there with them. "Let me have that tape recorder," he asked of Aaron. "I have an idea."

"What?" Aaron asked, before handing it over.

"I'm going to try to communicate with it," he replied. Aaron sighed, then gave him the device after setting it at the right spot, so as to prevent any accidental tape-overs. Greg took the player and hit the record button. His voice was recorded on the Study tape for the very first time.

"........Can you please tell us who you are again ................ Can you please tell us who you are?...... And why you're bothering us........... We just want to know............. Are you there?............ Please answer, if you're willing............" He stopped the recording. He played it back, and they listened intently, but nothing else was recorded.

"It looks like it said everything it wanted to say," Greg concluded.

"You'll never know," Zeb said, quoting Bennett, then settled back into bed. "If you don't mind, I'm going to try to get back to sleep... I'm exhausted."

"What?! How... How can you...!?" Greg stammered, but Aaron eased him.

"Let him sleep, Greg," he said. "Perhaps Zeb is not as surprised as we, for he knew Wendell personally." Zeb returned to his slumber.

"I'm going to call Derik," Greg said.

"What? Now, at this hour?" Aaron asked.

"That's right," Greg answered. He dug in his bag for his cell phone, and after retrieving it, called Derik's cell phone. It went right to voice-mail, and Greg left a message.
"Uh, Derik... It's about three in the morning... and, uh... the reason I'm calling is... we think we just figured it all out... What all of the harassment at Aaron's has been... I'll leave it at that, for now. I'll talk to you later, and God bless," Greg said, turning off his phone. He and Aaron sat and let out a heavy long breath.

"I believe your opportunity has come, my friend," Aaron told him. Greg's forehead wrinkled in worry and confusion. "To the Study. It may very well be our last chance together."
Greg let out a long and unsteady breath.

"Sure... I don't think I'll be able to be as professional sounding as you, but..."

"Don't worry about that," Aaron said, with a slight chuckle. "I'm as flustered as you... I'm sure I'll have trouble too..." he readied the tape, making sure not to record over the object of the discussion. "You ready?" he asked Greg.

"Whenever you are," Greg answered. Aaron hit the record button, and they began their discussion. First Aaron introduced Greg, then explained the cause for Greg's personal recording. This led to explaining the object of interest - the recording from 'beyond.' Now they discussed the possible meanings, as they had already done with Zeb. Greg emphasized the possibility of Wendell's spirit being the cause of the recording. He then had an insight, linking Wendell to a much broader phenomenon - that of the otherworldly 'harassments' that had been plaguing them for over a year now. "Perhaps the fate of this person, Wendell, was damnation... and it is his lingering spirit that has troubled us so many nights... I don't know what else to think... I don't suppose anything could be done about it... Aaron may have already said how any aid from the outside world may prove to be harmful to your parents' efforts in selling this house..."

"I have," Aaron said.

"I guess there's nothing that can be done, other than ignore it..." Greg sighed. Aaron also wanted to discuss the event in the context of Tryst and all the thoughts that had come up during the time of those discussions.

"This entity, this spirit, would seem to throw all the theories of the Doctor right back in his face," Aaron said. "But I remember he said that Wendell had become imbedded in a very deep and sacred stage in Tryst... Could he have simply been absorbed into something larger, I wonder? Maybe Wendell is not the sole cause of all the horrific things that have occurred here, but he is undoubtedly a major factor."

"We had been waiting for such revelations for a long time," Greg said. "Now we are finally learning more... Things truly are coming to a culmination." And soon there was little more to say. Aaron stopped the recording, they returned to their places, turned off the light, and talked about it quietly until they both fell asleep.

There was a discussion in the den the next day about the previous night's events. Aaron brought the tape recorder into the room and hit record once the discussion was well under way. Zeb's main point was that the spirit of Wendell in the house, however it got there, did not explain everything, and was more likely only a part of a greater phenomenon. This phenomenon, despite its violent tendencies and moments where fears would be played upon and minds were ridiculed, was not necessarily an evil one. It still seemed possible to him that it could be nothing more than the minds of the individuals in Tryst that created a context for the experiences. The reading of the Scary Book seemed like a major factor... Perhaps the world in this Book, the world to which they had devoted so much thought and whose intrigue often left them nauseous with angst, was what they now somehow desired... and this was being fulfilled in Tryst.

"Like the phenomena within that world, actually," Zeb began. "So many of these seem unrelated and yet we know they are all subsumed within some single Problem... Is it not the same with us?" The others waited to hear his wisdom. "The house at the end of the street and all the insanity associated with it in particular, the forest and the effects it seems to have on people... and the Shadow Man..." Greg shuddered. "And the manifold anomalies here at this house... prods, noises, portals, voices on the phone, faces on the wall, and let's not forget our nocturnal visitors that so love to party on our rooftop or in our basement... All of these things seem unrelated yet are some-how all a part of our developing relationship within Tryst..." Greg let out a long sigh.

"Shew... Then I guess we *don't* know anything..." he said, winning some ironic chuckles from the others.

"We just have to take care not to make assumptions, and be careful when trying to point to a single cause...for all we know there could be many separate causes..." The others were a bit confused now. Zeb detected this and attempted to ex-plain. "In other words, as far as this world is concerned, these different things may have separate and unrelated causes, but in the context of our relationship to the Absurd, they all serve to bring us toward one cause, one end."

"It sure sounds like a will of some kind would have to be behind all of it, guiding everything like that..." Greg said. "And I just can't help but think this will is malicious... I put my trust in God... I don't desire to be guided by a will that throws jugs, creates portals and puts faces on walls..." Zeb shook his head, but Aaron cried out. He slumped into the couch, dropping his head into his hands.

"Aaron?..." Zeb asked. Light streamed in through the windows, creating deep shadows on Aaron's despondent face. Tears glistened in his eyes as he slowly raised his head. Every-one waited.

"You were right, Greg... I... remember now.... I remem-ber everything..." Aaron said.

"What?!" Greg asked with great concern. "What did you

suddenly remember?!"

"The face... The face of evil I beheld that dreadful night..." The memory had come out of repression, as inexplicably as it had been put there. He had an idea of what triggered the memory, and nothing else. The others listened in silence as he explained. "When Greg mentioned the face... in the context of a will – that's what did it... I don't know how it brought the memory back, but it was this context that was so apparent as I looked into the face... I knew that it not merely another random aberration, even more than a nebulous consciousness creating a face to invoke fear: At that moment, I knew that I was seeing the face of the entity itself..." Greg dropped his head now.

"I never knew how to describe what I sensed... But you say it perfectly... I didn't look so deeply while it was happening. Maybe that's the only reason I was able to remember the experience... You were probably so disturbed by your realization that you were forced to forget it lest you suffer great psychological damage..."

"I don't know," Aaron sighed, wiping his face. "All I know is that there was a will behind that face, ridiculing me, and it is still present... It may not be showing itself as fully, but that face is always there on the wall, faintly... A constant reminder..."

"You see, Zeb, he had a close encounter with the entity," Greg said, rocking in the chair. He was a dark silhouette to Aaron as he sat in front of the windows.

"I don't mean to undermine his experience or challenge what he believes, but still this entity could be part of something greater..." Zeb said. "Perhaps there is some evil presence here. We can't let that stop our search for answers." Greg settled in the chair. Aaron still sat slouched, running his fingers through his ruffled hair.

"When exactly did you first notice that face?" Greg asked Zeb, squinting through his glasses. Zeb crossed his arms and looked up in thought.

"It was about twelve years ago, I guess," Zeb answered.

"Around the time of Wendell..." Greg said.

241

"Yeah, I guess around the time of his strange visit... It wasn't even me, actually, that noticed it," Zeb said. Greg looked at him in wonder, thinking Aaron must have been the one then. But Zeb surprised him. "It was Lars."

"Lars?" Greg asked, leaning back and banging into the windowsill. Aaron nodded, and sat up.

"Yeah," Zeb continued. "He first saw the smaller face below it... 'Look at that alien,' he said to me. Then we both kind of looked at the rest, and, together, saw the rest of the image," Zeb said, and the tape recorder clicked off here, having run out of space. "We could hardly believe it... It's so amazing that an image, accidentally painted, could be the representation of a person or a consciousness."

"I know," Greg said. "Did the will's coming into existence coincide with the creation of the image, I wonder, or was the will already there, and chose to be shown in such a way?"

"It's hard to say... I'm still not completely convinced that there is even consciousness in it," Zeb said, looking at Aaron. "I can understand why you would have felt that way, but I am a philosopher, and feelings don't prove anything to me... It could easily be that our own fear of the face – for it can't be denied that we already held a fear – caused it to be given life for a moment, as brief as it was. This would simply be a sign, a sign that we draw nearer to whatever it is week seek within Tryst... a way of showing us that we were right in fearing it..."

"But why would we even fear it, then?" Aaron asked. "It would be a mere coincidence that it looks like a face, nothing more. It would mean that it was mockery, what Greg and I saw, mockery of our fear."

"We really have no idea," Zeb said. "It might not be mere coincidence. There might be something fearsome within it... but it could have been something else that made the face become so visible that night...In this case, something could be mocking a legitimate fear... one fearsome entity mocking another. But there's no reason to doubt what I said earlier, either. I believe we are right in fearing it, it's just hard to say what caused the face to do what it did."

"Wow..." Greg sighed, shaking dizziness from his head.

"I don't know what to think."

"All we can do is let things happen as they will," Aaron said. "It is out of our control."

Later, Greg and Aaron were in Aaron's room, when Aaron looked at his wooden mannequins. The larger of these was positioned as if it were hiding behind the coffee can that held spare change and reaching for the top, while the other stood on the corner of the dresser, in mid-stride apparently.

"Hey, Greg," Aaron said. "Did you happen to arrange those models, as they are?" He pointed to the wooden beings. "I know you've arranged them before, but to me it seems that they had changed position some time during the week, when neither you nor Derik was here." Greg looked at the figurines then back at Aaron with an expression of caution.

"No, Aaron... I'm sorry," he said. "They seem to be moving on their own." They both laughed.

"I guess my mom moved them or something," Aaron said, and they began to leave the room. Then Greg noticed something that was new to him. On the insides of the doorway, there were large I-hooks driven into the wood, and small chains hung from them. There were four in all, two at head level, and two at waist level. He grabbed Aaron, pointing, for it seemed to have no purpose, nor had he remembered it being there.

"Don't worry, Greg," Aaron said laughing. "I had a piece of exercise equipment hooked up there a while ago. I can't remember now how it attached, but that's all it is."

"I wonder why I never saw it before...?" Greg asked himself aloud, walking out.

"I don't know," Aaron said with a shrug, and followed his friend. "I've forgotten how to know."

# CHAPTER FOURTEEN

## Remnants of Fear

Though some unexplainable events had transpired which had already left behind permanent traces, such as those that had been recorded on Derik's camera and Aaron's tape recorder, others would come whose significance lay in neither the brothers' behavior nor some ethereal voice. One of these would again be captured on camera, while the other would leave behind something more tangible. There were several interesting experiences that came shortly before and thereby created the context for the approaching Fear.

Derik sat on the floor of Aaron's family room, with the Book open in front of him. He was nearing the final chapter and was determined to finish before he would go home the next day. Night had fallen, and the windows were covered. A noise was heard now and again from somewhere close, perhaps on the deck. It was the sound of a squeak, like that of a rusty bicycle wheel. Whenever the group was silent, the noise would stop. But sure enough, whenever the reading resumed, the squeaking continued. One time, the wood stove, which stood between the recliners where Aaron and Zeb sat, rang out with a boom, as if something inside popped. It was so loud and unexpected that Aaron nearly jumped out of his chair. This had happened before, they now remembered.[5] Derik continued reading.

Nearly an hour went by uninterrupted. Zeb was falling asleep now, when suddenly the TV-dinner table that stood next to his chair suddenly rose several feet into the air, then flew several feet across the room. It landed with a crash next to Derik, who wailed in terror as he jumped away.

"What the hell just happened?!" Derik cried out. Greg simply stared at the little table lying there, and then stared at a bewildered Zeb.

"I think that table just got thrown," Zeb said, rubbing his eyes. Now he saw them staring at him, their faces bursting with fearful frustration. Everybody else already knew that it was the table that had been thrown. Aaron cured Zeb's ignorance by explaining what he could.

"I saw what happened, out of the corner of my eyes," Aaron said. "I thought it was Zeb who was getting up so I didn't look until it got thrown. When this happened, though, I realized that it was the table that rose..."

"As Derik nears the end, things keep getting worse up here... Like the night he finished the last Book, when we saw the Red Line..." Greg said. Derik nodded, pointing at him in agreement, for he was still speechless. "When we get him started on the zombie game, we should play it downstairs...

---

[5] .    This was not the only occurrence of hearing a 'squeaking' while in the family room. It actually happened on several occasions, but always in the family room, and always at night. Two other incidents in the family room are noteworthy and occurred around the same time. The more recent of these may have even occurred on the same night the TV table was thrown. An afghan, which was lain over the back of the recliner, was suddenly thrown over Aaron's head, who sat on the floor with his back to the base of the recliner. It landed in the middle of the floor in front of everybody. The earlier incident occurred when only Greg was visiting. He and Zeb sat at the table, talking, while Aaron lay on the couch, resting. Aaron left the room for a moment and when he returned, found a Cat-in-the-Hat doll (one he had known about) sitting on the floor with its back against the base of the sofa, staring at him. He asked Zeb and Greg, who remained talking and were oblivious to the doll, if it was a joke on their part. When they discovered it, they were quick to flee the room. A blanket was thrown over it, and it was later returned to the shelf where it belonged. Some time later, Aaron's mother took this doll to school to give it to one of the children but returned home still holding it. Strangely, she could not bring herself to get rid of it.

I'm beginning to think that the 'troubles' are actually worse up here."

"I've always thought that," Zeb began. "And what I fear of this room has yet to fully manifest."

"I can't think about going in the basement right now," Derik muttered. "Maybe next time."

"We're not going down now, Derik," Greg said in growing frustration. "You're not even going to finish the Book this visit."

"I don't know, I'm almost on the last chapter," Derik said. In reality, Greg was afraid that Derik would finish the Book without him, because he had to leave very early the next day.

"You don't understand how hard the reading gets in the last chapter – it's very cryptic. It requires many read-throughs to find meaning in it," he said, now trying to stall the reading until the next visit.

"I think I can do it," Derik said. Greg shook his head defiantly, but said nothing more, realizing the entire conversation had gone off on a tangent. Derik read a little longer, and the squeaking could still be heard every once in a while. Weariness soon came over them despite the coffee they had drunk earlier, and the reading was indeed getting harder. It was not the best time to try to finish it. "I'll finish it tomorrow," Derik said to the others. They grabbed some blankets and walked to the bedroom.

"I guess you need a pillow again," Aaron asked Derik, who nodded and followed him into the bedroom. Derik took notice of the chains hanging from the doorway. He laughed nervously and pointed at them. Aaron shook his head.

"Greg had the same reaction," he began. "I don't know why you guys haven't seen it before."

"Well, what is it then?!" Derik asked.

"It's just something for some exercise equipment if I remember correctly. It's been there for a while; I don't know why everybody's noticing it now."

"If you say so," Derik said.

"Now, I've got something to show you." He pointed to

the wooden mannequins. "See what I mean? Somebody keeps moving them."

"Yeah...It's crouched behind your coffee can..." Derik said, staring intently. "And the other one is about to fall off the corner of your dresser... It wasn't me, if you were curious." Aaron shook his head and grabbed the pillow for Derik and handed it to him. They left the room and piled into Zeb's.

It was indeed a crowded space now.

"I have a really bad feeling about tonight," Greg said. "We're all together and after what happened last time... I just know I'm going to be up all night." The others sighed and nodded somberly. Derik had been informed of the haunting during the previous visit from Greg. The recording had not been played for him, and he didn't particularly want to hear it either. His friends were understanding here and kept the tape away from the room. Except for an occasional scrape or pound, the night went surprisingly undisturbed.

The next day Derik resumed his reading, in an effort to finish the Book before he left. Greg gave a final word of dissuasion and left for work.

"It's weird reading this without Greg, and during the day at that," Derik said.

"I think you'll be able to finish. I'll offer my insights," Zeb said.

"It's too bad he won't be around to hear you finish," Aaron said, sitting down next to Derik. "But perhaps it is for the best."

Sooner than any had imagined, and in a moment of both relief and longing, Derik finished the Book.[6] He put it back on the shelf and fell back into the chair.

---

[6] The 'Scary Book' is not the actual name for that which occupied so much of the author's and other characters' thoughts and time during these years. But for the essence of the experience to be accurately understood by the general audience, it has been described thus. Doing this relayed the feelings and general environment of the people involved quite faithfully and helped maintain the atmosphere by preventing dangerous assumptions.

"I can't believe it's done," he said. "This is all it's been for well over a year now... and now it's over."

"Yeah, for now anyway," Aaron said. "I'm sure, with the way so much is left unexplained, there will be more someday."

"It will be good to take a nice long break," Derik said, drawing in a deep breath. "Besides, I want to start that video-game you keep talking about."

"Yeah, right now your main idea of horror probably comes from the Book, but the horror in this game is of a totally different kind," Aaron explained. "It is a very real and objective horror, with scientific implications. I'm sure you'll be inspired to create movies in its theme, like you have been with the Book." Derik laughed nervously and they talked now of other things.

Derik had brought with him the Star Wars DVD trilogy, which was a fairly new release. There were some bonus features that neither he nor the brothers had yet seen. So they decided to watch this until Derik had to leave.

"I can't believe we're still watching Star Wars, after all these years," Zeb reminisced. "Not to sound like a *total* nerd, but this house has lived alongside with the Star Wars saga. Both came into existence around the same time. It's hard to believe the final movie is about to be released."

"Yeah, that's weird," Derik said. "I never really thought about that. Just the fact that the final movie is coming out was hard for me to believe." The special feature ended but there were others, still. It had been some time since Derik dwelt on that wondrous world. It reminded him of the days when great fantasy occupied his mind, rather than the gloom of the Book. It was hard to appreciate the latter, when such strong feelings were present. It rekindled his ambition to create epic films, but it would not be enough to keep him from creating movies that contained actual footage of the surreal experiences at Aaron's house.

After Derik left, he remembered he had left the DVD

boxed set at Aaron's. He would be in the area later that evening, and decided to pick it up then, in a surprise visit. Aaron woke up from a nap hearing Derik's voice in the living room, talking to Zeb. He wondered if he was still dreaming. After a moment he knew he was as conscious of his surroundings as he had ever been and greeted Derik.

"Came back to get my DVDs," Derik said, smiling.

"I didn't even know you left them here," Aaron said, surprised. "Well it looks like you found them." The three sat in the living room and talked for a while. The room had become grey with twilight, yet no one seemed to want a light. Then a noise came into their consciousness. To Derik, it sounded like a bunch of moaning, coming from somewhere deep in the house.

"Did you hear that?!" Derik gasped. He could hardly believe he was experiencing something like this on such a short visit. Zeb looked troubled, but unsure.

"I thought I heard something, but..." he began.

"I thought I heard barking dogs, somewhere outside but close still," Aaron said. He guessed the neighbor's dog was having some friends of his own over.

"No... It was pretty clear... It sounded like moaning!" Derik said, now shaking.

"Geez!" Zeb exclaimed, shaking his head. "And as soon as you come back over!" Derik pulled back his long hair nervously. They had a hard time continuing the conversation. Aaron figured it was a good time to show Derik something he had not seen before. This was the ghostly recording he and Greg managed to capture several weeks earlier. Uneasiness grew in Derik as he heard the disturbing tape-recording for the first time. He then made a horrifying realization.

"That's the same voice that I heard on the phone that one time!" he cried, while Aaron tried to remember.

"Which one again?" he said, beginning to laugh. "I'm sorry, there have been so many voices... Go on."

"The one that said 'It is what it is', remember? The one that pretended like it was you?" he asked.

"Oh, yeah..." Aaron said. "I nearly forgot about that.

Could it be... the same entity speaking? Could it be... Wendell?" Derik shook his head without an answer, but only a sigh. As Derik got ready to leave, and the three stood by the piano, a loud groan was heard in the hallway. They jumped back but saw nothing which would provide a source for the painful noise.

"I better leave now," Derik stammered. The others nodded and followed him to the porch. "Maybe I'll bring my camera next time to do some more filming. I'll see ya, guys." The walk in the dark to his car was not the easiest thing to do, but it was a relief once he was driving away. Strangely, he felt a little homesick as he left. Even Aaron's was better than the apartment in which he would soon be sleeping.

As Derik lay in bed, a horrible dread came over him. He did not understand what brought it on, but it was among the strongest he had ever felt. Invaders, he thought... Watchers... These were the objects of his fear, and he knew they were Zeb's as well. He finally was understanding Zeb's dread. His small apartment room suddenly became a prison, one set up for study, and he found himself paralyzed in the darkness. There was no manifestation of the senses, that night, but it would mark a point at which a dread was felt that would never be equaled.

Regarding such manifestations, one of the most flagrant was also, interestingly enough, harder to believe – only to outsiders of course. The mark it had left behind was one of the only things that let them know the event had even occurred in any objective sense. Derik's video camera was the target for this particular mark, and the strike could not have been more well-placed.

The friends in Tryst were gathered in Aaron's family room one weekend evening while Dan and Carson were visiting. Derik toyed with his camera for a while as they made plans for the evening.

"We should use that camera to watch our backs, like

Greg was saying," Derik began. "We should set it up and just let it roll. Who knows, maybe something will show up in the playback, like the portal did for you." He had been wanting to let the tape record the basement steps for some time now. Maybe, just maybe, he would capture something that would once and for all confirm that the portals had been real beyond all doubt. And if not, at least they would know that the space behind them as they played their game was free of poltergeists, zombies, or whatever else it was they feared might irrupt into existence in that basement.

He prepared the camera but would wait until the rest of the family went to bed before setting it up, so as not to be in anyone's way. They went into the basement and took their seats. They were about to play the horror game here as they had planned last time, but now they were simply talking. They could not help but acknowledge the ever-approaching breaking of their fellowship.

"This may sound a bit funny, but your house feels like home to me, almost," Derik said.

Greg nodded. "Yeah, me too actually," he said. But Derik shook his head.

"It's more than that though," he began. "I feel like I was destined to be here, like I was always meant to be here..." The others looked at him in silence. "It's almost as if... being here... fulfills some childhood dream..."

They started the game now. It didn't take long for Derik to get a sense for this new kind of horror. Refreshingly, it was more of a classic horror story, with a scientific bend. It was only because of Derik's first powerful exposure to horror being that of the Scary Book that made this other type of horror 'new'. At first, he described it as being 'cheesy' but that was only because he was used to the cryptic nature of the Scary Book and its subtle artistry. The horror of this game was more of 'this world' and emphasized the feeling of being caught in the middle of randomly juxtaposed conditions, those which isolate one and leave him to fight for survival in a dangerous and horrifying scenario.

They went upstairs for a break. It had been dark for

some time now, and all the lights in the house were off. Everyone else had gone to bed.

"Alright, I'm going to set it up now," Derik said, pulling out the tripod. He stood it at the top of the stairs, aiming the camera down them, just as Aaron had done when capturing the portal. "If we hear any noises behind us, maybe we'll be able to look at this and see what it was."

"Yeah, hopefully," Zeb said. "I'm not sure if it works like that." They descended the stairs as the camera watched them. They left the stairwell light on, so the camera could see and so they would not be left in complete darkness. Even the comfortable carpet was not enough to make the basement a cozy place for them. In fact, the carpet softened any noise, and this made them even more nervous. But as they played, and immersed themselves into the mood of that world, they thought about these others fears less and less.

It was hard to imagine anything anomalous happening while Greg and the brothers enjoyed their reunion with this simpler, more tangible fear. This did not keep it from surfacing, however. A safe area was reached in the game, and they simply listened to its therapeutic music, which served, quite unexpectedly, to create a sense of impermanence and dread. Greg left the others for a moment to get a drink and returned after a moment. He sat and wrapped himself in a blanket and continued watching as Derik found himself reluctant to leave the safe haven. He neared the virtual door, still listening to the soothing tune, and now had almost enough courage to face his fears.

It was at this moment that he and everybody else suddenly became aware of a different type of music. It faded into their consciousness, and no one knew exactly when they first heard it, but they now knew that they were all experiencing it as they stared at each other in utter terror. What they heard was unclear, as was its location: it was music-like, but whiney and warped, and only Zeb wondered if it could have been the game. Aaron wasted no time in fleeing the basement, and the others were quick to follow.

Up the stairs they ran, Derik leaping from the side and being the second to run past the camera. They took refuge in the family room, shutting the door behind them and dropping to the floor. Much to their dismay, they all continued hearing the noise, and listened with mouths agape. Now they were certain it was some form of music.

"It keeps going!" Greg cried.

"Did the game fry?!" Zeb asked, his lips trembling. Derik shook his head.

"I don't think..." he began. "It came from behind us..." Aaron dropped his head into his hands.

"Are we...in hell?" he asked in despair, still hearing the whining sound.

"Don't say that!" Greg growled, through chattering teeth.[7]

"Are you guys still hearing it?" Zeg asked.

"Yes!" Greg wailed. "It sounds like a robotic – "

"I can't believe this!" Aaron interrupted. "And we're the only ones hearing it, apparently!" He jumped to his feet now. "I may regret doing this, but I'm going to head right for the source." The others reached out to stop him, but the door was now open. They would not be left behind and nor would they let Aaron go by himself, so they jumped up followed him.

As Aaron walked through the doorway and looked down the stairs, he was lost for words as he beheld something most bothersome.

"Um, um, um!...?..." he cried, as Greg ran up to see what he was pointing at. A red ball, about the size of a basketball, sat at the bottom of the steps, a mysterious mark of some unseen event... unseen by all eyes save the camera's. Knowing the ball was not there before, Greg let out a scream as he beheld this, triggering Hazel into a torrent of barks.

Down the basement stairs Aaron ran, filled with both

---

[7]      If one watches the footage seen in the video online titled "Red Ball Horror" he will notice that something else was happening, too, while they sat in the family room. Apparently, Derik saw something on the television screen. Nobody seemed to care, and nobody involved remembers what it was. The television was off, and one can only imagine what he saw on the screen.

utter dread and determination. He jumped over the ball, looking over to the television first to see that it was still functioning. It was. He flipped on the light that lit the back of the cellar, and quickly scanned the room, listening for the direction of the music. It seemed to come from the right, back near the poker table section and it grew louder as he approached this area. The others followed right behind, Derik now holding the camera in front of him and seeing Aaron stop in his tracks as he stared at the table. Greg, with knife in hand, moved forward, and now beheld what Aaron could hardly believe. The radio, which the group often used to supplement their role-playing games, was apparently the source of the noise. Dropping his knife onto the slate tiles, Greg approached the radio and noticed that the tape player on the device was playing. In an act of final desperation, he reached out with a trembling arm and stopped it. Everyone stood in his place, shaken, simply looking at each other in utter horror and amazement. Derik moved forward with the camera, resisting his tremble as best as he could.

Aaron's mother was now heard shouting from the top of the stairs. "Doggone it!! This is getting a little ridiculous!" She cried, and now Hazel began barking. "Everyone's trying to sleep!" The young men looked at each other in amazement, then Aaron hollered back.

"It, uh, won't happen again," he said, hoping it was true. How could she have heard only the scream, everybody wondered?

"Be upstairs with Zeb in five minutes. You're both going to talk to your father and I!" she shouted back, and returned upstairs, even as Hazel continued barking.

"Zeb, you better go up now and get Hazel to stop barking," Aaron said, gesturing him to move quickly so the terrier wouldn't wake anybody else up. "Tell mom I'll be up in a minute." It was probably too late in the evening, but Zeb had said earlier that Lars might be dropping by – perhaps it was only him at the door.

"No! Please, Zeb!" Greg called after him, one arm stretched out. But Zeb had left to deal with the barking situation, leaving Greg no choice but to spin around and join Aaron and Derik as they resumed their own surreal one. He hit the eject button and pulled out a tape, looking at it in confusion.

"Mozart?" he said, giving it to Greg. Greg looked at it in disgust, then showed it to Derik and the camera with a shaky hand. Zeb returned in a moment.

"Hazel was going ballistic at the door! She just kept clawing at it like she knew something was out there!" he said, out of breath and visibly flustered. "No one was there. I'm sorry for leaving you all but I needed to secure the Western Front." They apparently were in no mood for jokes.

"The noise was a tape playing," Aaron said with a shaky voice. Zeb looked at them in wonder. "Mozart in particular."

"What?! It hardly sounded like music!" Zeb said.

"Play it again, Aaron," Greg said, handing him the cassette. Aaron did this reluctantly, only because he, too, was curious as to whether the strange noise would continue. Indeed it did. Derik stopped the camera now.

"It's still like that!" Derik stammered. "Listen, though... You can hear some kind of melody underneath the warped sound..." He was right. It really was the music of Mozart, only distorted and now a horrible perversion of his work.

"It wasn't the game that fried, Zeb... but this radio!" Aaron said.

"It may just be the tape," Derik said. Aaron nodded, and first they tried the actual radio. It worked fine. Now they tried the same tape upstairs, on the other tape player. Now it sounded fine.

"But it shouldn't have even started playing in the first place!" Greg said. Then he remembered the red ball, and the fact that the camera had been there recording from the beginning. "And *that* was not there before!" He pointed at the enigmatic ball. "What the hell is it, anyway? I've never seen a ball like that."

"It's a medicine ball for strength training, but it hasn't been used in years," Zeb explained. "I'm not even sure where it's been all this time."

"It *would* be red..." Greg observed darkly.

"Well, wherever it came from, we have to play back this footage... Something happened down there, and only the camera has the answer." They all agreed and after checking the basement for any intruders or pranksters, moved into the family room.

"Zeb and I have to see what the parents want, we shouldn't be long," Aaron sighed. "Don't you dare watch that footage without us!"

"We'll be praying for you," Greg joked. "And don't worry – we're done with dares." Derik rewound the footage, and powered down his camera, and the two waited for their friends to return in perhaps the most horrible silence they had yet known.

Aaron and Zeb's mother gestured for her children to come into the bedroom where they both knew their father was waiting. They entered, and as she shut the door behind them they saw their father sitting on the bed in his night clothes, obviously having been recently woken.

"Did your mother explain that you and your friends woke everyone up? Not just your mother and I, but Dan and Carson, too. You know about Carson's bed-wetting problem. Your screaming must have caused him to have another accident." Aaron and Zeb put on the most remorseful faces they could muster. Presently their hearts were pounding too fast as a result of the prior mayhem to truly reflect on the grievance they had caused.

"We're sorry, we really are. We got too worked up with that game I guess," Zeb began.

"Sorry for waking you both. And sorry about Carson," Aaron added.

"Your father works long hours, Aaron," his mother scolded him. "I think you need to start showing a little more respect around here."

"I do, though! You must know that," Aaron argued. His mother wasn't having it.

"I want to see it."

"Okay. I will be more considerate. I'm really sorry."

"Alright then. But you're grounded for a month." Aaron

choked.

"Grounded? You can't be serious! That's crazy, I'm nineteen!" He was nearly laughing. That was a mistake.

"If you say one more goddamn thing like that to your mother, you'll be wishing you were only grounded," Mr. Eldritch growled. He had become scarier than phantom-Mozart. "You're grounded for two months."

"I said I was sorry! You guys don't get it! The stuff you sleep right through every other time – "

"Now its three months," Mrs. Eldritch declared. Aaron's head fell in silence. His father continued now.

"You can't keep doing these sleep-over things. Video-games, playing in the woods, and always reading that goofy book... None of that is going to come in handy when you're on your own. And you never know when that might be. You know that your mother and I would love for you to move to Virginia with us, but you must realize that this wouldn't be forever." Was it a tear Aaron saw his mother rub from her eye when her husband said this?

"I'm not going to Virginia with you. And I'm not going back to college. I've told you both that."

"The Kentucky land, right. And what do you think you'll do with that? Do you know how hard it is to start a homestead from nothing? Have you used your time to develop all of those skills you'll be needing for that?" Aaron's silence was answer enough. Truth be told, he hadn't given it as much thought as he should have. But given the recent circumstances, it was difficult to find time for 'real-world' problems when 'alternative-world' ones abounded. "I'm not saying you don't have what it takes. You do. You know we think the world of you both. Maybe some of it is our fault, too. But maybe you can take the next three months and really think about what you want to do with your life."

"Okay, Dad," was all Aaron could manage.

"The same goes for you, too, Zeb," their father continued. "I can't believe I even need to be saying these things to you anymore. There's a lot you need to start thinking about. The job's a start but you won't always have your aunt's place to fall back on. Some friends your own age might do you some good too." Zeb had likely not been so offended since his confrontation with Wendell himself.

"I see. Well it's good to know you have so much faith in me. I mean, why wouldn't you after all the support you gave me through high school?" The sarcasm could've been sliced with the knife Greg left lying on the basement tiles. Aaron was on the verge of telling all.

"No, Zeb, you aren't going to do that," his mother said, angry once more. But he only shook his head contemptuously and left the room. Now Aaron was alone with his parents.

"We love you," Mr. Eldritch said. "Your friends can leave in the morning. I hope you can absorb some of the things we've discussed here. We just want a little more respect. And for God's sake, no more screaming!" That got a small smile out of their son.

"Okay. I love you too."

"You may go. Goodnight." And with that he left the room. It would take some months before the words truly set in, but eventually he would find some wisdom in his parents' words. Whether Zeb had ever taken more than offense from that conversation he would not know for many years.

The folding doors of the family room burst open and it was all Greg and Derik could do to keep from screaming again – and undoubtedly bringing a rain of parental hellfire down upon them all. To their relief it was only Aaron and Zeb, who clearly didn't want to talk about the chat in the bedroom.

"Are you going to be alright, Zeb?" Derik asked concernedly. Aaron's brother was looking rather severe.

"I'm fine. Let me just sit for a minute. There are rare moments when my mind can no longer handle the juxtaposition of so many alien things coming together, without a bit of rest. This is one of those times." And so everyone sat for a quarter hour or so in near silence, until they were ready to return to the mystery that had ruptured any remaining order and logic still clinging to Attica Drive.

The young men gathered round the video recorder as

Derik booted it up and navigated its controls. Hitting play revealed he had rewound the tape too far, and carefully moved forward, near to the moment when they had heard the distorted music of the cassette tape spontaneously play. Now he pressed the resume button and the playback started.

The friends could be heard in the sound that was picked up, as they played the videogame. As they had expected, there was no ball at the bottom of the stairwell. They waited with dreadful anxiety as the moment drew nearer. After all, they were still feeling the effects of the real thing. But they heard something that none of them had expected. A throaty voice was heard whisper. "...*arakesh*..." it said, and very clearly as if spoken right into the microphone.

"What!?" Derik cried, looking at the others, who could only stare back with mouths gaping. "There was a voice!" Greg nodded slowly.

"Play it again," he said slowly. Derik did this, and it was confirmed.

"It almost sounds like... you, Greg," Aaron said. Greg shook his head obstinately.

"You always say that, but it never does," Greg retaliated. "It doesn't sound like any of us."

"We need to go further back," Derik said. "We may have missed a lot."

"Let's just see the rest, first," Zeb suggested. "Let's review the material that will reveal what we first wanted to know." Derik agreed to this. He let it continue playing. Now they heard the voice speak again, but this time it spoke a command.

"*Greg... You must go to Marakesh,*" it whispered. As it spoke, Greg was seen run up the stairs to get his drink, slipping by the camera. If it had been a person speaking, surely Greg would have seen him at this point. But he did not. He returned to the basement, and even as he descended with his drink, the voice again spoke. "Greg..." it uttered.

Now the men looked at Greg in disbelief. "We wouldn't have even known about this is it weren't for the camera!" Zeb said. "Then again, it might have only been the camera being there that made things happen the way they did..."

"What did the voice say, anyway!?" Greg cried. "Where did it say I need to go?" Again Derik replayed it, verifying the words. "Marakesh? What is that?" No one knew. "And I know whose voice that sounds like..." They looked at him in anticipation. "Dan." Their eyes went wide hearing this. Derik nodded, his lips parted, while the brothers looked less sure.

"Maybe a little," Derik began. "I actually think it sounds more like Aaron, but obviously he was sitting right there with us."

"I didn't want to push it sounding like Greg too much for the same reason," Aaron said.

"I don't think it sounds like anybody I've heard before..." Zeb said. "But what could that mean if it is Dan's voice? Could he have done all this?" The comment was met with Greg's evolved brand of incredulity; a mixture of fear, doubt, and amusement in the face of absurdity.

"Come on, Zeb, you know better," he said. "I don't think Dan did this in any normal way, but it is definitely his voice. That's all I'm saying. Besides, he couldn't have been in two places at once."

"Right, because nobody's ever been accused of having a double around here," Aaron joked. "But seriously, what's with the focus on Greg, all of a sudden?" The others shrugged, and Derik resumed playback. Now, they heard the whining music begin, and it was just as they remembered. They noticed now that it in fact was hardly music-like, at first. Several seconds later, Aaron came running around the left corner, followed by the others, and Derik leapt up in front just as they had remembered. Now knots formed in their stomach, for they knew they would soon behold that to which they had been ignorant - the introduction of the ball. How would it enter the camera? Would it suddenly appear? Would it roll down the steps, or from the side, maybe? Or would something... else ... place it there? If Lars had indeed been involved, Aaron thought, surely he would have been captured by the camera, unless of course he had rolled it from the right-hand side where one might be able to enter and escape the basement through the back door. The camera continued to record, as the men were heard from the family room, talking in distress.

They continued watching the playback, the suspense being almost unbearable. And now, surprising them all and filling them with terror, they watched as the ball suddenly rolled into the picture, from the left side and from where they had just run. The men wailed in horror upon seeing this.

"Right from where we had been!!" Greg cried out. "I don't even remember seeing that ball anywhere around!" Derik let out a groan in a moment of nauseating fear. Moments later in the recording, the family room door opened, and Aaron was heard gasping followed by a scream from Greg, just as they had done. The rest of the video went exactly as they had remembered, and it was very disturbing to watch. The feelings of the people on the video were the exact feelings the men still had, only heightened now with their new knowledge.

"I can't believe we have this on video," Derik stammered.

"Yeah," Greg agreed in disgust. "We actually have a horrific and unexplainable experience recorded for all to see! I can't believe it either..."

"And I don't even care anymore. You can show that to anybody you want," Aaron said with resolve. "It's time for people to know." After taking a moment to calm a bit, they rewound the footage way back to the beginning, and listened out for anything else. It proved to be a long and tedious process, with many play backs and requiring extreme attentiveness.

"Let's listen to the rest tomorrow," Zeb suggested.

"It will have to be early. I'm grounded, remember?"

"Oh, right. Well, it will have to wait then," Zeb sighed.

"Yeah, sorry guys," Aaron said to his guests. "Apparently you guys have to be gone by noon tomorrow. You're not in trouble or anything. It's just part of my punishment apparently."

"Shew, your parents mean business," Greg said with a look of shock. Derik, as was customary, had little to say and it would likely take some days before he could put his feelings into words, but it was clear that everything had brought on considerable exhaustion - Mr. and Mrs. Eldritchs' long-awaited response to the nightly horrors was only mildly amusing and became only one more ingredient in the ever-expanding enigma that was Aaron's house. Then he realized he was still hearing the background music of the video game emanating from the basement.

"The game is still on down there. We may as well try to calm down and finish up with the game." They descended the stairs, very carefully, staring at the ball which was still in its place. It seemed to put Zeb into a funny mood, and he simply wanted to pretend the ball didn't exist. He overcame this state shortly, and they were soon sitting by the television. "Well, now that I'm here I don't know if I'll be able to concentrate on the game after all," Derik said as the others laughed. He could only keep watching the footage in awe. "I'm going to show this to everybody." He hit the rewind and play buttons several more times.

"You know, that actually won't prove anything," Zeb said. The others looked at him curiously. He continued. "One could easily say that we were actors, and had some friends down here doing the various things. You know, somebody there ready to hit play, and somebody here to roll the ball, and somebody upstairs to talk into the microphone."

"Someone to throw all those bits of dust around," Greg joked in his classically serious tone that suggested it might not be a joke at all. "We would have seen all these people, of course, but could have pretended not to." Derik sighed now.

"Well I'm going to show them anyway," he said. "I'm sure they'll give me the benefit of the doubt." He could not have been more wrong.

The next week, he showed numerous people at his college this video. All of them suspected the group of simply acting, just as Zeb had said. With no one believing him, Derik was distraught, and felt horribly alone. Only one person believed he was not acting but attributed the radio phenomena to be some random electrical malfunction. He must have subconsciously ignored the ball rolling out from an isolated section of the basement. For if one observes this footage carefully, he will see that the camera is aimed at the only passage from the left part of the basement to the rest of the house. With that said, one will understand that the basement had been unoccupied and should realize that nothing which obeys natural laws of science could have been there to roll the ball. Incredibly, the footage had, by virtue of its replayability, become available, and continues to be as an online video, for anyone to see would he or she so choose. Whatever occurred that night, it seems likely that it happened *because* the camera was there. Rather than the camera capturing something that would have happened regardless, it seems that its presence was inherently involved in the determination of the phenomena that manifested before it. The camera allowed for a more elaborate and disturbing experience, and Tryst had decided that these would be used to provide Derik with just enough evidence to know that the portals, and likely everything else, had been real all along, without allowing him the pleasure of being able to say he had 'caught one'. As they would all eventually understand, there is nothing to be 'caught' in the world of Tryst, for all is provided - if not already held within oneself.

The day after the recording was done, Aaron approached Dan. He asked him if he knew anything about a 'Marakesh'. Surprisingly, he did. "It's a middle-eastern city, near Casablanca. I don't know much else," he said. Greg was there to hear this.

"What would be the reason to go there, I wonder?" Greg said to Aaron in both disgust and wonder. Later Aaron decided to just ask Dan if he was the one to speak the words into the microphone, without saying much about the recording itself. He didn't seem to know what Aaron was talking about. Greg shook his head when they left the room. "I don't know why you even asked. It wasn't the Dan we see before us now that spoke those words. You should know that by now."

"You mean... a doppelgänger?" Aaron asked. Greg

shrugged.

"Maybe," he said. "Who knows? Maybe it wasn't even his voice. But Dan knows about Marakesh, and his focus is world history, you tell me. Perhaps his double has similar interests and offers insights that he alone could." Aaron shrugged.

Because of, among other things, Aaron's being grounded, it was a few months before another visit was made by Derik or Greg. Greg was the first to visit since the Red Ball Incident as it came to be called. The first thing he noticed as he walked through the house, aside from the parents being gone, was the austerity that seemed to have washed over their home while he was away. It was hard for him to pinpoint what exactly was missing, but Aaron told him it was mostly pictures and mirrors. "All the stuff that usually isn't seen has already been packed," Aaron explained. "Now it's time to start packing away the major things, the things that have made this house what it is in our minds, as a *percept*."

"Why the rush all the sudden?" Greg asked.

"My parents finally found a buyer," Aaron said sadly. "It was weird, actually, how easy it was. Basically, somebody at my dad's work was talking about his desire to move and the type of house he wanted. Everything he said fit the description of our house just perfectly, and my dad nearly flipped out. So he told him that he was looking to sell his house, and when he described it to him, the guy wanted to see it as soon as he could. He's been here a couple times, actually, and they're working through all of the red tape now."

"It seems like all this came out of nowhere," Greg said, sighing.

"It did, Greg..." Aaron said. "It did come from nowhere."

When sitting in Aaron's room, Greg noticed the small wooden mannequin was now on the desk, the same desk where its big brother stood. "The smaller one wasn't on that desk before," he said. Aaron looked at it inquisitively.

"Are you sure?... I thought it was right on the corner

like that last time you saw it," Aaron said.

"It was on the corner... of the dresser," Greg began. "Now it's on the corner of the desk, closer to the bigger one. And I think the big one moved, too."

"I thought you guys said it was crouching. It still is," Aaron said, looking at it.

"It may be crouching, still, but now it's on top of the coffee can..." Greg said. "Before it was crouched behind it, almost like it was hiding... and I could have sworn that it used to be lying flat at one point."

"I don't know. It's hard to remember when so much time goes by," Aaron said. Could the figurines really be moving on their own? It certainly seemed possible at this point. But what could it mean? There seemed to be no pattern at all. All they could do was wait.

That night, Greg decided he would try to sleep in the family room. It couldn't be worse than Zeb's room, he figured. He had the pull-out sofa all to himself, and even enjoyed the company of Hazel. Making sure the window blinds were drawn, he closed the family room door, locked the side doors and turned off the light. He lay down, but now realized that the halogen light over the sink would give him trouble sleeping, with its white light glaring down on him through the sliding window over the television. He got out of bed, turned on a lamp light and cautiously entered the kitchen. Quickly, he turned off the light and withdrew back into the family room. He turned the lamp off once more, and now lay in darkness. As his eyes focused, he became aware of two pale squares on the ceiling. The skylights, he guessed. He stared at these with dread, until he fell asleep.

But the subtle growl of Hazel woke him some time in the deep night. He wasn't even sure he had heard it, until she again growled softly. Just as a knot began to form in his stomach, he heard a terrible feminine shriek cry out from the kitchen. Hazel now growled excitedly at the door, as she would do when a stranger was present. Greg was frozen in fear and could do nothing but wait. Now he was wishing he had the others with him. He lay still and silent, trying to stay awake and alert for as long as he could, but could only keep this up for so long. Soon he was asleep and did not wake up until daylight filled the room. He would not try it again.

A certain voice would speak one last time before the inevitable dissolving of this world in which the friends shared. It was over the phone some time later, while Derik spoke with Aaron.

"I'm pretty sure my wood figurines are moving, Derik," Aaron told him. "They must be moving so slowly... I never really notice it, but between the things you and Greg have said, I know that they are in different places than they used to be."

"Are you serious?... Where are they now?" Derik gulped.

"Well, I don't think they've moved since Greg saw them... The smaller one's standing near the corner of the desk, on top of a book... It's gotten closer to the larger one," Aaron described, hearing Derik sigh. "And the larger one... I'm pretty sure it wasn't like this when you saw it... is standing hunched on top of the coffee can. Greg noticed this."

"Wow, they *are* moving!" Derik said. "I know it wasn't like that before."

"I just can't figure it out... It's almost as if – as if you gave them life, Derik: gave them life by putting them in your movie..." Aaron said under his breath. Derik did not have long to think about this, as he was now hearing a sort of mechanical noise over the phone, clanking repetitively. He figured it was a waste of time, but he asked Aaron anyway.

"What's that noise?" he asked.

"*IT IS WHAT IS NOT, AND I...*" a familiarly deep and staticky voice broke in, eliciting a scream from Derik. Unfortunately, the shriek, which Aaron heard, caused Aaron to start talking to Derik in desperate inquiry, obscuring the voice.

"Wait, stop talking!" Derik cried. But as Aaron quieted, the voice was heard fading away, until it was no more. "No..." Derik moaned. "I missed it..."

"Is it alright to talk?! What just happened?!" Aaron

cried. Derik did his best to explain the experience. "I heard neither the first noise nor the voice," Aaron said. "You say it was the same voice as the other two?... My gosh..."

"But do you realize? It said something different than it did the first time..." Derik began. "At first, it said 'it is what it is' and now, now... 'it is what is not'? What does it even mean?!" The friends analyzed its possible meanings for some time.

"To say the first seems redundant... yet you still found meaning in it, since your art teacher says it so often... This second statement, however, suggests something else. I can't help but see the Nothing emerge as I speak those words... Think about it. What is not, is nothing, right? If you heard it the right way, then the voice is claiming that what is – being – is the same as what is not: Nothing... They are one and the same..." A feeling of lightheadedness came over him, as he left his room, phone still at his ear, and stared down the bare hallway. His very home was deteriorating before him...it was itself becoming nothing... He looked back to his room, which retained every physical appearance of being the same room that he had always known, yet something was different now, something in its very essence. He saw it as a corpse for a moment, devoid of its soul. His room was Nothing. Had it become nothing?... Or was it always nothing? He heard Derik speaking over the phone but couldn't seem to focus.

"Are you okay?" he now heard Derik say.

"Yeah... I think I just find more meaning in those words than you... You know, the two statements don't necessarily contradict one another..." Aaron said weakly.

"They don't?" he asked.

"No," Aaron said. "They don't." They remained silent for a moment. "Listen, I'm feeling a little sick. I need to go... I'm going to lie down on... my bed..." Aaron hung up and eased himself upon what he pretended to be such: his bed... what now *was* his bed, as much as it could be. He lay there staring at the small wooden imitators, until he passed into a gentle slumber.

Nothing deemed as noteworthy occurred now for many weeks. The two friends visited the brothers now and again, as the days of spring quickly passed by. A rough date had since been set for the move, which was determined to be a day in early July, around Independence Day. Surely it would set Aaron free from a long session of torment and pain. Even for Zeb and Dan, who both lived away from home, would experience an upheaval, for it was indeed their home, still. Each time Greg and Derik would visit, they would notice more and more things missing, and see the piles of packed goods grow larger. Still, the bedrooms remained unchanged for the most part, now small oases of a former world in a desert of nothingness. The only objects that caught Greg's eyes here were the long chains that hung from Aaron's doorway with silent portent.

"They're definitely getting longer, Aaron," Greg said, taking hold of one and running it through his hand. "You're going to find yourself chained inside, one of these days." They laughed and looked to the wooden figurines. "They don't seem to have moved... The one on top may have straightened up a bit, but the other one is still by that coin on the book."

"Yeah, I put that coin there as a marker to keep track of the movements," Aaron explained. "Now it seems that they aren't moving at all."

The nights that were endured, however, didn't undergo any significant changes. This is not to say that they weren't horribly frightening, but the aberrant phenomena were kept mainly to certain forms, those of a tactile nature being the most unwelcome. It was not until the latter days of spring that several new anomalies would introduce themselves, one of which would remain.

The four friends were again bunking in Zeb's room, which was now felt more claustrophobic than ever. Hazel lay at the foot of Zeb's bed, a cumbersome annoyance given the circumstances. Aaron lay on the top bunk, while his guests took the floor, clustered tightly against each other. The room was relatively 'inactive' and Derik was nearing sleep when he felt a cold, wet touch upon his cheek. He immediately sat up, groping in the darkness, but had no immediate answer. He ordered Zeb to turn on the light and described what happened. Now he took notice of Hazel, who still lay asleep.

"Do you think it could have been her?" Derik asked in desperation. "You know, her nose? It looks a little wet..." Zeb laughed as he shook his head.

"Come on, Derik..." he began, looking now at the canine of interest. "She doesn't behave like that... Look at her... She's sound asleep. Besides, I would have felt her get up, and she didn't."

"Well..." Derik said in submission. Zeb turned the light off, and Derik lay back down. It was some time later, after several gentle pokes and prods, when Derik and Greg, the only two awake at the time, heard what sounded like a weak harmonica strike two notes, one low and one high. It seemed to come from the top corner of the room, though each heard it at an opposite end. They didn't bother waking the brothers up, though they did quietly talk about it with each other.

Now the most intriguing aberration would irrupt. First, Greg felt a hand, with individual fingers even, take hold of his leg. The hand immediately let go as Greg lashed out to grab it, as he yelled out. "Ha! Zeb!..." he said, for it was so hand-like that, even though he didn't see Zeb do it, was sure that it was he that had grabbed him. "Something must have possessed him... I felt his every finger."

"How are you so sure it was him?" Derik asked. Greg had no good answer to this. Zeb rolled over in bed, still asleep. If it was him, he had no memory of it. Anyhow, this was not what they soon found so incredible. Because now, after several minutes, Derik felt a sort of grip on his ankle, but when he moved to go for a grab, he felt whatever was there fall off, to the side of his leg. He lay still, looking toward his feet in darkness. "Uh, Zeb, turn on the light..." he said, for his eyes were set to see whatever it was the moment the light would go on. Zeb was asleep and didn't hear him.

"What's wrong, Derik?" Greg asked him.

"Something was on my leg, and, uh, it's still by my leg!" he said. Now Greg understood the seriousness of the matter.

"Zeb!" he shouted. Zeb jumped with a groan, and now Aaron sat up in fear. Again, Greg shouted. "Turn on the light!" Zeb did this in aggravation, and for once, much to all of their surprise, the light actually revealed something. A charred and severed hand lay at Derik's feet.

They stared more with shock than anything else, but Aaron was most frightened of all. What would this hand do, he wondered, and where did it come from? Greg was ill at ease but managed to find some amusement in the absurdity. He had reached a point where almost nothing, now, could maintain a feeling of shock. Derik, meanwhile, sat there spellbound by the empirical quality of this aberration – he knew the weight of the object was too light to be that of a real flesh-and-blood hand, and soon they all realized that it was actually a strange sort of mannequin hand. It was indeed charred, and soiled, too, they noticed, as Derik grabbed it and examined it.

"I can't believe you're touching that thing!" Aaron cried, leaning over the rail. "There's no way I would ever do that!... I mean, it – it came from another world!" But the physicality was what seemed to disillusion Derik into discrediting it for a prank. He looked at it, nearly laughing, only shock holding him back.

"I'm starting to go back to the hoax idea," he said, eliciting a groan from Aaron. Greg understood, but disagreed.

"Come on, Derik, we're past that..." he said, giving him a pat on the shoulder. "Just take it for what it is. That's all we can do."

"I just can't believe this is here!" Derik stammered, now wondering if he was dreaming.

They all took a closer look. It actually was a silly-looking hand, with odd proportions, but still having an opposable thumb. A joint of sorts was here, allowing the thumb to swivel, as if it was meant to grab. "Did we catch it then?" Zeb asked in bewilderment. "Is this what has been harassing us?"

"It just dropped dead..." Aaron added. But Greg shook his head.

"I don't think so... I see this as just another example of mockery... It may have even been provided to appease us, to seem like an explanation... when it really isn't..." Derik sighed in disgust. Little did he realize he had just cast into oblivion three years of desperate searching.

"Derik... you may have just made the most significant observation yet – and at the same time closed the book on our Study," Zeb said with an air of reverence.

"How do you mean?"

"We know something now," Zeb explained. "We know that we will never be able to bottle these phenomena. We will never be in a position of leverage, in which we become the scrutinizer and it becomes the subject." The others looked on, with both clarity and fear.

"He's right," Greg said. "No matter what we try, be it a video recorder, a tape recorder, a Study – all will be taken within Tryst, and made part of it. It will never reveal itself the way we demand it; it will never allow itself to be captured."

"Geez!..." Derik laughed in bewilderment. He put a hand to his head. "I... I'm dizzy."

"The Study failed. We should have known this after the Red Ball Incident. But we were too stubborn. We should be thankful, really. We will no longer spend hours and hours in vain, seeking to dissect that which cannot be contained." Everyone looked at the absurd hand now.

"What are we going to do with it?" he asked, amazed that he even had to ask the question.

"I'll have nothing to do with it," Aaron said. "Take it... or better yet, burn it. I hate that thing, and I don't want it to exist." Derik recognized this fervor in his friend. But he was the more curious type.

"I'll take it home."

"Don't expect this to make anybody believe your stories," Zeb said. "It will just make them think you're even crazier." Derik nodded, as he put it into a plastic bag.

"Good," Greg told him. "We'll hear the bag rustle if it tries anything funny." Zeb took off his glasses and the light went next. They spoke to each other for some time now, in soft voices that belied their amazement of having acquired a hand from the world of the Absurd.

"I feel sick that it's even in the room with us," Aaron said. "I'm having a really hard time accepting it." Greg eased his mind as best he could, but there was really nothing that could be done. Only the annihilation of the hand could do this... or maybe sleepiness. Surprisingly they did begin to fall asleep now, but the manifestations were not over. For now, a metallic crinkling was heard over Zeb, followed by a kind of sputtering noise. Zeb cried out and flipped the light on himself. Lying on his chest was a severed hand, like that which was in the bag, but this time it held a crushed soda can. Derik immediately checked the bag to see if there was still a hand inside, while Zeb carefully lifted the object off him. The hand was still in the bag, and now they knew that Zeb now held a second one. Even more interesting, this new one was not an exact duplicate. The first was a left hand, and now this one was a right hand. But it was not a perfect mirror image. Each had its own unique attributes, though both were silly-looking albeit burnt. They stared in disbelief as the hand still held the can.

"Are you wet, Zeb?" Greg asked. "We heard the soda spilling all over the place!" Zeb felt all over his bed, feeling only dry sheets.

"All dry!" he exclaimed. Now they noticed something stranger, as Zeb took the can from the hand. Though it was crushed, the lid remained unopened.

"Weird!" Aaron clamored. "Let me see that!" Zeb handed it to him, and Aaron took it with a look of disgust. The whole thing nauseated him, and he threw the can in disgust. An anvil of Zeb's sat on the floor, and the can bounced off it with a ring.

"Careful, you fool!" Greg told him, and he grabbed the can himself now. He looked it over carefully, finding nothing out of the ordinary besides its vacated interior.

"Could it have come out of the factory like this?" Aaron asked.

"I don't know... It's the most reasonable explanation I suppose," Zeb said. "I just don't know!" He tossed both the can and the hand to Derik. "Here! They're yours!" Derik laughed nervously and, after taking a good look at them for himself, put them into the bag with the other hand. Now he had a complete bag of oddities, one made possible only by the Eldritchs' house. But there was one more observation to be made.

Greg pointed at the wall to the side of the bed, on Zeb's left side. There he saw a simple drawing, almost a scribble, as if done by a very young child. It was made by some dark and chalky substance.

"That wasn't there before!" Greg started. "That hand was drawing on the wall while we were lying in darkness! And apparently with its charred finger, no less!" Zeb's lips trembled as he was lost for words, staring at the image. It looked something like a face with arms and legs, with a triangle beside it. All these things would continue to exist as remnants of Fear, but one more remains, and this is reserved for the final chapter.

# CHAPTER FIFTEEN

## Game of Fear

The day of the move was fast approaching. Desolation was taking hold of the house, and its 'activity level' seemed to have diminished a great deal. Only the small wooden mannequin seemed to have a trace of otherworldliness in it, as its movement was now certain: it was more than an inch away from the coin Aaron had set by it. As for the plastic hands, they remained at Derik's house, still charred and devoid of life.

He failed to hide them from his family, though he hadn't exactly made a sincere effort. He had forgotten to remove them from the car, and his father saw their fingers curling out from the bag. After he had Derik explain what they were, he had but one thing to say. "They certainly aren't normal mannequin hands...They look like they come from a larger figure."

Zebulon thought less and less of home, despite his knowledge that he would soon never see it again. Even sadder, he found himself forgetting about the woods. To make matters still worse, his aunt, with whom he lived, gave him the nauseating and laborious chore of collecting rocks from the woods to add to her garden - it was the last way he wanted to remember the place of dreams and adventure.

His aunt learned of this idea when Zeb mentioned that his brother had been doing it; Dan, not Aaron. Dan had recently made a hobby of this: bringing his trailer and filling it with boulders every weekend he came. He would usually get an early start, making many trips deep into the forest and scrubbing them clean late into the evening. It was hard for his brothers and Aaron's friends to grasp initially, but his infatuation made it apparent that there was a deep desire to take parts of home with him, wherever he went. Perhaps he was more disturbed by the move than anyone else. "I should have started this a long time ago," he said.

Greg and Derik had both become more open with others regarding the aberrations at Aaron's house. Greg, specifically, had engaged in several discussions with various priests and parishioners. These left him more and more convinced that demons were at work there. Whether or not he was correct in thinking this, he and his friends would find themselves participating in the foulest of games, a game whose rules belong to Tryst.

While it had been known for some time that their friends were moving, Greg and Derik were now facing the reality of this fact. Soon, a whole lifestyle would change and a routine that had become nothing less than expected would reveal its insecure existence. Aaron, on the other hand, was almost in a state of denial. All he thought about was getting through the work week and enjoying his free time as best he could. The packing he was forced to do was nothing more to him than a typical chore: perhaps he already saw his home as nothing, and the packing had no effect on this attitude. In any case, his two friends visited one particular weekend, for they knew time was running out, and now observed that the house was barer than ever. Only the most cumbersome and essential housewares remained, such as those of the kitchen, and other objects like furniture, televisions, and beds. It was barely hospitable, but this was not the parents' concern: they had left for one last business trip regarding their future house. The stay was enjoyable nevertheless, perhaps more so, as the men savored the passing moments. That night, however, would not be so enjoyable. Except for the most unique of aberrations, almost every one of these that had so far been experienced would surface. This would still not prepare them for what was to come.

Aaron lay on his sleeping bag with Greg next to him, heads closest to the window and farthest from the closet. Zeb, as he never gave up his spot, again lay in the bottom bed of the bunk bed, while Derik took the top. It did not take long for the more subtle signs of paranormal activity to be noticed, such as scuffles, taps, tugs and scrapes. These things were now more nuisances than anything, and it was unfortunate that they had not yet learned to understand such phenomena as being a precursor to greater horrors. For now, not only was the bed shaking, but so was the closet as well as the doorknob and the dangling handles of every drawer. It was obviously not a tremor, as no vibrations were felt in the floor on which Greg and Aaron lay. Rarely was everything shaking at once, but it was usually more than one thing at a time. It did not end here.

Soon, though still infrequently, everybody was feeling prods and nudges. But this type of physical communion would not remain crude and limited. Rather, it would be elevated to a more forthright and invasive level of manifestation. As Aaron was finally drifting off into sleep, his body began to be pulled under the bed. He was not aware of this happening, as he felt no gripping force. It was only Greg, who felt the sheets being pulled away from him, who reached out and felt Aaron's body sliding away. Reacting quickly, he lashed out and grabbed him by the shirt, and managed to pull him back into place. The grab understandably startled Aaron, and he immediately woke. In the darkness, and feeling the pull, he did not initially understand what was happening.

"You were being pulled under the bed, Aaron..." Greg whispered, still holding tight. "I pulled you back."

"I didn't even feel it... It was so gentle..." Aaron sighed. "What would have happened? What's so bad about going under the bed, I wonder?..." Now he thought of this fear that so many children share, and he could only wonder.

"Well, I'm going to hold on to you, just in case," Greg said. "Now that we know it can happen, we have to be safe." Aaron managed to return to sleep like this. But not ten minutes later, Greg, whose grip was loosening in his weariness, felt Aaron's body begin to lift off the floor. He immediately tightened his grip, able to feel that Aaron's back was now more than a foot over him, being pulled toward the window behind them. "Get back here!" he shouted with a pull.

Again, Aaron had remained unconscious, and only after hearing the shout did he wake. He dropped to the floor, utterly terrified, for he could have been falling from any height as far he knew.

"It happened again?!" he cried, gripping the side of the bed as hard as he could. "Why me?!" Greg sighed without an answer, still holding onto him.

"I don't know, but I'm not going to let you go floating out of here," he said. It seemed ridiculous that he even had to say it.

"It's what happened to me when I was little," Aaron reminded his friend. "After all these years, it's happening again." He let out a quivering sigh. "Initially, I was hoping that maybe you were just confused, being in the dark - but this time I actually dropped down!"

"It was very clear to me," Greg said. "It was obvious that I was pulling you back down to Earth." Aaron managed to laugh, though terrified. Now Zeb was awake, hearing all the commotion.

"You said you were floating?!" he gasped. He doubted he had heard them right. Much to his surprise, they verified this guess of his. "Wow, it's getting pretty crazy in here, then." Greg laughed at the sheer absurdity of it all.

"Yeah, and you managed to sleep through it like you always do," he explained. "I'll never understand how you do it."

"Apparently Derik's still asleep. I guess he hasn't been too troubled," Zeb observed.

"I wonder if he's okay..." Greg said. "Turn the light on for a moment, Zeb, I just want to check on him." Zeb did this, but the question was not answered in the way that was expected. Instead, the three first noticed that one of the drawers was pulled open, and Greg cried out in fear. This cry incidentally woke Derik, who now leaned over the rail.

"Aren't you guys ever going to sleep?" he asked, rubbing

his eyes.

"Just go back to bed, Derik... You have no idea what's been going on," Greg said, pushing the drawer closed. "The forces in this room are greater than they have ever been..." He lay back down, as did the others. The light went off and they made another attempt at sleep. They talked for a little bit, easing the transition from this world to the one of dreams. But then something happened which made Aaron wonder if he was already dreaming, as he talked to Zeb.

"It's hard to explain in simple words the feelings I have when things like this happen," he said to his brother. He heard only a grunt from Zeb and guessed he was now too tired to talk. "All I can say, I guess, is that it's all quite creepy," he finished, but at this very moment he heard a voice, almost like Zeb's, speak very near to his ears, as if the mouth was right over him.

"*Very creepy...*" the voice said, and Aaron wailed in horror, lashing out then retreating under his covers like a frightened child. Neither Greg nor Zeb seemed to understand what gave Aaron such a fright, and he did his best to explain it.

"It sounded like you, Zeb... but sarcastic and even silly..." Aaron whispered unsteadily. Zeb sighed, not able to provide an explanation.

"I think I may have heard it," Greg said.

"It was right in front of me... All of the sudden, you know? I can't believe it wasn't like that for you..." Aaron said. After a moment in thought, Aaron had only one guess. "Some head was hovering right over me." Now he did his best to fall back asleep. But not more than five minutes later, he heard a harsh and whispering voice, again right over him. Again, out of instinct, he lashed his hand out. This time, however, he felt his palm slap something cold and fleshy. It felt like a face, yet, except for the smacking sound, it made no noise in response to the slap. Now the moment his hand made contact, before he could even gasp, he gave a shove, and felt the head-like object gently give way and leave his now-outstretched arm. Now he shrieked in horror.

"What was that smack!?" Greg asked, still awake.

"Did you hear that whispering?..." Aaron asked weakly.

"I may have... I was so tired..." Greg said.

"Well, I lashed out, a-and... hit a face!" Aaron stammered.

"You... *hit* it?!" Greg asked in disbelief.

"Yeah!... and... I shoved it away," Aaron groaned. "It was like a head in zero-gravity."

"We're going to have a lot to tell Derik tomorrow. At least he's not having any problems," Greg mused. At the moment only two were asleep. Hopefully, Aaron thought, he would soon join the others. And this he achieved, for some time. Greg was still holding onto Aaron, and it is impossible to say what would have happened if he had not maintained this steadfastness in caution. For a third and final time, Greg felt Aaron's body lift off the floor, and begin to float toward the closet now. He did not hesitate for one moment to pull him back to his place, and again Aaron dropped with a pound. It woke him for a moment, but since Greg said nothing, Aaron guessed that it he had simply jumped in his sleep and returned to a slumber he had not entirely left. On this night, only Greg would know what had happened. Still, the most threatening force had yet to manifest.

Static irrupted out from nowhere some time in the deep night. Immediately following this was the sound of boisterous cheering and applause. And now, in fulfillment of the acclamation, came the ostentatious voice of a host. *"Welcome back to Tryst everybody!!!!!"* The phantom crowd went wild. *"Now that all the contestants are where they need to be, let's get started!! Zeb was supposed to be with us, but unfortunately he is not here and may not be returning..."* At this moment, Greg flipped on the room light to find Aaron standing in terror, and Derik sitting up in bed with a hanging jaw. Zeb was nowhere to be seen.

"Zeb!" Aaron cried out. Derik jumped out of the bunk, and now they all listened together as they stared at Zeb's empty bed.

*"With that said, it's time to play a new game called*

*'Guess What's Inside the Closet'!!!"* the host said. The other-worldly audience, evidently primed with anticipation, roared with sadistic glee, calming only to allow their showman to continue. *"The rules of the game are simple: You have a minute after the buzz to guess what's inside the closet. Make your answer carefully! If you are right, a soul may be saved. But if not..."* and now a four-tone game-show sound was heard whine in a diminishing scale, the kind that usually indicates some failure. The voice said one final thing: *"Good luck!!!"* Seconds later, a loud and startling buzz sounded, and the pressure was on.

But contrary to what would typically happen in such stories, the men simply stood there shaking, already forgetting much that the voice had said. They had tried so hard to pay attention, but their horror overcame this. Aaron seemed to have the best memory, as he finally began to speak. "I just don't know what to do!... What did he say about saving a soul?! And where the hell is Zeb?!" he cried, ready to fall to his knees in submission. In futility the others, paralyzed with fear, strained their wills to their limits as they sought to move or speak. Finally,

"Something about the closet?" Derik had found his voice, much cracking and quivering notwithstanding. Aaron's eyes widened.

"Yes!! We need to guess... what's in the closet!..." he replied, looking around wildly.

"How much time do we have?!" Greg stammered. The others shook their heads.

"I don't remember right now," Aaron said. "I'm just too flustered... It was in minutes, I am sure, and maybe only one!" He dropped his head into his hands. "I'm no good under pressure like this! Greg... Derik... What's going to happen to us if we fail?" Now he was almost in tears. "And what's going to happen to Zeb?" At this moment Greg tried to open the closet, ignoring the rules of the game. It didn't budge. "What are you doing!?" Aaron cried. "We have to follow the rules! We have to make a guess..." Now Derik tried helping Greg. They pulled on the door as hard as they could, and it simply would not comply.

"We're running out of time guys! Just guess! What should we say?!" Aaron said, trying to think quickly.

"Zeb..." Greg uttered. And at this moment, the closet doors flew open, and out from it tumbled this very person. Everyone shrieked, unable to do more than watch him as he fell to the floor. He looked pale and sweaty and was shaking violently.

"Zeb!!" Aaron cried, dropping to his brother's aid. "Are you okay?! What happened?! How did you end up in there?!" But Zeb seemed to be delirious.

"Not so many questions, Aaron!" Greg shouted. "Just take care of him!" Soon Zeb began muttering, still distressed and apparently traumatized.

"A mind... a prying mind... So intelligent... Such inter-rogation... yet so... desperate..."

"Don't try to talk," Aaron told his brother. "You can explain it when you feel better... What can I do?"

"Nothing... Let me lie here for a moment..." he said. Derik knelt by him, putting a hand on Zeb's shoulder. He looked back to the open closet, then back at Zeb.

"We had a horrible experience as well..." Derik sighed, when Zeb looked a little better.

"What... did you see happening... to me?..." Zeb asked.

"You were in the closet..." Derik said. Zeb's teary eyes widened.

"The closet?... My mind was in an entirely different realm..." he said, with a distant look.

"And you wouldn't believe what we had to do to release you..." Aaron added.

"Release me?" Zeb asked, now sitting upright and rubbing his head. "I was set free... None of you had anything to do with it."

"Yet we were involved..." Greg began. "We had to, uh... play a sick game... We had to guess what was inside the closet."

"And when Greg gave your name for the answer, you popped out!" Aaron said. Derik nodded.

"Yeah, something took you, and we had to save you!" Derik said.

"Save your soul, the voice said..." Aaron explained.

"Voice?" Zeb asked. The others explained the nature of the game.

"The strangest part of all was the way the voice made it sound like you were supposed to be with us," Aaron told his brother. "I remember that clearly. I immediately became worried for you, and when the light went on I realized the voice wasn't joking... You were really gone... and yet you were the object of the game! The whole thing was sick..."

"My gosh... My experience was entirely different," Zeb began. "I was set face to face before some ultra-intelligence, a being much dissatisfied with me... We were communicating, but I can't remember the content of the discussion... I remember It was desperate for something... asking something of me that presumably only I could offer... "

"What thing?!" Derik choked. "And please tell me you didn't oblige!"

"An exchange of some kind took place. All of this was so clear at the time. But it is nearly all lost to me already. I'm sorry. Whatever it was, I was released..."

"Both of our experiences were related somehow," Aaron sighed. "You were the central object, in both... but how could it be both that we saved you and you were willfully released?"

"The interactions of worlds can be inconceivable," Zeb said. "It is a mystery we will most likely never comprehend."

"Could it be over, then?" Greg asked. "I wonder if that's it..."

"I guess we'll find out," Derik said, climbing back into the bunk. "After all that, I need to sleep!" Zeb laughed.

"That sounds like a good idea. Hopefully I'll wake up still in bed," he said.

"I think you will," Greg said. "I think our bodies have been moved around enough for one night."

"We aren't the same men we used to be, are we?" Aaron laughed. "Before, a bump in the night was enough to keep us up all hours of the night. Now, apparently, we'll chance a second abduction by an invisible game show guy," They bellowed out laughter that could have just as easily been the sound of insanity acknowledged at last. And with that, they climbed in bed, turned off the light, and slept the rest of the night.

The next morning, there was no sign of such a game having been played - only the participants' memories, which became cloudier with each passing moment, contributed any meaningfulness to behaving as if the events somehow still existed in time, like some eternal encore in a far-off ether. One thing and only one thing suggested a bit of lingering noumena: the movement of the wooden figurines.

This had occurred with significant progress. The small wooden figure was much closer to the larger one, now off the book and with an arm outstretched toward the base of its larger companion. And this larger one, which had stood hunched for some time on the top of the coffee can, was now upright with arms raised.

"We need to really pay attention to their movement," Greg said, eyes narrowing as he leaned in to study them. "It's probably very significant... It probably means so much..." Aaron nodded, and Derik shuddered, both apparently lost for words. As they left the room, Greg glanced at the hanging chains. They seemed to have remained unchanged, though he felt uncomfortable waiting near them and passed them as quickly as possible.

The two friends left together, as Aaron saw them off. "Only several weeks left... We need to get together one last time," Aaron said. They nodded, sadly, and left.

# CHAPTER SIXTEEN

## Rebirth

In some lonesome corridor at the warehouse, Aaron's supervisor approached him. "They came to help," he said very seriously. Aaron looked at him curiously.

"Huh?" he said. "What do you mean?" The thin man looked at him intently.

"They came to help," he repeated, and with that he turned and left Aaron to his work. Aaron was left to dwell on this comment, one he would never forget. It was totally out of character for his supervisor to speak so vaguely, but this did not mean the comment had no meaning. Perhaps it was not even the supervisor who spoke the words: he simply may have been a medium of sorts, or even perhaps a delusion of Aaron's. But the words had been spoken nonetheless. To what did they pertain? Who were 'they', why did they need to help and with what did they need to help? It would remain a mystery, though Aaron and his friends felt without a doubt that it was pertinent to their situation in some way. And it opened up a new possibility - one where two opposing forces were at work, in Aaron's house if nowhere else.

As the final days at home had come, Dan wished to see the forest one last time. His brothers went with him. They walked slowly, with heads held up toward the lofty canopy. Slowly, they passed the old forts, which, having been engineered poorly, were now in ruin. Their destination was the newest fort, atop the ridge.

"It's funny how well we built it, actually," Zeb began. "I mean, it's much more permanent than the others. At the time, we planned on building a very livable shelter." Of course, it was only a dream of fanciful youths. Now they made their way up the ridge and followed it, waiting for the large timbers to break through the foliage. Finally, something different from its surroundings was seen ahead, about where the fort would be. But something was wrong. As they drew closer, they saw that the timbers, which had always stood numerous and plumb, were now few and leaning. They ran up, only to find wreckage. Many poles were leaning, while others were ripped from the earth or broken in half.

"No..." Aaron said, caressing a broken pole and dropping his head. Zeb looked away.

"We really have nothing left here now..." he said. "It's sad to see it destroyed... But it's not like we were ever going to finish it, either..." They all wondered what had happened. It seemed that only a force of intent could deal such damage, for no natural disasters had struck recently. Yet the destruction was not complete.

"I guess it was just a bunch of kids..." Dan said. But he would then challenge his own naturalistic explanation with a more meaningful one. "They're telling us to go..." he said, looking around at all the trees. "It's tough love... They know that it's... over..."

"Even Star Wars is over... Everything is ending at once..." Zeb sighed. The brothers had recently seen at the theater the last film of what at the time was expected to be the last in the franchise, further solidifying the encompassing sense of finality. They stood by the stream now, until the day was late, recalling all of their fondest memories of this sacred place. Finally, the dark moment had come, and the men left – abandoned – the forest.

Derik and Greg arrived for a final visit. The first thing they noticed was a huge white cube sitting in the driveway. They parked their cars along the curb, in line with all the family cars which were now forced to park in the street as well due to the box. As the two friends walked up the driveway, they stared up at the solemn scene of the house. Here they both noticed two windowpanes of the large bow window flapping violently, like crazed eyes blinking wildly at them. This stopped as they drew closer, and Aaron greeted them after they knocked on the door.

He explained that the large box was holding most of the things from the house, and this would be taken to be stored at a warehouse until the new house was built. Evident of this was the emptiness within the house now. Nearly all the boxes that held such wares were now apparently in the large storage box, and even much of the furniture was gone. Only one table was left for eating, and Aaron's bed was now nothing more than a mattress on the floor.

Fortunately, Zeb's room was now much more open, and the bunk bed had not yet been dissembled. The house seemed rather lifeless, and Greg hoped that perhaps this would imply a decrease in 'activity', and a restful night's sleep.

Neither he nor Derik had experienced anything bizarre over the phone, a sign that the annihilation of the home was somehow tied with such aberrations. Aaron and Zeb had recently proposed this theory. They could only wonder what total annihilation would entail. For now, however, Aaron was sure that something... perhaps Tryst... was still at work, since the mannequins were still moving, though slower than ever. Now, as his friends verified, the larger one had thrown its arms up toward the heavens; its back arched. The smaller one was next to the coffee can, its arm outstretched toward the base of the larger one, and they were nearly making contact. "Look at this scene as a whole," Derik said, framing it with his fingers. "It's a wonderful composition, actually..." The others did not expect this and looked at him with disgust. Derik continued. "They have told some kind of story... I can only imagine what's going on right *now*..."

"Or what is yet to happen..." Aaron added. For the time being, staring at them would reveal nothing more.

Most of the evening was spent looking through a box of

drawings, most of which were Zeb's from years ago. Perusing these did little to ease their spirits but curiosity, after so many months of desperation for answers, saw the men proceed as if without conscious choice. On top were some oil pastel drawings. One was a scene of a bedroom, at night apparently, as it made use of many contrasting shades and colors. It looked vaguely like Zeb's bedroom, and many willowy, beige beings stood within it, casting long shadows and surrounding the bed. A stiff figure lay here, unaware of the watchers. "This actually isn't mine... Lucinda drew this one for me..." Zeb explained, removing it to reveal the next. The image was the bust of a hooded figure, with a chubby, noseless, blue face bearing a wide grin. Zeb's friends looked at him worriedly. "I drew this during the same discussion..." he said. "And this one too." He put this aside and lifted the next. Done in colored pencil, it portrayed a young boy, from behind, as he held the hand of a luminously red being. The being looked similar in shape to those of the first drawing, and together with the boy, they watched through a window the activities of a group of people inside a room. "That boy is me. When I was little I had a recurring dream. In it, I would befriend this red entity, who wanted me to show it around. That's us, looking at my mom having fun with her friends inside the house." He held it close, then dropped it. "Strange thing is, is that this room I saw in my dreams had not yet existed... It was the family room, which was added years later. Anyway, this drawing was done at the same time."

The next one appeared to have been illustrated by yet another hand. Much simpler than the others, it depicted several squiggly objects arising from the ground, whose tops widened into ungainly heads of some kind – this being evident from the twisted grimaces they bore. Above them, four triangles in the sky. And to the right, a small hand-written note that read 'You'll know the Way when you know the Hay. *So be wise.*' With that mixed expression of dread, bewilderment, and amusement that everyone had grown to love, Greg lift the drawing, studying it, and looked to Zeb for an explanation.

"That would be Bennett's work," Zeb revealed. And with

a shake of the head, added, "Your guess is as good as mine on that one." The large stack of drawings below was now only drawings from years past.

Several common themes could be seen in Zeb's drawings, though he failed to remember his reasoning behind them. Fantasy and science-fiction sketches were mixed throughout, but there were distinct themes that seemed to change with age. First was the period where he drew monsters with numerous heads. Then came a period where people were drawn with pig-like faces. This theme remained for some time, concurrently with others. One was characterized by these faces being half-shrouded. Finally, in one drawing, this half-face was unveiled, revealing a hideous side.

Then came a stage where giants dominated. Usually a large foot would be next to a house, or an animal. There were few of these, but next was a theme that dominated the rest for some time and did not make a recurrence until much later. This was an apparent intrigue with outer space, and space-ships. They were rather creative, considering the young age at which they had been drawn. At the center of one was a small planet, Earth. There was but one island on it, with a single house. This house was of a particular kind, and it was seen in other drawings. Surrounding the lone planet were many stars, and at the corner of the page, a single saucer-like craft. Another particularly interesting drawing was a sort of panoramic image of a wide, multi-leveled, and windowed space craft. There was a wide-headed being in each window, but only one had a human-like figure in it. This figure was shaking hands with the wide-headed being. It was not until a much later drawing, one done as a project for high school, that a certain face surprised them all. The drawing was very surreal, with many unique shapes and objects. The scene looked something like a graveyard, with monolithic forms protruding from the ground. Upon one of these stone-like objects was a face, thin-lipped, with large ebony and almond shaped eyes. Across from this was a shadowy figure with a coat and a wide-brimmed hat. Exchanging uneasy looks, everyone decided it was a good time to put the drawings away, for they believed they knew at least what this last figure represented. Exchanging small talk mostly now, it soon grew late.

Preparations were made for bed, now, and the guests could feel the sense finality all around them. "It's so bare in here... and so spacious now..." Greg noted in solemnity.

"The Nothing has nearly taken this house... just as we had known would happen as Derik filmed us talking... Even then, the Nothing was all around us. Now it has simply reared its ugly head." Aaron climbed to the top bunk.

"Let me sleep here one last time... I've done it for so many years...Now, with my friends, I will do it one last time," he said, climbing under the sheets. His friends said nothing, and simply climbed inside their sleeping bags. When everybody was settled, Zeb flipped off the light.

"With a bit of luck, maybe I won't get taken from my bed again," Zeb said, as understating the obvious so far had allowed him to compartmentalize his dread.

"I have a feeling it's all over..." Greg began. "I can't quite explain it... but I feel like the life of this house is intertwined with its relationship within Tryst... Now that this house has lost its being, perhaps it will also lose its tendency to be that threshold to the bizarre that we've come to know it to be."

"Yeah, maybe..." Zeb sighed. Their eyes had since adjusted to the darkness. Aaron lay in bliss, savoring the passing moments as he caressed his bed. His eyes were closed, but he detected light through their lids. As he opened his eyes, he saw a red glow coming from the vent over his head. This faded as he turned his head directly toward it. Derik must have seen it, too.

"Did you see that red glow up there, Greg?" Derik asked him.

"No," Greg answered. He tried to resist intrigue or fear. But Derik's fear and fascination with Aaron's house had not yet desensitized him.

"Did you, Aaron?" he asked. Aaron sighed.

"I think I saw a red glow coming from the vent..." he said.

"Oh no... More red...." Derik moaned. For some time now they lay in peace. Aaron fell into a blissful sleep, as had Zeb already. Only Derik and Greg were awake to hear the subtle signs of 'activity' begin. First was some small object that was thrown from one side of the room to the other.

"Maybe I was wrong about all that," Greg said. Derik sighed in acknowledgment. Now a patter could be heard from inside the closet. "No... Not the closet again..." he said. But this did not last long. The patter seemed to move to the wall, and it was heard, like a scamper, run up along the entire wall and across the ceiling.

"My gosh!" Derik cried as softly as he could. "Something definitely just ran across the roof!"

"Derik...would you be willing to join me in prayer?" Greg asked him. Derik grew hopeful hearing this.

"Yeah... Sounds good..." he answered. And pray they did. They began with common prayers, such as those taught to children at young ages. Interestingly, the frequency of 'activity' increased noticeably. Another object was tossed across the room, and now the closet began to shake, lasting for nearly a minute. The prayers continued, and not once did either ask for a light, for their strength was in something else now. Then a troubling phenomenon began. Suddenly, a voice similar to Zeb's was heard speak, and from his general direction.

"*Where are you going?*" the voice asked in a harsh and tense whisper. The two that were awake were quiet for a moment, waiting for more. There was no need to respond.

"*Nowhere...*" another voice answered in a similar tone. It sounded like Aaron's and came from his general direction. Derik and Greg resumed their prayers now, chanting even louder now. As if in response, Zeb's voice was heard speak again.

"*Stop that...*" it said. But the prayers continued, directed toward the voices now. They prayed for the brothers, asking that the brothers not be harmed and resist the possession it seemed to be.

"*Lies...*" Aaron's voice said. More things were thrown across the room, and then there was silence for a while. Still

291

the prayers endured. It was then that both noticed a soft tapping sound, from somewhere close. It seemed to them that it was mocking the prayer, as its rhythm was that of the prayer being spoken. Whatever the meaning was, it continued for some time until it all finally came to an End. The two friends had joined together more closely that night than they ever had and agreed to say nothing to the brothers regarding the cause for this.

"We can only pray for them..." Greg said. "Pray that they escape the clutches this house has on them."

"Right..." Derik said. And they drifted off into the last sleep they would ever find in that room.

Aaron's guests kept their secret and said little of the night they had endured. "Maybe you were right, Greg," Zeb said. "We seemed to find sleep much easier this last time." Only the two guests knew the truth. Greg was convinced that demons were present there and suggested one last time that a particular action be taken.

"Still, you should have this house blessed before you move," he told Aaron.

"Well, perhaps there's no need now, if there ever was," Aaron replied. Derik looked at Greg cautiously, but they said nothing more.

The rest of the stay went by quickly, just as had all of their journeys in Tryst. They faced now the reality of not only change, but annihilation. They stood outside by the wooden fence at the edge of the pasture, watching as horses grazed on patches of grass.

"I haven't even known you that long, yet this place has become my home," Derik said. The brothers laughed.

"It happens to everybody, trust me," Zeb said.

"All the role-playing we did in your basement... the forts we built in the woods..." Greg sighed. "I will truly miss all of it."

"Don't worry, guys. One day, we'll be playing D & D again, you can be sure of that," Aaron told his friend. "It won't be here, and it won't be near that forest, but such is the way of all things. In Time, the Nothing reigns supreme... Being itself undergoes constant change, and in the very process becomes undone... Staying here would only have kept us ignorant to that." Greg nodded, looking away.

"It's hard to imagine, after all these years, that my very home will fade away," Zeb said.

"I'm sure it's even harder for Dan." They moved under the shade of the maple tree now.

"I can't say I'll miss our nightly terrors," Greg said. Derik laughed.

"That's all I ever really knew!" Derik said. They all laughed.

"And again, I'm sorry for all of those foolish games, you two," Aaron told his friends.

"At the time, I could only think in the present. But now, looking back, I realize that telling the truth would have made things so much simpler..."

"But look at how it brought us all together so strongly," Greg said. "Though there have been dark times, we can't deny that it was *everything* that happened that made our friendships so strong. Perhaps this is Tryst... Us... All of us joined together, common in spirit."

"Perhaps," Aaron said. "*Something* happens when we get together."

"And yet there was something about the house which made it all possible..." Zeb said. "I guess the 'troubles' will die with our home. My guess is that the new residents will never know the horror – the wonder – that was known within those walls."

"A dying Tryst..." Aaron said softly. "It makes sense..."

"We are experience an uprooting, you might say," Greg said. "Perhaps this Tryst will live on."

"I thought you said you'll be glad to leave it all behind...?" Aaron said.

"Well... the bad things for sure... but it's hard to say if they were inseparable from the good things... It all seemed to go hand in hand..." Greg sighed.

"I know what you mean," Derik said. "In general, I must

say that I'll miss the adventure." They laughed with fearful faces at this statement but found themselves nodding in agreement.

"After all, isn't that what everyone desires?" Zeb asked, crossing his arms. "When this world becomes dull, anything else is better... Reality is rejected for alternate reality... It's hard to believe we found it."

"With the help of certain objective forces..." Greg muttered under his breath. "Well, I guess it's time for me to get going. What do you think Derik?" Derik shrugged.

"Yeah, we have some more packing to do, I guess. Dad needs our help for some of the heavier stuff," Aaron said.

They walked to the house and the guests gathered their things. Now they stood in an empty room that was once a living room.

"Alright then," Derik said. Now he smiled. "It was all worth it. And I would do it again... if I had to..." The others laughed.

"He's right," Greg said. "One life ends while another begins. Hopefully we will find happiness together again, in the future."

"There's always room for hope," Aaron said. Now he and Greg clasped hands. "Take care, friend!" Then Aaron put a hand on Derik's shoulder. "And you do the same," he told him.

"Good luck with your plans in Kentucky," Greg told the brothers. "I'll probably be joining you one day. After everything, I certainly don't see myself being absorbed into the gray fog that is the world of the masses."

"I hear you. Either way, we'll be able to stay in touch for a little while longer," Aaron said. His friends nodded.

"Sounds good," Greg said. "Now, Derik, let's leave this place... this nightmare... this home, sweet, home..." They stepped out the door, looking back, and after a gesture of farewell, walked to their cars. When out of earshot, Derik turned to Greg.

"You think they'll bless the house?" He turned to Greg, and they both now granted the rancher one last ambivalent gaze.

"Nah."

"See you at Church next Sunday?"

"Oh, definitely."

Wondering if he would ever again know friendship so true, Zeb sighed and turned, walking to his bedroom which, after so much horror, turmoil, and discovery, was now hardly a shade of its former self. Aaron, clinging to faith that they would unite again, stepped out onto the porch, and waved good-bye as his friends drove away, departing Attica Drive for the last time. It was hard for him to understand exactly what had just happened. Regardless, he understood that whenever their reunion would occur, and he knew it would, its essence would be unrecognizable; embryonic and at the mercy of the most subtle of mutations. Wishing to meditate in silence, he turned and went to his room.

There, he beheld something most unsettling. First, he saw tiny carven pieces of wood scattered across the floor. As he traced their source, his eyes fell upon the desk's surface, the stage for the wooden figurines. He immediately called Greg's cell phone.

"Hey, what's up already?" Greg asked, not two miles away.

"You didn't... uh... do anything to my wood figures, did you?" Aaron asked.

"No... Why...?"

"Well, I'm, uh... standing here looking at them... or, what's left...The small one is demolished..."

"Woah..." Greg said.

"Its ligaments are stretched, like it exploded... Its head is missing, and pieces of its body are all over my floor..."

"What about the big one?" Greg asked.

"Well, it's whole... but..."

"But what?..." Greg asked.

"It's dead," Aaron said. "That's the best way to put it. It looks like it went completely limp and slumped lifelessly. It kind of looks like the way Derik positioned it for his video, you know, real sad and depressed... but it looks more like it just died, and went limp. It's stiff now, and I guess I can still use it... but the little one..."

"You're going to keep the big one?" Greg asked.

"Yeah. I bought it as a replacement for the small one, after Alex ripped its arm off..." Aaron said. "I'll be glad when I have time to use it, actually."

"I guess that makes sense. Derik still has those hands..." Greg remembered. "It can't be any worse than that."

"Well anyway, that's all I wanted to say... I knew you would want to hear," Aaron said.

"Yeah... I was wondering what would happen to them... Thanks," Greg said. "Like you said, we'll keep in touch."

"Yup. I'll be sure to do that. See you later, friend," Aaron said.

"See ya, and God bless," Greg said. And that was the last conversation over the phone Aaron would have from the house on Attica Drive. He gathered the figurine pieces and lay on his mattress. With a deep breath, he shut his eyes and embraced the Nothing.

The next day Mr. Eldritch would have his sons help him with the rest of the furniture and equipment, as he had said. But before this, in the morning, he heard a funny noise coming from his bedroom.

"Do you hear that, Mary?" he asked his wife. Now Aaron heard it. Zeb was eating and paid no attention.

"What is that noise?" Aaron and his mother both asked. It was a sort of humming, or a buzz, that became louder as they drew near the large dresser. Mr. Eldritch opened the drawer from which the noise was heard. Out from it he pulled his electric shaver. It was buzzing loudly, shaking his hand.

"Weird..." he said, turning it off. "It was clicked on... I would have thought that someone would have had to manually do that." He put it back, closed the drawer and left the room with his wife. Aaron stood there, staring at the drawer.

'The last sign...' he thought to himself.

After moving most of the heavy things, the day was

spent mostly cleaning out the bedrooms; sifting through the drawers and separating what could be stored from what needed to be accessible. The large wood figurine was thrown into one of Aaron's drawers, while the pieces of the small one were trashed.[8] One by one, Aaron removed every object from his shelf, sorting them in a similar manner. Buried under some odds and ends, he found an old harmonica, whose mouthpiece was partially covered with pieces of tape. "Weird..." he said. "Something I did when I was little, I guess."

The Eldritchs had recently found a small rental cabin near their future house site; they would stay here while their house on the river was being built. Within a week, the large storage cube had been taken, and a rental truck had been filled with the remaining goods and emptied at the cabin.

Now the house on Attica Drive had nothing but a table and some mattresses. A feeling of déjà vu struck Aaron for an instant, though he gave it little thought. For now, in the driveway, he discovered a new storage cube – that of the new family's belongings. It was hard to not feel tread upon, as though invaders had breached his fort, but house and fort alike he had prepared himself for handing over.

Though there were many details to sort out, the premise was simple: he would be setting out for Kentucky to begin his homestead, and now filled his car with the most essential things – matches, string, pots, pans, coolers, tent, first-aid kit, axe, and a bundle of cash. His parents were heartbroken to see him do this, having held onto the hope that their youngest would accompany them to Virginia. The moment had come however, and Aaron had proved to be as stubborn as they had feared. Knowing he had made his choice, they could only offer their love, prayers, and encouragement. Zeb had also assured him. The two moved around the corner of the house away from their parents' eyes and ears.

"I'll be with you soon," he said.

---

[8]    The larger figurine is considered the last 'remnant of Fear'.

"Yeah... I guess no one knows when we'll be seeing each other again... but until then," Aaron said, and he clasped his brother's hand, "good luck, and take care."

"I will," Zeb said. "You do the same." Aaron looked up in thought.

"It sure was an adventure here. At the end of the day, I don't know if I would take anything back... not even the meetings with Mark..." he asked. Zeb shook his head. "Speaking of whom, have you heard from him lately?"

"For a while I hadn't. I was beginning to think he may have joined the stars," Zeb laughed cautiously, earning a chuckle from Aaron. "I meant to tell you last week, but he sent me a short letter. Said he was going to be busy for a while doing some research in New Mexico and may be making some waves in the news at some point."

"Huh. He's not one to rest often, is he?" Aaron joked. But his face grew more serious now. "We never learned much about him. I mean, think: for him, Tryst is one of who knows how many esoteric ideas! And yet this one had become so central for us..."

"At least we can say we found a center at all," Zeb opined. "Not all are so lucky."

"I used to be in constant search of it. Of meaning, at least," Aaron mused. His brother looked at him inquisitively, waiting. "Well, you know, everything had to come back to God in one way or another – the pinnacle for all purpose and significance, as it were. And I... I guess I just don't know if I can say that anymore."

"I see..." Still only Zeb's dark, studying gaze.

"Yeah... we grew up needing to give everything a story, and of course every story needs an author," Aaron began. "But what if we are the author? The only story here was the one we gave it and continue to give it. Or perhaps we choose to tell no story at all and come to terms with the fact that sometimes unexplainable things just *happen*." His brother nodded, though he would be mulling on that for a while. As they gave each other a warm if not bittersweet smile, Aaron concluded, "Now begins a new era, a new life, a new Tryst."

Together they came back from around the corner of the house and exchanged a few jokes and laughs as they joined their parents under the tree. After a bit of small talk, Aaron indicated it was time, and idled over to the car, his family following.

"I'll be praying for your safety, Aaron," his mother told him. "Please call us whenever you can, from a payphone, anything."

"We love you," his father said, holding back tears now.

"Yes, we do, dearly," his mother said wholeheartedly.

"And we believe in you," Mr. Eldritch admitted. "We always have. We just wanted to be sure you knew where you stood."

"I know. Thanks though. I'll remember that if things get tough. I love you both... We'll see each other again, sometime soon, I promise... Until then, goodbye!" And with that, Aaron, seated in the car, blew a kiss and eased down the driveway leaving it empty of everything but the new family's storage cube. He looked upon his home one last time, and then upon the forest, where his heart would always remain. Then, after waving goodbye to his family, he ventured into a new world, and watched in the rearview mirror as the old one shrank away into nothingness.

# About the Author

Aaron Eldritch was born and raised in the Piedmont region of Maryland, not far from Baltimore. An accomplished illustrator as well as author, he prefers to write about true events from his past. These stories provide some background for the surreal and unnerving renderings in his drawings. He now lives in the peaceful foothills of Kentucky and holds a B.A. in Fine Art.

See more from Aaron Eldritch by visiting:
www.aaroneldritch.com

Also be sure to watch footage of an actual paranormal event at:

**https://youtu.be/CX8Y9AzkibM**

CPSIA information can be obtained
at www.ICGtesting.com
Printed in the USA
LVHW031114141019
634125LV00001B/232/P